# EXPERT WITNESS

A Novel

## KAREN KNUTSON

Copyright © 2025 by Karen Knutson

ISBN: 978-1-966343-27-1  (hard cover)
        978-1-966343-28-8  (soft cover)
Knutson. Karen
Edited by: Amy Ashby

Warren Publishing
Charlotte, NC
www.warrenpublishing.net
Printed in the United States

*In fond memory of Jan Warner*

# Chapter 1

*Charlotte, North Carolina*
*November 6, 1996*

On the Wednesday morning Elle Larson was asked to do her medical evaluation, she opened the door to Charlie Blackwell's home and stared down an unlit hallway, giving her eyes and her attitude time to adjust. Tommy Sumpter had called her as she was pouring kibble into Mac's bowl and finishing her first cup of coffee. Sumpter—Mr. Blackwell's attorney and a father figure to Elle—was the elder law attorney who had referred the majority of her clients over the past five years. She took an uneasy breath and clenched her teeth. Whenever Sumpter referred new clients to her, family conflict always followed. Big time.

"Anybody home?" She checked her watch. It was nine thirty. As she made her way down the hallway, she shifted her briefcase strap higher on her shoulder and straightened her collar. *What now?* Well, first, she needed to find Charlie Blackwell. Then, later, she would ask Sumpter why no one was here to answer the door.

Seeing a door at the end of the hallway, she power walked the length of the hall. "Mr. Blackwell?" She opened the door a crack and stared into what looked like his bedroom, noting the children's photographs, an oil painting of an army soldier in uniform, and a backyard view of daylilies and flowering crepe myrtle. But overgrown weeds and a pool full of leaves were signs that all was not well. Charlie was a landscape architect, after all.

"Over here," came the faint sound of a man's voice.

Elle pushed the door open. At first, she barely recognized the figure who lay wrapped up like a mummy under a tightly tucked blanket. *What on earth?* Rushing to his bedside, she dropped her briefcase and pulled back the blanket. She raised her voice and spoke directly into his ear. "Elle Larson, the nurse practitioner. Remember? Your attorney, Tommy Sumpter, sent me."

She bent down and took his hand. Cold skin and blue nails. "Mr. Blackwell! How long have you been in bed like this?" When he didn't answer, she took his finger and applied hard pressure to his nail bed. She watched for a response.

His creased lids flickered as he struggled to open them, yet he barely reacted.

"Can you tell me what's going on?"

"Call me Charlie," he whispered.

Elle came back to his ear. "Okay, Charlie. Open your eyes. Are you taking any medication?"

"I don't know," he said, then stared at her.

She pulled a penlight from her pocket and directed the beam to his gray-blue irises. His pupils were pinpoint and nonreactive. *God almighty.* She didn't want to frighten him though. "I'm worried about you being alone here and trapped in this bed."

"Don't leave ..."

"I won't, I promise." She tucked the penlight back into her pocket. "We're gonna get you through this, Charlie." She pulled a stethoscope and blood pressure cuff from her briefcase, then wrapped and secured the cuff around his arm. When she looked back at him, he had closed his eyes. "Keep your eyes open, please." She pumped and listened, keeping her eyes trained on the gauge. His pressure was 80/44. She slid her fingers to the underside of his wrist. His radial pulse was below sixty; his respirations, twelve. "You just need to help me here, Charlie."

She turned to his bedside table, reached for the phone, and dialed 911. "Emergency. I need an ambulance, stat." She gave a quick report.

"Eighty-year-old Caucasian male. His vital signs are dangerously low. No, I don't know why, but you need to hurry … we only have minutes here." She directed the dispatcher to the side door, hung up the phone, and untucked the top sheet from his bed. Someone had mitered the top sheet corners by folding and tucking the sheet under his queen-size mattress and locking Charlie in place.

Elle pulled off the top sheet. An electric cord snaked up the front of his shirt. "Charlie, I need to listen to your heart." She unfastened his shirt buttons and carefully lifted a warm heating pad at the end of the cord. Five fentanyl patches, fastened like glue, were stuck to his hairy abdomen. Before she could think, she jumped back and dropped the heating pad to the floor.

*Enough fentanyl here to kill a horse.* In just minutes he'd be sliding into a coma. She grabbed the two nearest patches between her thumbs and index fingers, tearing them off, pulling his abdominal hair off as well. "I'm so, so sorry." He didn't move. After setting the patches inside-up on his bedside table, she tore off the other three, pulling away more abdominal hair.

Elle sprinted to the kitchen, her brain reeling off flashcards she'd memorized. *Fentanyl: one hundred times more potent than morphine.* In the kitchen, she swiped a dish towel from the sink, then ran to the freezer and loaded up as many ice cubes as the towel would hold. She noticed the coffee light was on. Three empty cups rested on the granite counter.

Running back to Charlie, she placed the ice against his bare abdomen and watched for a reaction. He didn't flinch. Her mind kept going back to her flashcards. *In patch form, fentanyl is released slowly, then absorbed by the top layer of skin before entering the bloodstream.* But this new transdermal way of delivery she'd only seen used with terminally ill patients. She pressed the towel firmer against his abdomen. At least the ice would slow the drug's absorption.

His face was now ashen, his lips purple. She shook his shoulders. "Charlie! Open your eyes." She checked his blood pressure and listened to his heart using her stethoscope, keeping the ice in place with one hand. Finally, a siren.

"Keep breathing … please keep breathing." A chill shivered through her skin. If he stopped breathing, she'd have to start CPR.

The ambulance turned into the driveway, then footsteps creaked through the side door and down the hall. "Hold on, Charlie."

Seconds later, a female police officer entered the bedroom. She was very tall, had curly black hair pulled into a scrunchie on top of her head, and looked unflappable in her dark blue uniform.

"I'm Sergeant Harrigan, Charlotte-Mecklenburg Police Department." She looked from Charlie to Elle.

The floorboards creaked under the weight of heavy footsteps in the hall, and Harrigan moved out of the way. Two guys with thick shoulders and strong forearms maneuvered a stretcher through the bedroom doorway.

"His blood pressure's crashing. He's losing consciousness," Elle said, still not moving the ice.

The paramedics ran to Charlie's bedside. Elle jerked her free hand toward the resealable bag holding the five Fentanyl patches and showed them her evidence.

"We'll take it from here," the older paramedic said. He placed a face mask on Charlie and started up the portable oxygen. The younger paramedic started an IV, and they both rolled Charlie onto the wheeled stretcher, rushing him through the house, out the side door, and into the ambulance.

Elle ran after them, recounting the events that led up to her 911 call as she watched the first paramedic give Charlie Narcan and the second paramedic jump into the ambulance and rev the engine. "Tell the ED physician that we don't know who put the fentanyl patches on Charlie's abdomen," she shouted as they put the ambulance in reverse.

The driver gave Elle a nod and pulled out of the drive. Harrigan asked her how she happened to be visiting Charlie.

"His attorney, Tommy Sumpter, hired me to make a surprise visit ASAP. He usually calls me early, speeding down the interstate to his office in Charlotte—sometimes for a client evaluation, sometimes for setting up care in the home." She regretted using the word speeding with a police officer. She licked her dry lips. "I'm sure he was doing the speed limit."

"Why do you think he wanted a surprise visit?" Harrigan asked, her face relaxed, with a voice that commanded respect.

Elle thought for a moment. "All he said was that Charlie was scheduled to see him this morning, but that Charlie's son, Robbie, called and told him that Charlie couldn't make the appointment."

"Sounds like Tommy Sumpter didn't give you much to go on."

Elle frowned and looked down at her hands. They were shaking. She wondered why Sumpter hadn't told her more—why he'd asked her to drop everything. He'd never done that before.

She heard Harrigan's voice again. "How did you get in?"

"I knocked and rang the doorbell," Elle said, trying to remember, now that there was time to reflect on what had happened before she knew there was a medical emergency. She drew in a deep breath. "When there was no answer, I tried the side door. It was unlocked, so I walked in."

Harrigan pulled out a small notebook and began taking notes. "Did the victim say what happened?"

Elle shook her head. "He was too sedated. He could barely talk."

"Any possibility he may remember what happened?"

"We won't know until the fentanyl's out of his system."

"So, what's your story here—did you know the victim before today?"

Elle told Harrigan how they met five years ago. She had just opened her private practice as a care manager when she attended Charlie's reception.

Harrigan glanced over at her, her dark eyes calm.

"He was retiring, and the community was honoring him as a local hero. For years, he had planted parks and gardens around the state." Elle smiled, remembering Charlie's stories about Charlotte before it was a city. "He's also a local historian." She had been surprised to learn the country's first gold rush started in North Carolina, and how Charlotte's old mine shafts and mysterious tunnels were still hiding far below the city.

Back in the kitchen, Elle called Sumpter on the cordless house phone. "Somebody intentionally overdosed Charlie Blackwell," she told him when he answered. She explained the mysterious fentanyl patches. "Like five tiles across in a Scrabble game."

"Holy shit, Elle!"

"It was freakin' weird. It's against the law to give fentanyl without a doctor's order, but there were only two drugs listed on the fax you sent me: hydrochlorothiazide and lisinopril—both for high blood pressure—not bad considering he's eighty years old."

"Who's there now?" Sumpter said.

"Sergeant Harrigan." Elle looked around for her briefcase; it was still in the bedroom.

Sumpter kept talking. "Charlie Blackwell married one month ago. After the wedding, his new wife, Susan, fired all of the help and filed for guardianship."

"Seems like a perfect way to flush a new marriage down the toilet."

He laughed.

She was being serious, if a little sarcastic, but his laughter released some of the tension in her shoulders.

"Susan set up new caregivers in the home, and Charlie's now contesting the guardianship," he said. "I'll need your testimony at the hearing."

She shivered. It was the courtroom thing she hated. God knows what the opposing counsel would do. After finding her carotid arteries, they'd go after her with the biggest scalpel they could find. "Sumpter, can we talk about this later? I've gotta get to the emergency department."

"Hold on, hear me out. When I talked to Robbie, he told me that he and his wife stopped by to see Charlie and meet with Susan. That was early this morning."

Elle frowned. "That explains the three coffee cups."

"Robbie said that Susan left for work at eight forty-five; he and Peggy left about nine fifteen."

"They left him here alone?" she asked.

"Not intentionally. Charlie's caregiver, Mary Beth, went home sick around three this morning. She has type one diabetes and needed more insulin. She told Susan she'd be back by nine."

"Well, no one was here at nine thirty," Elle said. "Sumpter, I need to meet with Charlie's emergency physician."

"Tell you what. I'll stop by the emergency department with a copy of the medical records."

"I need to tell him what I've seen here—"

"You'll get to do your assessment, just not today. Besides, he has the paramedics' report."

"The paramedics report their own observations. There's no guarantee that they'll even see the treating physician … they may report to one of the ED nurses." She shook her head. "Their report won't include everything I know … what I've discovered here." Her face flushed. "Plus, I always follow my clients to the hospital. Someone needs to stay with Charlie."

"Elle, you're the only witness," Sumpter said.

She started to protest again but stopped and bit her lip. Sumpter had referred this case to her, and she didn't want to let him down.

"Don't touch anything without gloves. This is a goddamn crime scene now. I need your home evaluation for the hearing. The police need to let you walk through with them this one time. They won't let you come back into a crime scene."

"My prints are on the door." She looked around the room. Her prints were on the freezer door and counter as well. She caught sight of Sergeant Harrigan, who had walked back into the kitchen. "My fingerprints are all over the fentanyl patches."

"Show the police those patches as physical evidence," Sumpter said. "I want you to look for Mary Beth Abbott—see why she didn't come back to work. Go to her house first. It's only ten minutes away." He gave her Mary Beth's address on Windemere Street.

"Now?"

"As soon as you finish your home evaluation. Remember, we need evidence for the court hearing."

"No problem," she said, immediately thinking it was a problem, but the insistence in his voice was loud and clear. And it made sense that if Mary Beth wasn't feeling well, she most likely was at home.

"Now I need to talk to Sergeant Harrigan. I'll see you in my office later."

Elle put her hand over the receiver. She hoped her connection with Sumpter would give her some credibility with Harrigan. She handed over the phone and heard Sumpter request that Elle be allowed to complete the home evaluation.

Elle bent over to catch her breath. Her adrenaline had been going full blast and was starting to make a slow fall after the rush. She slid into a kitchen chair and looked at her watch. It was almost ten thirty. *Where is the freakin' caregiver?*

Harrigan moved outside and inspected windows and doors while talking on the phone. Elle walked to the street and stood under the tall willow oaks. She listened to the low hum of tires and an occasional honk from the cars that zoomed by. Since her introduction to Charlie Blackwell five years ago, Elle had admired him. She loved that, like her dad, he was a World War II veteran. He even reminded her of her dad: the handsome face and gray-blue eyes.

She'd often wondered about Charlie's home. After all, the street he lived on was one of the oldest and loveliest in all of Charlotte. And when she drove by, his house was the one that reminded her of a brick fortress standing in the shadows: the canopy of willow oaks, a hundred feet tall, like a wooded glen in some Brothers Grimm fairytale.

She looked back at his house, her shoulders sagging. At first, it had seemed idyllic, a time capsule of old Charlotte: the small, safe neighborhood, the tree-lined, curved streets, the white columns and slate-gabled rooftops. She'd come here with the notion of doing her evaluation and writing up her report. But now, she'd never look at this place in the same way.

From the side door, Elle watched a big white Chevy van pull up Charlie's drive. The door opened. Dressed in a uniform and black boots, Elle's friend David stepped out, unmistakable with his spiked, bleached hair and friendly face flecked with freckles from summers at the beach and laugh lines around his deep blue eyes. At five foot ten, he was five inches taller than Elle, though he looked shorter standing next to the gun-packing Harrigan.

"Sorry I'm late—my team's processing a scene across town," David said, his neck and shoulders straining under the weight of his camera equipment.

"Is Detective Slater on his way? Told him we've got something fishy," Harrigan said. "Might be attempted murder."

"Slater'll get here as soon as he can." David shot Harrigan a jaded look. "We're spread way too thin this morning." He readjusted the camera strap on his shoulder, setting down a kit of some kind on the floor.

"Elle Larson, this is David Cauley, one of our shift supervisors for the crime scene unit." Harrigan turned to David. "Mr. Blackwell's attorney thinks Elle can help us understand what's happened here. Detective Slater gave his approval for a quick look around so she can tell us what she knows about the case."

David greeted Elle politely, breaking into a soft smile, then went about setting up his camera.

"It's great you're here," Elle said, relieved to see him. David was the first guy she met when she moved to Fourth Ward. Now he lived in a condo two blocks away from her, with the best skyline view of the city.

Harrigan looked from David to Elle. "Y'all know each other?"

"Not from the job," David said, his voice sounding professional.

Elle understood. They both separated work from home. They had to if they wanted to have any kind of a personal life.

"He lives on the other side of Fourth Ward Park. I see him sometimes when I walk my dog." She didn't say she'd been at his condo last night with a group of neighborhood friends, celebrating her twenty-ninth birthday with lit candles and chocolate cake.

David nodded. "Slater called and wanted me to get started—says he'll be calling the emergency physician shortly to get a status report on the victim."

"All the doors are locked except for this side door. No windows or doors have been forced, but we can't rule out a break-in, not with an open door." Harrigan looked at David. "Until we hear more, it's just going to be photos."

David was quick to answer. "Slater wants more than photos. He wants me to look for evidence and document everything I see."

Harrigan shrugged her shoulders. If she disagreed, she didn't say.

They moved to the kitchen. Elle was grateful that Harrigan had given her gloves and booties to put on over her shoes. David took pictures and Harrigan checked the refrigerator, cabinets, shelves, and two wastepaper baskets with gloved hands, in search of fentanyl wrappers.

"They come in a box of ten, which means another five could be floating around here," Elle said, trying to be helpful.

There was an opened quart of milk in the refrigerator, a couple of frozen dinners in the freezer, a few plates and glasses in a cabinet by the sink. David pulled open the pantry. Empty, except for a couple cans of chicken soup and a package of rice. Even though the kitchen was large and had a walk-in pantry, it was not well-stocked like Elle usually saw when people were cooking and eating at home.

Elle followed Harrigan to Charlie's bedroom, where David pulled open the double closet doors. The closet smelled like citrus and cedar. Three-piece suits, as well as a blue-and-white seersucker, were lined up on wooden hangers. David took pictures, then with a gloved hand checked pockets and poked through mod-patterned shirts of the sixties and earth-tone prints of the seventies. Charlie's closet was akin to a vintage clothing store.

"He's partial to colorful disco shirts," Harrigan said.

"Totally," Elle said, smiling at the thought of Charlie dancing disco.

Harrigan pulled out her flashlight and shined the beam on Charlie's shoes as David checked inside them, looking for anything hidden.

Elle remembered her briefcase next to Charlie's bed and retrieved it.

David checked the wastepaper baskets and medicine cabinet in Charlie's bathroom while Elle and Sergeant Harrigan looked on. Nothing. An empty med box, two razors, and a can of shaving cream sat on the sink. No prescription bottles anywhere.

"Looks like someone cleaned up before we got here," Elle said, surprised to find no evidence of his regular blood pressure meds.

They entered a second bedroom, and David opened a walk-in closet. A woman's navy sweater, pullover sweatshirt, and a pair of new jeans hung suspended from metal hooks. No shoes. The medicine cabinet in the attached bathroom was empty. No trash, soap, or shampoo.

"I bet Charlie's wife didn't sleep here last night," Elle said.

Harrigan checked her notes. "Susan's the new wife, right?"

Elle nodded as they crossed the hall into the caregiver's bedroom. The bed was made, and the closet was empty. David took pictures of two empty short-acting insulin bottles atop a maple dresser. Elle stared at a printed logbook with the insulin pump settings handwritten in the side margin; the date and time from this morning were recorded below the settings. A phone number had been written and underlined twice. She quickly wrote down the number.

"What's going on here?" Harrigan asked.

Elle looked at the sheet again and began reading the notes out loud. "Checked blood sugar: ketones positive. Checked pump settings, adjusted pump. Called rep, reviewed checklist, pump okay."

"So she's diabetic and takes insulin," Harrigan said, taking more notes.

Elle nodded. "Her blood sugar was high. Sounds like she couldn't bring it down. She called the rep and went through the steps of checking out the pump."

"Okay, so she goes home to get more insulin—"

"So she can either inject herself or refill the pump again," Elle said, nodding.

"So why didn't she come back?" Harrigan asked.

Elle shook her head and shrugged.

David put his camera down. "I'll collect the insulin bottles and the logbook, just in case." He placed the empty bottles and log in separate evidence envelopes.

"His wife hasn't moved in?" Harrigan asked.

"What woman lives in a place without her shoes?" Before Elle could say more, Harrigan's cell phone rang. There was a pause, and Harrigan stayed on the phone as they walked back to the kitchen, leaving David to take more pictures throughout the house.

"Yeah, the side door was unlocked when the nurse practitioner arrived." Harrigan's expression grew impatient. "I want it locked before I leave. We'll need investigators here now." Another pause and then, "Oh, I see."

Elle wondered what was happening.

Harrigan ended the call only to be interrupted by the ringing house phone. She picked up, listened briefly, and said thank-you before hanging up and turning to face Elle. "That was Susan Blackwell. Says she'll be here in thirty minutes and doesn't want to see you. Says you're on opposing sides of this legal battle."

"She's the one who filed for guardianship," Elle said, giving Harrigan a puzzled look and frowning. "I just want what's best for Charlie Blackwell."

"So does everybody and their mama." Harrigan rolled her eyes and smiled for the first time, showing her straight white teeth. "What exactly do you think happened here?"

Elle paused in the doorway. "Someone slipped into Charlie's bedroom while he was sleeping." She stood for another minute and did a quick calculation in her head. "The peak effect of one fentanyl patch is about twelve hours—adjust for five patches. Probably took four to five hours before his respiratory distress kicked in." She couldn't be sure about the heating pad, but considering how it sped up absorption, she could make an educated guess. "I'd say those patches were put on between four and five this morning."

"Okay, so you come along, see these patches, take them off," Harrigan said. "And the suspect doesn't even stick around to see that it's done?"

"No one knew I was coming. Sumpter wanted it that way."

"Seems like a dopey way to kill somebody," Harrigan said.

"Or carefully planned. It would have worked if I hadn't interfered."

"How so?" Harrigan asked, shifting her weight from one foot to the other.

"Someone could have returned later, pulled off the patches, and no one would be the wiser. It would have looked like a natural death."

"Unless an autopsy was ordered," Harrigan said.

"Funny, right? And even though things went wrong, the person who did this got away." Elle looked at her watch. It was after 11 a.m.

Harrigan shook her head, scowling. She didn't look convinced. "That first call was Detective Slater. He called the victim's emergency physician. The good news is your client's going to make it; that's bad news for your theory though."

"What do you mean?"

"The emergency physician gave him a diagnosis of self-inflicted overdose."

"Charlie did not do this!" She was surprised at the anger in her voice and pulled off her latex gloves. "So, this attempted murder is no longer a crime scene?"

"It's *not* attempted murder, and *that's* why it's no longer a crime scene. Listen, this is a small, quiet neighborhood. We don't have a problem with violent crime here—"

Elle interrupted her. "Then the doctor who made that diagnosis didn't have the whole story." She bit her lip, not wanting to say something she'd regret. "This is a perfect collision! The doctor is acting on the information he has, and your office is acting on the information you have."

David walked into the kitchen, talking on his cell phone. "Yeah, things aren't adding up." He looked at Harrigan and ended the call. "That's Detective Slater again. He agrees that things look suspicious. I'll take the evidence in case something changes and we need it."

Elle handed David the plastic bag holding the fentanyl patches. She also handed him the heating pad. "Talk to you later." She hoisted her briefcase over her shoulder and headed for the side door. As Harrigan walked her to the door, Elle gave her head a slow shake. She paused, pulling off her gloves and booties, then tucked them into her briefcase. "I hope it doesn't take another crime scene for you to believe me."

# Chapter 2

When Elle reached Mary Beth's neighborhood on Sharon Amity Road, she gripped the wheel of her Volvo family station wagon and slowed down. She hoped that Mary Beth had fixed her insulin problems and was still at home. Ahead on Windemere, a frenetic puppy chased his tail in circles, a reminder that Mac would be waiting for his midday walk. Twenty yards up on the right, she spotted a brick bungalow, set back, with a detached garage in need of repair. She looked at her watch, 11:40 a.m. Sumpter was right: It was a ten-minute drive from Charlie's.

The house was dark and partly concealed by longleaf pines and a narrow, twisting driveway. Elle braked as a breeze blew the scent of pine needles through her open window. She made her way up the secluded driveway and pulled to the left of a silver two-door sedan. Thank God, Mary Beth was home. Drawing to a stop, she organized her thoughts: *Mary Beth must have talked to Charlie last night, helped him get ready for bed, and checked on him at three o'clock this morning before she went home.*

Elle glanced into the sedan's driver's side window. Under the shadows, a woman sat in the driver's seat. Her hair was pulled back in a single braid, and her head leaned against the window. But that was all Elle could see. Yet something about the body's stillness forced her to hurry. She killed the engine and ran around the car, yanking its passenger door open. "Mary Beth?"

She held her breath as she slid across the vinyl seat and swung her legs over a large purse on the floor. She turned face-to-face with Mary Beth and was greeted by half-open, soft brown eyes, as if a ghost were looking past her. A thin gray film covered each eye. Taking a deep breath, a fruity, acetone smell hit Elle's nose—one of the symptoms of high blood sugar.

"Mary Beth?" Elle leaned forward, fingers searching for a carotid artery. She was too late. Mary Beth's skin was cold, and she had no pulse. Slender and fair, like a sleeping Disney princess, only her beautiful face had turned a gray pallor.

She recognized the signs of death long after respirations had stopped. After cardiac arrest and brain death … and now lividity and rigor mortis. A shiver ran through her, like spiders crawling up her spine. People were expected to die in the hospital or at home where the surprise of it could be controlled, not in their own driveway.

Elle opened the purse on the floor and found a driver's license in a worn leather wallet. Mary Beth Abbot. Twenty-three. She wondered if Mary Beth's spirit was somehow still hovering inside the car. "I know this is crazy—we've never met. I wasn't even sure you'd be home." Tears welled up. "Oh my God … oh my God. Mary Beth, what happened to you?"

Elle closed her eyes. From somewhere in her subconscious mind, an oncoming van slammed into the driver's side of her parents' car … an explosion … a sensation of cartwheels, rolling and spinning … She opened her eyes, reached out her hand, and yelled, "Stop!" The image had come suddenly, accompanied by the pain of grief and guilt she usually felt, having survived the crash. Her heart raced. That Mary Beth's death should trigger the worst time in her life was not surprising to her. It wasn't the first time the terrible memory had come back to her. She turned her face away and took two deep breaths.

Elle heard a loud squeal of tires and took a look out the back window in time to see a red Ford van with a woman at the wheel turning toward them in the driveway without slowing down. Jumping out of the car, Elle waved her arms in the air to get the driver's attention. At the last second, the van braked and screeched to a halt, sending gravel flying.

A ruddy-faced man lurched forward in his wheelchair and snapped back as the van swerved to the left and brought the back passenger window into better view. Elle heard him groan through the open window where his wheelchair was strapped down in the back. Thank God he was wearing a chest strap and seat belt.

"Damn it, Peggy! What the hell are you doing?"

"I didn't see the cars, Rob," the woman said, shaking her light brown ponytail.

"Your driving is making me crazy!" he said.

"Shit!" She got out of the van and walked to where Elle was standing. "Peggy Blackwell. This is my husband, Robbie. Are you okay?" Peggy's brown eyes peered at her, then looked back at Robbie.

Elle straightened her shoulders and introduced herself. "I'm okay, but we're too late. Mary Beth is dead." She shook her head. "I need to call the police, but I don't have a phone."

"Damn it." Peggy pulled out her cell phone and handed it over. "You were the one who called the ambulance for Charlie this morning. Susan called to let me know."

Elle dialed 911 for the second time that morning, taking in Peggy's watery eyes darkened with heavy mascara. Peggy made no effort to walk over to Mary Beth's car.

After the call, Elle approached Robbie's side of the van and took a deep breath. So this was Charlie's son and his wife. *I wonder why they are here.*

"Why didn't you start CPR?" he asked, his gray-blue eyes flashing.

*The same eyes as Charlie.* "She's been dead for more than an hour," she said gently. "More like two or three hours."

"I need to talk to the police," Robbie yelled to his wife.

Peggy opened the passenger door and released his tie-downs. She returned to the driver's seat and lowered the ramp into position. It made a grinding and screeching noise, like two rusty metals rubbing against each other.

Robbie started to roll out and stopped. "Peggy!"

"Now what?"

"Are you trying to kill me?"

"Jesus, Robbie."

"You've lowered the ramp down to the ground."

Peggy laughed nervously as she adjusted the ramp back to the midway position, parallel with the floor of the van, and waited while Robbie steered his electric wheelchair onto the ramp. Then she lowered Robbie to the ground.

Elle moved to the side of his electric chair. Robbie was dressed in a casual knit sports shirt, clean khakis, and slides for shoes. She recognized a spinal cord injury that had left him mostly paralyzed from the neck down. It must have been incomplete since he still had some movement of his arms and legs.

Peggy walked over and joined them. "Want your cigarette now?" she asked him.

"Let's hold off a minute," Robbie said, his anger softening.

While they waited for the police to arrive, Elle asked Robbie a few questions. "How long have you known Mary Beth?"

"Only for, like, the past month," he said. "But we know she's been diabetic since age nine. Her blood sugar goes up and down like a rollercoaster."

"She's relied on an insulin pump to keep her blood sugar stable for the past two years," Peggy said, blowing her small, upturned nose with a tissue.

"She's young," Elle said.

"Too young," Peggy said.

"She's twenty-three," Robbie said, defensively. "Besides, she was willing to live in as Daddy's caregiver, five days a week."

"I think it's been too much responsibility," Peggy said, keeping her eyes on Elle.

"You know how hard it is to find live-in caregivers," Robbie said.

Elle decided to keep quiet and just listen.

"Mary Beth started working a month ago when Susan fired Charlie's previous caregivers, Geena Louise and Florence," Peggy said, gesturing with her hands. "Robbie asked Susan if he could interview the new replacements."

"And after the interview, I gave Mary Beth a thumbs-up," Robbie said.

"Has she missed work before?" Elle asked.

"Not as far as I know," Robbie told her, moving his electric chair closer.

"I think Mary Beth tried to help Charlie die by suicide," Peggy said, her voice icy with judgment.

Elle was surprised by Peggy's accusation. *Going from a self-inflicted overdose of fentanyl to assisted suicide?* Based on the lack of physical evidence left behind, Elle didn't want to assume either story, and motioned for Peggy to continue.

"If Mary Beth had to leave work early," Peggy said, "that's probably when she put those patches on and left him to die."

"Where's this coming from?" Robbie sighed. "Her diabetes was out of control."

Peggy shook her head in disapproval. "Why did you hire a young girl with no experience and serious health problems of her own?" She turned her gaze back to Elle. "Mary Beth was the only one staying in the house with Charlie during the week."

"You have no idea what's going on here." Robbie paused, looking at Peggy. "Daddy doesn't want a guardian." He turned to Elle as he backed up his chair. "And I'm supporting his wishes ... I'm meeting with his attorney in just a few, actually."

Sirens sounded in the distance. Elle glanced at Robbie. He braced himself and winced. She could tell he respected Mary Beth. Maybe he didn't like her reputation being trashed.

"I need that smoke now," he said to his wife. "Elle, we'll be by the van."

Elle nodded. "Thanks for letting me use your phone. I'm grateful you came by," she said. "I'm so sorry about Mary Beth."

Two police cars pulled up. As the uniformed officers approached, Elle waved them over to Mary Beth's car and they started setting up the scene.

Elle looked at her watch and leaned against her trunk, wondering how long she would be there.

Within the hour, a six-foot-tall officer wearing mirrored sunglasses stepped out of a dark unmarked car and parked on the right side of the driveway. He walked with a swagger to where the police were working, and after talking with them and viewing the body, he made a phone call. He walked over, keeping his hand on his firearm, and gave Elle a polite smile.

"Mike Slater, detective with the Mecklenburg County PD," he said in what sounded like a Philly accent. He clenched his jaw as he gave Elle his card. "I called the medical examiner."

Elle introduced herself as they shook hands. Her neck was warm under his stare, although she couldn't see his eyes. "I made the call to you guys. Mary Beth Abbot—you'll find her purse on the floor of the passenger seat. I checked her driver's license."

Detective Slater pulled out his notepad and pen. "I need your name and phone number in case I need to talk to you again." After writing the information down, he looked at the couple near the van, then back at Elle. "Did the three of you come together?"

"No, I arrived first," Elle said. "That's Robbie Blackwell. Mary Beth worked for his dad … and that's his wife, Peggy." She didn't say that this was her first meeting with them as well. "Robbie and Peggy arrived five minutes after me."

"Has the family been notified?"

"Not that I know of," Elle said. "All I know is that Mary Beth lives here. Robbie might have the number for Mary Beth's family." Her stomach burned from the memories of her car accident six years ago—her leg in a cast, waking up after surgery, being told that her parents hadn't survived the crash. It was her brother, Peter, and Aunt Sara who told Elle she was the only survivor. She couldn't bear to think about Mary Beth's family being broken by the awful news of the young woman's death.

Across the way, a crime scene technician was bending over Mary Beth's body. Detective Slater tapped his pen on the notepad, drawing Elle's attention back to him. "So how do you know the victim?" he asked.

"I don't. Her client's attorney asked me to find out why she didn't show up for work this morning." She hated Detective Slater's mirrored sunglasses.

"And what do you think happened?" he wondered, his voice steady.

She paused, thinking about her crazy morning. She told him about her visit to Charlie Blackwell: the fentanyl patches, his plea for help before the ambulance arrived, Mary Beth's empty insulin bottles, and her handwritten note that was turned over to David Cauley. "This case feels like it's going down a dark hole."

Slater nodded. "I was assigned to that case this morning but couldn't get there." He studied Elle for a long time. "I was across town pushing around a guy who beat the living crap out of his wife."

She didn't know what to make of Slater's tough talk and fought the impulse to ask. Truthfully, her head was spinning from all the events of the day. She inhaled a slow, shaky breath.

"Are you okay?" Slater asked.

Elle heard voices coming from the silver car and glanced back at the medical examiner leaning over Mary Beth's body. "No," she said. "Mary Beth dies on the same day Charlie Blackwell ends up in a coma?" She raised her shoulders in question. "Strange, right?"

Elle drove to Presbyterian Hospital, parked, and quickly ran to the hospital entrance. Whoosh! The electronic doors opened and the medicinal smell—a whiff of antiseptic—welcomed her. She loved the smell of hospitals and knowing that they were there for you when you absolutely needed them. It was like coming home as she stepped inside. Phones rang. The intercom crackled, "Paging the charge nurse, stat, to the doctor's desk."

She stopped at the registration desk and asked for an outside line from the on-duty desk clerk, a burly guy with a body like a sumo wrestler.

"Hey, Elle, what are you doing here today?" he asked, handing her the phone as if they were best friends.

"I'm here to see a patient," she said while dialing.

When Sumpter answered, Elle told him about Mary Beth. "She must have passed out pulling up her drive. She never made it to the house."

"Elle, I'm sorry, but I had to send you—"

She stopped him. "Charlie's son and his wife arrived minutes after me. It sounds like Robbie had a working relationship with Mary Beth."

"Well," Sumpter began, "Robbie does have Charlie's health care power of attorney, so that makes sense. Where's Mary Beth's body now?"

"She was with the medical examiner when I left."

"And Sergeant Harrigan?"

"She was waiting at Charlie's house to talk to Susan." Elle dodged out of the way of a transport stretcher racing a patient through the hallway. She told Sumpter about Charlie's initial diagnosis of self-inflicted overdose and heard his deep sigh over the phone.

"No lucky breaks today," he said.

The desk clerk shot her an impatient look as his phone lines started to ring. She smiled at him gratefully.

"Gotta go. I'll keep you posted." She handed the phone back to the clerk and thanked him. If only she hadn't been so late. If only she had been able to talk to Dr. Geller first, maybe he wouldn't have given Charlie that diagnosis of self-inflicted overdose.

She spotted Dr. Josh Geller walking toward the middle of the emergency department. His head bobbed about, like a duck treading water on rough waves. With brown curly hair as rumpled as his khaki pants, he looked like he had woken up that morning, slipped on his lab coat, and driven to work, straightaway. With a look of "Don't bother me," he turned the other way when he saw Elle.

She swallowed the lump in her throat. Dr. Geller pushed her buttons. Just a week ago, he told her, "I don't have time to care about my patients' lives. What I care about is the fifteen minutes I spend—diagnosis and treatment. Period."

"Do all doctors think that way?" she had asked.

"They do. That's the way we're forced to think. Now out of my way."

And she still felt the sting of his very first words to her, when she introduced herself a year ago.

"There's no glamour in geriatrics, and no one will pay you for your services," he had said. "I bet you won't survive another year."

She told him she was perfectly capable of surviving without his help. Though she initially thought him attractive, any interest in him had melted away that day from his antagonistic comments about her business. She was proud of her independent practice even though Geller had never referred a single patient to her.

She had started small and slow, letting the number of clients and their families help her decide how fast to grow. By six months, she had used up all of her start-up capital, and cash flow was really tight. That first year had been the worst. Fear about the Gulf War, the recession, and her brother Peter joining the military and leaving for Bosnia; fear about providing services not reimbursed by third-party payment; fear about playing in the big leagues—the list went on and on. But now, what gave her an edge—even though she was an outsider—was collaborating with physicians like Charlie's grumpy doctor. All the more reason she hated being late.

Walking toward the nurse's desk, Elle fidgeted with her copy of Sumpter's signed consent form and pulled out her notes.

Mary, the charge nurse, came over. She wore navy scrubs and placed a hand on Elle's shoulder. "Glad you're here," she said and hugged her with one arm.

"I see he's busy," Elle said.

"We're always busy this time of year. Kids are back in school. We've got colds and flu, on top of today's emergencies."

"Charlie Blackwell?" Elle asked and handed Mary her copy of the consent form.

"He's the third overdose since seven a.m. And this is Josh's fifth day on. Good luck," Mary said, shaking her head.

"I've never seen Josh Geller when he wasn't grumpy," Elle said and smiled back.

She held an affinity for hospital nurses—a shared kinship that reminded her of her own hospital days as she worked her way through undergrad and grad school—as though she could go to any hospital and always feel welcome. Josh Geller was a different story. "You know, Mary, I don't think I've ever seen him smile."

"There's a new Starbucks across the street," Mary said, chuckling. "He may warm up to a nonfat latte and three shots of espresso." She squeezed Elle's shoulder again. "It's worth a try."

Elle thanked her and made a quick beeline toward Dr. Geller. She wasn't going to leave until he heard her out.

He picked up a clipboard from the rack and headed for Charlie Blackwell's room. She ran to intercept him so they could talk. His legs were longer, but she was closer. As she stood waiting for him in front of the glass doors, Elle peeked in. Charlie's eyes were closed. His breathing was regular; he appeared to be sleeping.

"You're late, Larson," Dr. Geller said, standing behind her.

She whirled around. "I'm sorry. The police insisted on talking to me."

He mumbled something under his breath.

She held one arm across the doorway, blocking him. "Dr. Geller, it's complicated. His paid caregiver is dead. I found her, in front of her house, in her car. And Charlie's overdose was not self-inflicted."

He raised his eyebrows, uncovering sleepy brown eyes.

"Evidence?"

"I found five fentanyl patches on his abdomen, a heating pad over the patches to speed up the absorption, and the top sheet and blanket tucked under the mattress using mitered corners."

His impatient eyes stayed fixed on hers. She studied them, hoping his logical mind was taking this in.

He reached for her arm to move her aside, but she didn't budge.

"None of the fentanyl wrappers were found at the scene." She squared her shoulders. "If it was self-inflicted, where are they?"

"Did you see someone?" he asked and backed up slowly.

"No, he was home alone when I got there—"

"Your point?" he interrupted.

She kept up her steady gaze. "There's no way he could have mitered the corners of his sheet and blanket, not after getting into bed first. And who puts a heating pad over five fentanyl patches?"

"No witnesses," he said, writing notes on the patient record.

She didn't move. Why was he so hard on her?

"And we've got two separate drug issues here." He pulled a lab report from his clipboard and showed her the results. "We ran a drug screen; looks like he's been taking oxycodone and clonazepam as well."

She dropped her eyes and glanced at the levels of oxycodone and clonazepam in his system. "Your self-inflicted diagnosis means Charlie's house is no longer a crime scene. The police have stopped investigating—"

He interrupted her again. "My first patient today was dropped off at the door by his mother. She was so exasperated with his drug addiction that she left him here. Now why is it always on me? Don't people have responsibility for their own behavior?"

"Of course they do," Elle said, listening attentively, "but I'm telling you, Charlie Blackwell did *not do this*."

"And I'm telling you to back away," he said. "Now." He opened the sliding glass door. The room was stocked with surgical supplies, monitors, oxygen, and suction, like a mini-hospital prepared for a disaster.

Elle moved aside, then snuck into the room behind him and tripped over a chair. "I'm sorry," she said as she knocked down suture trays and a wrist splint. The cardiac monitor beeped and blinked as she placed the supplies back on the shelf. Charlie did not respond.

"Why is it you won't listen to me?" she whispered, not wanting to be overheard by Charlie. She held up her notes. "Here, read what happened."

Dr. Geller made no move to take her notes. He washed his hands at the sink, approached the bedside, and glanced at the monitor. "Mr. Blackwell, I'm Dr. Geller. I'm going to examine you again. Can you wake up for me?"

"He prefers to be called Charlie," Elle said, trying to recover her composure.

Charlie's eyes fluttered open. "Okay," he finally said, then closed his eyes again.

Elle watched as Dr. Geller worked. He pulled his stethoscope from around his neck and listened to the different areas of Charlie's heart. Then he ran his fingertips over Charlie's abdomen and palpated his liver and spleen. He checked the pulses in his neck, arms, and legs. When he finished, he stood up and glanced over at her. "How do I know you didn't put those patches on Mr. Blackwell?"

"Evidence?" Her face burned hot. Why would he accuse her of being a suspect? She shot him a frosty glance. She would have it out with him one day, but not here in the ED. He was Charlie's physician and Charlie depended on her, and that meant depending on her to work with his physician too.

Charlie opened his eyes again. "Doc, I thought I was dying. This young nurse saved me."

Blinking, Elle walked over and touched Charlie's shoulder. His kindness was like cool water flowing around her, taking some of the heat away. Bleary-eyed, she looked at him. Wisps of white hair were plastered around his face. He still looked pale, but his color was improving. "Charlie, who did this?"

The sliding door opened. Mary stood next to a woman in an elegant satin dress and blue high heels.

"Mrs. Blackwell—" Mary began before the woman interrupted her.

"Charlie, my *dear* Charlie," Susan Blackwell said as she swished to her husband's bedside. She brushed her cheek against his. "I was so worried."

Elle's eyes were drawn to Susan's overall poise and her striking stilettos. She looked to be about twenty years younger than her husband. Gravity had settled around her face, softening her once youthful features and blurring the lines between her neck and chin. Her skin looked as though she had spent the morning carefully getting ready for the day. Even with age, her easy smile and dark eyes exuded charm.

"Mrs. Blackwell, I'm Dr. Geller. Your husband is stable now. Would you like to sit with him?" He pulled up a chair next to the bed and gestured for her to sit.

Elle took a step back as Mrs. Blackwell lowered herself to the chair with the grace of a movie star.

"Please, call me Susan." She gently took her husband's hand.

"Susan, this is Elle Larson," Dr. Geller said.

"Pleased to meet you," Elle said and extended her hand. She could smell the hint of Susan's floral perfume.

Susan refused Elle's hand but offered Dr. Geller an inviting smile. "I'm sorry, I didn't realize she was here."

Elle sighed. "Did you get a chance to talk to Sergeant Harrigan?" she asked.

Susan kept her focus on Dr. Geller. "I'm the petitioner for Charlie's guardianship hearing. I'm sure you know what that means?"

"You're the person filing the action," Geller said. "You must think he needs a guardian."

"My attorney won't allow me to talk to her until the hearing's over," Susan said bluntly. "She's on the other side."

"Miss Larson's been asked to evaluate your husband," Geller said. "That's all."

"My attorney told me that she's trying to come between Charlie and me," Susan said with a sniff.

Elle's face flushed. "No, no," she said, slowly shaking her head. "That's not my role here."

Charlie's eyes fluttered again. He looked up at Elle. "I've done nothing wrong." He lifted his head and let it fall back.

"Charlie, you need some rest … and time to get those drugs out of your system," Elle said wearily.

Dr. Geller looked from Susan to Mary and loosened his tie. "Mary, would you stay with her while I see my next patient?"

Mary nodded and moved next to Susan.

"And find out what medications Charlie's been taking." Dr. Geller motioned to Elle.

She looked at Charlie one more time and followed Geller out of the room. She had wanted to ask Susan questions, but this was Dr. Geller's domain. She was okay with being an outsider and working for herself and for the client. If she worked here, she'd be supervised by the perpetually rude Josh Geller. *Ugh!* Still, she had to get through to him.

"Why don't I go over to the new Starbucks and bring us some coffee?"

"I'm sorry, I don't have time to talk," Dr. Geller said.

She stood, waiting while he finished his note … feeling like the girl in class with her hand raised, unrecognized and invisible. She had to make him see her more clearly. She straightened up and gave him an angry look. "Robbie is Charlie's power of attorney, not Susan."

"What?" he snapped.

"Seriously, I'm just telling you what I know and what happened to Charlie." She circled her eyes with her thumbs and index fingers. "What I saw with my own two eyes."

"Chill out, Elle—"

She interrupted him. "Chill out? I don't think so. Someone is trying to kill Charlie Blackwell!" Elle turned around and walked out in a huff.

# Chapter 3

Sumpter took an early lunch and spent the hour leaning back in his chair, reading yesterday's election results in *The Charlotte Observer*. He had never liked Bob Dole's plan to slash Medicare and Social Security, but Clinton, again?

"I can't believe it!" he shouted to his wife as she buzzed a call through.

"Morning!" he said, picking up the phone.

"Tommy Sumpter?"

"Sumpter here," he said in a calmer voice as he folded up the newspaper.

"Robbie Blackwell, sir. I'm sorry, we're running late. Our morning has been a disaster."

Sumpter scanned his calendar and looked at his watch. It was 12:45 p.m. He didn't like holding appointments for late clients, but Charlie Blackwell was contesting guardianship. He needed Sumpter's help and needed it right away. But he also needed to see how much information he could get from Robbie without giving away too much. "I can hold your appointment for another ten minutes. I need to be in court this afternoon."

"We're pulling in right now," Robbie said. "Daddy's in the hospital and his caregiver, Mary Beth, was found dead in her car this morning."

Sumpter feigned ignorance once again. "I'm sorry, Robbie." He straightened up and maneuvered his chair closer to the desk.

"The cops are still waiting for the coroner's report."

As much as Sumpter wanted to trust Robbie, unbelievable things happened during contested guardianships, and he was far too busy to let a family member get the best of him. "Well, I trust Elle Larson can tell us what's going on. She'll be our boots on the ground going into the hearing," he said and hung up the phone.

Sumpter opened the new case file and sat back as images from the late fifties began popping into his head. He'd been a teenager in high school when Charlie Blackwell was farming his late parents' land along the Catawba River and the Duke Power Company began planning how to dam up the river to make way for Lake Norman.

Walking over to his office window, he unlocked the sash and balled up the front page of the *Observer*. Julie poked her pretty head from behind his office door as he pitched the newspaper wad into the trash. He grinned at her. "Remember when Duke Power secretly bought thousands of acres that would later be flooded to create Lake Norman?"

Julie thought for a moment. "Farms were selling at rock-bottom prices, right?"

He nodded, his eyes holding her attention. "Lower than eighty dollars an acre, but Charlie Blackwell refused to sell."

"I remember that." She opened the door wider. "Speaking of Charlie, his son and daughter-in-law are here."

Sumpter paused and closed the case file. "Charlie was smart. In the end, the Blackwell farm was the last to be sold—and at the highest price. Charlie made a fortune."

She smiled at him. "I'll hold your calls."

"That's fine, hon; show them in."

Sumpter walked over to his conference table as Julie made the introductions. The resemblance shocked him. Intelligent eyes, strong chin … Robbie looked like the spittin' image of his dad when he was young.

Using a joystick, Robbie drove his electric wheelchair into the office and, with the skill of a Ferrari driver, backed up to a corner and parked at the far end of the table.

Sumpter stepped toward him and curled his own hand around Robbie's flaccid fingers. Robbie's wife winced as if she wanted no part of their meeting. She remained standing and stared at her husband. An awkward silence filled the room.

Finally, Peggy made eye contact with Sumpter. "These are the power of attorney documents you requested," she said, handing him the papers from her shoulder bag. "Charlie wants to talk to you about his will."

"Daddy has the original will at home in his safe," Robbie said. "He wanted you to have a copy."

"Thank you," Sumpter said. He filed the papers in the case folder he'd brought to the table, then looked back and forth between the husband and wife. "I could use some caffeine. Coffee?"

Peggy's eyes darted around the office as she shifted her weight from one hip to the other.

"Sure, I'd like a cup," Robbie said.

"I'll help him with that," Peggy said.

Sumpter pulled out a chair for Peggy and left the room. He returned and handed Peggy two steaming cups, one at a time, and sat down across from them. "So how did the two of you meet?" he said, wanting to make Peggy more comfortable. She was grabbing a plastic straw from her purse and setting up Robbie's coffee in his cupholder.

Robbie took a couple of sips through his straw. "Vietnam. I was starting my first tour of duty when I took shrapnel."

"He was airlifted to a military hospital for surgery," Peggy said.

Robbie nodded. "She was my ICU nurse for the first four weeks." He paused and smiled at her. "She followed me home."

"He asked me to move in and take care of him," Peggy said, her face relaxing. "How's that for a proposal?"

Sumpter gave them both a smile. "Did you get drafted after high school?"

"No, I went to college … I was twenty-one when Mother died. After that, I left school and joined the marines."

Peggy stood and thanked Sumpter for the coffee. "I'll be in the waiting room, Robbie," she said and then left abruptly.

"She hates talking to attorneys," Robbie said.

"It's a mistake for her not to be here."

"Look, we're not the Waltons," Robbie said glancing at him. "What she wants and what I want are different. She's supporting the petition for guardianship."

Sumpter grabbed his legal pad. This was a surprise. He imagined Robbie and Peggy on the same side. He didn't like the sound of this, although the next visit was plenty of time to hear what Peggy had to say. And maybe Robbie would be more forthcoming, talking to him alone. He watched as Robbie's leg started jumping up and down and went into spasm. He could see that every minute was a struggle. Yet with help from his wife, he managed quite well. "Well, I want to thank you for serving in the military and protecting our country." He wanted to spend some time talking to Robbie about his disability, but there just wasn't time today.

"So now what?" Robbie asked impatiently.

Sumpter swallowed a gulp of coffee and looked at Robbie. "As I told you, Elle Larson is a nurse practitioner. She specializes in assessing clients regarding their cognitive function and reviewing their medical records. She works with dementia clients every day." He paused, expecting Robbie to comment, but when he didn't, he continued explaining. "As a care manager, Charlie is her client too. She needs to first determine if your daddy can attend the hearing. Then I'll need to know if we need additional medical experts to testify."

"I don't trust experts," Robbie said, shaking his head.

Sumpter cleared his throat. He didn't like that Robbie was suspicious of Elle, but tough shit. "I accepted Charlie's case on the condition that Elle evaluate him at home. Then she needs to meet with family members, formal and informal caregivers, and any other professionals that have impacted Charlie's care."

Robbie shrugged his shoulders. "Well, I only want to deal with you."

"I understand, but her role is not negotiable. Robbie, you signed our consent forms."

Robbie's face looked exhausted. He nodded. "Well, she's already met with me. Like I said, I only want to deal with you."

Sumpter frowned and took a deep breath. There was no point in arguing. He simply needed to show Robbie what he and Elle could do to help Charlie. "Good. I need to ask you some routine questions. First, how did you find out about Charlie and Susan's wedding a month ago?"

"Susan called me." Robbie's leg suddenly went into spasm again. "October 6, the day she and Daddy were married. I didn't believe her at first. I was at home with Peggy when she called."

"So before the wedding, how long had it been since you'd seen him?"

"A month, maybe. I live in South Carolina. Rock Hill. I mean ... it's difficult for me to travel."

Sumpter took notes as Robbie talked. "The wedding?"

"They went to the courthouse. I was surprised Daddy didn't want more of a family affair, but it was only the two of them."

"Marriage is a contract, Robbie. Was it legal? That's what I need to know."

"I asked Peggy to call the justice of the peace—whatever the hell you call that guy."

"That's right, justice of the peace. He's also called a magistrate." Sumpter watched Robbie reposition himself, to take the pressure off his hips.

"He married them all right ... an hour before we called him."

"So you didn't know they were getting married?"

"That's right, sir, they didn't tell us," Robbie said. "Maybe they told Melinda ... my sister."

"Wouldn't she have told you?"

"We don't talk," Robbie said.

Sumpter took the copy of Charlie's will and began reading it. The will predated his divorce and divided his assets three ways between Amy, Robbie, and Melinda. So he hadn't updated his will to reflect his new marriage. "Has Susan seen this?"

"No, and Daddy doesn't want that. She may want to change the will. I can also tell you that this inheritance was unexpected by Melinda. That's really why she's coming home for a visit."

Sumpter looked at his watch. His next appointment was waiting. "I can get the marriage license from Susan's attorney, but I'd like to talk to your daddy about these documents."

Robbie nodded and swayed back and forth in his wheelchair. "If he dies, his estate goes into a trust. I'm just wondering … he's eighty and a World War II survivor. I just need to know this marriage is the right thing for him."

"And whether it's legal. As long as he consented, he meets the age requirement." Sumpter wondered if Robbie was more worried about the will than the marriage.

"What's the age requirement?" Robbie asked.

Sumpter smiled. "Eighteen in North Carolina."

"Then that's not a problem," Robbie said, rolling his eyes and smiling for the first time.

"Have you been back to the farm since it was sold?"

"Hell no!" Robbie gave him a surprised look. "You couldn't pay me a million bucks to go back there."

"No?"

"You know, over thirty-two thousand acres of farms, houses, and trees went under water when the dam created Lake Norman."

"Right."

"Most everyone I know had to leave. My granddaddy's farmland went under the lake as well." Robbie was shaking his head. "After Mother died and the farm sold … it was never home again. So no, I don't want to talk about that damn farm."

Sumpter stood and patted Robbie's shoulder, then watched him drive his electric chair out of the office. He thought about his life with Julie on Lake Norman. At any given time, there were thousands of residents like them who lived there. Paved streets, lakeside shops—a far cry from

Charlie Blackwell's farmland along the river. So why did he have this sinking feeling about this case?

It was 3:30 p.m. when Elle walked into Sumpter's mahogany-paneled office and waved to Julie, who was talking on the phone. Julie had worked in the same office as her husband for the past thirteen years. Pretty and petite, her sweater sleeves pushed up to her elbows, Julie looked ten years younger than her husband. In Elle's mind, Julie was the secret to Sumpter's well-organized law practice.

"He was a wild man," Julie had once told her. "Hard driving, hard drinking—drove to work on his motorcycle. No hobbies, just work." But when Julie came into his life, he settled down, and they married soon after.

"Hi, I'm a little early," Elle said once Julie was off the phone.

Julie frowned as her gaze swept over Elle's face. "Are you okay?"

"Just shaken after seeing Charlie and Mary Beth." She fought back tears.

"Oh, honey! Go sit, and I'll make a fresh pot of coffee. Tommy's just finishing up in court and not terribly happy."

Elle thanked her and walked down the short hallway to the waiting room, where several silver-haired clients were waiting. She sat by a lady in a sage-green coat and matching hat who was reading *The New York Times*.

A few minutes later, Sumpter stormed through the front door and down the hallway. "Shit, shit, shit! What a fucking waste of time."

Elle couldn't help but smile. He was cursing like a sailor with all these people in earshot. Sumpter turned the corner, looking sophisticated in his dark suit and conservative haircut. Medium build with naturally brown hair mixed with gray, Sumpter looked older than his picture, which was displayed on every promotional brochure in the waiting room. Elle often teased him about this, but he refused to change his photo.

Sumpter stopped dead in his tracks and looked up. His silver-haired audience was waiting and watching. Slowly they stood and cheered. Those without walkers or canes began clapping their hands.

Elle stood and clapped along. With the aging of the population, elder-care had become a number-one issue, and Sumpter had been making guest appearances on *Senior Focus*, a weekly radio talk show. Apparently, he had developed quite a following. If swearing didn't lessen the pain he was feeling from whatever happened in court, this standing ovation couldn't hurt. She felt her own energy lifting.

His face turned crimson, but he took a bow.

"My apologies, ladies and gentlemen. And thank you for your vote of confidence." He hesitated before going on. "I need to talk to my colleague for a minute. I thank you for waiting."

Sumpter motioned for Elle to follow him to his office. He shook her hand as she walked through his door.

"Bad afternoon?"

"Goes with the territory," he said, nodding his head.

"Nice to see you in action." She tried to cover her exhaustion as she dropped into a leather chair near the end of his conference table and made herself comfortable on the soft, cool leather. Julie and Sumpter were childless, and while they all three maintained a certain degree of professionalism, Elle felt an invisible blanket wrapped around her whenever she was here. Their office was home away from home.

"I like coming over here when I'm having a bad day—you never bark at me," she said.

"There's always a first time." He plucked a legal folder from his desk and sat across from her, quickly leafing through his notes.

Julie first opened the door with her elbow, then placed a mug of fresh coffee in front of each of them and hurried out to answer the ringing phone. Sumpter loosened his burgundy tie and picked up his mug. "Good thing we both drink it black," he said, taking a sip.

Elle cradled the mug with both hands. "Well, even if you did bark at me, I'd come here just for a cup of Julie's French roast."

Sumpter leaned back and breathed out a long sigh. "This is going to be a tough case," he said. "Abuse is an invisible crime." There was a tiredness to his voice. "Most cases are never reported. We track reports of child abuse, but hell, we have no way of tracking elder abuse."

"Are we talking about Charlie?"

"Yes. Studies show that older men like Charlie have the same risk of abuse as older women."

"So you also suspect foul play?"

"I always suspect foul play."

She nodded, uneasy. So that's why he wanted the emergency visit to Charlie. "Tell me again about Susan?"

"Well, she's sixty to his eighty. She works full time as the scheduler for a company called Compassionate Care and Prayer, and right now she can't take time off. Her attorney says she's moving in a little at a time."

"I saw no evidence of that in his house," she said. "Is she his second wife?"

"No, Susan's his third. His first wife died back in 1960." Sumpter paused, then added, "Charlie remarried a couple of years later."

"And the name of his second wife?"

"Amy."

"And when did he divorce Amy?" Elle asked, still wondering about the first wife.

"A month ago, after a twelve-month separation. He turned around and married Susan the next day."

"You're not practicing divorce law again, are you?"

He smiled at her. "Of course not. My heart couldn't take it. Besides, after my heart attack, going into elder law was the best decision I ever made."

"Next to marrying Julie."

"That's right, next to marrying Julie." He pursed his lips and glanced down at the case file. "So, let's get these relationships figured out."

Parent-child relationships could be thrown off balance easily, especially with a new marriage. Even if Charlie didn't expect to get help from his children, it still would be nice to have their blessing.

"Does the new wife have any children?"

"I don't know. I do know that Susan's an old friend of Charlie's. As a realtor, she helped Charlie sell his farm, back in 1960. I also know his ex-wife, Amy, has a son from a previous marriage. She's temporarily living with him in Davidson."

"Okay," Elle said, "so Charlie requires care while his new wife is working and in the process of moving in. His recently divorced wife lives thirty minutes away. He has a son and daughter from his first marriage, his second wife has a son from her first marriage, and we don't know about family from the third marriage."

"Well, there are no kids between the two of them."

Elle shook her head and tried to hide a smile. She could always count on Sumpter for comic relief.

Sumpter tapped a piece of paper with his finger. "Here's a report from the bank's trust officer ... he claimed the ex-wife pocketed a large sum of money. Apparently, Charlie came into the bank with her and requested to withdraw fifty thousand dollars. The teller gave him the money. Later, the trust officer called him at home to follow up. Charlie said he didn't remember. Amy told the trust officer she didn't know anything about it."

Elle sipped her coffee and thought about her clients with dementia. She was eager to assess Charlie's level of cognitive functioning. Exploitation, if it was going to happen, usually started quickly once the cognitive impairment set in. "How are his children looking at this?" she asked.

"Robbie and Melinda, from his first marriage—"

"I met Robbie today ... in Mary Beth's driveway." It was weird talking about Mary Beth as though she were still alive. This morning was so surreal.

He nodded. "His children don't understand the issues here."

"What do you mean?"

"Like competency, capacity, undue influence."

"Oh, the guardianship issues. Well, tell me what you'd like me to do," Elle said, not sure she fully understood the issues either ... not from a legal perspective.

"Interview family members, caregivers, anyone who's had a relationship with Charlie—do your evaluation and write your report."

"I can do the interviews, but Charlie won't be ready till next week. He was too sedated to be evaluated. I still need to assess his cognitive impairment: his hearing, vision, arm and leg function. Can he stand and walk? I really don't know."

"That's okay, we've got time." He paused and looked at her with worry in his eyes. "Look, I know today was rough. We're contesting this case—there are always surprises along the way. We want them out now … before the hearing. I don't want any surprises later."

"I'll do the best I can," she said, wondering if the caffeine was enough to carry her through the rest of the day.

"Remember, you're building our case, and if anything scares you," Sumpter said, smiling kindly at her, "call me."

"Hey, my knees tremble every time I step inside the courthouse." She was still freaking out from this morning, but she needed to prove she was up to the task. She wanted him to be proud of the work she was doing.

He smiled and pulled out the consent form signed by Charlie's son that he had faxed to her.

"Do you trust Robbie?" she asked.

"At this point, I trust no one. Robbie's a way for us to get in the door, Elle. My client is Charlie Blackwell, and so is yours."

"I understand. Can I get a copy of his medical records?"

"Drop by at noon on Friday. I'll make sure that Julie has a copy of everything for you."

"Awesome," she said, thinking the records might help her connect the dots and clear up her questions. She looked at her watch. "Anything else?"

"Can you pick up Melinda from the airport tomorrow?"

"Charlie's daughter? Sure, what time?"

"She's taking the red-eye from San Francisco." He handed Elle a copy of Melinda's trip confirmation. "She gets in at seven thirty."

"You bet—"

"You won't be able to facilitate a family meeting," Sumpter said, interrupting her. "But maybe she can give you some insight into the family dynamics."

"Thanks, Sumpter." She loved that he could set this up, help her find her way through the case. "Is that it?" She folded the piece of paper into her purse. Sumpter usually had a joke or a story to tell her after they finished their work.

He pondered her question for a few seconds and frowned. "My first guardianship hearing … it was a case where the court appointed a son as guardian for his mother. She had dementia and couldn't really tell us what had been going on. Without going into detail, we found out later that the son had been abusing and exploiting his mother for years. The case still haunts me to this day."

"I'm sorry," she said, not knowing what else to say, then blurted out, "How awful."

He didn't respond.

"Sometimes things are freakin' out of our control," she said, thinking about this morning and how easy it could have been to screw up a case.

"And sometimes, even us old skeptics can be fooled into thinking someone's telling the truth."

Elle glanced at Sumpter. He looked more serious than usual. She picked up her briefcase, her purse, and said goodbye, then quietly walked out the door. Across from his office the courthouse loomed large, like an ominous cloud against a clear bright sky. The hair stood up on the back of her neck. She hoped it was not a premonition of things to come. *Time to get out of here.*

# Chapter 4

The shadow in his doorway startled Charlie. The intercom going off in the hall sounded like a fire alarm, even with his hearing loss.

"Code blue for ICU. Nurse emergency in Labor and Delivery."

It gave him the jitters. He didn't remember moving to this new room with its fluorescent lights and liquid menu. He didn't remember much about the emergency room, other than having been naked and cold and the doctor ordering him to open his eyes. The nurses must have taken his clothes and wrapped him in a gown that gaped in the back. It upset him that he didn't remember all of that.

He struggled to sit up. He untangled the tubing that connected his arm to IV fluids and leaned forward to see his blurry image in the mirror above the sink: his hair, mostly gone; his face, gaunt, like a shell-shocked soldier about to face another battle.

Robbie was reclined in his wheelchair by the side of the bed, his hands jerking, much like they had since Robbie's war injury.

"Nobody taught us how to come back from war, did they Robbie?" he mused, leaning back against his pillow.

Robbie opened his eyes. "No, sir," he said, shaking his head.

Charlie thought about the years before Vietnam, the lines that were drawn during Robbie's childhood, those years of him fighting with Melinda. It wasn't the friendly kind of sibling rivalry—more like two kids at war—and he had tried to intervene. There's no more important relationship than to have a brother or a sister, he used to tell them.

He still felt guilty when he thought about that advice. Maybe because Robbie and Melinda had never learned to get along … and all those years when Charlie's first wife, Carol, had blamed him for her own unhappiness. He didn't exactly make up for her depression. She was so depressed that she eventually took her own life. But he had battled demons, too, and still did. And now he faced going to court to find out if he was crazy, on top of everything else.

"Daddy, I'm sorry about what happened after my accident," Robbie said, moving his wheelchair closer so Charlie could hear. "I knew you loved me … I did. It's just that I was struggling in rehab and needed to be around people who were positive … who could encourage me. I had to step back … especially from Melinda."

"I remember," Charlie said, his voice cracking. Before his injury, Robbie had been selfish and angry. But the tragedy changed him for the better. And he met Peggy.

Charlie paused for a second, looking around the room. "Where's Peggy?"

"She ran out to do a couple of errands. She'll be back in an hour or two."

Charlie nodded, trying to get comfortable in the bed. "You know I always supported you and the war."

"I know," Robbie said before Charlie could go on, "but Melinda and her friends were against it."

"After Vietnam … after your mother died, Melinda wanted to get as far away as possible."

"She called me crazy while I was still dealing with Vietnam in my head."

Charlie slowly shook his head. "It's a pain that can tear you apart inside," he said, knowing what was lost in the war and locked away.

"It did … especially coming home."

Robbie avoided looking at him. Charlie pushed back his blanket and remembered back—anti-war riots everywhere; Robbie coming home in a wheelchair, only to find his sister leading a college protest.

"I'm sorry I haven't seen you much until recently," Robbie said.

Here they were, grown men and still letting hurt feelings get in the way; still drawing those stupid lines. And then there was Amy. And their wedding. Tears filled his eyes. He didn't understand his kids' reaction to her ... as if they were ashamed of her. He wondered if the loss of their mother was a boundary they couldn't cross, so they pulled back and rarely stayed in touch. "I never knew Amy and I were heading for divorce. I want you to know I loved her, Robbie." Jesus, he missed his old life with her.

"But you two were separated for a year?"

"She had been in the hospital all of those months, then staying with her son in Davidson until she recovered."

"Who told you that?" Robbie asked.

"Amy told me. She never said a word about the divorce. It wasn't until I received the papers to sign," he said, his voice shaky with emotion. "What would have happened if I hadn't called you a month ago?"

"I'm grateful you did. Sounds like you aren't over her." Robbie looked closely at him. "So ... why *did* you marry Susan?"

Charlie held back more tears. How could he not have known that Amy wanted out? For the past year, he remembered only glimpses of his days: swallowing blood pressure pills and struggling to walk. Even his wedding day a month ago ... he didn't remember much of it. *What kind of man doesn't remember getting married?* He gripped his blanket. "I don't know, Robbie. I can't remember, and it's scaring the hell out of me."

"It's okay," Robbie said. "I'll help you figure this out."

Charlie reached over and put his hand on Robbie's shoulder. "I've missed you." It was good to have Robbie fighting for him. With Tommy Sumpter's help, they would erase some of those old lines and make things right.

Drifting in and out of sleep, Charlie woke to the sounds of war. Lights flashed in the dark. Guns fired. The smell of death was all around. He couldn't remember what happened, but things had gone wrong. The fog that surrounded him obscured the small village just over the Czechoslovakian border. It was sucking up his oxygen. He couldn't see the enemy and dove to the ground for cover, looking down at the hole punctured through his arm. He was wounded. He would have to fight wounded. He fought back a scream. Blood spurted from his arm and spattered everywhere. Then a familiar voice—

"Daddy, Daddy, *it's me*, Robbie. You're in the hospital. Nurse, nurse, please help! He's pulled out his IV!"

"Fight for your life," Charlie yelled. "There's no turning back!"

Alone in his bed, Charlie looked around the sterile room. He hated that nothing in the hospital was familiar. He had difficulty using his call button, adjusting the damn bed—that was uncomfortable to begin with—but the sounds were the worst. Even the bleeps and blips of his IV machine sounded like an alarm clock going off in his ear.

He sat up on the too-firm mattress, picked up *The Charlotte Observer*, and looked at the weather report. He couldn't read the fine print but knew from his window that the sky had been clear and the days were growing shorter. Right now, it was already dark. He glanced at the business section and tucked it back in the paper. It was still Wednesday, according to the whiteboard on his wall ... that meant today was his first day of sleep interruptions—nurses checking his vital signs and the lab folks drawing his blood. The hospital was bustling with people, but for him it meant waiting for a nurse so he could go to the bathroom. He pushed away his intense longing to be home.

Susan passed through his doorway and walked to the mirror. "Dear Charlie."

He watched as she pulled a brush out of her big shoulder bag, fluffed her hair, and applied more makeup.

"I've been to the beauty shop this afternoon, then shopping at the mall. I'm excited to show you my new haircut and cashmere sweater," she said, her voice hopeful, as though she was certain of the future. And now she was applying her lipstick.

"This is my favorite color, Scarlett O'Hara Red. You apply it with a brush to create rosebud lips."

"I see," he said. She was taking her own sweet time. Makeup had never interested him, anyway. He liked a more natural look.

Susan moved a chair to the corner, where she could be closer to him yet still face the doorway.

"Did you take the day off from work?" He couldn't bring himself to resent Susan. After all, she had convinced him years ago to sell the family farm. She did whatever she could to close the deal. And he was grateful she had helped him. But he didn't love her.

"I did," she said, breaking into her Scarlett O'Hara smile. "It's been a tough day." She reached for his hand. "Robbie told me you were delusional and pulled out your IV—"

"No!" he barked at her. "It was a flashback … the war." His chest swelled, and he swiped her hand away. What did she know about the nightmares he faced?

She sighed and lowered her arm. "Your doctor says it's acute confusion and dementia, made worse by being in the hospital."

"Well, if this is dementia, Robbie has it too. Only his confusion is from Vietnam, not Europe." Still, he believed his brain was now getting better. Every hour. If only he could go home to put his memories back together; it wasn't going to happen here.

He watched Susan walk to the doorway, peer down the hallway, and close the heavy door quietly. She looked back at him. "I talked to our attorney about the fentanyl patches."

"I have my own attorney, Susan."

She sat back down. "You could have died, Charlie. I let him know the fentanyl must have come from Mary Beth."

He closed his eyes and tried to remember the fentanyl patches. Nothing came to him, but he didn't want to believe Mary Beth had been drugging him. "What are you saying?" He shook his head and looked at her.

"Well, that woman Elle Larson found Mary Beth in her car today. She was dead." Susan leaned back in her chair. "Robbie called me at work to let me know what happened and why Mary Beth didn't come back to the house. I think Mary Beth put the fentanyl patches on you and then took her own life."

"Holy hell, Susan. Are you damn sure?" He stared at her for a second and squirmed in his bed. "Of course not."

"And Elle Larson stopped by our house ... unannounced," she said in a loud voice.

"You'll have to speak up," he said, even though he thought he had heard her. *I can't believe this is happening to me.*

"Well, she could get her hands on fentanyl too."

Charlie stopped her with his raised hand. He didn't answer. He couldn't think clearly. Not with her. People paid attention to Susan, even if he himself disagreed with her. But he wasn't afraid of Susan or Elle Larson either. And he hadn't been afraid of Mary Beth. He would listen to the advice of Sumpter. Sumpter would protect him.

Charlie looked at the closed door. "I hate it here, Susan. I need to go home."

"I'll see what I can do. In the meantime ..."

He watched Susan's hands from his peripheral vision as best as he could. She quickly popped the cap off a pill bottle, hidden inside her big shoulder bag. She pulled out what looked like two pills and reached out to him, the pills in one hand, holding a glass of water in the other.

She leaned forward. His nose caught a whiff of her perfume, reminding him of Amy.

"We're going to be okay, Charlie," she said in his ear. "You and me ... we're going to be okay."

There was a knock at the door.

"Mr. Blackwell, I'm here to take your blood pressure," his nurse called out and walked over to his bed.

He watched Susan pull back her hand and quietly pop the pills in her mouth. His nurse took out her cuff and stethoscope and kept silent as she rapidly pumped up his arm. When it was tight, she listened, and he watched as the cuff slowly deflated. He looked at her in expectation.

"Your blood pressure's elevated," she said and wrote some numbers on her clipboard. "We need to watch that carefully."

"Thank you," he said as the nurse headed toward the door.

She stopped to say something but hesitated, glancing between Susan and Charlie. With a friendly smile, she spoke in a loud voice that he could hear. "Mrs. Blackwell, the hospital won't allow you to give your husband any of his medications."

"No, no, this was not for Charlie," Susan said. "It was for my headache. I was just showing him what I'm taking."

Charlie blinked. He didn't know what to say.

"Can I get you more water?" the nurse asked Susan.

Susan shook her head and thanked her.

"I'll stop by again later," the nurse said, and she was gone.

Charlie watched the doorway as Susan drifted off to sleep in her chair. He remembered how she'd looked like an actress in her early twenties. At first, she'd been so charming. Sexy. Attractive. And now? God knows she could still act. And because she looked like an older version of Vivien Leigh and Lana Turner, he had a hunch that she could go to great lengths to get what she wanted. He was hoping she could help him plan his hospital escape.

In the late evening, after skating at the Ice House, Elle was back home, sitting on her carpeted stairway, sipping a glass of red wine and icing her right knee with Mac by her side. She had been skating mostly for physical therapy to strengthen the ligaments that had been sprained in the car accident and were now healed. Skating also helped her relax and forget about work—at least for an hour. And because the Ice House wasn't insulated, the cold rink reminded her of winters in Illinois.

She was thinking about Charlie and wondering how the rest of his day had gone when her phone rang.

"Can you hear me? Elle?"

"Hey, Peter ... there's some static, but I can hear you!" The familiar voice made her smile. She summoned an image of her younger brother in his flak vest, helmet, and full uniform. It had been almost a year since they'd seen each other.

"I miss you."

"I miss you too. How are you doing?"

"Not being able to leave the base is driving me nuts—it's like I'm in prison!"

"Please be safe," she said, wishing he wasn't in some small remote village halfway around the globe. Peter had been deployed to Bosnia as part of a peacekeeping force last year. While he had reassured her that the people in Bosnia wanted peace, the news in the *Observer* gave her the opposite impression.

"So, how's that five-year-old *terrierist?*" he asked.

She looked over her shoulder and smiled at Mac. "He's sitting right here ... on guard, like you." She turned and wrapped her free arm around Mac's neck. "When are you coming home?" she said quietly, before he could ask how she was doing. She'd had the day from hell and didn't want Peter worrying about her. Plus, the whole day was too confusing, and they only had a few minutes to talk.

"I don't know yet, but the first thing I'm gonna do is put my arms around both of you guys."

Tears filled her eyes. Mac reached over and began licking her, giving her a sticky face. "If only we could give you a hug."

"I just needed to hear your voice, Elle."

Peter's voice spoke right to her heart ... best friends and memories of home. He sounded more like her dad every time they talked—deeper, hoarser from smoking cigarettes every day.

He used to call her on military phones, but the static prevented them from having real conversations. So he began running his calls through a private carrier, spending half of what he earned each month to support AT&T.

"I know it's expensive for you," she said. "Call me collect—at least we can chat for ten minutes once a week." She couldn't tell him how alone she felt, not without making him feel worse.

"Are you still having nightmares?"

"Sometimes," she said, which was sort of true, but she had been hiding her PTSD from him since the accident. He was her baby brother, and she didn't want him to worry.

"We've got guys like that here—the ones who have seen the most combat. Elle, you need to get some counseling."

She sighed. "Peter, I did all the rehab and counseling back then ... I'm fine. Besides, I don't have time with this new case I've taken on."

When they said goodbye, Elle turned and looked at a framed picture on the mantle of two school kids looking up at the camera. Elle, wearing a mortarboard, her thick hair pushed behind her ears; Peter in braces and a striped summer shirt, his hair almost white from the sun. Two smiling faces from far happier times.

Peter had still been in high school the day Elle graduated from her nurse practitioner program. Six months after that happy day, their parents were killed in the car accident. What followed were days on end when she and Peter acted like strangers to each other, going through the motions of other people's lives.

He was a junior in high school when he announced he was exploring a move to Charlotte. Elle had been sitting at their kitchen table that cold April day with a carton of ice cream and a spoon. "Charlotte?" she asked. It sounded like the end of the earth. A new life? It made no sense. "You know, Mom was hoping you'd go to a Lutheran college, like Augustana." When he didn't answer, she finished the carton of ice cream.

"Everyone grieves differently," their family doctor later told her.

The next year, Peter was accepted at the recently coed Queens College, just after his eighteenth birthday. He told her he needed to leave their tragedy behind and start life again. Not wanting to be left behind, she followed him to Charlotte and tried hard to move forward too. And now? Standing at a crossroads, she was still straddling their old and new lives, whereas Peter had moved on, again.

"I wouldn't have moved so far away from home, Mac," she said, after taking a slow sip of wine.

Mac surprised her with a low-throated growl. Instantly, he was on all four feet. She looked up as his black-and-tan body raced down the stairs, making a noisy racket of snarling growls. He jumped on the door, clawing with his front legs, barking over and over. As she headed down the stairs, balancing her almost-empty wine glass without spilling, she looked up long enough to see a face pressed into the glass window of the front door.

"Jeez!" She jumped, the wine glass trembling in her hand. A man in a dark hoodie … she couldn't really make out his face, except for White skin and dark eyes that glared at her in fear. Mac continued making a racket as the stranger bolted off the porch into darkness and disappeared around the corner of Eighth and Pine.

*Who would come here so late at night?* Elle thought about calling the police, but after her long and exhausting day, she just wanted to sleep. She closed her eyes. Her whole body was tired. *It's not like the guy tried to break in. Mac scared him off.* "Great job, Mac." She bent down and ran her hands through his curly hair. He stopped barking at the sound of her voice.

She walked to the kitchen and put her glass in the stainless sink and began her nightly routine of checking the deadbolt locks on the front and back doors. She moved from the dining room to the living room and closed the shutters, making sure the windows were locked.

Up in the bedroom, Mac continued to growl. She was grateful he was her protection, but the visual image of that face pressed in the window wasn't going away. Therapy taught her that the shock of her parents' death had caused her to be on guard, that she overreacted at the possibility of sudden surprises. Any time she felt that panic, she needed to step back, calm herself down, and engage in the coping skills she was taught.

Before Elle got ready for bed, she punched in the code on the security panel above her bedside table and made a decision. She would tell David what happened. She would also use the security system every night ... at least until the Charlie Blackwell case was over.

# Chapter 5
*Thursday*

Elle's Fourth Ward townhouse sat squarely on the corner of Eighth and Pine and faced a city park. She had moved into the neighborhood of tall Victorians with their wrap porches five years ago, when a colorful restoration of the old painted ladies was underway. While her townhouse had a small footprint, it was three stories high, and she couldn't imagine a better view and location. Still, she struggled to pay the rent.

As she stood in her jeans and a T-shirt, pouring her first cup of coffee, Mac dragged his leash into the kitchen. She bent down and kissed his ear, pressing it to the side of his head. "Okay puppy, let's go."

She stepped off the front porch and approached the park with coffee in one hand and Mac out front, his leash in her other hand. It was their early morning caffeine and sniff walk. The air was crisp and smelled like spicy crab soup from Alexander Michael's restaurant around the corner. She loved these morning walks in the heart of things. It was like living in a small town within a big city and being part of the New South. Best of all, Mac's daytime and nighttime walks had forced her to meet her neighbors. The small neighborhoods created the illusion of safety. But Elle knew only too well how safety and security could be taken away in an instant and change a life forever. These days, only Mac made her feel safe.

They passed a businessman in a dark striped suit toting a briefcase, rushing to his Uptown office. A bearded man with matted hair and layers of old clothes sat on a metal park bench, reading the Thursday paper. A black labradoodle sniffed the monkey grass that lined the brick sidewalk with her owner in tow. Mac charged forward, greeting everyone with the same enthusiasm, then lifted his leg and marked the surrounding trees and bushes to claim the park as his.

By the time they came back home, Elle's house phone was ringing. She ran through the hallway and answered it.

"Aren't you out of bed yet?"

"What?" she groaned as she struggled to make the phone cord reach to the pantry where she stored Mac's kibble.

"It's time you invest in the new technology, Elle. A cell phone—you need a cell phone!"

"David, I have a pager." She opened the pantry door.

"I've had my cell phone since they came out in January. I just flip it open. I'm telling you, it'll revolutionize your business."

"That's what you said about my laptop. My clients don't use cell phones. I can't even get them to leave messages on my office phone."

"You need to work on that, missy. What if Charlie Blackwell's house phone hadn't worked yesterday?"

Push and pull. He was right about Charlie. And what about Mary Beth? *What would I have done if Peggy's cell phone hadn't been available?* Elle hadn't talked to David about that yet. "What are you doing tonight?"

"I'm fixing to shop for your cell phone."

David had picked out her Gateway 2000 that ran on Office 95 and Windows 95, showed her how to set up QuickBooks, and signed her up for Timeslips so she could bill for time. After installing Microsoft Mail, they set up her schedule and stored all of her passwords and websites. A cell phone sounded like the best next step.

"It's a plan. Let's talk later."

After they hung up, her phone rang again. "Hello?" It was David again.

"Hey, missy, something I forgot to tell you."

She was filling up Mac's bowl and spilled his kibble. Mac stepped in and nibbled from the floor. The doorbell chimed. "Can you hold a sec," she said and set the phone down as Mac raced down the hallway, growling as he ran. There was David at the window … still holding his phone to his ear. She grabbed Mac by his collar and opened the door.

"See, if you had a cell phone, we could still be talking." David handed over a brown paper bag, smiling. He flipped his phone shut as she gripped the bag and stared down into it.

"Biscuits?"

"The bread for every Southern meal. Perfect: tall and light as a feather."

She waved him inside. "Your grandmother's recipe?"

He nodded and leaned against the door. "I made them yesterday. Had the afternoon off."

"There's something I need to tell you, David. You won't believe what happened after our visit to Charlie Blackwell's." She told him about finding Mary Beth. Then she told him about the stranger in her window.

He listened and gave her a sympathetic look. "Did you call the police?"

She rolled her eyes. "Come and sit down. I'll fix you a cup of tea and tell you the whole story."

He glanced at his watch and raised his hand. "Save it. If I stay, the traffic will make me late for work. We'll talk tonight after the cell phone shopping," he said, opening the front door.

"Okay, okay!" She knew she was in good hands with him. "I'll take you out to dinner!" She laughed as Mac tried to follow him out the door, chewing the last of his kibble on the way.

At 8 a.m. Elle sat down at the kitchen bar with one of David's golden-brown biscuits after slathering it with honey butter and mixed berry jam. Southerners loved their biscuits, and in David's home, his grandmother's recipe was a beloved member of the family. Unfolding the *Observer*, Elle spread the newspaper out in sections and flipped to the obituary page.

Since starting her company, she had become an avid obituary reader, grateful when she didn't see any of her clients' names. Most obituaries were tiny, while a few were half a page, like those of singer Ella Fitzgerald or civil rights activist Barbara Jordan, who had died earlier in the year.

She scanned the page and nibbled on her biscuit. Writing the summary of someone's life was like trying to condense a novel into a bumper sticker.

Even the smallest obituary was a tribute to a life well lived, like Pearl, who had died peacefully, a cherished mother of three children and six grandchildren. Generous to a fault, Pearl's quiet demeanor and strength of character touched many and continued to inspire her family to this day. The next was Joe. He was a United States Army veteran of the Korean War and a talented trumpet player; always quick with a bad joke, Joe made people happy. Whether someone's years were spent as a baseball player, a piano player, or the first Black marine in World War II, Elle found the stories amazing and loved reading about the lives of unfamiliar characters, how they lived, and how they were remembered.

Elle read the next obituary and stopped. ABBOT, MARY BETH. She stuffed the rest of the biscuit in her mouth. *Who are you, Mary Beth?* She swallowed and pored over the text.

**ABBOT,** MARY BETH

Mary Beth Abbot, twenty-three, third-year nursing student, passed away suddenly on November 6 of complications from diabetes, a disease she suffered from since childhood. Her favorite food: tomato sandwiches. Mary Beth was a bit of a shopaholic and, like Judge Judy from her favorite TV show, wasn't afraid to speak her mind. She is survived by her mother, a member of *The Charlotte Observer* family. A private service will be held for the family. In lieu of flowers, donations may be made in Mary Beth's name to the Juvenile Diabetes Research Foundation.

Elle folded the newspaper. So Mary Beth's mother worked for the *Observer*. That explained the expedited printing of her daughter's obituary. Mary Beth's life was cut short by "complications from diabetes." But why? What exactly had happened? Okay ... if she died from ketoacidosis, from her blood sugar and blood acid levels spiraling up out of control, then it must have been a faulty insulin pump. Mary Beth had probably been wearing the faulty pump when she drove home to get more insulin. But wait, Mary Beth's note said, "pump okay."

According to the obituary, Mary Beth had been a third-year nursing student. She would know how to work the pump, so it must have been a problem with the insulin. Elle thought about the empty insulin bottles she and David discovered yesterday. Had she missed something? What if someone had taken insulin out of the bottles and put something else in its place? Elle stood and moved to her kitchen phone. Had someone tried to harm Mary Beth? Her fingers trembled as she punched in the police department's number. Her next stop was David's office.

Within an hour, Elle stood in front of David's personal locker in the Crime Scene Unit. They were listening to the election news on the radio as he inventoried the supplies he loaded up every day: fingerprint kits, tape for print cards, swabs for DNA, distilled water, brushes, and 35 mm film for shooting pictures.

"I'm hoping the days of Don't ask, don't tell are almost over," he said, pausing to glance at her. "I remember the first time Clinton was elected. He and Gore were promising to stop the harassment of gays in the military. That was four years ago."

Elle heard footsteps and turned to see Kate Harrigan walk through the door with a folder in her hand.

Kate looked at David. "Enjoy your afternoon off?"

He switched the radio off and nodded. "Caught up on sleep."

Elle pulled out Mary Beth's obituary and handed it to Kate.

Kate quickly skimmed it, then peered at Elle. "What are you doing here?"

"I'm a consultant on the Charlie Blackwell case, remember? We saw the empty insulin bottles on the caregiver's dresser ... and Mary Beth's note in the logbook? The pump was working, right? So, what if that wasn't insulin in those bottles? What if the bottles were tampered with?"

"What do you think, we've got a mass murderer running around Char—"

David interrupted. "Kate, can you fill me in?"

"That's why I'm here." She shook the file. "I have the report."

Elle shifted her hip and leaned against the wall.

Kate placed Mary Beth's obituary in the folder. "Apparently, Elle was first on the scene again."

"Who was called out?" David asked.

"Patrol and detective units. No obvious signs of trauma," Kate said. "Nothing suspicious, but one of your guys was still called. The victim had type one diabetes."

"Was she wearing an insulin pump?" Elle wondered.

Kate looked down at the report. "Yes, and it was collected."

"What about her car?" David asked.

"Processed in her driveway. Medical examiner did an external exam and took her body back to his office." She flipped a page. "He said she died from ketoacidosis, a complication of her diabetes."

"Autopsy?" David asked.

"Nope." She handed David the folder.

"No autopsy?" Elle asked, raising her voice. "How can he say the investigation is complete if he didn't test the pump?"

David scanned the report. "Why was your division involved?"

"We weren't, but like you, I responded to the Charlie Blackwell call yesterday."

He rubbed his eyes and nodded. "God bless those officers in the Providence Division. They don't get murders in Myers Park. But when a minor crime occurs there, the residents need the National Guard to come out."

"I think there's a connection here," Elle said, watching David close his locker.

"So you're afraid someone's tampered with the insulin," Kate said, jumping in. "That's David's department."

"Hey, I don't chase down suspects and make arrests," he half-joked in response. "Usually, it's one of the detectives that gets me involved."

He looked up at Kate. "No requests so far, but it couldn't hurt to test the insulin in the pump."

David slammed his locker shut and grabbed his bag. "Elle, with someone dying that young, Homicide routinely gets involved, and the chain of evidence follows, documented by the detective. It's a collaborative effort." He smiled at Kate. "We're looking at two cases here ... sounds like Elle's looking at one."

Kate nodded. "I think you're both a little crazy."

He chuckled. "You might want to spend more time with her and find out for yourself."

Twenty minutes later, Elle was sitting in David's office across from his desk while he took a break. "Let me tell you something about Kate. She was the first Black female police officer in the department. Her hardball style and ability to get along with the guys is why she's been promoted to Sergeant."

Elle nodded. "I can handle hardball. I saw a show on *Law and Order*—"

David interrupted her. "Wanna hear my gripe about TV crime investigations? They never have any paperwork. Not to mention that criminals are being educated by these shows. It makes my job more difficult."

"What do you mean?" she asked, eager to understand his role.

"For crime scene investigators, the paperwork is never-ending; there're separate property control sheets for each piece of evidence. For a major crime scene that involved guns and money, thirty or forty property sheets are needed—all in separate places."

"Are you investigating any young victims, like Mary Beth?"

He didn't need to rack his brain to answer. "Over the weekend, I had a rape victim who was only ten. She looked at me, hurt and broken. The kind of hurt you can only see in the eyes of a child who's been betrayed. When she went to the hospital to meet with the sexual assault nurse, I had to strip search the suspect. Full Monty. Head hairs, pubic hairs, penile swabs. I was expected to pull fifty head hairs, fifty combings, and the same with pubic hairs."

"More paperwork, right?"

"You're getting the picture. That is my responsibility, distasteful as it is. Anyway, I pulled more than twice what I needed." He smiled at her, his eyes watery. "It wasn't justice, but it sure the hell made me feel better."

Kate knocked on David's open door and stood in the doorway.

"You don't waste any time," he said as she held up a form, waving it in the air. He motioned her to sit next to Elle.

"I don't have time," she said. "Detective Slater signed the paperwork to test the insulin pump." She smiled and raised an eyebrow. "I think he has an eye on Miss Elle here."

David shot her a look of surprise.

"Just remember I did this for you." Kate placed the paperwork on his desk before heading out.

Elle glanced down. Mary Beth Abbot. Was she going out on a limb here? Probably. But she was standing up for Mary Beth, much like David had found a way to stand up for the little girl in his other case. She followed him down to the basement property room with its vaults for handguns and automatic rifles, vaults for drugs, locked safes for money, and coolers for blood, followed by towers of metal shelves—thousands of general items, all secured and tagged for evidence.

David raised his hand to stop her entry. "Can you stand right here?"

"Sure." Standing in the doorway, she watched him pick up a box from a shelf.

"Mary Beth's insulin pump. I have ten minutes to look for the fentanyl patches."

Elle thought about the two victims. Looking at them separately, she could see why Kate thought the first victim had overdosed on fentanyl and the second had died from a faulty insulin pump, especially if Mary Beth's diabetes was as unstable as the medical examiner reported. But taken together? One victim caring for the other. Both taking medication. One too much, the other not enough. Her shoulders tensed, and her palms were sweaty as David tightened his grip on the box. If only this room could talk.

After purchasing a cell phone for Elle, David drove them to Fenwick's, their local go-to place when the weather was nice. "This is dining, Carolina style," David said. Dressed in a crisp cotton shirt tucked into his khakis, he pulled out a chair for Elle at an outside table.

She removed her boxy black jacket and folded it over her chair. It was a warm November night, and the breeze smelled like cedar and smoke.

"Thank you." Elle sat as he scooted her chair in and took a seat across from her. There were six outside tables tucked under a purple-and-gray striped awning. She loved the purple neon lights along the roofline and tiny white lights around the windows, a casual yet elegant glow to the front of the building. David ordered two glasses of champagne and fried oysters to start.

The oysters were seasoned with pepper and tasted like the sea. "Mmmm," Elle said, washing the crunchy morsels down with champagne.

"Frying food is a real skill," David said, tasting the fried pickles that garnished their plates. "You have to be a Southerner to do it right."

"That's what keeps statin drugs in business," she said, trying hard not to smile.

After drinking their champagne and talking about her cell phone, they ordered the Thursday-night special: a half-off bottle of pinot noir and roast chicken smothered in pimento cheese.

Elle was happy that the wine was half price since she was planning to pay for dinner. It was a splurge, but it was the least she could do for David. She would use the credit card that she used to pay off her student loan and business expenses when the company had a tight month.

Their friendly waitress, Wanda, delivered a basket of sweet potato biscuits, and David gave an appreciative moan.

"You make freakin' biscuits every weekend," she said to David, stuffing a large bite of buttered biscuit in her mouth.

He grinned and made a funny face.

"What?" she asked, raising her eyebrows.

"Just lookin'," he said as she took another bite. "In addition to your being very opinionated and surprisingly strong—but clumsy—I've never seen a woman with such a voracious appetite."

"Well, my parents did teach me how to think for myself." Elle shook her head and leaned forward, finishing the last mouthwatering bite. "I think you're trouble."

As they ate, Elle asked David about the number of reported cases of elder abuse.

"What brings that up?" he wondered.

"My new client."

"Charlie Blackwell?"

She nodded.

"It's rare that we get an elder abuse case reported. Usually, it's child abuse."

There was something upsetting about his answer, and a hint of sadness flickered across his face before he glanced away from her. "What are you worried about?"

He hesitated briefly, then sighed. "My niece is eleven and my nephew is twelve. Seeing what I see ... adults duping kids ... it's ugly."

"You worry about kids, and I worry about older people. What a pair of worriers we are."

He nodded. "We're getting old before our time."

"As long as we get a break like tonight ..." She didn't know how to finish her thought and decided to switch gears. "Tell me about Detective Slater. Is he single?"

David sat up straight and stared at her with stern blue eyes. "Elle, he's not right for you."

Her face turned red. It wasn't that she was *really* looking, but still, she was curious. "Ouch?"

"I like to think we have a kinder, gentler police force in Charlotte ... it has to do with the people here and their expectations."

Now she was confused. "Doesn't he work with you?"

David exhaled. "Yes, Slater and I have worked together over the past couple of years, and he likes working with me. He's good at solving crimes and gathering evidence but not very good with relationships. He worked for years in Philly before moving here. Let's just say, he's proud of his Philly toughness."

"You mean the Charlotte police aren't tough?"

"They are, but Slater is gritty ... he's too coarse for you." David hesitated and shook his head. "Back in Philly, he backhanded people who talked back to him ... We don't hit people here in Charlotte. They wouldn't stand for it. You wouldn't either."

Her eyes softened. He was as Southern as sweet tea, sitting there, talking in his classy accent. The long *i* in "either" was drawn out, and he pronounced their city's name "Chahlotte," like *Gone with the Wind*. Far was "fah" and Myers Park was "Maahhs Paahhk."

Elle smiled and picked up her drink. "I have a question for you, Mr. Historian. Charlie Blackwell became wealthy after selling his farm. It was before the dam was finished. I'm trying to get some background." She leaned close. "What do you know about Duke Power buying land along the Catawba River?"

David chuckled and relaxed back in his chair. As their food arrived, he gave her a history lesson on Duke's plan to harness water power along the river, how the growth around Charlotte increased the need for more electricity. "The building of the dam led to overbuying farmland and then selling it as expensive lakefront property after the lake was completed," he said.

"You mean Duke Power turned around and resold the farmland as lakefront property?"

He nodded, taking a large forkful of his chicken.

"Doesn't sound fair," Elle said, imagining what it was like to be a farmer back then.

"We still ended up with Lake Norman."

Elle almost choked as she swallowed a mouthful of pimento cheese.

"Hey, life isn't fair, Elle." He shrugged.

"Tell me about it," she said, pointing her glass at him. "Speaking of not fair ... the physician who evaluated Charlie Blackwell didn't want to hear my observations about the fentanyl patches."

"I'm gonna start by sending your patches to the crime lab."

"I'm grateful, David—I really wish you were still involved in the Blackwell case."

"We can't prevent all crime, Elle. That's what you're askin' for."

"I know."

"We can't handle the caseload we have. Sometimes we have no officers to answer 911 calls."

Elle didn't know what to say. She sighed.

"What's wrong," David asked her.

"I don't know?" She shook her head and thought of possible ways she could screw up this case. "I think I'm in over my head." She leaned over and whispered, "I've never been an expert witness in a contested guardianship before—"

"I thought you told me you had?"

"Expert witness, yes; never contested. It's freakin' me out."

He dabbed his mouth with his napkin and tossed it on the table. "I'm confused. You're used to families who disagree ...."

She tried to think of the best way to explain. She was right at home setting up care to help someone. But in court, it was different. "If I screw up, it could mean all of Charlie's rights could be taken away." She frowned, thinking. "Or, if I screw up, the wrong person could become his guardian, and I'll be as miserable as Charlie."

They sat there in silence. Elle placed her own napkin on her plate and made eye contact with Wanda. David tried to intercept the bill, but Elle pushed her credit card past him.

"Please let me. You're always helping me," she said in a sudden rush of emotion.

He gently squeezed her hand and grinned. "Next time, just buy me a glass of champagne!"

David stood up and pulled out her chair. She hugged him hard as they said goodnight.

# Chapter 6
*Friday*

Elle stood outside of baggage claim and leaned against her family station wagon. The sun warmed her face. The sky had turned different shades of blue that people here called Carolina blue. She held up her handmade Melinda Blackwell sign and checked her watch. Seven thirty, right on time.

The temperature was pushing seventy. She was grateful for her white cotton blouse and knee-length skirt. Her black blazer would come off as soon as she introduced herself. She listened to her mother's voice in her head: "There's no such thing as bad weather. You just need to dress for it." But fall weather in the Midwest was never like this. By the end of October, kids back home were wearing winter coats under their Halloween costumes. By late November, it often snowed and was bitterly cold. But here in Charlotte, fall always arrived late.

Elle watched passengers move out of baggage claim. One by one, they piled through the glass door and glanced at her sign without recognition. She unbuttoned her blazer and rolled her shoulders to relieve the tension, then thought of Sumpter's caution: "I always suspect foul play." Why had Melinda not come home in twenty years? And why was she now back?

A heavyset woman with an overpacked suitcase limped to the sidewalk. Her eyes focused on Elle's sign. She was shorter than Elle with big red hair and dressed in a loose-fitting paisley top. Elle stepped up to the sidewalk and moved toward the puffy-faced Melinda and the sweet smell of Aqua Net. Spider veins ballooned across Melinda's face, and her bloodshot hazel eyes were the same color as the men's in her family.

Elle offered her photo ID for examination, then smiled and shook Melinda's hand. "Here, let me help you."

"I could have taken a taxi."

"Your father's attorney wanted me to meet you." She opened the passenger door and lifted the heavy bag into the back of her wagon.

Melinda turned and scrutinized her. "What is it you do, exactly?" She gave no indication that she was getting into the car.

Elle thought for a minute. She didn't want to say anything controversial that might scare her away. "I coordinate care for aging family members, kind of a concierge in crisis. I've been asked to help Charlie and your family."

"Well, bless your heart. My family's crazier'n all-get-out. I can't even stand to be in the same room with my brother."

Elle peeled off her jacket and folded it in the back seat. She didn't say what she had learned over five years: that her business thrived on the crises of families, that weird fights between adult kids over favoritism and lack of trust were common, and that contested guardianships could tear families apart.

Once Melinda settled in, Elle slid into the driver's seat and started the engine. "We're having such warm weather," Elle began, trying to make pleasant conversation.

"And I put all my summer clothes away."

Elle lowered the front windows halfway and followed the cars out from the terminal.

Melinda opened her flip phone and punched in a call. "Hey, Susan. I'm on my way. What? It was the only direct flight with an open seat in the exit row. Yes, I sat in the window seat."

Elle listened quietly. Clearly, Melinda had a comfortable relationship with Susan. When Melinda hung up, Elle glanced over and smiled. "So how was your flight?"

"I hate to fly. Usually I'm doin' the white-knuckle ride, if you know what I mean."

"I do," Elle said, nodding her head and trying to provide some support, some trust. "How long will you be staying?"

"Depends on the guardianship."

Elle glanced at her. "Are you here through the hearing?"

Melinda gazed out the window. "If I can stand it."

"What do you mean?" Elle asked.

"Like I told you. I don't get along with my family."

They drove along Airport Drive with the front windows down. Elle drew in a breath of fresh air and wondered what Melinda wanted from her visit.

"These red Bradford pears make me think about our old farmhouse," Melinda said. "The long, winding drive I crossed to catch the school bus. I had a psychedelic purple bedroom and posters of Woodstock and Bob Dylan." She stayed quiet for a few minutes. Her voice became husky. "It was a warm fall day like this when I moved away."

The view out the car window changed suddenly, from red pear trees to barbed-wire fences and a junkyard. Wilkinson Boulevard, the shortest route from the airport, was still an eyesore. Its decaying warehouses were slowly being replaced by new development. Elle sped up as they approached the city.

"I see the topless bars and retail gun stores are still here." Melinda shook her head. "I can't say I miss this place."

They exited onto the beltway that wrapped the city like a bracelet. Several new skyscrapers loomed ahead. At the center was a tower of glass rising to a multitiered silver crown, like some postmodern building out of a science fiction movie.

"Can you avoid the Uptown rush?" Melinda asked. "I'm in a hurry."

"Sure." Elle guided them past the city skyline on their left. "So when did you leave Charlotte?"

"After Mother died. I was twenty ... dropped out of school and drove to California in a VW camper with my boyfriend."

"Jeez, that's a big move."

"It was a big commitment. We married just before he started medical school."

Elle listened quietly as she turned off at the Third Street exit.

"I supported him through his residency. We settled into a small house in San Francisco after he started his endocrinology practice. On my son's fifteenth birthday, I discovered my husband was having an affair. Then my son was diagnosed with attention deficit and drug addiction."

"I'm so sorry."

"Now I'm divorced and manage a small inn overlooking the Napa River on the Silverado Trail."

"What about your relationship with your dad when you were young?"

"My parents' relationship was on the rocks, and Daddy just wasn't there for me," she said. "I'm fifty-six, and it's taken years of therapy for me to understand that Mother, in all her unhappiness, drove a wedge between us. Then after she died, the police department had detectives follow him around."

"Why was that?" Elle asked.

"He was a primary suspect at first, until they determined Mother's death was a suicide. But I'm trying not to be angry at Daddy anymore. He's had enough unhappiness."

"I'm sorry to hear about your mother," Elle said, thinking of the heartbreak of having your own mom die by suicide. She was relieved that Melinda was comfortable with her.

Melinda talked about her mother's depression and how her suicide had happened while she and Robbie were away at college. "I've cried enough," she said as tears welled up in her eyes. "It won't bring her back. All I know is the problems became worse for me when Mother died and Daddy sold the farm. If Daddy had just talked to us back then, I wouldn't have spent the last twenty holidays alone with my kid who doesn't even know his granddaddy."

Elle wound her way past Queens Road. "What about Susan?" she asked, hoping Melinda would continue talking.

Melinda's expression turned soft. "Susan loves Daddy ... has cared about him all along."

"That's important, isn't it?" Elle asked, nodding. "Real affection and support."

"She was friends with Daddy even back when Mother died. She was supportive of me and my brother too. And now she takes Daddy to doctor visits and supervises his caregivers. God knows, I couldn't do it. Robbie can't. He can't even take care of himself."

"It must have been tough on you, going it alone." Elle turned onto Queens Road West.

"It's too dark to think about," Melinda said defensively.

Under the shadow of the willow oaks, Elle pulled into Charlie's driveway. She parked the car, then glanced at Melinda.

Melinda shot her a suspicious look. "You were hired by Daddy's attorney, right?"

"Right, so Charlie's my client too."

"Daddy's eighty. He doesn't understand what he needs."

"Melinda, what if your daddy is capable of making his wishes known?"

"It was Robbie who went to see the attorney, not Daddy. Robbie thinks he's the only one who can do this—he's always wanted control. Yet Susan's been doing all the work."

Elle needed to find a way to build trust here and not increase Melinda's defensiveness. "Help me understand, Melinda. When did your daddy start showing changes in behavior?"

"Three to four weeks ago. Susan called me several times. Each time she put Daddy on the phone, and each time I talked to him, he sounded more confused."

"How's Susan holding up?"

"It's been difficult for her," Melinda said. "I was surprised at their quick marriage ... but Susan did us all a favor. It's just that now, Daddy's aggressive behavior has pushed Susan to her limit. That's why she asked to meet me and Robbie. I knew I had to come, reassure Susan, see Daddy before he no longer recognizes me."

"And what would you like to see happen?"

"If only Susan could be the buffer between me and Robbie. Susan knows what to say. I try not to make Robbie angry, but that's like steppin' on a hidden land mine in some battlefield and hopin' it won't blow up." She opened her passenger door. "I'm just so fuckin' tired of fightin' everybody's war."

Elle got out, too, and retrieved Melinda's bag from the back of her wagon. She attempted to bring the bag into the house, but Melinda stopped her.

"Susan doesn't want to see you."

Elle could hear Melinda's voice turn cold. Before she left, Elle thanked her for talking to her. She let her know Charlie would have twenty-four-hour care as long as he was still in the hospital.

"Is he that bad?" Melinda asked, grabbing her bag and limping to the side door.

"No, but the narcotics have made him more confused and unsteady on his feet. We just want to make sure he doesn't fall." She felt a chill as Melinda walked inside, dragging her bag behind her, without saying thank-you or goodbye.


Charlie Blackwell couldn't remember the last time he had been hospitalized. It may have been during the war as a young officer when he was just twenty-nine. He sat up in bed and leaned against his pillow as Melinda sat beside him. He had an instinct she was watching his every move, as if she were seeing him for the first time. He was feeling better, but still hated being here. Hospitals were where you went to die.

Melinda had gained a lot of weight, he guessed, from the tent-like paisley top she wore. She looked a lot like her mother. She had Carol's curly red-and-gray hair. Besides her looks, she also shared her mother's moodiness. His daughter was smart, but she was like a balloon with a giant empty space inside. One prick, and she instantly deflated.

He closed his eyes. He was still glad to see her. Melinda was only twenty when she lost her mother. Such a young age. And at a time when he thought they would have pulled together as a family, Charlie had found himself alone. The wedge that existed between him and his children was only driven deeper.

"I don't think I'm going to be around much longer, Mel," he said.

"Daddy—"

Melinda was interrupted by a knock at the door. Charlie glanced right, with his side vision, to see a young woman with sandy blonde hair and light blue eyes standing in the doorway. He recognized her but couldn't think of her name.

"Hi, Mr. Blackwell. Elle Larson. Remember me?"

He watched her balance a tray of steaming cups with both hands. He was glad she had introduced herself again.

"Come in, doll," he said, waving her closer, "and call me Charlie." He started to grin. "I'm not the big bad wolf—hard of hearing and macular degeneration. The middle of my vision is the worst. My side vision is better, especially the left side."

"He's going to lose it all, eventually," Melinda said.

"Elle, meet my daughter, Melinda. She's the optimist in the family." He watched as Elle smiled and placed the coffee, cream, and sugar on the bedside table. He was pleased that he'd made her smile. Elle handed Melinda a cup.

"Cream, sugar?" Elle asked as she moved an empty chair next to the left side of his bed and sat down.

"I'll take two of those sugars," he said and watched as she emptied the packets into his cup. "Can you share a cry with us? This will be my last year."

"He's been saying that all morning," Melinda said, unsmiling.

"I keep thinking this year will be my last." He told his story about serving under General Patton during World War II, the rivers they had crossed—some more than once, like the Moselle and the Rhine—swift currents in cold water, under enemy fire. "They made me an officer," he said proudly. "I was one of Patton's assistants several weeks before the war started; just damn lucky he liked me."

"Daddy, you think about that war all the time," Melinda said, "but I don't think that's why she's here."

Charlie looked up at Elle and Melinda. The days when he was home had been confusing and lonely. He had lost track of time, but these few minutes here with them had cheered him up.

"I did want to ask you a few questions," Elle said and handed him his thick glasses.

"Fire away." His brain felt clearer than it had been in months. He positioned his glasses on his face and his trembling fingers around the warm cup. He took a sip. "Ahhh, so good."

Elle pulled a reading card from the pocket of her blazer. "Look at this card, Charlie, and tell me what you see."

He put the coffee back on the over-bed table. "The lines are a little blurry and move around. There's a black hole in the middle."

"How long have you been wearing these glasses?" Elle asked.

Charlie thought he'd been wearing the same glasses for the past five or six years but wasn't sure. "I quit driving three years ago because of my vision. That's all I know."

"Do you have a magnifier?"

"No."

"I'm going to request to have your hearing and vision evaluated and bring in a magnifier. Okay?"

He nodded, wondering if he had neglected his health.

"Charlie, do you know where you are?" Elle asked.

On the wall in front of him was a whiteboard with the day of the week and the date, written in big black letters. He turned his head to the side.

Friday, November 8, 1996. Looking at the date, he wondered how he would spend Thanksgiving. He read the name of the hospital.

"Presbyterian."

"And what time of day?"

He glanced up at the wall clock then back at Elle. "Ten thirty," he said with a grin.

"Do you know why you're here?"

"Somebody's trying to take advantage of an old man with white hair."

"Daddy, do you remember what happened Wednesday morning that brought you to the hospital?" Melinda asked.

Charlie took another sip. "Good coffee," he said, seeing flashes of Elle coming to the house, flashes of the emergency room where he saw her again, some time with Robbie, and now, waking up to Melinda sitting next to him. He settled his coffee cup down on the bedside table.

"It's hard to know what you've missed if you don't remember it," he said, watching Elle's bright eyes stare back at him. Nothing over the past year had made sense now that he thought about it.

"You've been taking a lot of medication," Elle said, her voice reassuring. "Now that you're off of it, you may remember more."

He tried to hold on to what she was saying, knowing it might be gone the next time she asked him.

"A couple more questions, Charlie."

"Sure, but you'll have to speak up. I can't hear you that well," he said.

She moved closer, leaned in, and raised her voice. "Do you remember the medication patches on your belly?"

"Patches?"

Elle nodded. "The patches are put on one at a time. You peel off the liner and press them onto your skin," she said.

"I don't remember." Charlie moved uneasily in his bed. "I wouldn't be able to see well enough to peel off those liners either."

She touched his shoulder, reassuring him. She knew he hadn't put the patches on himself. "Can you remember anyone else putting patches on you?"

"When was this?" he asked.

"Early Wednesday morning," Elle said.

He shook his head. She was a good listener. Nice voice. Kind hands. "You're not from the South, are you?" he asked.

"No—"

"I can just tell."

"I grew up in a small town north of Chicago. Charlie, do you remember getting married a month ago?"

Again, he shook his head.

"So when did you first meet Susan?"

He looked out the small window at the far end of the room. The sun was shining in. He liked this young woman. But what could she do? Good God almighty! He had so many ghosts from the past. He closed his eyes and thought of Susan, when she had walked into their farmhouse with a contract and a bottle of wine that night so many years ago. The way she smiled, the misery he felt, the struggles with Carol, and trying to make a go of the farm. It was like the war in his mind. Flashbacks, guilt, gratitude, resentment for all that was terrible, and feeling unloved and lonely—all at the same time. He opened his eyes. "I met Susan back in 1960. I had been busy planting on the farm. It was a spring weekend, and my first wife, Carol, had gone to stay with her mother who lived a couple of miles—"

"I thought Susan was your friend before that?" Melinda interjected.

"I only knew her as a realtor, honey. She wanted to sell the farm for us."

"What happened?" Melinda asked.

"Well, I didn't sign a contract to sell the farm that night. The next day, your mother came home, and we discussed it."

"Do you remember the name of the real estate company?" Elle asked, sipping her coffee.

"No, I don't, but you could ask Gordon Thomas. Gordon bought our farm. He would know."

"Gordon owns a company called North Carolina Mineral Resources," Melinda added. "You can find him in the phone book."

Charlie remembered how responsible he felt, pressuring his wife to sell the farm. "I thought a move might help with her depression, give us a new start." He hesitated before going on. "She took her life the next day." He remembered the pain of calling Robbie and Melinda. He looked at Elle, his eyes filling with tears. "The kids were away at college at the time."

"We came home the next day. You put the farm up for sale the next week," Melinda added, "just after Mother's funeral."

"And that fall you moved to California," Charlie said.

"Daddy, did Mother know that Susan had been to the house?"

He shook his head. "Only that she dropped off a contract, not that she stayed the night."

Melinda stood up and stared at him, her eyes wide. "Susan told me you were having an affair. She never said it was with *her.*"

Charlie shrugged as Elle choked on her coffee. He looked down at his hands. "Melinda, it wasn't an affair."

"We never talked about this," Melinda said, shaking her head and moving toward the door.

"What was there to talk about?" Charlie asked, realizing he had disappointed his daughter once again. "You and your brother had just lost your mother."

# Chapter 7

Tommy Sumpter sat at his desk for a rare noon lunch and loosened his tie. Julie set a fresh cup of hot coffee and a grilled chicken salad in front of him.

"The waiting room's clear except for your one o'clock, and she's an hour early," Julie said as she picked up a folded document from the top of his inbox and placed it on his desk. "And Doug Kilpatrick's résumé is here, compliments of Doug Kilpatrick."

Sumpter unbuttoned the collar of his shirt and thought how pretty his wife looked in her black cardigan and pale blue skirt. Sometimes, in the early days, he would watch her work as she scheduled new clients on the phone and he ate his lunch with her behind her desk. But these days, sharing a meal together happened only at the end of their workday. "Bring in your salad and sit next to me," he said. "We have a few minutes."

As Julie walked out, he picked up the copy of Doug Kilpatrick's résumé and thumbed through the document, wondering why Susan Blackwell hired the Harvard attorney. Kilpatrick had represented some of Charlotte's most prominent and wealthy divorcées. The forty-six-year-old trial lawyer had made quite a name for himself. This was not spelled out in his résumé, but Sumpter knew his reputation. Hell, everyone in the state knew Kilpatrick's reputation. Kilpatrick's success in the courtroom meant he could devote himself to the rich and famous looking to end their unhappy marriages, and he could make himself rich in the process.

"Give me another heart attack," Sumpter said as Julie returned. He finished leafing through the résumé, shaking his head. "This is a guardianship hearing, not divorce court."

Julie sat down and placed her coffee and salad next to his. "You're worried about Elle, aren't you?" she asked, cutting her grilled chicken into pieces.

"Well, look at what's happened." Sumpter pitched the résumé across his desk.

Julie laid her hand on his arm. "And look at how she's handled things. How much harder would this case be if she weren't out in the field working with you?"

He sipped his coffee thoughtfully. Charlie Blackwell would have died, and the problems with this case would have died with him. He took a bite of grilled chicken. "I just wish she didn't have to testify."

"I thought you said she was a believable witness."

"She is." He sensed Julie wanted to keep their conversation going and smiled at her, suddenly feeling tired. "I just have a bad feeling about this case."

"Are you worried about how she'll do in the courtroom?"

"You're damn right. She'll struggle with how much to hold back when Kilpatrick cross-examines her."

"And that's a problem?" Julie asked.

"She'll see it as a problem." He thought for a moment. Elle deeply analyzed everything, looking back, digging deeper—she saw things and connected the dots like a finely tuned sensor. But she didn't anticipate future problems. Kilpatrick was clever. He was also a mean bully and Elle was naive. He thought how the courtroom unnerved her. "She's incredibly young, Julie. She doesn't wear a suit of armor." He frowned. "Kilpatrick will try to break her, and she won't see it coming."

Julie narrowed her eyes and stood up. "Sure, she's young, but he sounds unethical."

"More like cutthroat, and he knows how to use the law to win. Don't get me wrong. He's skillful." Sumpter stared off into space. "He's also a damn egomaniac."

"She'll be fine, Tom."

"Kilpatrick is friends with the judge and thinks he has all of the aces in his hand."

"Then you need to play your cards right."

"I'm not sure I can protect her."

"Elle is young and healthy." Julie furrowed her brows. "You're the one I'm worried about. Isn't this why you went into elder law, so you wouldn't have to share the courtroom with guys like Kilpatrick?"

Sumpter looked at the concern on his wife's pretty face. She was right. While most of his divorce and custody cases had settled, it was when they went to court that he had a real battle. A couple of his clients had been financially ruined because their cases went on for years. But that was all before his heart attack.

"I have no choice this time." He finished the last of his salad. "Kilpatrick's been paid seventy-five thousand up front by the new Mrs. Blackwell."

"How can she afford him?"

"What's it to her? She's spending Charlie's money," he said, shaking his head. "I can only imagine the hours Kilpatrick is racking up."

"What happens when it's over?"

"If the guardianship's imposed, the guardian of the estate will be ordered to pay all legal fees from Charlie's assets."

"Maybe you could do something about that," Julie said, picking up his plate and kissing the top of his head before heading for the ringing phone.

"I'll talk to the judge," Sumpter said as she walked away. He wondered again if the petition was brought in good faith. Elle would help him answer that question. She didn't know it yet, but she would be his secret wild card to play.

It was 12:30 p.m. when Elle dropped by Sumpter's office to pick up Charlie's medical records. This time, there was only one person in the waiting room: the same elderly lady with the sage-green coat and matching hat. Her frizzy, blue-tinged hair stuck out under the brim.

Elle thought about Charlie while she waited. His long-term memory was good. He couldn't remember what medications he was taking, but he pretty much knew he was in the hospital and why he was there. He remembered the names of his wives and kids—the horrible things too, like his first wife's suicide and being in the war.

Elle's dad had been just nineteen when he served under General Patton in the Third Army. While he rarely talked about the war, there were those few times, like when he drank too much and said he didn't like the general personally but respected him; he praised Patton as the best fighting general of World War II. She had been eager to learn about his wartime experience, especially when she was learning about post-traumatic stress in nursing school. But he couldn't go there. He had created this closed-off emotional room, like the proverbial Pandora's box, where he put all of those painful memories under lock and key. The war had changed him forever ... how he related to her mom, to Peter ... how he related to her. She knew he felt things deeply, even though he had secrets he couldn't share with her, kind of like Charlie and Melinda.

Elle's shoulders were tight. Charlie may have hidden secrets from his family—even from himself—but did he also have secrets about this case that she needed to know?

"Thanks for seeing me," Elle said as Julie ushered her into Sumpter's office. She pulled up a chair across from his desk and sat down.

"You need a cup of coffee," Julie said and was gone.

Sumpter took in her appearance, noting she looked tired but strong nonetheless. "How was your trip to the airport?"

She shook her head. "Melinda has sharp elbows. She seems hostile. I think she's scared."

Sumpter nodded. "This is the first time she's been here in a long time. When you see her again, tell her I said hello ... Now tell me about Charlie."

Sumpter had a client in the waiting room and didn't have much time, so Elle quickly told him Charlie's story. "Swears he didn't know he was marrying Susan. He actually thought he was remarrying his second wife, Amy."

Sumpter frowned and extended a document for her to read. "Aren't those symptoms of early Alzheimer's disease?"

"They can be," she said. "But not remembering details of a wedding is different than thinking you were about to marry someone else." Elle scanned the document. It was a marriage license. She looked at the signatures and didn't know what to say.

"Doug Kilpatrick faxed me a copy this morning," Sumpter said, giving her a puzzled look. "Apparently, Charlie was happy to sign."

"Has anyone talked to Charlie about all this?" Elle asked.

Sumpter shook his head. "Did Charlie remember you?"

"He pretty much remembered me coming to his bedroom at home but not going to the hospital, and only glimpses of the emergency department. He recognized me later this morning in his hospital room."

"What do you make of all this?"

She sat up and felt like a juggler—a lot of questions in the air and no answers. Not yet anyway. She crossed her hands on his desk. "He was given a lethal dose of fentanyl, and if I hadn't pulled off those patches and called 911, he would have died. I understand why he wouldn't remember much of my first visit."

"You think it's the narcotic."

She nodded. "Two additional drugs, oxycodone and clonazepam, were found in his blood tests as well." She held up three fingers. "Three controlled drugs and no orders for any of them."

"How long before you can evaluate Charlie's mental status?"

"Until the drugs are no longer a factor; I'm shooting for Monday."

"So how did the damn drugs get in the house?" Sumpter asked, pounding the corner of his desk with the palm of his hand.

Elle jumped. "We don't know. I'd like to talk to his caregivers—follow up on the drugs and other things Charlie doesn't remember—and Amy too. He told me that Amy left him. When I asked him why, he said he didn't know."

"Talk to Amy as soon as you can set it up and any key relationships with people Charlie trusts," Sumpter said, looking at his watch. "We only have one week, and I need your written report by next Friday."

Elle gave him a searching look.

"We're taking an eighty-year-old businessman, who's always been his own boss, into a courtroom, into this contested guardianship case. There's a lot of medical information we don't know. I'm counting on you to get it right."

Julie came in with Elle's coffee and a message for Sumpter. He read the message and frowned while Elle cradled the cup in both hands.

"First, you need to prepare Elle," Julie said, pointing at his calendar. "Your schedule is booked for the rest of the week."

"Can you get Elle's copy of the medical records and tell Robbie I'll get back to him? And Julie, can you get Elle a copy of the medical letter written by Dr. Woodham? The one that supports the petition for guardianship?" He winked at his wife. "I just need ten minutes to work this witness in the shed."

Again, Julie was out the door.

Elle didn't understand what he meant exactly by "work the witness in the shed" but thought he was about to give her a ten-minute lesson on witness preparation. She pulled a new notebook and pen from her briefcase.

"You work on the medical piece," Sumpter said, standing up, "and I'll work on the legal plan." He handed her a copy of the North Carolina guardianship law from his desk and walked over to his office window as colorful fall leaves fluttered to the grass. "If a person lacks sufficient capacity to manage his own affairs or to make or communicate important decisions regarding his person, family, or property, he can be found to be incompetent," he recited by memory. He turned to look at her. "Just remember, capacity and competency are not the same thing."

Elle bent over, looking carefully at Sumpter's handout. "Capacity is a clinical term. Won't Dr. Woodham's medical letter answer these questions about Charlie's capacity?"

"You need to answer the capacity questions too. But it's better if you don't read Dr. Woodham's medical letter until after you do your own evaluation. I don't want you to be influenced by what he says."

"But the competency/incompetency question—"

"Yes, it's a legal one." Sumpter furrowed his brows. "Only the judge can make that decision in court. However, the judge usually takes recommendations from all of the medical evaluations."

Before she could ask for advice on defending herself from the opposing counsel, Sumpter began coaching her on things to remember during her testimony.

She wrote notes as fast as she could: *Be very succinct. It's not a conversation. Just answer the question and stop. Don't embellish. The worst thing you can do is to contradict yourself. "I don't recall" is a perfectly good answer. Always pause after the question. As Charlie's attorney, I need a chance to object. Try not to touch your face or play with your hair—that's distracting.*

"And let me know when I can talk to Charlie in the hospital," he said, walking back to his desk.

"Will do." She knew this was his signal they needed to finish up.

"And let me know how your evaluation compares to the medical letter written by Dr. Woodham."

"I'll be happy to," she said, curious about the letter. She set her empty coffee cup on his desk, then tucked her notebook and the North Carolina definition of guardianship carefully into her briefcase.

"That will also prepare you for cross-examination."

"Thanks, Sumpter," she said, standing up, feeling the extra boost of caffeine and an anxious twinge triggered by the words "cross-examination."

Elle hurried into her office building with a bag of Bojangles' chicken and biscuits in one hand and her briefcase and purse in the other. It was 2 p.m., and her brain had been signaling hunger for the past two hours.

Back in the day, the Johnston building—with its arched, coffered ceilings and marble lobby—had been the city's tallest skyscraper at fifteen stories. Two upper stories were added later. Now the historic building was concealed in a skyline of towers, one reaching sixty stories high.

Elle's care management company shared the sixteenth floor with a small law firm, a dating service, and Executive Services, a small office next to hers that housed a receptionist to answer phones for the seventeen companies in the building. Elle's office was tiny, but she got a huge price break as the space was so small—too small to rent to other companies but perfect for her—the size of a large closet. And the sweetheart deal was paying Executive Services only $200 a month to answer her phone, Monday through Friday.

She opened the door and set her purse and briefcase on her desk. Usually, she stopped at Executive Services to pick up her messages, but she was too hungry. Not waiting to sit down, she took a big bite of a warm chicken biscuit. The crispy-crunchy coating and tender chicken had never tasted so good.

A chiseled face peered around her door, startling her.

"Grady Ainesworth, Executive Services. I made a pot of coffee if you'd like a cup," he said in a friendly voice.

"Thanks, maybe later," she said after swallowing. "Are you covering Sally?" She scrutinized the pale-faced boy, his pierced ear and wavy brown hair. He was skinny, though his loose-fitting jeans and Led Zeppelin T-shirt tried to hide it.

"Sally quit yesterday," he said, smiling and extending a long, thin hand.

"Elle Larson," she said and gave Grady a warm handshake. "So talk to me."

"I'm the landlord's son. I'm twenty-two, just quit college, and moved home. Daddy-O offered me the job last night." He gave her a tight-lipped smile. "My life's going to shit, so there you have it."

Elle laughed as she took off her blazer. She felt the weight of her own day lifting. As much as she had a fondness for the old Johnston building, it was the sense of belonging in this bustling city that was the best part of having an office Uptown. The only downside of Executive Services was staff turnover. Sally was the second receptionist to leave in the past month, and that was pretty average.

"Busy?" Elle asked, as Grady handed over several pink slips. She was not about to tell him what kind of week she'd had, for fear that he'd be scared away and the next to leave.

"Phone's been ringing off the wall for you. Will Morgan called three times."

"Did he say why?" she asked, giving him her full attention.

"Just that he's unhappy."

"Unhappy with me?"

"Unhappy that his brother is his power of attorney. Says he doesn't even like his brother. Says he'll only talk to you."

She was relieved that was all. Suddenly, she wanted to have a little fun with the landlord's kid. "He should have thought of that when he decided to make his brother his power of attorney, don't you think?"

"I don't know," Grady said. "I wouldn't trust my brother as far as I could throw him."

Elle chuckled. That sounded like something she would say. The kid seemed good-humored and bright. It would be nice having someone younger than her in the building. The phone rang next door.

Grady turned. "Peace," he said and hurried out to answer the call.

Elle sat down, crammed into her tiny desk next to a table with two chairs, and began returning phone calls, starting with Will Morgan. By

5 p.m., she had finished her second chicken biscuit and made her last phone call. She opened her flower-decaled laptop, slipped off her flats, and started a new document, *Blackwell Case: Unanswered Questions*. Like in a traditional mystery, she needed to know whodunit. Until the police department had proof of a crime, they weren't going to be out there stopping the crime from happening again, and that would be too late to help her and Charlie out. Her first overall question: *Who tried to murder Charlie?* Okay, so she knew how it was done—fentanyl patches.

She quickly typed as each question popped into her head: *Who was knowledgeable about fentanyl? Who had access to prescription fentanyl? And who had the opportunity to come into Charlie's home during the early morning hours and slap those patches on his abdomen? Who had the knowledge that a heating pad would speed up absorption of the drug?*

Her mind turned to Mary Beth: *Who was knowledgeable about insulin and the use of an insulin pump? Who had access to Mary Beth's insulin at Charlie's home?* She saved the document and printed the page, then pinned it onto her message board below her desk where no one else could see it. She told herself to breathe. She could hear Sumpter's warning that any answers to her questions needed to be proven with evidence. There were other loud questions in her head, and she closed her eyes. *How can I think my way out of testifying? But then who would protect Charlie?*

She changed gears and opened up her assessment document, typing in her evaluation of Charlie's vision and hearing.

Grady peered around the corner. "Can I talk to you?" he asked, giving her a questioning look. He walked his lanky frame over to her.

"Sure, I'm just finishing up here." It was five thirty and Elle wanted to leave early. She usually worked from eight to six, and three nights a week she skated at the Pineville Ice House. More than ever, skating had become the only hour of her waking day when she wasn't thinking about work.

"Your clients sure do like to talk when they call in." Grady smiled at her.

She laughed. "When people call a care manager, they like to tell their story because they need help, but they usually don't know what part of their story is most important."

"I like talking to them ... and I think they like talking to me." He looked down and started reading the top page of her assessment. "This a case you're working on?"

"Yup." She saved her document and closed her laptop. "This is confidential information, Grady. You can't be reading it without my permission."

He nodded and was quiet for a moment, his face earnest. "I thought all old people had vision problems ..."

She tried to suppress a smile. "Nope. But when they do, it can decrease their ability to recognize faces and objects. Vision is about sixty-five percent of our sensory input. It affects taking medications, driving, food preparation—"

"Not exactly life or death," he said, interrupting her.

Elle thought for a minute. "What if you had hearing loss and you couldn't use your phone or drive? What if you had difficulty understanding speech and became withdrawn and depressed? And what if the symptoms of your vision and hearing loss were being blamed on Alzheimer's disease?"

"I'd get help," Grady said. "Speaking of ... do you need any help here? I just don't have enough to do."

She studied him while reaching for her purse and briefcase. He seemed smart, and she heard a gentle voice when he talked on the phone. She could use the help—setting up interviews and checking references on the paid caregivers who had worked with Charlie. But tonight, she was going to the Ice House for some skating under colorful lights with DJ music. She had just enough time to take Mac for a walk and feed him dinner before heading to the rink.

"It's disco night at the Ice House."

"Disco is so seventies," Grady said, scrunching up his face.

"I was born in '67. Growing up in the seventies, it was all about disco." Elle smiled. A thought popped into her head. "Let's meet Sunday morning then, say ten a.m. Dilworth Coffee House."

"Awesome. Thanks."

"This is a big case for me that's going to court. I guess you could say it's a life-or-death kind of case." She stiffened, thinking of the paramedics and emergency team that helped her. "It was only because we intervened that he survived."

"What about the police?"

"The police aren't investigating anymore, and I need to find a way to pull in some help. So welcome to the team."

"Will catch you Sunday." Grady looked at her with excitement in his eyes and practically skipped out of the room.

Elle turned off the lights and locked the door behind her. She'd been hired to write a report and now to testify in court. So why did she feel like this case was so much more than being an expert witness in a court hearing?

# Chapter 8
*Saturday*

Elle woke up to Mac standing with his front paws balanced on her bed. He licked her face, calmly jumped on the bed, and with his wet black nose, gave her a nuzzle. Light peeked through the shutters as she squeezed her eyes closed and turned over, burying her head deeper under the covers. She loved Saturday mornings and the extra hours of sleep.

Mac forced his wiry muzzle under the duvet and began pushing the comforter to the end of the bed. Elle thought about this past week. Things had fallen apart and caught her off guard. But Mac was letting her know that today couldn't be as bad. No way.

Elle took Mac for his morning walk, fed him his kibble, and still wearing jeans and her CHICAGO LOVES DA BLUES T-shirt, crawled back into bed, being careful not to spill her second cup of coffee. She hadn't made any plans for the day except to read Charlie's medical records and see him later at the hospital. Mac looked at her with four feet in the air while lying on his back across the duvet cover rumpled up at the end of the bed. When he was a puppy, he used to demand all of her attention and hated being left behind when she went to work. He would pull clothes out of the laundry basket and drag T-shirts, underwear, and dirty socks around the house as if he loved her smell and would somehow find her in her smelly clothes. Now five years old, he was content to lie next to her while she worked at home. But he still went through her dirty laundry if she left him alone for too long.

Opening her briefcase, she pulled out an armful of medical records and stacked them faceup on the right side of the bed. "Mac, we've got one hour," she said as he flopped over to be closer to her. Elle stretched out her legs and sat back against the headboard.

Based on years of reading medical records, Elle read these like a crime novel: Charlie was the central character, the unsolved mystery examined by his doctors—only his story was read in reverse. The most recent visit came first, followed by the visit preceding, until the first visit was read at the end of the story. Like an author's carefully crafted plot, physician notes reflected a talent for storytelling and problem-solving, something few people got to see unless they were clinical professionals.

"Mmmm," she said out loud to Mac. "Charlie was seen just two weeks ago, on October 20, by Daniel Woodham, board certified in internal medicine."

Mac's tail thumped on the bed.

Elle didn't know Dr. Woodham, but he had been Charlie's primary care physician for just over a month and had seen his patient twice. His notes were handwritten, with an almost-illegible scrawl of a pen that required careful reading.

The rest of the notes were written by Dr. Parker, whose handwriting showed a tremor. She knew Dr. Parker. He had retired in his seventies with Parkinson's disease, following a busy Medicare practice in Charlotte for over forty years. From notes every six months, it looked like he had been Charlie's primary care physician for the past several years.

Elle went back to Dr. Woodham's notes and reread them slowly, letting the words sink in. Charlie's new wife, Susan, described her husband's memory impairment as gradual, accelerating over the past two weeks of their marriage.

"That's hardly gradual!"

Mac's tail thumped again.

According to Susan, Charlie had started having difficulty recalling names. More recently, he was getting Susan mixed up with his ex-wife,

Amy. He was unable to take his medications and had become more aggressive and physically violent with his wife and paid caregivers. He was unable to handle his finances and accused Amy of stealing his money. So after she and Charlie were married, Susan changed out the caregivers who were working with him. Charlie apparently remained very friendly to people, even when he didn't know who they were.

Elle sipped her coffee, thinking. *Hmmm ... new doctor, new wife.* Did the new Mrs. Blackwell tell Dr. Woodham everything that was going on? Of course not. They'd only been married a month. Yet Susan gave a pretty thorough history of his memory difficulties. It was all there. Time of onset ... progression of symptoms. There was no mention of other family members having the disease. She probably didn't know that.

"This puzzles me, Mac. No mention of a dementia workup. No order for lab work, an MRI, or CT scan."

Mac raised his head at the mention of his name, then rolled on his back again as Elle rubbed his belly and sipped her coffee. She opened her laptop and started taking notes: *What did Charlie have to say? No mention of Charlie's comments in the physician's notes.* She was still reading when the phone rang.

"Morning, Elle. How's it going?"

"Hi, Sumpter. I'm reviewing Charlie's records now."

"Any surprises?"

"Well, Dr. Woodham stopped short of a dementia workup. No neurological exam, no neuroimaging, but there's a written diagnosis of Alzheimer's disease very clearly at the end of his note."

"Anything else?" Sumpter asked.

"Give me a minute." Elle leafed through the notes again. The patient's chief complaint was followed by the history of the present illness, the overall medical history, and finally the physical exam performed at the time of the visit. Then came the lab, X-rays, and other tests. She knew the format by heart.

She leafed to the back of the stack, looking for lab tests. Thyroid and B12 were the biggies, as hyperthyroidism or hypothyroidism and vitamin deficiencies were treatable but could temporarily prevent the brain from working properly. She paused for a moment. "No order or test results anywhere." She typed *No blood work or neuroimaging studies.*

She quickly scanned Dr. Woodham's previous note from just over a month ago. This had been their first meeting. The note began with an entry of *poorly controlled hypertension.*

"There's no mention of memory impairment on Dr. Woodham's first visit ... little in the way of medical history other than his hypertension." He had listened to Charlie's heart and lungs, which sounded normal.

"So what do you make of this?" Sumpter asked.

Elle looked up at Mac, feeling like a magnet trying to pull out the things that didn't quite fit. "He needs a dementia workup, preferably by a neurologist who specializes in dementia. Alzheimer's is a disease of exclusion; other problems need to be ruled out."

"Set it up as soon as you can, and try to find out why this didn't happen."

"Sure thing, and Sumpter? The neurologist would be your best expert witness."

"You were the first witness on the case. I still need you."

Elle hesitated for a moment. She didn't want Sumpter to sense her reluctance. He might think she was a coward. Plus, the neurologist would be the main expert. She looked down at a note by Dr. Parker on September 5, 1994. "No mention of Alzheimer's disease by Dr. Parker."

Mac was happily asleep, eyes rolled back, snoring away without a care in the world. Elle took a sip of her now-cold coffee and read on.

"There's a gap of over a year between Mr. Blackwell's last visit with Dr. Parker and his first visit with Dr. Woodham," she said.

"Elle, I want you to meet with the ex-Mrs. Blackwell. Ask her what she knows. Ask the caregivers what they know. Let me know if you find out anything else from the records."

"Sure, have a good weekend," she said and heard his phone click.

She reviewed Dr. Parker's notes more thoroughly, searching for a diagnosis of Alzheimer's disease or any mention of cognitive impairment and found none. Her eyes turned to the lab report from blood drawn at the September 5 visit, showing a low level of vitamin B12. She paged through to find the physician progress note that corresponded to the lab work on September 5. There was no further note from Dr. Parker or reference to the B12 deficiency, although there was a "no show" visit on October 5, 1994. She compared Dr. Woodham's notes to Dr. Parker's but found no mention of the B12 deficiency. People with low levels of B12 had a higher risk of dementia, but a B12 deficiency was also very treatable. A small number of her clients had received regular B12 injections followed by ongoing oral supplements and experienced significant improvement in their cognitive functioning. "For Pete's sake, give him some B12," she said to Mac, as he raised his sleepy head and thumped his tail once more.

She opened her laptop to the Blackwell Case: Unanswered Questions file and added more questions. *Why hadn't Charlie seen a primary care physician in well over a year, given that he had high blood pressure? Was he taking his blood pressure medication? Who switched Charlie to Dr. Woodham as his new PCP?* She typed in *missing doctor visits* and *change in primary care provider* and added *no dementia workup or follow-up on the B12 deficiency* to her comments corresponding to Dr. Woodham's visit.

She glanced at the clock on her bedside table: 9:40 a.m. Things didn't add up. Welcome to the crazy world of Charlie Blackwell. She needed to move forward, like the medical records she was reading, while finding her way back to the beginning of the story.

Charlie Blackwell sat on the side of his hospital bed and finished two pieces of buttered toast and soft scrambled eggs. The food tasted surprisingly good. He glanced with his side vision to see a blurry but familiar figure knocking on his door. It was that young nurse practitioner who had rescued him at home.

"Hey, doll, come in."

"Good morning, Charlie."

Charlie watched her walk to the sink and wash her hands, close enough for him to hear her. She was wearing a long-sleeved print shirt and khakis.

Elle walked over to his bedside. "What happened to the caregiver? She was scheduled to start this morning."

"Susan canceled her. Susan and Melinda are going to take turns coming in." Charlie read her ID badge. "Elle Larson," he said, as if repeating her name would help him remember.

They shook hands. Her hand was warm, but she was frowning, trying to mask the disappointment on her face.

"I'll need to let Sumpter know," Elle said.

"How hard can it be to sit and watch me?" He pushed the bedside table away from his bed. "You tell Sumpter I'd rather be here with my family than some stranger."

"Okay, Charlie. I'll let him know." She raised her eyebrows. "So how are you feeling?"

"Like somebody slipped something in my drink and I've been waking up, wondering what the hell happened."

She pulled a chair up close to him and sat down.

He realized how much stronger he felt, though. It was good to be alive. He had survived something big and was grateful in a way that he couldn't put into words. He looked up at Elle, who still looked a little blurry. "But better than I have in a long time."

"The paramedics gave you Narcan. It's a drug that blocked the narcotics in your system. You were awake in minutes. It's like giving sugar to a diabetic."

"Thanks for savin' me." His eyes clouded with tears.

"Well, it was a team effort."

There was a comforting sound to her voice that told Charlie she understood. "Know what General Patton said about teamwork?"

"No, what?"

"An army lives, eats, sleeps, fights as a team. This individuality stuff is a bunch of crap." He watched a smile spread from the corners of her downturned mouth.

"Charlie, you've been taking three drugs that have not been prescribed by your doctor. Two powerful painkillers and one sedative. Do you have any idea why?"

"Oh God," he said, shaking his head. Who would have given him these damn drugs without his doctor's approval? Someone should have explained all of this to Elle, but he didn't know who that would be. "I've had help at home. They give me my pills every day." He stretched his tired back. "Y'all need to talk about this."

"The caregivers give you your pills every day. Is that because you forget to take your medicine?"

"No, I can't see the fine print on those prescription bottles."

"Is there any reason someone would want to give you an overdose of fentanyl?"

"No!" Charlie shouted, shaking his head again. "The people I've hired have been very good to me." He could not think of anyone who wanted him out of the way.

"Your lab work looks good now. But when you came to the emergency department, you were taking enough pain medication to be lethal. So unless you did this to yourself …"

"No recollection of any pain," Charlie said, thinking back. "But I would never take my own life."

Elle met his gaze. "How have you been feeling this past year?"

"Tired … dizzy … mostly sleeping. Then Wednesday, I thought I was at death's door." He paused. "And then this sweet young nurse was helping me."

"You remember it happened on Wednesday. That's great. What exactly do you remember about that morning?" she asked, smiling again.

"Well, I remember waking up to the sound of a woman's voice." He was enjoying her attention, although the mysterious puzzles of his life had always been hard to explain—it's the reason he usually kept them secret. He thought hard. "She asked if she could come in and opened the door. I thought I was hallucinating. You know, flashbacks from the war."

Elle nodded. "Go on."

"The room was filled with fog. That fog presses against me and makes it hard to breathe. I remember trying to move against a hot blanket—I heard her voice again." Charlie smiled and thought about what else he remembered: Elle's thick bangs, a fair-skinned face, and light eyes peeking around the door. She apologized for coming in, but he was too tired to respond. He thought he was dying, and she was there to help him. He had learned to fight back fears of death during the war, but this would be okay. Better here, warm in his own bed, than in a cold, wet, and snow-filled foxhole a world away. If it was his time … he was ready. And he had his own Nordic messenger to take him wherever it was that dead warriors went. "Then I drifted away. I guess I was surprised that an old soldier like me was gettin' into heaven."

"Well, this isn't exactly heaven, but I'm glad you're here. Just—"

Charlie interrupted her before she could go on. "I don't know what happened. I wish I did. But I can't lie in bed all day and think about it." He wanted to head home. "So what's the plan?"

"A neurologist is going to see you Monday and run some tests."

"Hey, I'm eighty," Charlie said and glanced at Elle, feeling impatient. "One day, this old soldier ain't gonna get up. But till that day comes, I need to keep movin'."

"I'll ask your doctor to make sure a physical therapist works with you while you're here." She narrowed her eyes. "Charlie, here's the deal … you're not safe going home. Not until we can figure this out. If you stay here, we can at least protect you until the court hearing."

He was not going to stay here a minute longer than was absolutely necessary, but he would keep that to himself till after his evaluation. In the meantime, he wanted to change the subject and cheer himself up. "You know that young doctor who treated me when I first came in?"

"You mean Josh Geller in the emergency department?"

"Right. Be nice to him. I think he could use your help," Charlie said and gave her a wink.

# Chapter 9
*Sunday*

Elle rested her steaming latte on a secluded table by the window, sat down, and placed her folder of notes in front of her. She liked the local Dilworth Coffee House. It was comfortable, laid-back, the service was slow, and she could always find a table. Plus, the strong coffee was the best in Charlotte.

As she watched the pedestrians from the neighborhood come in for their morning joe, she called Grady. "I'm smelling ground coffee beans."

"Where are you?" Grady asked, sounding half asleep.

"Dilworth Coffee." She took a sip of her latte.

"I'll be there at ten," he said, yawning.

"What's your favorite?"

"Cappuccino."

"Great," Elle said, moving to the line in front of the register. "Two shots of espresso?"

"Make it three."

"I've saved a spot by the window."

A couple of minutes after ten, Grady pulled out a chair and sat down in front of his cappuccino, his still-damp hair waving across his pale face. Tall and thin, he wore Dr. Martens and a short-sleeved T-shirt with a moon over the ocean on the front. Elle wondered if he was anemic.

"You look tired," Elle said.

"Sister Hazel—heard of 'em?"

Elle thought of last summer's boyfriend at the beach where she first saw Ken Block on stage strumming his beat-up guitar while they stood in a packed house shouting out the chorus. "Sister Hazel, 'All for You,' right?"

"Saw them at South End last night. They are da bomb, like poetry. I am sick of grunge bands. Too much negativity."

"Da bomb," Elle repeated with a smile.

"You know how the band got its name?"

"A local woman who ran a homeless shelter."

He nodded. "Yes! She's also a Baptist minister."

Elle glanced at her watch. She was meeting David later, so she had to get the ball rolling here. She curled her hands around her latte and peered at Grady. "So are you sure you wanna work with me?"

"Yeah! From what I've seen, I think what you do is awesome," Grady said, breaking into an eager smile.

She smiled back. After getting spurned by Susan, Robbie, and Josh this week, it was refreshing to see someone so enthusiastic about working with her. Elle looked around to make sure no one was listening. "When a client wants to hire a private caregiver, we always screen them first. Monday morning, I'll show you how we do our regular reference checks and criminal background checks, how to look for driving and credit card problems." She handed him a computerized list of paid caregivers. "This case is going to court in a week."

Grady lowered his voice, his face solemn. "One question, first. Where did the narcotics come from?"

Elle picked up her copy of the caregiver list. Her eyes widened. "How did you know about the narcotics?"

"Just a hunch." He raised his hands as if to defend himself. "Hey, I was into grunge music for a while. Drugs were like a badge of honor."

"But I'm bound by client confidentiality, Grady. That means you can't talk about this case to anyone. Okay?"

"Did you know ... Charlotte's gang leaders traffic narcotics from their jail cells?" He leaned forward gesturing with his hands.

Elle's eyes widened farther. "Now you're scaring me." She sipped her latte for support. "The narcotics were never prescribed for Charlie."

His face was filled with excitement. "That's what I mean. If we start poking around—"

Elle interrupted. "We're talking fentanyl patches, not cocaine."

"Still, we need a source," Grady said.

Elle felt a red flag going up and slowly placed her list back on the table. *He's just eager. Trying to figure out who he is ... what he's going to be. I was like that too, at his age.*

"Grady, I need to introduce you to a friend of mine. He's a crime scene investigator. That might be your calling, but we're a care management company."

"I thought this case was going to court ..."

"All the more reason it needs to be done by the book. I'd like you to screen the paid caregivers. I'll focus on family members and friends and places that provide pain relief or anesthesia," she said.

"You mean like hospitals?"

Elle nodded. "But that's not why you're here." She pointed to the names on the list in front of him. "I need you to screen these people here."

"Okay, and then what?"

"Grady, let me be clear: The hospitals can't talk to you about missing fentanyl." Was she making a mistake asking the landlord's son for help? She watched him scan the list and stretch his hands on the table.

Grady slumped in his chair; his mouth turned down. "Doing these background checks doesn't sound like I'm helpin' y'all much ..."

"They're a priority for Charlie. Then you can schedule the caregivers for appointments in the office. I need to interview each one."

Grady was silent for a moment, and Elle took the opportunity to help him understand. "The physician who examined Charlie said he overdosed. He called it self-inflicted, so the police stopped their investigation." She sighed, wondering if she said too much. She imagined Grady trying to investigate the case on his own, and his father as her landlord asking her to vacate the building.

"I'm just saying, if you found out who had access to the narcotics, we could figure out who has motive," he said.

Elle shook her head. "Seriously, if we find that a crime has been committed, we'll get the police involved. What I want us to do"—she gestured between the two of them—"is stay one or two steps ahead of the crime. Doesn't that make us the real crime fighters?"

Elle and Grady read over the list. She stopped and scratched out the first two names on both their lists with her pen.

"Mr. and Mrs. Caylo were a husband-and-wife team who worked for Charlie for a number of years," she said, shifting Grady's paper back to its place in front of him.

"What did they do?"

"Mrs. Caylo cleaned the house and prepared meals. Mr. Caylo maintained the yard and the last year drove Charlie around wherever he needed to go."

"Why wasn't Charlie driving?" Grady asked.

"His vision was worse from macular degeneration, and he failed his driver's test. That was three years ago."

"So why cross them off the list?"

"They moved back to the Philippines two years ago." She tapped the pen on the next name on the list. "That's when Geena Louise Dixon was hired."

"So Geena Louise worked with Charlie the longest?" Grady asked.

"The longest in the past two years. A month ago, when Susan married Charlie, Geena Louise was the first to go." Elle paused. *This kid is smart. He's asking good questions.* "From what I've been told, Geena Louise still visits Charlie from time to time."

"How did Charlie find these people?" Grady asked and pushed the hair off his forehead.

The coffee house was bustling now. Across the room, the line at the register was getting longer. Elle lowered her voice. Soon it would be hard to have a private conversation. "Compassionate Care and Prayer."

He squinted and frowned. "Huh?"

She wondered how to best explain while tightening Grady's focus on the task at hand. There were home care agencies and home health agencies, caregiver registries, and staffing agencies. Some were highly regulated; others were not. And then there was The Underground. "Compassionate Care and Prayer isn't licensed; it's just a handful of caregivers who decided to work together and give themselves a name. Administrators from the retirement communities call them The Underground because they travel around from one community to another, banging on doors, getting hired off the street."

"What's wrong with being unlicensed?" he asked.

"It's not legal to provide hands-on care in North Carolina without a home care license, and Charlie requires hands-on care. They began working with Charlie in 1994. What I want you to do is check the references for the caregivers who have worked with Charlie over the past two years. Then see what you can find out about Compassionate Care and Prayer. I want to know how they screen their caregivers and what kind of other cases they handle."

"Sure," Grady said, making notes along his copy of the list.

"Ya know, when I moved to Charlotte and started my company, no one asked about my credentials," Elle said as she played with her cup, moving it in circles. She chuckled softly. "People asked me if I was baptized though, and where I went to church."

He barked out a laugh. "Welcome to the Bible Belt," he said. "What church y'all go to?"

Elle smiled, pleased that she made him laugh.

Grady opened a sling-style bag and pulled out two oatmeal cookies wrapped in plastic and gave Elle one.

"Thanks," Elle said, unwrapping and breaking off a piece of the cookie. "A total of four caregivers have worked with Charlie over the past two years: Geena Louise and Florence Benson, from 1994 until a month ago; Mary Beth Abbot and Jane Hale only since he married Susan." She popped the morsel into her mouth.

"So, for the last month?"

"That's right," Elle said, then finished the cookie. "And Mary Beth died this past Wednesday morning . . . complications from diabetes." She didn't tell him about finding Mary Beth's body in her driveway. It was still too weird.

Grady offered her a second cookie. "I made these yesterday. I've plenty more at home."

Elle thanked him and slipped the cookie into her purse.

"What about Charlie's kids?" Grady asked.

Elle nodded. "I've been checking out Robbie and Melinda."

They spoke for a few more minutes as they finished their coffees, then Elle told him she had to head out. She placed the empty cups on the counter and grabbed her folder from Grady. She hitched her purse higher on her shoulder as they walked out. "Right now, I'm not comfortable with any of these people working with Charlie," she said, a haunted look sweeping over her face. Estranged family ... no one watching. Charlie separated for a year, then divorced and married the next day. Elle shivered and whispered, "It's our responsibility to keep Charlie safe."

Elle was spending Sunday afternoon with David, who had invited her to a boat party on North Harbor's Davidson Landing. She said goodbye to Mac and grabbed her backpack and her meatball appetizer as David's Porsche, its faded red paint and dented fender, pulled up to her house.

"Can't we just do something fun that doesn't involve work?" Elle asked.

"It's not a work party," he said, opening the passenger door for her. "It's a cruise on Lake Norman, and the forecast is seventy and sunny—the last warm weekend before the weather turns cold."

"I thought you said you got a last-minute invite from a work friend." She settled into her seat.

"Right, but I hardly know the guy." He raised his eyebrows and smiled. "I happened to see him last week. It's not like anyone else from the police department will be there. C'mon, it's a thirty-minute drive."

"Okay, okay, it'll be nice to watch the sunset," she said and smiled back.

Though David kept his sexual orientation under his hat, he was inclusive where Elle was concerned. She tried to include him as well, though he knew far more people in Charlotte than she did. It was nobody's business but his own that David was gay. But it was always in the back of her mind when they were out in public. What if she slipped up and gave him away? She'd never forgive herself. Some people wondered about their relationship. Were they friends? More than friends? Being his friend meant keeping his secrets. It was like helping him hide in plain sight.

"There's someone I want you to meet," he said, putting on his sunglasses. "We're getting there early."

The air was warm and dry as David drove north on Interstate 77 with the windows down.

"A friend?" Elle rolled her eyes.

"Not tellin'. Did you know this car can go from zero to sixty in less than five seconds?"

"I believe you, but please don't show me. My week's been weird enough," she said, thinking how life had turned upside down since Wednesday. "I just want to be safe."

"That's obvious by the car you drive."

"Hey, my Volvo brought me to Charlotte, right?"

Just before Exit 30, they crossed over Lake Norman. The sun shimmered across the rippling water. Burnt red, yellow, and orange trees reflected around the lake.

"I can just imagine you coming across the Blue Ridge Parkway in your white refrigerator on wheels," he said with a hint of a smile.

She laughed.

"Here she comes. Charlotte, brace yourself," he said leaning against his steering wheel.

"So why did you get this car?" she asked, trying to put the focus back on him.

"Dream car ... red has always been my favorite color. I was only twenty-four. An act of self-expression, I guess."

She couldn't help but smile. David could make her laugh until she was in tears. He was like a good book, a colorful gift to her from the universe. This was going to be a good day.

The party boat was anchored at the marina in a deep-water cove. David carried his cooler with two champagne bottles on ice. Elle followed, balancing her backpack and a casserole dish of Norwegian meatballs.

"You're the first to arrive," Captain Brian said, helping them onboard and directing them to the front deck.

Elle spotted the DJ setting up his music equipment.

"First things first," David said. "Champagne."

They found a comfortable spot on the starboard side of the boat. He sat down next to her, their legs dangling above the water as the boat rocked gently and waves lapped against the hull. Elle watched him pour the bubbling gold into glass flutes.

"Did I ever tell you that I drink to get social?" she mused.

"You?" He raised his eyebrows.

"Funny, right?"

He nodded.

"I'm a nervous wreck in a crowd of strangers." She scanned the shoreline. It wasn't Lake Michigan; still, it was an awesome place on the water. The old Blackwell farm was down the road from the lake ... somewhere in the direction of the Cowans Ford Dam. She just didn't know where. She was about to ask David if he knew when a tall guy with dark brown hair appeared from nowhere. He was facing away from her, bending his long legs—the kind of legs that made for great extensions on the ice rink. He sat down next to David.

"Josh Geller, meet Elle Larson," David said.

Josh turned. He was wearing a white T-shirt that said DOCTORS DO IT IN CODE. She gave his hand a quick shake. "How do you two know each other?" Elle asked.

"I sometimes run into him when he's collecting evidence in the emergency department," Josh said, stroking his close-cut beard. "Like last week."

Elle frowned. Her last words to Dr. Geller in the ED were, "Someone is trying to kill Charlie Blackwell!" She whispered in David's ear, "No way. He treats me like I'm contagious."

"Don't be so hateful," David whispered back.

She scowled and clenched her teeth, not wanting to say something she'd regret.

David pulled out a third champagne flute from his pack. He poured Josh a glass and refilled Elle's glass to the top.

"*Skål*," she said, slightly bowing her head in the Scandinavian ritual of her family. She took a cold gulp, met both of their eyes, and gave another nod.

David clinked her glass and looked at Josh. "Happy Birthday, Josh."

Elle swallowed hard. She really wished David had mentioned all of this.

"*L'Chaim*," Josh said, and they clinked their glasses together.

An awkward silence followed, then Josh swung the conversation to a topic Elle could sink her teeth into: health care. He described the hospital systems in Charlotte and how they were buying up other hospitals and adding physicians as employees.

"With Clinton still in office, physicians are running scared," he said. "I've never seen anything like it. Groups are being bought up left and right. We have one public community hospital, but they all say they're nonprofit." He held a finger up and took a long sip of his champagne.

"Hospitals are becoming machines. Just swipe your insurance card and lie there. We'll take care of the rest."

Elle forced a laugh, and David scowled at her.

"I knew you were irreverent," she said, feeling less restrained than when they were in a work setting.

"I already feel like I've been at this too long ... and I've only been in practice a couple of years!" Josh said, shaking his head. "My cynicism is coming through. I love the words *public* and *nonprofit*, like they have some altruistic meaning. It makes me nuts."

"Cynical, and you're only turning thirty," Elle said, raising her eyebrows.

"It's just that you can throw words around, and they don't necessarily mean anything. The Catholic Church used to mean something," Josh said, raising his empty glass for emphasis, "and now it means pedophiles."

"I think y'all need a little more champagne if we're going to continue this conversation," David said and began to top off everyone's glass.

Elle chuckled. *David the peacemaker.*

"What drives you crazy, Elle?" Josh asked, peering around David's body.

A guy like him drove her crazy, but here she was seeing a different side to him. She was starting to enjoy the banter, the fall breeze, and especially the champagne.

"Well?" David prompted, waiting for her to answer.

"I guess the stereotypes about old people. I mean, when I bring an older client to the emergency department and the staff see wrinkles and white hair, nine times out of ten they ask me which nursing home ... it just makes my job so much harder."

"What do you think, Josh?" David asked.

"I'm glad you brought her as your guest." He smiled at her, showing his white teeth.

Before she could respond, a couple of shirtless guys came up and said hello.

David grinned as he stood up and moved on to talk to the newcomers.

Elle heard David ask, "Where y'all from?"

Anxious to fill in the silence, Elle asked, "Did you get your latte on Wednesday? You were with a patient ..."

His gold-brown eyes searched hers. "Yes, I did. Even though it was cold by the time I got to it." He shook his head. "I definitely needed the caffeine."

Their boat was anchored next to a boathouse with an orange tile roof, a hundred yards offshore. Elle had only been to Sumpter's house twice, and both times had been in the backyard.

"The attorney I work with has a place right here." She pointed to the shoreline and tried to keep the conversation light. "Tommy Sumpter. He referred Charlie Blackwell to me." She spotted Sumpter's white speedboat, *Knot Guilty*, moored alongside his pier. "That's it."

Josh scoffed. "*Knot Guilty*. Definitely an attorney," he said. "Speaking of Charlie, I checked in on him this morning."

She studied Josh carefully. He had a dimpled chin and his hair, tousled by the wind, curled around his face. "How's he doing?"

"Much better, but he's micromanaging from his hospital bed. He said I should be nice to you."

Elle smiled at him and caught an intensity in his eyes. Funny. Yesterday, Charlie had told her to be nice to Josh. She didn't know what to make of that. The wind blew her hair into her face, and she pushed it back behind her ears.

"So how did you end up in Charlotte?" he asked, breaking the silence.

She gave him a weak smile. Whew! She was feeling the buzz from her champagne. "Five years ago, I followed my younger brother here."

Josh shifted his body closer to her. "Five years ... Let's see, that would have been after the Gulf War broke out and we went into the recession?"

"Yeah, funny, right? Not the best time to start my company." She didn't tell him that she had wondered every day for the first three years if she had made the right decision.

"Where's your brother now?"

"After the start of Desert Storm, he lost interest in Queens College and joined the army." She recalled her tearful goodbye to Peter the day he left for boot camp.

"Your parents okay with that?"

She shook her head. "It was after my parents died. I was in a car accident with my parents before we moved to Charlotte. I suppose Peter was running away, but he was the only immediate family I had ... I didn't want to be left behind."

"I'm so sorry."

She nodded. "Head-on collision; it all happened so fast ... I hear." Repressed feelings started to well up, and she wished she had worn her sunglasses. She still had to be so careful when she talked about it.

"I lost my father a couple of years ago to a heart attack," Josh said, sounding genuinely concerned. "And I'm still not over it; can't imagine losing both parents at the same time."

Elle breathed deep. "So, you know ..."

He nodded with a sad smile.

"My brother was only eighteen; I was a month shy of my twenty-third birthday." She looked away as her eyes began to water. "I can't remember any of it, really. Peter and my Aunt Sara told me my parents had extensive injuries. They both lost too much blood. All I got was a broken leg and sprained ligaments ... and a concussion."

"Sounds like you were lucky."

It was the most connection they'd had since they met. She found herself talking without wanting to. "The day it happened, my car wouldn't start. So my parents agreed to drive me to work." It was funny how she could talk about the accident more easily than the grief—the emptiest kind of loneliness she couldn't put into words. "It's still hard to talk about."

"Where's your brother's base?" he asked, seeming to take her cue.

"Some mountaintop in Bosnia controlled by the Serbs. I pray every night that he comes home soon."

"And your Aunt Sara?"

"She lives in Oslo, Norway—she's the black sheep of the family."

"Why is that?"

"Oh, I don't know … she's an atheist and rolls her own cigarettes. She was part of the resistance during World War II and hid guns in her parents' basement without them knowing." Thinking about Aunt Sara brought a smile to her face.

He chuckled. "And what do you think of her?"

"Aunt Sara? The best ever. She's coming for Thanksgiving."

He looked confused. "But Thanksgiving's an American holiday …"

"Yes, but Peter and I are her only family."

Josh nodded. He pulled himself into a cross-legged position and tapped his fingers on his shoe as he struggled to say something to her. "Look Elle, I owe you an apology," he finally said with a heavy sigh. "At work … you've caught me during some terrible moments. The ED is short staffed and we're seeing a tidal wave of patients coming in the door … an increasing number are getting addicted to drugs. I get so overwhelmed … I can barely get through the day. I think, what am I doing in medicine?"

"I accept your apology. I didn't know."

"And then I see you—"

"I hated being late," she quietly interrupted. "I thought you'd want to hear firsthand about Charlie Blackwell."

"I did hear you …"

"I see, even though you resisted?" She started to smile.

He touched her wrist, his soft eyes pleading. "I'm not always so horrible…"

Elle looked down into the lower deck. She hadn't seen this coming. "I think it's time to go in," she said, mindful of a strange awkwardness developing. She stood quickly and suddenly was lightheaded. "It's getting cold."

She sprinted to the cabin below, hearing Josh's steps behind her. The breeze blew through the open door. David was standing along the wall, chatting with someone she didn't know. She smiled and waved. More of Josh's friends were coming onboard and wishing him a happy birthday.

He greeted one guest after another as they placed their dishes next to the fresh jumbo shrimp, her meatballs, and a rich-looking chocolate cake already on the table.

She glanced at Josh, grateful for their conversation. The afternoon sun began sinking on the water as the sensual voice of Michael Jackson singing "Rock with You" flowed like liquid through the crowd. The party was starting.

# Chapter 10
*Monday*

Elle left her neighborhood before the Veterans Day parade started. A line of American flags, floats, bands, and classic cars with veterans in uniform were lining up along Tryon Street as honking cars and banners added to the festive noise. The sun came out and the crowd cheered loudly. It was another warm November day.

Shortly after nine o'clock, Elle walked inside Presbyterian Hospital and took the elevator up to the sixth floor. Dressed in a loose-fitting Marimekko print dress, a gift from her Aunt Sara, Elle unbuttoned her sweater and wandered over to the reception desk to say hi to Amanda. Elle was on a first-name basis with most of the daytime regulars in Neurology, and Amanda was her favorite.

"How's Charlie?" Elle asked.

"Trying to be the"—Amanda raised her hand to make the *V* sign. "His new glasses are here. We're still waiting on the magnifying glass."

Elle thanked her and walked down to Charlie's room. He was sitting in a chair by the window wearing a white dress shirt, dark pants, and Velcro-closure running shoes. Elle walked in and washed her hands at the sink, scrubbing with liquid soap. "It's good to see you out of that bed." She smiled at Charlie.

"Hey, doll, you're getting to be a familiar face around here," he said in his slow Southern accent. "How do you like my glasses?"

His hair was combed back, and his gray-blue eyes looked clear in his new glasses, even though she probably didn't look clear to him. He looked stronger.

"They look great," she said, admiring his brown frames. She was hoping he'd fully recovered and they could get back to business—the reason she'd been hired. She pulled up a chair and faced him, sitting close enough to be heard. "Any improvement in your vision?"

"Not really. The eye doctor told me my macular degeneration is worse. But I've had my shower, my breakfast, and physical therapy." He rose slowly and looked at her proudly, his feet planted in a wide stance. "They've got me on a tight schedule, and I'm walking again."

"Yes!" Elle moved her chair out of the way and watched him walk around the room, turn around, and walk back to his chair, his gait awkward but deliberate, his legs stiff and slow. "How's the food?" she asked when he was settled.

"Coffee's not as good as the cup you brought me the other day."

She laughed. "I'll bring you more coffee." She told him about the parade. "You risked your life for our country," she said quietly, her voice becoming husky.

He waved her off. "We were lucky. General Patton always said that courage is fear holding on a minute longer."

She really liked this guy—his courage, his kindness. "So tell me about yourself," she said, dragging her chair back in front of him.

"Sure," he said and paused to gather his thoughts. He told her how he'd grown up poor, as the third generation of farmers along the Catawba River. He talked about being an outstanding swimmer in high school. "I started dating my first wife before the war. Her parents owned the farm across the river."

Elle grinned. "She married the boy across the river instead of the boy next door?"

He nodded. "We waited to get married until the war was over. I thought if I got married and started a family of my own, my life would become more meaningful again." He looked out the window and paused before going on. "We struggled in so many ways. I had nightmares ... flashbacks. I drank too much. It was a marriage of convenience for both of us."

"Did you own the farm at that point?" Elle asked, trying to understand his past and adjustment back to farm life following the war.

"No, not until I inherited it. Carol and I moved in with my parents so I could run the family farm. I took business classes at night—the GI Bill. My wife took care of my parents until they died. It wasn't until Carol died and I sold the farm that I made any money."

He described his move to Charlotte, his landscape business, planting parks and gardens, and the Carol Blackwell Memorial Fund he started in honor of his first wife. "I still owe so much more than I can ever give back. I sometimes wonder, 'Why me?'"

Elle would have loved to talk with him all day, but a quick look at the time—10 a.m.—told her she needed to move on if she was going to stay on schedule. She grabbed some items from her bag. "I need to ask you some memory questions, Charlie." It was always tricky evaluating someone's cognitive function, but she wanted to explain what she was doing. "Let's see if your memory has improved, now that the drugs are out of your system, okay?"

"Fire away."

Elle used a general screening tool that focused on concrete thinking skills but didn't test the more abstract executive function skills that would require a more comprehensive neuropsych evaluation. Charlie worked slowly but gave her his full attention.

On a blank piece of paper, Elle drew a circle. She asked him to draw in the numbers on the clock face, inside the circle. When he finished, she asked him to draw the clock hands at 2:45. He tended to give up easily, though he gave his best effort when she encouraged him. He told her the numbers looked blurry because of his vision, and he couldn't see well enough to set the clock. When she pressed him further, he looked embarrassed.

"I used to read the newspaper every day." He blew out a frustrated breath. "Now I just go through the motions as my vision keeps getting worse. I don't want to tell anyone, not with the hearing next week."

Elle smiled and touched his shoulder. "Vision loss doesn't mean you need a guardian, Charlie."

The Geriatric Depression Scale took less than ten minutes. Her biggest challenge was his visual difficulty that limited his responses to some of the questions. Thirty minutes into her evaluation, she knew his cognitive impairment was mild, he had good language skills, and he was not depressed. She was relieved ... relieved and happy for him. In spite of the chaos going on around them, she reminded herself that she could still do good work. "Awesome, Charlie."

But anxiety was written all over his face. "Last year is still mostly blank." He shook his head. "It's like amnesia, just for one year." He leaned forward. "I know you're trying to help me ... I'm sorry I can't remember more."

"Charlie, you're doing much better now. Certain drugs like narcotics, sedatives—they make it harder for the brain to form new memories. Were you taking narcotics or sedatives last year?"

He thought for a minute, shaking his head. "If I was, I didn't know it."

She could almost see his wheels turning. "If you were, you may never remember the things that happened during that time." Then it hit her; those memories were never stored. "It's like writing your thoughts on a computer and not hitting save before closing the document."

"I had one of the first computers built ... one of the first calculators too. It stood about five feet high. I paid about a thousand dollars for that machine," he said, his smile reaching his friendly eyes. "So what's next?"

She rifled through her briefcase. "The neurologist will see you next, at eleven a.m. That's Dr. George Norris. Then, Dr. Singleton will do some additional testing at one." She patted his hand gently. "You're pretty much in for a full day. Oh, would you do me a favor?"

"Sure, doll. Anything."

"Let Dr. Norris know I'll stop by his office at three thirty."

"Three thirty."

"You're doing great, Charlie," she said and shook his hand. He gave her a firm grasp with both hands. To her, his story was as heroic as it was heartbreaking.

Sitting in her Volvo in the hospital parking lot, Elle listened to the ambulance sirens as they made their approach to the emergency department. A tremble started at her knees. A minute later she was nauseated and dizzy. Were her fears from the accident years ago now triggered by new events? She rolled down her window and waited for her symptoms to clear. "Breathe. In. Out. You can do this." She repeated the mantra.

Elle found Dr. Woodham's medical letter in her briefcase and quickly read the single page, typed on his letterhead and dated October 20, 1996. He was listed as the only physician in the practice. She read the letter again more slowly. She reread the letter a third time, only this time out loud:

> Due to Alzheimer's disease, Charlie Blackwell has been noncompliant in taking his medications. He does not shower or change his clothes and recently has become more aggressive and physically violent with his wife and caregivers when they try to help and care for him. He is obsessed with movies about guns and violence. He is unable to care for himself and is not competent to make decisions about his care.

Dr. Woodham further stated the Alzheimer's disease would progressively become worse and that Charlie was not capable of handling his affairs.

Elle turned and looked out the window. There was a lot of smoke here. What had Sumpter asked her ... to read the letter only after she finished her own evaluation? Sure, Sumpter wanted her to come to her own conclusions. Did he also want her to find problems with the doctor's evaluation?

She turned on her engine, letting the air conditioning cool her off, and tucked the letter back in her briefcase. Charlie seemed so much better than Dr. Woodham had described. And why did he give Charlie a diagnosis of

Alzheimer's disease when he hadn't even done a dementia workup? Elle closed her eyes. Deep in her thoughts was another rub. The typical course of Alzheimer's was one of progressive decline, and it developed slowly. It often took twenty to twenty-five years to develop. She opened her eyes. Then why did Dr. Woodham's medical records go from no symptoms or difficulties in activities of daily living during one visit to Charlie not being able to care for himself only one month later?

Elle pulled out of the parking lot and floored the gas, even though she didn't speed … ever. *Breathe. Breathe.* She had to get away from these ambulances. Mac needed a walk, and the leftover meatballs were calling her. After lunch, she would stop at Rite Aid and have a talk with Charlie's pharmacist. Then it was on to see Dr. Norris. She couldn't wait to hear what he had to say.

At three thirty that afternoon, Elle was back on the hospital elevator, heading to the sixth floor. Her cell phone rang. "I'm here," she said after opening up her phone and walking into the Neurology Unit.

"Running late," George Norris said.

"No rush." Music was playing, and people milled around the front desk, which was piled high with gifts.

"It's George's birthday," Amanda said. She handed Elle a slice of frosted chocolate cake on a paper plate.

"Thanks. I love chocolate." She also loved Amanda's gray hair—premature for a woman in her thirties, but it gave her an aura of wisdom. "All these people work here?"

Amanda shrugged her shoulders. "Everyone likes George."

Elle felt the tug of her own memories from when she'd worked in the hospital during graduate school, recalling the benefit of a dedicated staff pulling together.

"Here to see Charlie Blackwell?" Amanda asked.

Elle shook her head. "Dr. Norris this time." She couldn't bring herself to call him George. Was it their age difference? *More out of respect for his role*, she thought.

Amanda circled an arm around Elle's back and gently nudged her forward. "C'mon. Let me see if I can get his attention."

They made their way through the crowd to Dr. Norris's office. Amanda left her as Dr. Norris pushed his way in and closed the door behind him. Salt-and-pepper hair, a slim mustache, and a goatee that made his round face look longer, the doctor's button, pinned to his lab coat, read Fifty and Like Fine Wine, Aging to Perfection.

"I really don't like all of this attention," he said, extending his hand. "I guess that's what happens when you see patients in every department."

"Happy birthday," Elle said.

He nodded in thanks. "Charlie Blackwell told me you'd be stopping by." He motioned for her to sit in the chair next to his desk.

"I'm so glad he remembered." She sat beside him and settled her briefcase on the floor.

Dr. Norris was one of a handful of Black physicians in Charlotte, and the only Black neurologist she knew. He was often the last stop for a number of her clients with difficult diagnostic problems. He was all about deduction, with a keen eye for detail.

"Did you know our patient saw several months of combat in the war, remembered hearing a blast, and woke up days later?" he asked.

Elle shook her head. "He also doesn't remember most of this past year."

"Yes, I'm worried about that."

"Dr. Woodham diagnosed him with Alzheimer's disease."

He was quiet for a moment. "Charlie Blackwell presents with sudden symptoms, based on his history and my testing—more like mild vascular dementia." He shook his head. "I've asked Dr. Singleton to do additional neuropsych testing. Do you know Lynne Singleton?"

"I do," Elle said, although she hadn't seen Lynne since the birth of her new baby girl. "We've worked together before."

"Good. I've asked her to stop by so the three of us can talk."

"I understand you're testifying as the primary expert," Elle said, glad they were in this together.

He nodded. "Dr. Singleton will be in court too. That makes three of us." He began to tell her about his visit with Charlie and Susan. "Susan was practically hysterical and didn't like what I had to say. She wanted me to say that Charlie is incompetent—before I even started my evaluation."

"Susan's not happy that I'm working with Charlie. Originally, I was going to meet with you and Charlie." Elle shrugged her shoulders. "She stopped it."

"So she came instead," Dr. Norris said.

She nodded. She knew he didn't judge. That's why she was anxious to hear what he had to say about Charlie. "Sounds like Susan tried to influence you."

"You know I can't allow that. I made her leave … I did agree to order Depakote."

"I know some physicians prescribe Depakote to treat agitation in Alzheimer's, but won't that affect his attention span … his memory?" A knot formed in Elle's stomach.

"Yes, but Susan told me how aggressive he's been. She can't manage him at home."

Elle looked at him. "I just don't see it."

"Elle, you're suggesting Dr. Woodham is fabricating Charlie's illness?"

She felt tired and it was only Monday. Closing her eyes for a moment, she could see the doctor's dilemma. It wasn't her role to influence him either. There was so much more that Elle could tell him, but it was important for the hearing that Dr. Norris be unbiased. Still, she had a duty to warn him. "I just have concern about the Depakote." She pulled out her copy of Charlie's medical records and passed them into his hands.

"It's just the history doesn't match—and it's not just that. I found Charlie with five fentanyl patches on his abdomen when I made my first home visit. He had a drug screen in the ED that also showed oxycodone and clonazepam in his system."

Dr. Norris raised his bushy eyebrows and looked at her with concern. "I saw that on Josh Geller's note; probably contributed to Charlie's delirium."

"And Charlie goes to court one week from today."

She watched as he carefully took the documents and read Dr. Woodham's office notes, his medical letter, and the petition for guardianship. He followed along with his right index finger, placing each document on his desk, one at a time. He picked up his own notes and examined them side by side.

"Josh Geller said to watch out for you," he said, his brown eyes dancing as he looked at her. "Says you can be *quite* convincing."

Elle blushed, surprised Josh Geller had talked about her. She watched Dr. Norris write an order to cancel the Depakote and took a deep, audible breath. There was a knock at the door.

Lynne Singleton had come in for the day to evaluate Charlie, wearing a lab coat over navy slacks and a bright red silk top. She had classic Persian features: black hair and large dark eyes. She entered the office in a whirlwind. "I had a two-year-old running track around the house this morning while I was trying to get her dressed. My mornings are quite entertaining."

Elle laughed. She liked Dr. Singleton; she was confident without being pushy. "Congrats on having another girl. You look great."

Dr. Singleton crinkled her nose like she disagreed. "That's right, the last time you saw me, I was huge. How are you, Elle? George?" She shook hands with her and then Dr. Norris.

Dr. Norris sat behind his desk, leaned back, and folded his hands over his stomach. "How's our patient?"

Sitting beside Elle, Dr. Singleton filled them in on her evaluation. She agreed with Dr. Norris that Charlie had a mild dementia and it was more likely vascular than Alzheimer's disease.

"His CT scan showed a small piece of shrapnel lodged in his skull," Dr. Norris said.

"Shrapnel!" Elle said, imagining what Charlie must have experienced to have metal lodged in his skull. She took out her notebook and started taking notes.

"The CT scan takes hundreds of 3-D pictures," Dr. Norris said. He held up an image from Charlie's chart and pointed to the shrapnel. "You can see where it stopped before entering the brain."

"An old war wound," Dr. Singleton agreed.

"So, no injury to his brain?" Elle asked.

"Not from shrapnel—the blast probably caused a concussion. But look here," Dr. Norris said. "See that?" He handed Elle the CT scan and pointed at the small area of scattered white matter on the image. "Mini-strokes. These tiny hemorrhages look white on the CT. He has mild vascular dementia."

Elle held the image up close and placed it back on his desk.

"Charlie had a hard time analyzing problems and developing solutions during my testing. His language skills were intact ... he speaks and writes very well," Dr. Singleton said. "That's consistent with Dr. Norris's findings of vascular dementia."

"What about the Alzheimer's disease?" Elle asked. "You saw Dr. Woodham's letter."

"Memory problems are too quickly diagnosed as Alzheimer's," Dr. Singleton said. "Do you know Dr. Woodham?"

"No," Elle said.

They both looked at Dr. Norris.

"Has Dr. Woodham filed other petitions for guardianship?" Dr. Singleton asked. "I've never had any referrals from him."

Dr. Norris shook his head. "Nobody I know."

"His office is in Charlotte, off of Providence Road," Elle said. "I saw the address on the bottom of his medical letter."

"Vascular dementia is often caused by high blood pressure," Dr. Norris said. "What do we know about Charlie's blood pressure medications?"

Elle flipped back a few pages in her notebook. She explained that she had stopped by Charlie's pharmacy on Providence Road that morning and talked to his pharmacist. "It's been six months since his diuretic and ace inhibitor were renewed."

"Well, that's a problem," Dr. Norris said. "We need to get his blood pressure under control and start him on some daily aspirin to prevent this from getting worse. Other drugs?"

Elle shook her head. "Nothing prescribed, other than his blood pressure drugs."

Dr. Norris threw Elle a look of concern. "That's not reassuring … can you check on this?"

"I'll be talking to caregivers and the rest of his family. Once I find out who's been setting up his med box, I'll let you know. What do you think about the guardianship petition?"

"It doesn't accurately reflect his diagnosis," Dr. Norris said.

"I agree," Dr. Singleton added, nodding her head. "It doesn't reflect his current level of functioning either."

Elle finally had what she needed to finish her report. She tucked her notebook back in her briefcase. Mini-strokes—she had seen the evidence for herself. She had never seen shrapnel on a CT scan before. *Awesome!*

As they wrapped up, Elle thanked them for their help and shook their hands again. She was grateful for their comradery, for including her as part of the unified team. For the first time since the case began, some of the weight lifted from her shoulders. She would chat with Sumpter later. There was one more person to see. She picked up her briefcase, the shoulder strap feeling lighter, and headed out the door.

For the second time in a week, David pulled out a chair for Elle at an outside table at Fenwick's. They sat and listened to Wanda describe the homemade dessert specials. Tonight, Wanda was helping keep the regulars at the inside tables and bar happy while waiting on their outside table as well. Elle glanced around at the empty tables. It was a slow Monday, just before dinner hour, plus the temperature was cooling off. She was glad she had worn her aunt's hand-knit scarf.

"In addition to our regular desserts, we have pecan cream pie, chocolate Kahlúa pie, key lime pie, and New Orleans-style bread pudding with whiskey sauce," Wanda said in her soothing voice.

Elle asked her to repeat the choices, knowing each one had been made from scratch.

"Elle, you're the only person I know who spends thirty minutes going over desserts, then orders your favorite anyway."

She stuck out her tongue when Wanda wasn't watching.

He chuckled. "We'll both have the bread pudding," David told Wanda.

While they waited for their desserts, Elle told him about Dr. Norris and Dr. Singleton. "They agree that Charlie doesn't require guardianship ... and they disagree with Dr. Woodham's diagnosis of Alzheimer's disease." She wanted to celebrate.

Wanda was back in five minutes with two plates of warm bread pudding.

"I think I'd like to hang a crystal chandelier over my dining table," David said, describing the Venetian plaster and faux painting project he was planning for his dining room.

She loved hearing him talk about the old estates, the formal gardens, and life in the past. "You were born in the wrong century."

"I think so too," he said with a grin.

"You won't catch me living back then. It's hard enough being a woman now."

"Speaking of now, how did things go last night with Josh?"

She swallowed a big spoonful of bread pudding and made a face at him. Her feelings for Josh were confusing. She leaned against the table. "How often do you see him?"

"Not much. I saw him last week when he told me he was celebrating the Big Three-O with a boat party. I told him I had plans, and he said to bring you along." David started on his dessert. "I thought he was a ten."

"He pretty much gives me a hard time."

"Duh, how else would you know he likes you?"

"But with me he's miserable, so—"

"He didn't look miserable yesterday. You, however …"

"I mean when I see him in the ED," Elle said.

"You're twenty-nine and single, not even dating."

She shook her head at David's matchmaking.

"Why don't you have a boyfriend?" he asked her softly.

His question made her uncomfortable. She hadn't been able to keep a boyfriend since her parents died. Maybe she just didn't want to go through any more heartbreak. "Hey, the prince riding in on a white horse isn't for me. There's no such thing as happy ever after."

"Well, while you try and figure things out for yourself, I want to ask you a favor."

She studied his boyish face, the freckles evenly sprinkled across his nose, eyeing him suspiciously. "What kind of favor?"

"I'd like you to help me find someone."

"You were flirting with one of the guys on the boat yesterday. Did you know him?"

"No and yes. Unlike you, I'll talk to people I don't know, but you're not the only one who likes to play hard to get."

"Mmmm," she said and took another bite of her bread pudding.

"Don't get me wrong. I've hooked up for sex, but those relationships never go anywhere. Elle, I'm pushing thirty. I'd like to have a normal life," he said, keeping his voice low.

"So, what I pretty much hear—"

"If I just wanted sex, I could go home and look at porn."

"I'm still back at flirting and playing hard to get," she said and smiled in her kindest way. She didn't want to make too much fun, knowing he was serious. She put her hand on her chest. "Me? Play matchmaker?"

"You're a good judge of people. I know there's somebody out there for me. I don't know who or where, but I have faith that someone will come along. I want what everyone else wants … a relationship with someone I can build a future with."

"Of course I'll help," she said. "Can I change the subject for a minute?" She pulled her sweater closed.

"What's up?" he asked between bites.

"Okay, Mister Historian, tell me about gold being discovered here."

He looked at her suspiciously. "Is this a test?"

"No, I had a phone call this morning with the guy who bought Charlie Blackwell's farm years ago. Nice guy … said he was a geologist. He told me he was waiting for a second gold rush. Anyway, I'm scheduled to meet with him tomorrow and thought if anybody knew, it would be you."

"You mean you've lived here, missy, and didn't know the first gold was found right here in North Carolina!?" he said with a dramatic wave of his hand.

She did know that. The little bit of gold history she knew had come from Charlie Blackwell's reception five years ago. But David was enjoying giving her a hard time, so she just took another bite of dessert. The whiskey sauce was to die for. She liked this tiny restaurant with the big smiles and good food.

"It was about fifty years before the California Gold Rush. So you didn't know, did ya?"

"Where in North Carolina?" she asked.

"The Reed Gold Mine, off of Albemarle Road. It's just a forty-minute drive from here. If you'd like, we can take a ride out there. They still let you pan for gold at the mine."

"Sounds fun. Have you heard anything about a second gold rush?"

"There are always people speculating, Elle. Gold still exists in the veins of these abandoned mines. When inflation rises, the price of gold goes up. Who wouldn't like to have another million-dollar industry right here where you could get rich quick?"

"Let's go there," she said, polishing off the last of her bread pudding. "Maybe one of us will get lucky."

# Chapter 11
*Tuesday*

Wearing old gym shorts and a long-sleeved T-shirt, George Norris started down the pathway to his backyard garden that ended with a corner fountain and the sound of gurgling water. The sun was barely breaking through the morning darkness as he stooped to smell a couple of fragrant roses just beginning to open. At last count, he had over a hundred rose bushes. And at this point in November, the blooms were larger and grew more slowly because of the cooler Charlotte nights. On weekends he sprayed, his garage devoted to antifungals and fertilizers. But during the week, he watered and watched his roses grow, never knowing which ones were going to bloom the best, last the longest, fade, or make a miraculous comeback when the conditions were exactly right. He thought of his garden as a way of giving a little joy to other people, and he'd planned to bring a bouquet to his staff this morning and thank them for his birthday party.

George loved this fifteen minutes of early daybreak, when his backyard turned into a tapestry of color and no one was around. As he cut long stems and added roses to the bucket of warm water, he thought about Charlie Blackwell. He had less time than he wanted before Charlie's hearing, but at least he was prepared to address Charlie's needs. He had stayed late last night and written his evaluation. He even faxed Elle a copy. So why was he borrowing trouble at the end of the day? He was still asking himself the same question this morning. Had he missed something in his evaluation? Doctors always worried about missing things. At least the good ones did.

George opened the screen door to the porch and let it hit his backside as he entered. Only when he made his way back to the kitchen and looked out the window did he see a shadow gliding toward the house. The screen door creaked. From the kitchen he saw no one. "Honey?"

Silence.

*Good.* His wife was sleeping in this morning. Then he heard footsteps on the porch. As he watched the kitchen doorway, a stranger in casual clothes and a hoodie emerged. *Jesus.* His heart pounded. The visitor had gloved hands, black-and-white sneakers—nothing about the man's thin profile was familiar.

A second later the man raised a gun.

"Please, my wife is having a baby." George tried to catch his breath. "You can have anything you want—"

The gun flashed. George fell backward, dropping the bucket to the tiled floor in one slow motion.

The police department's Providence Division was small, covering sixteen square miles including the historic Myers Park, a wealthy neighborhood with beautiful tree-lined streets, the biggest homes, and a decades-old reputation of being the safest place in Charlotte. David Cauley leaned forward and maneuvered his unit's mobile van into the steep drive, the engine sounding like marbles in a coffee can. Tuesday morning, a hell of a way to start the day, like taking a drink from a firehose.

*Holy shit.*

A sobbing woman in her nightgown was in the middle of the driveway, being consoled by Kate Harrigan. Mrs. Norris looked about thirty-five and, based on the size of her belly, near the end of her pregnancy. *Dammit.* David braked and lowered the window. "Kate?" Unspoken words conveyed his offer to help.

Harrigan barely looked up as she wrapped a blanket around the wife's shoulders. "The crowd's getting bigger. I'm calling for backup," she said.

David nodded. Two patrol officers prevented nine or ten neighbors and a reporter on the sidewalk from entering the scene. People huddled behind yellow tape as they talked to a reporter from the news crew.

"Welcome to the shit show," David said under his breath. He heard one woman say the neighbors were shaken by this kind of crime.

"North Charlotte, yes," the woman said, crying into the camera. "But not here in our neighborhood."

"We need more police officers on our street," another said. "Stay inside and lock your doors."

The first neighbor talked nervously to the camera. "Tell them we need more police now."

A reporter from the *Observer* motioned him over, and David raised his hand. He didn't want to get caught on TV. Physicians didn't usually get shot in Charlotte ... and this was the first physician on his watch.

David strained to see the house. Enormous boxwoods and a grove of trees hid the stone bungalow from view. An easy place to hide a crime, though crimes with firearms were never a problem here.

Accelerating, he cut around a couple of squad cars parked in the drive, then crested the top of the steep incline and parked next to the house. The van radio squawked, and his cell phone rang with an incoming call. Crazy. At times like this, he was glad he was a multitasker. It fit his job to be able to focus on so many details at once.

He checked his messages. Elle was returning his call. Only now was not a good time. Stepping outside, he clipped the phone back to his belt and walked to the back of the house where a big, angular Carter Lewis—his evidence technician—was bent over, examining the back-porch floor and working the scene with detectives Mike Slater and Scott Mullen, two of Homicide's best.

"Whatcha got?" David asked as he ducked under the tape and stepped inside the small porch. He heard Slater and Mullen comparing theories in the kitchen through the open door.

"We don't know why he was shot. The call came in as attempted robbery." Slater looked up, his sunglasses resting on his Roman nose.

"Who robs someone at six in the morning?" David picked up a pair of gloves and pulled them on. He bent over and scuffed his shoes into the booties.

"Looks like a botched robbery," Mullen said, his thick black hair sticking up in a crew cut.

"The victim forgets to lock the screen door," Slater said. "The suspect walks into the porch and is confronted by the victim as he enters the kitchen."

"The victim was shot once in the head and found here." Mullen pointed to the kitchen floor. "He was still alive when they transported him to Presbyterian Hospital."

"Detective Scully's at the ED to talk to the victim when he wakes up," Slater added.

David went over to the pooled stain on the tile, bent down, and sat on his heels. He looked at the scattered roses, water, and empty bucket and then stood to examine the blood spray on the cabinet over the sink.

"The paramedic actually sounded encouraging—reminded us that when a gunshot injury to the head bleeds, it's because of so many blood vessels close to the surface of the face and scalp," Mullen said.

"The victim's wife found him." Slater glanced at David, narrowing his eyes and frowning. "The shot woke her up. Said she was asleep in their bedroom. She ran into the driveway, screaming after discovering him and calling 911."

"She also saw someone running into the woods to Edgehill Park, not far from the old Duke Mansion," Mullen said. "A masked man with a backpack, running all over hell's half acre. A number of officers were sent over yonder," he said.

David glanced at the backyard, ending in tall trees. "Trees in front and back." Too many ways for the suspect to escape.

"No suspect yet," Slater added, shaking his head.

"Weapon? Anything left behind?" David asked.

"No weapon, but we did find one shell casing," Lewis called out from the porch, holding his flashlight at an angle, while dusting for fingerprints on the doorframe.

"You've got the casing?" David said.

Lewis nodded, raising a manila envelope.

David lowered his brows. "Lewis, get the firearms examiner to take high-res pictures—"

"I'll take it to the lab," Lewis said.

"Security was off," Slater said. "Victim's wife said he's out in his rose garden most every morning. Looks like the suspect entered the kitchen."

"Okay, so the suspect walks up behind the victim and points his gun?" David was not surprised by the anger in his own voice.

"Our victim must have turned around and boom, he's out before he has time to think. The roses never made it to the vase." Slater's eyes looked impatient. "What else do you know?"

"The victim turned fifty yesterday," David said. "Finished evaluating a hospital patient scheduled for a court hearing next week. He was the primary expert for the case."

"Is this the Charlie Blackwell case?" Lewis stepped into the kitchen and ran a hand over his blonde buzz cut.

David nodded, thinking back on his conversation with Elle last night.

Slater's cell phone rang. "It's Scully." He picked up the call and stared out the kitchen window as he listened.

Everyone was quiet. David watched Slater with anticipation.

Slater's mouth turned downward. "Does his wife know?" His voice was solemn. He placed the phone on his chest and looked at the team. "Our victim just died in the ED—never regained consciousness."

Mullen broke the silence. "A guy who grows roses, about to be a father ..."

David's phone rang. He looked at the number. It was Rachel Harper, the new evidence tech who was sent to the ED to work with Detective Scully and retrieve the projectile once the victim was out of surgery. "You okay?" He had been supervising her for the past six weeks and was impressed with her initiative.

"Chaotic scene—bloody floor, packages from supplies."

David walked carefully through the kitchen. "Where are you?"

"Outside his bed in the ED—the curtain's pulled. I can hear the nurses talking."

He heard a catch in her voice. "Take the clothing for evidence, Rachel, and anything like cigarettes, ChapStick, cell phone. We'll need pre-autopsy photographs of injuries, any markings, and buccal swabs. I'll be there as soon as I can." He hoped his instructions snapped her back to focus on her responsibilities.

"Yes, sir ... Autopsy's tomorrow."

"That's pretty routine. Detectives won't be present; we'll do postmortem fingerprints of the deceased after."

"I'd like to go with you."

"This your first time?"

"Yes, sir."

He imagined processing the body, covered with white sheets. On the surface: civility and calm. Below the surface: conflict and violence. Sometimes, there was blood on the sheets. The morgue was always dark. And they would sit and wait in a miniature waiting room before taking the victim's fingerprints. He shuddered. At least he could be there to support Rachel.

"Okay, I'll see you tomorrow."

Carter Lewis walked into the kitchen where David stood next to Slater at the sink.

"I hope we catch this bastard," Slater said.

David clipped his phone back to his belt and looked at his watch. He needed to stop by and see Elle after this. He took no comfort in letting her know but didn't want her learning about her colleague's death on the news. What agonized him the most? The suspect was still on the loose. He pulled off one glove and fumbled with the other. "This was no botched burglary." He turned and looked at Slater, his hands still trembling. "Can I ask you for a favor?"

# Chapter 12

Elle was sitting on the large wraparound porch with Gordon Thomas, overlooking his winding driveway. It was ten in the morning, and he was the only appointment she had scheduled today. *Oh, happy Tuesday.* She had the rest of the day to catch her breath and work on the Blackwell report.

The old farmhouse smelled like a fresh coat of paint. At one time, this original house had been part of the Blackwell farm. She tried to imagine Charlie sitting here as a young man. She breathed in the fragrance of fall apples as Mr. Thomas pointed out his favorite trees: pecan trees, fruit trees, and Southern red oaks that bordered each side of the drive.

At seventy-six, with short white hair, Mr. Thomas was tall and stooped but still muscular for his age. He talked with his hands. Big hands. Hands that worked in the dirt and looked for gold.

Elle thought of her dad. He'd had big hands too—hands that held hers—and also liked to grow things. It had been her job to help water his summer garden.

"I was born and raised in Davidson County and was looking for a place to come home to. Bought this land over thirty-five years ago … 1960."

Elle settled back on the porch swing. She knew he was in no hurry. This is what she loved about her job. She took a sip of sweet tea. A coffee drinker herself, she appreciated his Southern hospitality, even if she wasn't big on sweetened drinks.

"Just finished college and was working as a state geologist. I knew there was gold on this property." He turned and looked at her, unruly eyebrows raised. "Did you know that North Carolina started the gold mining industry?"

"Well, I didn't until I moved to Charlotte. I thought the gold rush started in California." She gently rocked the swing.

"That's what a lot of folks think. But it ain't so. The first gold was found over yonder in Cabarrus County," he said, pointing north. His keen eyes looked out over his land with pride. "First gold in this entire country," he said, putting both hands together around an imaginary mass. "Discovered by a twelve-year-old boy named Conrad Reed."

"At the Reed Gold Mine," Elle said, recalling her conversation with David last night.

"It was a warm spring day in 1799," Thomas said, closing his eyes.

Elle could see this was a story he loved to tell. She slowly sipped more tea and let herself relax.

"Conrad was fishing with his brother and sister on their farm and saw this shiny, seventeen-pound gold rock in the water. The kids carried the heavy rock home. And that's how the first gold rush in America started."

"Can you imagine finding gold on your property?" Elle asked.

Mr. Thomas opened his eyes and changed his position, trying to get more comfortable. "I most certainly can, young lady. What's funny though, is Conrad's father never relied on mining for money. John Reed was a farmer at heart. It wasn't until the crops were in and the stream had nearly dried up late in summer that he took up his pick and pan. Yet it was gold that made his family rich." He turned and smiled at Elle.

"Were there other mines around here?" she asked.

"Oh sure. All the way up to Greensboro. I even have an old mine here."

She perked up. "You do?"

"Yes, ma'am. There were over fifty gold mines in North Carolina. The largest, though, were right here, around Charlotte."

"So what happened?"

"Well, that's another story now. A lot longer than your pretty ears have time to hear ... and I know that's not why you came to see me," he said with a wink. "You didn't know that once upon a time, Charlotte was this quiet little village supported by gold. Did you?"

She smiled back at him. She didn't know, but it was starting to make sense to her.

"Well, the Great Depression brought hard times. By the time I bought this place, North Carolina gold mining was dying out. You see, speculating where to find gold is risky. It's made some people around here rich and others poor."

"I know, right?" Elle said, thinking about the growth of Charlotte.

"Mining was sometimes a dirty business," Mr. Thomas said. "Easy gold attracted a lot of different people to this area back then. Some people neglected their farms, drank too much, and gambled. Slave labor was used too. Even back when I bought this place, the South was still segregated."

Elle grimaced. North Carolina had incredible natural resources. But the right place at the right time for the Reed family was also the wrong place at the wrong time for Black Americans. She sighed and wondered how much had changed in people's minds.

"It's no coincidence that Charlotte's the second-largest banking center in the country," Mr. Thomas said.

"So, the gold brought the mines, and the mines brought the banks?"

"That's right. And mark my words, Miss Elle. We'll have another gold rush in North Carolina. Why, it's just a matter of time that we find gold on my property."

"Well, I hope you have a lucky accident like Conrad Reed."

He laughed. "I'm too old to mine now, but Melinda Blackwell has talked about helping with the farm here someday. She's darn sure about still finding gold in the veins of my abandoned mine."

Elle stopped swinging.

He looked at her sheepishly as though he had given away too much. "No more nuggets sittin' in the creek beds, though. Most of the gold now is deeper underground and harder to reach."

"Your secret's safe with me, Mr. Thomas." She mimed zipping her mouth shut.

"We're just waiting for inflation to rise and gold prices to go up, so it's worth our while to go after it."

Elle tried to hide her excitement. *Is that what this guardianship is about—gold? But why would Melinda be involved? And how is Charlie mixed up with this?* She tamped down her natural curiosity. The core of her clinical training was to investigate and make judgments on factual information. She placed her glass of tea on the side table. "Mr. Thomas, do you mind if I ask a few more questions?"

"I'll be happy to help if I can, young lady."

"I'm working with Charlie Blackwell and his attorney."

"Well, I'll be damned," he said, looking surprised.

"I was hoping you could tell me about your purchase of the farm here."

He nodded slowly and closed his eyes again. "Well, let's see ... Charlie's first wife was in her forties when she committed suicide." He leaned forward, opened his eyes, and pointed midway between the driveway and the garden. "The newspaper said she shot herself, early in the day, right here on the lawn."

Elle looked where Mr. Thomas was pointing, not twenty feet away. Her heart started pounding. She imagined Carol Blackwell enveloped in a dark cloud of depression. The confusion—not knowing where to turn—like trying to walk underwater. But why would she walk to the middle of her yard and in the brightness of day to take her own life?

Elle turned to look at Mr. Thomas. "Where did she get the gun?"

"I read she kept a gun in her bedside table," he said, returning her gaze.

*How freakin' awful for Charlie ... for Robbie and Melinda.* "Were there any witnesses?"

"At the time, she was home alone with the housekeeper. The housekeeper called Charlie afterward, but no one saw Carol pull the trigger, if that's what you're asking. Charlie was here minutes later, but it was too late for him to do anything."

He stood up and stretched the stiffness out of his knees, shifted from side to side. "I've got a little somethin' to show you," he said and shuffled into his house. When he returned, he handed her a newspaper article and sat back in his rocker. "I've saved this. Charlie was in the paper after he sold me his farm."

Elle looked down at the yellowed newspaper and a picture of Charlie, his wife, and two kids. She read the headline and then the article that described how his wife had shot herself in the head. She didn't think she could ever move into a house that had experienced a death like this, maybe for fear that it wasn't suicide.

"Was there a suicide note?"

"They never found one. A cop was on the scene just minutes later." Mr. Thomas shook his head, rocking back and forth in his chair. "But Carol was already gone."

Elle looked again at the article. The story was just as he described it. New info she learned was that Charlie was cleared from being a suspect, and the police never found any other reason to investigate. She finished taking notes and handed back his article.

"Do you think Charlie killed her?" he asked.

Elle fiddled with her pen a moment before responding. "No, why?"

"Well, the husband is the first to be suspected. He was a suspect in the beginning. I thought maybe that's why you're here."

"Oh, no. I've been asked to interview Charlie's family members and friends," Elle said. "You know, Charlie married his third wife a month ago."

"Well, his first marriage wasn't a happy one." He looked around and frowned. "Sometimes I wonder if the house is haunted … like her ghost is after me fer buyin' this place."

"Really?" Elle felt butterflies in her stomach as her heart beat faster. She wondered if he saw doors open or slam closed but was afraid to ask.

He settled farther back in his rocker. "Anyway, Jackson Walker sold me the farm, and Charlie Blackwell moved to Charlotte. That's pretty much what I know."

"And what do you know about Susan Blackwell? Sorry, she was Susan Porter back then. She was the realtor working for Mr. Walker at the time you bought this place, right?"

"She was never a realtor. Not for Jackson."

"Well, Charlie and his family are under the impression—"

"Jackson started his company a couple of months before I bought this place," he told her, his face marked with impatience. "Susan showed up for an interview with Jackson."

"Was she from around here?"

"No, she was a young gal from Rock Hill, South Carolina. Old Jackson hired her on as an assistant. It was just the two of them." He shook his head again. "She only worked with him a coupla weeks. Have you actually spoken with Susan?"

"I met her last week in the ED, but she was only talking to Charlie's doctor. I'm still waiting for her attorney to give me permission to talk to her."

"Well, when you talk with her ... you'll understand."

"Understand?" She was confused by his vagueness.

He closed his eyes again. "She was beautiful. Beautiful and charming and ..."

Elle waited for him to finish his sentence, but he didn't. "And what?" she said.

"And persuasive. She could be downright persuasive." He hesitated. "That's about all I can remember."

"Is that positive or negative?"

"Everything I know, miss, is secondhand, and frankly I don't know what to believe. I don't pass along rumors." He looked at her seriously. "But I do believe in ghosts."

"Do you think Jackson Walker would be willing to talk to me?" She sensed he pretty much was trying to scare her and didn't want to talk about Susan.

"Jackson closed his office and left his wife two weeks after I bought this place. People thought he was in over his head. He couldn't compete with Duke Power and with the dam going in and Lake Norman ... let's just say, he missed his business opportunity."

"Wow. Are you saying he disappeared?"

"That, he did. His wife called the cops, but they didn't do too much back then when husbands ran away from home." He chuckled. "His wife is still around. I think I've got her number in the house. Let me get it for you."

Elle drank the rest of her tea before he came back with the number. *Too sweet.* While coffee was king where she came from, sweet tea was the elixir of the gods in North Carolina, even if she didn't get it.

"I'll call her and tell her I suggested you give her a ring," Mr. Thomas said. "She still lives here in Davidson."

"Thanks, Mr. Thomas. I really appreciate your time," Elle said. She put away her notepad and handed him her business card.

"Pretty lady, I want you to think about the streets in Charlotte when you drive home today. Those streets are paved in gold."

"Sounds like another story."

"I'll save that one for next time."

Elle thanked him for the sweet tea. This was starting to feel freakin' weird. Melinda had talked to Mr. Thomas about helping with the farm someday. He said Susan was beautiful, and charming, and persuasive. "Persuasive," she said out loud as she pulled out of his driveway. There was something about the way he had said that word that caused her to wonder if there was more to the story.

Elle spent Tuesday afternoon working on the Blackwell report, aware that the judge and attorneys would read it over before the hearing started. The goal was to have the final edits finished on Friday. She was saving the document when Grady poked his head into her office. He was dressed for another Sister Hazel concert, with a picture of their first studio album printed on his white T-shirt.

"Special delivery, a fax from Dr. Norris. It came in last night."

He handed her the fax with a handwritten note from Dr. Norris on the cover sheet.

"Sure explains Charlie's problems, doesn't it?"

"Thanks, Grady. You know it's confidential, right?" She wished he had asked her before reading Dr. Norris's evaluation of Charlie.

Grady nodded with a shy grin and moved his thin frame to her conference table. She read the note from Dr. Norris.

Elle,

For all you've done here and your willingness to share your special talents, THANK YOU! The sad truth is, for every Charlie Blackwell who gets help, there are four or five people who have no help at all and suffer alone.

Enjoyed working with you again, George Norris

*How nice of him,* she thought, savoring his words.

"The caregivers' criminal background checks are done," Grady said.

It took her a second to change gears. "You've been to the courthouse?"

He nodded, inflating his chest and grinning with self-importance.

"That was fast," she said, putting down the faxed report. Only yesterday she had shown Grady how to check references and go to the courthouse for criminal background checks.

He sat down and placed a folder in front of her. "I called the clerk's office a million times with no answer, so I just walked over on my lunch break."

"What did you think of the courthouse?"

His eyes lit up. "Da bomb."

He shared a copy of the background checks on two of the paid caregivers. "Florence Benson filed a criminal complaint against her husband for hitting her over the head with a phone, and Jane Hale went to the hospital after her boyfriend broke her arm. Does this give them motive?"

"What?" Elle asked, glancing at the forms. "I need to be reminded when these two worked for Charlie."

Grady handed her his summary sheet. "Okay, Florence Benson worked with Charlie for two years. She was let go a month ago and now works as a temporary staff replacement in a doctor's office. Jane Hale has only worked with Charlie for the past month, weekends only."

Elle nodded her head. "Now I remember. Florence Benson and Geena Louise were fired when Susan and Charlie were married." Elle returned to the background checks.

"Sounds like abuse to me," Grady said, his brows furrowed.

Elle sighed. "These reports are background checks, not arrest records. We check the caregiver's background as one of our screening steps to make sure that it's safe to place that person in the client's home. Plus, it looks like these two women were victims of domestic violence, not the other way around." She smiled at him. He liked to play armchair detective. "Neither were criminally charged. Even so, the incidents show up on the report, making it harder to find work through an agency."

Grady nodded. "Jane and Florence are scheduled for interviews on Thursday. Both of them want more hours," he said. "Geena Louise is currently working with Amy Blackwell, Charlie's ex-wife. She'll get back to me when she knows her days off."

"Was there anything on Mary Beth, the caregiver found dead in her driveway?"

Before she could finish, he handed her two background reports. "Clean. Nothing on Geena Louise either," he said with a sheepish look on his face. "I've got some information on their little underground ring."

"You mean Compassionate Care and Prayer?" Elle smiled again. While Grady's overreaching nature might be annoying, he was really getting into helping her.

"Yeah, they only have a couple of their own clients. The rest of their work is filling in for hospice or doctor clinics when they need more staffing.

I also found out that Susan is staying in an apartment off of Randolph Road while she's in the process of moving in with Charlie."

The phone rang.

"Elle Larson and Associates." Grady put his hand over the mouthpiece. "David. Says he needs to talk to you."

Elle took the phone. "Hey, what's up?"

"Can I come up?"

"You're in the building?" She heard the phone click and waited for him to call again.

Before she knew it, there was a knock. She opened the door and looked up at David's face, surprised by his grave expression. Standing next to him was a tall man in a police uniform with slicked-back hair and a nose burned from too much sun. She recognized the detective from Mary Beth's crime scene, his eyes hidden by mirrored sunglasses.

Elle turned to Grady. "This is David, crime scene investigator with the Charlotte PD."

David shook Grady's hand and glanced at her apprehensively. "Elle, I think you know Detective Slater, Homicide Unit."

"Mike Slater, right?" Elle said.

He nodded. "Can we speak to you privately?"

"Sure," Elle said as Grady, looking disappointed, left her office. She closed the door and crossed her arms.

"We're here about a doctor, George Norris?" Slater said. "Understand you were working with him ..."

She nodded. "Yes, he's the primary witness for Charlie Blackwell's hearing next Monday."

Slater lowered his head.

"He's super smart. In fact, our case pretty much rests on his testimony .... is he ... okay?"

"He was shot at home, Miss Larson. He died this morning."

"He's ... what?" She stared straight ahead, shock flooding through her veins like ice. She froze and didn't hear the rest.

"Elle?" David asked.

Her stomach rumbled, a queasy sour taste rising up in her mouth. *Something's wrong. This can't be right.* She found herself kneeling on all fours, supported by David's grip on her arm, and gagged into the wastebasket. He steadied her until she stopped.

"You okay?"

"Oh my God ... why?" She struggled to her feet.

David handed her a tissue and met her gaze. "I didn't want you hearing it on the news tonight—"

"I've known him since I moved to Charlotte." Her voice quivered as she dabbed her eyes and blew her nose.

"Detective Slater has a few questions," David said.

"How'd this happen?" Elle asked.

He ignored her question. "I told him you were also testifying in court."

She nodded. "I was in Dr. Norris's office yesterday, working on the case." She looked from David to Detective Slater. "You think there's a connection?"

David's freckled face betrayed his concern.

"I would like to contact the other expert witness," Slater said.

She nodded. "That would be Dr. Singleton." Elle wrote down her phone number and gave it to him.

"You need to be careful—" David said.

"You think I'm in danger?"

"If Dr. Norris was a target as a result of this case you're working on ..." He folded his arms.

She shook her head. It was a shift to think about her own immediate safety when Charlie's safety had been at the top of her list. Sure, her credibility had been threatened before, but never her physical well-being.

She walked to her desk and showed them the faxed note from Dr. Norris. "I don't know what to do." Her own work with Dr. Norris was over. She took a deep breath.

David gave her a sharp look. "In the meantime, you need to have security cameras set up outside your house. I can help you with that. One pointing at your front door and another, your side door."

"Jeez, David. I've got Mac."

"Elle, Mac is hardly—"

"Mac makes me feel safe," she interrupted, desperately wanting to be with her dog. David was scaring her—her colleague, Dr. Norris, gone forever. What about his family? His staff? More grief and hardship. Elle looked at David and Detective Slater. She thanked them for stopping by and telling her in person. "David, whatever you need to do is okay with me. I really need to go home right now."

Hidden behind the Pineville Burger King, the Ice House looked like an industrial warehouse, not a skating rink. The sun was sinking as Elle spun her car into the parking lot and turned off NPR, distracted by the experts debating why President Clinton had been reelected. She pulled her car into a parking space close to the building and killed the engine. The queasiness in her stomach was still there. She bundled up in her knit scarf, pulled on her hooded jacket, and wiped away the tears.

Skating was therapy and kept her strong. "And now Dr. Norris," she whispered. She opened her car door, gathered her skates, and walked to the entrance.

The rink smelled like sweat from the hockey game that had just ended. Driving the Zamboni, a dark-haired man scraped up ice and sprayed water that filled up the leftover holes from the game. Skaters waited impatiently as he finished and the ice hardened. Elle laced up her skates and looked at the wall clock: seven o'clock.

Once the ice was ready, the rink went dark, and immediately, colorful strobe lights turned on and off to the seventies classic, "I Will Survive." Teenagers and kids, yelling to friends, poured onto the ice and began dancing counterclockwise.

The cold air was inviting. She warmed up to the strong beat of "Funky Town," skating in circles as she pushed away the stress of another horrible day—like taking drugs for pain, temporary but grateful relief.

She picked up speed. With each stroke and every turn, her brain totally focused on the edge of her blade. Suddenly, she felt a tug and was pulled back by the hood of her coat by someone behind her. She struggled to pull away, then screamed as her blades failed to hold the ice and her legs skated out from under her. Her body strained out of control, the rink spinning as she propelled into midair. Her mind was suspended; it was as though her brain was spinning faster than the rest of her. Instinctively, she spread her hands as she landed, and her palms scraped across the ice, then curled up to protect her head as she skidded toward the long boards. She spun around and slammed her back into the boards.

Slowly, she moved her arms and legs. Her right leg was numb, her right hand was cut, and her back was throbbing. She managed to get to one knee and up on one skate, then the other. What happened? She hadn't seen anyone—just felt the pull. She looked around. No one seemed to have noticed. Finding the doorway, she limped off the ice.

Elle unlaced her skates and went to the pro shop to get her skates sharpened. She wanted an excuse to let the young manager know what happened.

"Disco Nights are always crowded," he said after she explained the incident.

Elle could see how it would be easy for some weirdo to move around the rink, especially when the regular lights were off and the jarring strobe lights were flashing. "I could have ended up with a concussion, or worse, a brain injury," she said, still breathing heavily.

"I'll make an announcement," he said, his face now worried at her flash of anger.

She limped to the heated snack bar, sat there, and studied her knee. It felt like another injury of a ligament she had previously sprained.

A voice over the loud speaker yelled, "If anyone saw the skater who pulled down the woman in a red-hooded jacket, please come to the pro shop immediately."

She ordered hot chocolate. Her dad's face came to mind. "Whenever you fall, you've got to get up and try again." She thought about home—skating on her small neighborhood lake, near Lake Michigan. The double blades at age five and six … how they iced over, making it impossible to stand. She and her brother skated with wobbly ankles and short, choppy steps, constantly chasing their balance. When they held hands, both of them would fall, arms flailing as they tried to stay upright.

What she remembered most was skating on clear ice. Dad helped the older boys in the neighborhood make giant sail kites. The wind blew them across the entire lake as they stood perfectly still on their hockey skates. Mom, gliding carefree on figure skates, holding Elle's hands, steadying her balance. She felt a sudden yearning for her parents and wished she and Peter were home to share a cup of hot chocolate. *Sweet and bitter at the same time.*

As she sat watching the skaters dance to the Bee Gees, holding her steaming cocoa, she thought about David's concern for her safety. It spooked her given what had happened to George Norris today. Creepy that someone had yanked her down and disappeared. She shivered. She would skate again, just not tonight. And she would do what Sumpter had asked her to do: interview Charlie's family members, friends, and finish her report. With only six days to go, she needed more answers—now.

# Chapter 13
*Wednesday*

Elle limped halfway up the carpeted stairwell, carrying a bag of ice and her fresh cup of coffee. "I'm okay, Mac," she said, turning around. An impatient pair of eyes stared up at her from the bottom of the stairs. She sat down, forearms to knees, her eyes filling up with tears as he lumbered up the stairs, one foot at a time, making a clumping sound, to sit beside her. She iced her bruised knee and sipped her coffee.

She had pulled on a T-shirt and jeans and taken Mac for his first walk in the park at 7 a.m. and then fed him while she ate her morning oatmeal. He usually took a nap on her bed while she showered and dressed for work. But this morning she wasn't ready to leave home and start the day. She tried humming backup to "In My Life" with her mom's favorite, Judy Collins, and thought about how her own life had changed.

It had been a rough night. In the haze of sleep, she dreamed about Mom and Dad. Although she couldn't remember the dream, she woke up with them in the family car, heading toward that fateful collision—feeling overwhelmed and indecisive, triggered most likely by the death of Dr. Norris. She mourned in pieces, sometimes with the old sense of being a family again. And then there was the spill on the ice last night.

Mac licked her face, and she patted his head, then limped down to the kitchen and picked up the morning paper. Under Charlotte Crime on the first page was a large photo of Dr. Norris and his wife inside their home. Then a brief story of his murder. The community response spilled out over two additional pages.

COMMUNITY ON EDGE AFTER KILLING

The small idyllic neighborhood and historic district of Myers Park has been shattered by the brutal murder of Charlotte neurologist George Norris. Dr. Norris was found unresponsive in his home by his wife in the 800 block of Edgehill Road. No arrests have been made.

She looked down at Mac, now lying on the kitchen floor, feet up. She eased herself next to him with the front section of the paper and read out loud while rubbing his belly.

Past police data showed that Myers Park had the lowest crime level in Charlotte. But the unsolved murder has rocked the neighborhood, causing residents to look over their shoulders, a chilling reminder that the neighborhood remains vulnerable.

She read the rest of the article slowly and to herself.

While a good working relationship existed with the Providence Division police, also known as Baker One, resident requests for increased police patrols have not been honored since the murder of Dr. Norris.

There was a picture of a neighbor, sitting on his front porch, looking out over his neighborhood. He was head of the neighborhood watch program and was quoted as saying he encouraged residents to look out for each other, keep their homes well lit and report burglars immediately, such as the one suspected of ambushing Dr. Norris.

Elle rubbed Mac's belly again and kissed the top of his head. She wondered what the residents would say if they knew about Charlie's attempted murder or about Mary Beth Abbot—all in less than a week.

She waited until nine o'clock before calling Mrs. Walker. The phone rang twice before a woman answered in a soft, tremulous voice.

"Mrs. Walker?"

"Yes?"

"My name is Elle Larson. I was wondering if I could meet with you?"

"Gordon told me you would be calling. I'm sorry, but I can't help you."

Elle could hear Mrs. Walker fighting for her breath and the vibrating hum of portable oxygen in the background. "Did you know Susan Porter?"

"I didn't work ... with my husband. Susan ... was in her early twenties ... and didn't—she didn't have the experience he needed. She only worked with him ... for two weeks or so ... that was thirty-six years ago." Mrs. Walker stopped for a minute to catch her breath. "My husband left me shortly after that—cashed his commission check and took our money with him."

"Did you ever hear from him again?"

"Sorry I can't help you, miss; I've been ill. But ... but that mean bastard never even said goodbye." Mrs. Walker hung up the phone.

Elle sat thinking. Clearly Mrs. Walker thought she'd been dumped, that her husband intentionally slipped away so she'd never find him again.

Mac rolled over and wagged his tail.

"Blind alley," she said and patted his head.

He met her gaze, hopped up, and grabbed his leash.

"Okay, one quick walk. Then I've gotta go."

When Elle left Charlotte, she drove north to Davidson Landing, where Amy Blackwell now lived. Lake Norman sparkled in the sun, just a short walk from the marina where Elle had partied with Josh and David last Sunday. People were still wearing summer clothes, even though it was almost mid-November, and days from now, all the brilliant-colored leaves would be gone.

She followed a lane to the lakeside condo and knocked on the front door, where a petite woman in a neck scarf and wool trousers was waiting for her.

"Bonjour," she said. "*Je suis* Amy Blackwell."

Elle extended her hand and introduced herself. "*Mon français est horrible.*"

Mrs. Blackwell was pretty—mid-seventies with soft, watery eyes, maybe five feet tall, and extremely thin.

A plain woman, wearing a white uniform, walked up from behind, carrying a steaming pot of coffee.

"Geena Louise, how nice to finally meet you," Elle said, hoping to break the tension.

"Miss Amy's son wants you to promise that you won't upset her." Geena Louise looked at Elle with furrowed brows and wary eyes set in a bare face.

Elle nodded and said nothing back. She exchanged glances with Mrs. Blackwell, who led her to the living room, where she sat down under an old French painting and patted the cushion next to her. Elle sank into the sofa, still feeling the bruises from her fall last night, and placed her purse on the floor.

"Please call me Amy. It would be too confusing to call me Mrs. Blackwell, yes?"

Elle smiled, listening to her lyrical accent and that breathy sound at the end of her words that sounded so sexy, so French, like poetry. Her English was excellent.

"My son does worry about me. You see, I have heart failure … sometimes, my heart is too weak to pump enough blood out to my body. I am doing better, yes?"

Geena Louise set the coffeepot down on a small table and excused herself as they made themselves comfortable in front of a coffee table spread with breads, jellies, and chocolate cookies.

Amy leaned in close and whispered, "Wednesday is shopping day ... I hope she remembers we need more milk. I told Geena Louise it was okay to meet you, but I wanted our conversation to be private." She sighed. "I don't want my son upset ... she tells him too much of my business."

Elle hid her disappointment. She was hoping to interview Geena Louise, but that would need to wait another day. *I need to hear Amy's story first.*

"Let's start with coffee, yes?"

Elle looked into Amy's soft brown eyes. "I can't thank you enough for taking the time to talk to me."

Amy smiled and poured a cup for Elle and a cup for herself. "We like it strong."

"It's perfect," Elle said, after taking a sip.

"Go ahead, try the bread. My first job was working in a bakery. I still love fresh-baked bread."

Elle sliced a piece of bread from the loaf and placed it on a small plate that she balanced on her knees.

Amy turned to the painting hanging above them—little orange rooftops like random dabs of paint. "During the war, many European families sent their old people and small children out of the big cities."

Elle applied a thin layer of butter and jam to her bread and looked at the painting.

"I was French and my parents' only child ... and because they worried the bombing would come to our city, I was sent to the small village of Zhuri in Czechoslovakia. My aunt and uncle owned a bakery. Can you see? It's right here." She moved her finger across the painting and pointed to a small patch of color: a little house, touches of green trees, the mountains in the background. "And that's where I met Charlie."

Elle followed with her eyes. "When was that?"

"Let's see, Charlie came to Zhuri in 1945. He was an officer. His last battle was in our little village. It was the last day of the war." She took some short breaths. "And now the village is no longer there."

"What happened?" Elle asked, dying to know about this part of the world her dad had traveled when he was only nineteen. Her dad had seen too much combat, though, and never talked about the war.

"Gone." She paused. "Everyone had to leave."

Elle looked at her expectantly.

"Do you know about Zhuri?"

Elle shook her head.

"The Russians rewrote history during the Cold War. You won't find our village mentioned anywhere in the books." She cleared her throat and with a small shake of her head continued her story. "Charlie and I met the day the war was over. I had washed the front windows of the bakery that morning, inside and out. Then I put cakes and breads in the window. At six a.m. I rode my bicycle to the houses in the village, rang their doorbells, and left their bread by the door."

Elle sipped her coffee.

"When I returned on my bike, my aunt suggested I take the American soldier some coffee. She thought he looked like such a nice young man."

"And that was Charlie?"

Amy nodded wistfully. "He showed me how he heated his food in his canteen cup. I've often thought about that cup and how I filled it with his first cup of strong French coffee that morning."

Elle leaned her head to one side, still smiling. "That must have been so crazy ... romantic, yet scary too."

"He was kind to me, and a good-looking American." She shook her head with a soft laugh. "Life was crazy back then. The day before, I had been hiding in the basement for hours and hours while the fighting between American and German soldiers went house to house. The next day the war was over, and we were falling in love."

Elle took a bite of what tasted like caraway seeds, poppy seeds, butter, and berry jam. The bread was warm, with a chewy crust, fresh from the oven. She took a sip of coffee. "*Tusen takk*—that's 'a million thanks' in Norwegian. I don't know how to say it in French."

"*Merci beaucoup.* It's sourdough rye. We keep the starter going, and Geena Louise bakes me a loaf every week.

"Charlie loved my sourdough," Amy said with a soft smile. "We had a short courtship—four days while he was in Zhuri. But then his regiment was ordered back into Germany. I was Catholic, and he was Protestant. The only way I could have left the country was to marry him in Germany. That's how it was back then, but I was so young."

"So when did you marry?"

"Not until 1962. Seventeen years later. You see, we never thought we would see each other again. Charlie married Carol after the war. After she died in 1960, he reconnected with me. I lost my first husband to cancer. When I finally came to Charlotte, we married at Saint Peter's." Amy handed Elle a black-and-white picture that was sitting on the coffee table.

"Saint Peter's Episcopal Church? That's right down the street from me in Fourth Ward." Elle leaned over to see the wedding couple standing in front of the Victorian Gothic church's huge doors that were now painted red.

Amy poured Elle a second cup of coffee, her fingers still trembling.

*Remember her CHF.* Elle didn't want to push; still, there were questions she needed to ask. "So when did Charlie start needing help in the home?" She picked up the fine china cup with one hand, steadied it in her other, and took a couple of sips.

"Yes, well, that was probably two years ago. In the beginning, he only needed help to set up his two blood pressure pills."

"Was he forgetting to take them?"

"No, but his macular degeneration had progressed. He couldn't see the names on the prescription bottles. He also gave up driving three years ago."

Elle waited for her to go on.

"Once we started having help, Charlie began sleeping more, having more nightmares and flashbacks. After he got sick, his behavior changed. Some nights in bed, he would kick me so hard, I'd have bruises on my legs in the morning."

"Was he ever aggressive or physically violent with you when he wasn't having flashbacks?" Elle asked, stretching her sore right leg under the coffee table.

"Oh no. He worried my heart could get worse if he thrashed about at night. I moved into the bedroom across the hall."

Elle's knee ached. "Did that help?"

Amy shook her head. "No, it made everything harder."

"In what way?"

"Charlie and I stopped talking as much."

"I want to be sure I understand—"

"You're straight and to the point," Amy said.

Elle shrugged. "I'm sorry … must be my Midwestern upbringing."

"Oh no, the French like to be frank. People in the South don't say what they think, not to your face anyway." Amy smiled, her eyes sparkling. "They're more like the English in that way."

Elle laughed and nibbled her bread.

"My heart was getting weaker. Charlie began sleeping all of the time. I stressed over him, telling the caregivers not to wake him when he was sleeping. My stress didn't help. I became breathless and started retaining fluid. We took to communicating through them and spending more time in our own bedrooms. The caregivers gradually took charge of running the household."

"Was Charlie taking any medication for anxiety or pain?" Elle asked.

"No, only for blood pressure."

"Did he have a drinking problem?"

"He told me he drank a lot when he came back from the war. It caused problems in his life when he was young, but he was done with that by the time we married. I mean he enjoyed a scotch before dinner, usually one scotch on the rocks."

Amy's breathing became more labored. "Did Robbie or Melinda help in any way?"

Amy shook her head. "His children were not happy he was marrying some strange woman from Eastern Europe." She leaned closer to Elle. "I think they thought I was a communist spy." She rolled her eyes. "They'd been on the outside of his life until after our divorce."

"Did you know they were calling him once or twice a week over the past two years, but rarely got to talk to him?"

Amy's eyes filled with tears. "Charlie pushed everyone away and stayed in his bedroom, wouldn't take phone calls from anyone."

"Did you personally take calls from Robbie or Melinda?"

"Oh no, they didn't trust me," she said, shaking her head. "The care-givers screened all the calls coming in."

"Well, it sounds like they may have been keeping Charlie from Robbie and Melinda too."

"What do you mean?" Amy asked.

*Be careful here.* Were Florence and Geena Louise trying to poison Amy and Charlie's relationship? Elle needed to explore her hunch without stressing Amy out. "Well, if Robbie and Melinda had talked to Charlie, they might have been more supportive."

Amy raised her hand as if to protest. "We had a happy marriage. He was a good husband," she said in a quivering voice. "There was no way I could fight what was going on. When he wanted a divorce, I collapsed and landed in the hospital with heart failure. I had to be hospitalized for weeks—that doesn't mean I ever stopped loving Charlie."

"I understand. Did Charlie ever tell you he wanted a divorce?"

Amy looked thoughtful for a moment, then shook her head. "No, the caregivers did." She stopped, fighting back more tears. "He never let go of the guilt he felt from his first wife's suicide, especially what it did to his children."

Elle put her plate down and leaned forward. "This must have been such a difficult time for you."

Amy took another moment, gazing into her coffee cup, then shook her head again. "I received the divorce papers to sign while I stayed here with my son after I was discharged from the hospital."

"Did the caregivers say anything else that made it harder for you during that time?" Elle asked, feeling her own heart start to pound.

"About a year and a half ago, Florence told me that Charlie thought I was after his money. I later found out that Florence was telling him that I thought he was after my money."

Elle could see how stressful this was for Amy. She was breathing hard, which meant her heart was beating fast. *Just get this over.* "When you first needed help for Charlie, how did you find Geena Louise and Florence?"

"Robbie's wife, Peggy. She worked for a hospice organization in Charlotte. Geena Louise and Florence were on the list of caregivers used by the agency."

"What about Susan?"

"She became the scheduler shortly after Geena Louise and Florence started. Before that it was Peggy. Scheduling a caregiver every day became too hard for Peggy, but Robbie didn't trust me to do it." She sighed.

Elle reached out and held her hand. She noticed that Amy had not touched her baked goods. "So will you be staying here from now on?"

Amy brightened up a bit. "Actually, I'm moving to The Pines soon. You've heard of it, yes?"

Elle nodded, encouragingly. "They have a new French chef who does all of their cooking."

Amy smiled. "That's a good enough reason to go there and still be close to my son."

Amy's dyspnea was getting worse.

"Are you okay?" Elle frowned.

Amy closed her eyes for a second, then looked at Elle. "Sometimes I wonder if I've been stupid. You think we were being manipulated, don't you?"

Elle avoided sharing her assumptions with Amy when she didn't have the facts. She didn't want to worry her. "I'm checking everything out, that's all."

"I do feel more breathless. I've got this twinge in my chest. It means I better lie down … to be safe. She smiled, weakly. But I don't panic anymore … not like I did before I was hospitalized."

Elle stood, put her hand out to Amy, and helped her to her feet.

Amy turned to her, taking short breaths. "I remember something else. It may help, yes?"

"Whatever you know could be extremely important."

"I believe Geena Louise told me that Compassionate Care and Prayer began looking for a permanent office and found space in Charlie's new doctor's office building."

"Dr. Woodham?"

"Dr. Woodham, that's his name."

Elle followed as Amy walked slowly to her bedroom and settled on her bed.

"Did you like my bread? The French will kill for baguettes, but I think this bread is best for breakfast."

"It was delicious."

Elle took another minute to say goodbye, then limped to the kitchen, stacking the delicate French plates in the sink as if they were made of glass. So Compassionate Care and Prayer had an office in Dr. Woodham's building. Her mind was racing. What was their relationship with Dr. Woodham?

Elle sat in Amy's driveway, staring out her windshield at the lake's waves splashing against the dock. Clouds were turning the water a murky gray. She wasn't sure how much time had passed when her phone rang.

"I still need to talk to Charlie," Sumpter said.

"Great timing. The drugs have cleared his system and he keeps improving." She heard him paging through his calendar.

"I can meet you at the hospital on Thursday afternoon?"

"I'm sorry. I have the memorial service for Dr. Norris at three."

"That's fine. I can't get away until five anyway, so I'll meet you then."

"Have a minute?" She summarized her conversation with Amy and took a deep breath.

"Good work. Any red flags?"

She thought of what Sumpter would want to know. "A couple of biggies: Amy never heard directly from Charlie that he wanted a divorce. Charlie said the same thing, yet both received divorce papers to sign. The last year or two, they started sleeping in separate bedrooms while the caregivers screened all calls coming in from Robbie and Melinda—not putting them through to Charlie or Amy. Strange, right?"

"Keep it going. We're building our case here, but we need actual evidence."

As encouraging as his words were, there was so much more to know, and she was still learning, but there were some things she did know that stabbed at her heart like a knife. She looked out again at the water that had lost its sparkle. "Sumpter, I believe Amy. The past medical records corroborate her story, until Dr. Woodham. And Amy was out of the picture by the time he came along."

# Chapter 14
*Thursday*

Elle closed the office door behind her and offered Florence Benson a seat. "Sorry it's so cramped in here," she said and pulled the small corner table out from the wall to create some more room.

"Goodness gracious." Florence winced as she placed her purse and well-worn Bible on the table and squeezed into the only chair at the table.

Elle offered her an oatmeal cookie from the plate Grady had placed on the table. Sure, she wanted to put Florence at ease, but she also needed to thread the needle differently. If one of the caregivers had intentionally kept Charlie from talking to Robbie or Melinda and had drugged him as well, that was far more important to figure out. She turned her desk chair to the table and slowly sat down, gently rubbing the spot under her knee brace. "So, tell me about yourself ... your work history."

Florence hesitated while taking a cookie between her short, thick fingers. "I'm from Charlotte. I live alone," she said in a wistful tone, her thin gray hair lying flat around her pale face. "I've worked for several home care agencies. What else do you want to know?"

"What made you decide to work for Compassionate Care and Prayer?" Elle began taking notes in her spiral notebook.

"I can make more money in twenty-four hours as a live-in," Florence said and examined her oatmeal cookie. "And it keeps me from getting lonely."

"It's not a legally incorporated company, you know."

"I guess." Florence gave Elle a dazed stare. "It's a faith-based company. People in the office start every morning with a prayer."

"When were you hired to work for Charlie Blackwell?"

"Miss Amy hired me back in '94. I worked the weekends and Geena Louise worked during the week."

Florence said she had never spoken to Mary Beth or Jane and had never worked with them. For the past month, she was staffing a doctor's office. Now she worked Monday and Fridays only.

"Are y'all interviewing everyone who worked with Mr. Charlie?"

"That's right," Elle said. "So why do you think Susan let you go?"

Florence shrugged and took a big bite of the cookie. She chewed slowly and squinted her eyes. "Once Susan married Mr. Charlie ... I just thought she wanted to choose her own caregivers."

"But Susan knew you, right?" Elle watched her carefully. "I mean ... as the scheduler, Susan already had a relationship with both of you."

"Yes, ma'am." Florence returned Elle's gaze with a blank look on her face.

"Doesn't Susan do all of the scheduling?"

"She does," Florence said matter-of-factly. "Like I said, Miss Amy hired me and Geena Louise two years ago, but I ain't lookin' to work with Mr. Charlie again."

When Florence offered nothing more, Elle went on. "Tell me about giving Charlie his medication."

"What do you mean?"

"When you worked there last year, what were the steps involved ... what were the pills you gave?"

"I handed his med box to him. The two little white pills were already set up. No one told me the names of those pills." Florence took another bite of cookie. "Y'all know I'm not a nurse, right?"

Elle nodded. "So, who set up the med box?"

Florence gave her another blank stare. "I couldn't say for sure. I always thought it was Miss Amy."

"Seriously?" Elle's face turned hot. "Amy and Charlie were separated last year."

"Then maybe it was Geena Louise."

"Florence, do you recall Charlie ever asking for pain medication or any sedating drugs?"

Florence shook her head no. "I only gave those two little pills for blood pressure."

"I know you haven't worked with Charlie for the past month, but have you had any recent contact with him or had any access to the drug fentanyl?

"What's fentanyl?"

Elle explained about the drug screen in the emergency department and the fentanyl, oxycodone, and clonazepam found in his system. "Look, these are all highly sedating medications."

"I haven't seen Mr. Charlie since I was asked to leave." Florence placed both hands on her Bible as if to gain strength. She described the spiral notebook that was kept in his bedroom where she wrote notes from her shift but didn't know who had the notebook. Someone in her office would probably know. She had been surprised by Mr. Charlie's divorce and marriage to Susan. And yes, she had heard that the new caregiver attended the ceremony, but no one else was there. She didn't even know that Mary Beth had died.

Elle closed her eyes. She was getting nowhere fast. *Stay calm.* Florence was polite in a weird way but not the least bit inquisitive, and she didn't express the kind of concern about Charlie that was expected from a seasoned caregiver. *Time to shake things up.*

Elle opened her eyes to see Florence nibbling around the edge of the cookie. "Why did you tell Charlie that Amy was after his money?"

"What makes you say that?" Florence looked away and pushed herself back in the chair with her free hand.

"I spoke with Amy yesterday."

Florence shook her head. "Maybe she was talking about Geena Louise. Remember, I only worked the weekends."

Elle wondered if that was true but decided she could always circle back and talk to Amy. "So when did Charlie start to need more help?"

Florence ate the last bite of cookie. "Over this last year, Mr. Charlie got to where he could hardly get out of bed."

"Why was that?" Elle asked.

"It was too hard for him to walk. After a while, he seemed to just give up."

"Why do you think he had a hard time walking?"

Silence.

Elle waited. Finally, Florence shrugged. "A man can't help gettin' old and not bein' able to walk."

Elle sat up straight in her chair. "Could it be all the sedating medications someone gave him?"

"Sorry, I don't know nothin' about that." She picked up the Bible and helped herself to another oatmeal cookie.

"Did you know that Charlie's blood pressure medicine hasn't been refilled for the past six months?"

Florence gave Elle another blank stare.

Elle decided to change the subject. Maybe Florence would remember something later, but it was doubtful. She opened the folder with Grady's notes from checking references. He'd added a five-by-seven glossy that he'd enlarged from the two-by-two photo embedded in her driver's license. *Nice work, Grady!*

She examined the photo carefully and picked up the criminal background check. "Can you tell me about this complaint against your husband?"

"He was fit to be tied when he found out I wanted a divorce," Florence said. "But he was cheatin' on me."

"I'm sorry—"

"It was the only time he ever hit me, and I called 911." Florence talked about not feeling supported by family and friends at the time, and that's when she'd started working for Compassionate Care and Prayer. "Just so you know, Mr. Charlie was never aggressive with me. He was so kind to everyone."

As they finished their meeting, Elle stood painfully on her right leg and pulled the table out farther from the wall. She didn't think Florence was lying, just not observant. She was also careless. Or was it her attitude about older people? Had Charlie been a young man, would she have worried about why he wasn't walking? Elle wanted to shake her, yell, or do something that would wake her up. Instead, she thanked her, limped to the door, and ushered her out of the office.

A woman in a brilliant purple dress and gold hoop earrings was crossing the hallway, moving toward Elle. She wore her thick black hair in a short cut with chunky bronze highlights.

"I'm Jane Hale," she said. Her soft Brown face gave no sign of recognition as she passed Florence, who was heading to the elevator.

"Please, come in." Elle shook Jane's hand and escorted her to the corner table.

Jane hung her shoulder bag over the chair, squeezed nervously against the wall, and smoothed out the fitted dress that highlighted the roundness of her body. She looked around the room and then at Elle. "Could y'all have a smaller office?"

"Sorry, I have no separate conference room." Elle slid into her chair and told her the women's bathroom was across the hall. She then offered Jane a cup of coffee and one of Grady's homemade cookies.

"No, thank you. Susan advised me not to talk to y'all," Jane said, her voice filled with tension. "But I haven't been called to work on another case since Mr. Charlie's hospitalization. I heard you were working with his attorney ... he wants what's best for him, right?"

"Absolutely," Elle said.

Jane told Elle that she and her ex-husband had a son in college. She lived near Park Road shopping center, and her parents lived down the street. She sang in her church choir when she wasn't working.

Elle hated to pressure Jane, but she had worked with Charlie until the day he was hospitalized. "We're trying to understand the staffing over the past couple of months. Let me ask you, why do you think Susan fired Geena Louise and Florence Benson?"

"Geena Louise was close to Mr. Charlie's ex-wife, Miss Amy," Jane said. "Susan told me she wanted to build her own team. Susan also needed to schedule Florence for some temporary staffing."

"And what's your relationship like with Susan?" Elle asked.

"We mainly talk about my schedule over the phone." Jane explained that she had helped out occasionally during the week when Mary Beth had a doctor's appointment but otherwise worked weekends only. "I've only worked with Mr. Charlie for the past four weeks."

"So, since the wedding," Elle said.

Jane nodded.

"Did you know Charlie and Susan were getting married?"

"No, I didn't. That was Mary Beth's first day on the job. I didn't know Mary Beth either." Jane sighed, the tears welling up in her dark eyes. "Can you imagine, first day on the job and you're the only witness at Mr. Charlie's wedding?"

Elle pushed the tissue box within reach and waited while she blotted her eyes and blew her nose. She seemed kind. "Did you know Dr. Woodham?"

Jane shook her head. "Soon after the wedding, Susan started taking Mr. Charlie to his doctor appointments."

"So why do you think someone put five fentanyl patches on Charlie?"

"Y'all know that for sure?"

Elle told her about finding the fentanyl patches and the two other sedating drugs discovered by the ED doctor. "The fentanyl alone was enough to kill a horse."

"I never saw no fentanyl. This ain't no case like that. Mr. Charlie only takes his blood pressure pills, that's all."

"Do you know the names of those pills?"

Jane shook her head no.

"So how do you know what you gave Charlie was for his blood pressure?"

"Susan told me. She said he was only to get his two little blood pressure pills from the med box twice a day." Jane shook her head. "Nothin' else."

"Look, I'm not here to threaten your job, Jane. I'm frustrated. Nobody seems to know what the drugs were that he was taking." Elle gave her a weak smile. At least Jane was more curious and engaged than Florence.

Jane began to tear up again. "I should have worked with Mr. Charlie last Wednesday after Mary Beth got sick." Her voice choked.

"Go on," Elle said.

"We usually covered each other so Susan didn't need to cover with someone else."

"You weren't asked to come in and cover when Mary Beth went home last Wednesday morning?"

"No," she said, twisting her hands together. Her voice trembled and she blotted her eyes with another tissue.

"When I arrived Wednesday morning, the side door was unlocked," Elle said.

Jane nodded. "It's always been that way ... like I said, I've only worked with the Blackwells for the past four weeks."

Elle was discouraged. Neither caregiver was aware of any sedating medications. Neither had heard about the fentanyl patches. Both had written notes every day but didn't know the whereabouts of the notebook that had always been in Charlie's bedroom.

Elle handed Jane a copy of her criminal background check. She paused while she waited for Jane to comment.

Jane put the copy down and pushed it back across the table, without looking at it. "My boyfriend was a huge mistake from the beginning. He beat the crap out of me, then lied and said I fell down the stairs."

"How badly were you hurt?" Elle asked, watching her take a few deep breaths in and out.

"Cuts and bruises. A broken rib."

"Good thing you were evaluated."

"Yeah, but it makes it hard to get work. Even though I did nothing wrong, it's now on my report for everyone to see."

"Jane, was Charlie ever physically violent with you?"

"Never, never." Jane reached for her bag and slipped it onto her shoulder. "I need to get home now. I have choir practice. Can I go?"

Elle looked up from the report to Jane's face. What was she not saying? "Sure, and thanks for coming here." She handed Jane her business card. "If you know anything at all, please tell me."

"Y'all don't think Mary Beth's death was an accident?" Jane tucked the card into her bag and moved out from the table.

Elle shook her hand. "No, I don't, and someone tried to murder Charlie ... Did you know, if you cover for someone else, you could be an accessory to the crime?"

Jane didn't answer, but her hands were visibly shaking as she walked out the door without a glance.

Elle sighed and thought about the two interviews. Neither caregiver had ever seen Charlie act aggressively or physically violent. That was the good thing. Of course, Florence and Jane only worked the weekends. Why was it that so much was still hidden? Murder or accident, the caregiver who knew the most was Mary Beth.

Elle ate the last two cookies, hardly tasting them. There had to be a way to get ahead of this case. It was time to widen the search.

Elle drove down West Main Street with Kate Harrigan in the passenger seat. Rock Hill, South Carolina, was twenty-five miles south of Charlotte and, according to Kate, was named for a solid hill of rock that was in the way of the railroad years ago.

"Naomi runs the lunch counter," Kate said as Elle parked at McCrory's Five and Dine. "If you ever want to know about anyone around these parts, just stop in and ask her."

Elle limped through the diner-like restaurant behind Kate and sat down at the counter.

"This ain't no ordinary lunch counter," Kate said, smiling at the tall Southern woman with bleached blond hair teased up in a beehive.

From behind the counter, Naomi ambled over to take their order as the last of the breakfast crowd was leaving.

Elle looked at her with curiosity while fingering the stainless steel and chrome counter. Naomi's hair looked crispy-hard, like it would hold up in a strong wind. Elle wondered how much hairspray it took to keep her hair up that high.

"Naomi's been working here since the sixties," Kate told her.

"Back then, y'all would not be sittin' at this counter together," Naomi said with a bright red smile.

"Hey, honey," she said, turning to Elle. "Kate's been telling me about you. You look kinda young to be doin' what you're doin'."

Elle smiled. She hated looking younger than her age. "Yeah, I hear that. It's nice to meet you."

"Tell her what happened here back in the sixties," Kate said.

"Black college kids. We couldn't serve 'em at the counter. And they refused to leave."

Elle felt a vague hint of recognition. She had never been to McCrory's but remembered hearing stories about the Woolworth lunch counter in Greensboro.

"I said to my boss, 'Lordy, don't make me turn them away.' But he was standin' over my shoulder. Said he didn't have a choice; it was the law. I thought we's gonna fight the Civil War all over again."

"They became the first to serve jail time," Kate said.

"Lordy, that's right. First in the country," Naomi added.

"How brave," Elle said, swiveling on her stool, unable to take her eyes off of Naomi's hair.

"And now she's the boss," Kate said, giving Naomi a nod.

Naomi's red smile grew wider. "Now what can I get you ladies today?"

Elle ordered a chocolate milkshake and Kate a sweet tea. They asked Naomi about Robbie and Peggy Blackwell.

"He don't come in here. Not with that fancy chair." She waved her arm as if to show there was not enough room for his wheelchair. "But I hear he's a good neighbor—good to his daddy, good to his wife. Why?"

Elle told Naomi about Charlie's recent marriage and her desire to find out more about his family.

"So who did he marry?"

When Elle told Naomi about his marriage to Susan Porter, she rolled her eyes and raised her dark penciled brows.

"Lordy, can't believe it! Don't you repeat this," she whispered, moving within inches of Elle's face as Elle drank some of her milkshake. "She's nothing but white trash. And even if she dresses up like a rich Southern Barbie, she's still white trash."

Elle smiled. *She is a hoot!* "You know Susan Porter?"

"Honey, folks talk in front of me while eating their burger and fries. They forget I'm here." She gave Elle another broad smile. "Keeps me from gettin' bored."

While they sipped on their drinks, Naomi stood behind the counter and told them about Susan coming in every month for the past year with a friend.

"Never leaves a tip. Last time she came in, she bounced a check."

"Do you know the friend?" Elle asked.

"Oh goodness no." Naomi paused. "Average height and weight, I'd say. She's White. It sounded like they was up to somethin'. All gussied up and nervous as two whores in church. You know she had a son," she said, mopping up the counter. "Woulda been maybe thirty."

"Who had a son?" Elle asked.

"Susan; hooked up with some mob guy in Philadelphia."

"Was she married?"

"Hell no. They had a son though—in and out of jail. Arrested on drug charges. The way I heard it, the heroin finally got to him, and he died. Maybe that's why she came back here."

"Who died, the son or the mob guy?" Elle asked.

"Mob guy."

"So when did Susan leave Rock Hill?"

"Long time ago; didn't come back till a couple of years ago."

Elle finished her milkshake and set the glass on the counter. "Did you ever meet her son or know his name?"

"No, he always lived in Philly, but I heard he changed his name after prison."

"I'll have another sweet tea, to go," Kate said.

Elle paid for their drinks and gave Naomi a ten-dollar tip. "Thank you—great milkshake," she said, staring back at her as she hobbled out the door on her sore knee.

The traffic was light on the drive back to Charlotte. Elle thought about Naomi's story and tried to imagine being told she couldn't be served at the counter. She had never asked Kate about her own experience. Kate seemed so independent and strong … making her own way at the police department.

Elle cleared her throat. "It's better now than when those Black students went to jail, right?"

Kate glanced at her. "Not much."

She told Elle about her first job in Charlotte, working as a home health aide. She had gone through her certified training program and was proud of what she accomplished. "Nobody ever told me that being White made for a better home health aide."

"People wanted someone White?" Elle asked, knowing that some of her own clients had requested White caregivers.

"I would hear people say, 'I hope I don't get that Black girl.' "

"So what did you do?"

"At first, I felt trapped. I wasn't raised that way, but then I've always felt like an outsider. Not quite Black like my papa or White like my mama."

Elle shook her head. She knew what it was like to feel like an outsider, like forever being out of place as a Midwestern Lutheran living in the South and like being the only twenty-nine-year-old she knew who had lost both of her parents. But losing your family was different than a lifetime of prejudice based on the color of your skin. Thank God, like Kate, her parents had taught her to think for herself.

"I was determined to change their minds … show them what I could do," Kate said. "In the end, though, people wouldn't give me a chance. Eventually, I didn't want to be an aide anymore."

"Jeez, I'm sorry. Why then a police officer?"

"I come from a law enforcement family. My papa was a Black cop. Mama was a White social worker. I'm privileged compared to most. If people have passed judgment on me, I'll assign someone else on my team to work with them."

"So Charlotte's not as progressive as people say it is?"

"White folks in Charlotte like to think so …"

"Well, look at you now. You've been promoted—"

"Elle, I'm the only Black female in a supervisory role. I'm still navigating a path from an outside point of view, and nothing exciting ever happens in the Providence Division."

"Until this week." Elle thought about an article she read in *The Charlotte Observer.* "The paper says our city is over thirty percent Black, and that we have a strong Black middle class."

"Wake up, girl. The editors at the *Observer* are White, and the middle class is disappearing. Black people account for sixty percent of traffic stops, pulled over by a mostly White police force. We're no different than other cities."

By the time Elle pulled into the prisoner entrance of the police station, Kate had finished talking, and Elle had been quiet for a while. A cloud hung over her head as she parked the car. She didn't question Kate's facts. After all, Kate had lived in Charlotte forever.

"I appreciate you talking to me," Elle said. God knows she and Kate were trying to make things better.

"You just need to learn how to kick ass." Kate held her gaze.

A thought popped into Elle's head. She sat up straight, looking out the window at the parked police cars and vans.

"Kate, I'd like to swing back to McCrory's with some pictures, see if Naomi can recognize the mystery friend who came in with Susan."

# Chapter 15

E lle pressed her full body weight against the heavy church door and opened it. She had never been to Friendship Missionary Baptist Church before, or any other Black church for that matter. She looked around. No one had arrived. She checked her watch. It was only 2:30 p.m., and the memorial service wasn't until three o'clock. Thank God, she was early.

She limped into a large community center and noticed a framed picture of Dr. Norris straight ahead, on a table along the wall. Several white candles were lit. Roses, lilies, and cards that held personal notes—an impromptu memorial, a reminder of a life cut short and the terrible way it had happened. She smelled the fragrance of roses and shivered, thinking about Dr. Norris.

She looked up to see an usher in a bright blue suit, clearing his throat and guarding the church door. He looked at her sternly.

"I'm here for Dr. Norris," she said, walking up to him. "His memorial service?"

"Would you please sign the guest book?" he asked in a somber voice. After she signed in, he asked her, "Presbyterian?"

"No, Lutheran."

"I mean did you work at Presbyterian Hospital, with Dr. Norris?"

"Oh, sorry. I'm not a hospital employee," Elle said, feeling her face flush. "I did refer clients to Dr. Norris, and he sometimes referred clients to me."

"You can sit behind the Norris family," he said, after they were in the church, pointing to the front pews.

She looked to the front of the church. The sanctuary was huge compared to her little Lutheran church back home. Wood-stained panels across the entire front wall formed a backdrop for two long rows of pipes for the organ and a large and simple cross. "I'd like to sit in back." She hesitated. "I like to listen to the choir from the back of the church."

He nodded and walked her over to a thickly padded wooden pew near the back wall.

"George Norris sang in the choir," he said, his dark brown eyes softening as he extended an open hand to the pew. "He's been coming to this church since we were boys, his parents too. We went to Sunday school together."

Elle nodded and sat down, painfully bending her stiff right knee. From here she could watch the people walking in without being obvious. She didn't know what to say. *Say the truth.* "He was the best neurologist in Charlotte," she said, her voice cracking.

He smiled at her and ushered in two Black women in colorful dresses and matching shoes. Their hats were serious, all feathered and sequined—nothing like she'd seen before. Three more ushers appeared in bright church suits as the organist began the prelude. By now, Presbyterian physicians and other hospital staff were arriving. She wasn't sure who she was looking for but was surprised by their number, given the hospital operated 24/7 and not everyone could take time off from work. Elle recognized Amanda with her bright-colored makeup.

The choir danced into the sanctuary, swaying and dipping to the clapping of the congregation and the sound of the organ and tambourine. They started singing "God Is in Control," working the crowd, soft and slow, then loud and fast, like in the song "Proud Mary." The house of God was rocking by the time the choir members took their place at the front of the church and faced the congregation with its huge number of White guests.

Mrs. Norris walked in, a gloved hand pressed over her heart, her pregnant belly the size of a basketball. She took a front seat with her family, looking lovely but absolutely devastated in her burgundy velvet dress.

Listening to the soulful singing of "Peace in the Valley," Elle's tears started to flow. *How strange* ... no casket. She knew Dr. Norris was still in the hospital morgue, his body cold and still. She tried not to let too much of it in.

Just before the first gospel song finished, Josh Geller rushed through the church doors. He looked slightly disheveled, like he needed a haircut but was far too busy to get one. He spotted Elle. She smiled and mouthed the words, "You're late."

"Can I sit with you?" he whispered.

"Only if you have tissues," she said.

He pulled a folded tissue from inside his coat and sat down. She wiped her runny nose and smelled the clean scent of his cologne, then felt his arm around her shoulder.

"You okay?" he asked.

"Just thinking about the people I've lost."

She noticed his red-rimmed eyes. Who else had he lost besides Dr. Norris and his father? Some of his emergency patients, for sure. He took care of his patients, and when they died, he was the last person they saw, and then he still had to talk to their families.

"Do not lose your faith," the pastor said, his voice strained. "Rather, think of our friend and brother dancing with our Lord."

"Praise Jesus!" shouted a woman from the congregation, followed by several spontaneous shouts of "Amen!"

During "Amazing Grace" everyone stood. Many raised their arms and swayed as they sang mournfully. Elle sang along softly and blinked away her tears. The service gave her something she couldn't describe, then the word came to her: *grace.*

When the service was over, they were ushered back into the community center.

"So how does this compare to your church?" Josh asked.

"Some things are similar ... we sing a couple of familiar hymns, and the pastor talks about the person's life. Have you ever been to a Lutheran church in the Midwest?"

"Never been invited," he said, smiling.

"We don't sway to the music, but we do the handshake of peace."

He raised his eyebrows.

"It's where you shake hands and say 'Peace be with you.' It's a small gesture." She turned toward him and softly shook his hand. "Very simple; you don't want too much emotion." She chuckled quietly. "How about you?"

"In Jewish funerals we have a blessing, you kick the dirt in, and you go eat," he said.

She smiled at his irreverence and suddenly thought about how *Twilight Zone* this all was. Just a couple of days ago, Dr. Norris had evaluated Charlie. Then she asked him not to order the Depakote, and now they were saying goodbye. She leaned in and whispered, "I could always count on Dr. Norris when I had a difficult case. What if he was murdered because someone didn't like the results of his evaluation?"

"What?" Josh searched her face, puzzled.

"His evaluation of Charlie Blackwell?"

Now he looked at her like she was insane. "I can't imagine someone doing that." He raised his hands, as if surrendering. "Hey, I'm a nice Jewish boy."

"Just like you can't imagine anyone using fentanyl as a weapon, right? I know it sounds crazy, but what if someone didn't want him to testify at Charlie's hearing?"

"Well, in case your conspiracy theory is right, Dr. Norris's autopsy was done yesterday. The pathologist extracted a bullet for ballistics." Josh's phone buzzed. "Look, Elle. I gotta go, but let's grab dinner one night?"

"Sure." She swallowed hard. *What's happening here?*

"Want me to walk you to your car?"

"Thanks, but I'm gonna stay."

"Peace be with you, Miss Larson," he said as he shook her hand, then pulled her into his arms for a brief second before walking to the parking lot.

The table against the wall was now overflowing with flowers, as if it had grown into one giant arrangement. Other flowers were stacked against the wall, a heartfelt hug in all of this sorrow. She could still feel Josh's arms around her and wanted to come back to this church again.

Elle looked around. A thin White man was standing back from the crowd, staring at her. He looked about thirty and was dressed like a rapper in his camouflage T-shirt and high-top sneakers that resembled Rorschach inkblots. For a moment, she felt an intrusion on her personal thoughts about Josh that she was still trying to savor.

The man slowly shook his head at her and rushed outside.

She stepped back, her sixth sense warning her to stay away from him. Was this the guy who stood in her doorway, staring at her and Mac? She watched him rush outside.

A tap on her shoulder made Elle jump. Jane Hale was standing behind her. "Jeez … you scared me, Jane."

Jane nodded, her hairline damp and her face perspiring. "Can we talk outside?" She looked over Elle's shoulder, not making eye contact.

"Sure." Elle followed her to her car.

"I went to see Mr. Charlie at the hospital," Jane said, opening the driver's door. "He thinks you can help him."

"He told you that?" she asked. Jane hadn't trusted her, but at least Jane trusted Charlie.

Jane scanned the parking lot and pulled a small paper bag out from under the driver's seat and placed it in Elle's hands. "I want to help Mr. Charlie too."

Elle lifted the leather-covered book out of the bag and started to leaf through the pages.

"Put that back," Jane said, looking around. "It's Mary Beth's diary."

Elle searched Jane's face and returned the diary to the bag. *I could hug you.* "How long have you had this?"

Jane shook her head. "About a week."

"Does anyone know you have this?"

"No ... somethin' made her afraid," Jane said and lowered her eyes. "She asked me to hold it for her."

"Is there anything else I should know?"

"Mary Beth shared a bit about her first day, when she took Charlie to his wedding. You'll want to read it. Oh, and Miss Elle—" Jane stopped, chewing her lip. "This ain't comin' from me, but word is gettin' around that you put those fentanyl patches on Mr. Charlie."

"No way!"

Jane moved into her driver's seat. "Our logbooks are missing, and they say you're responsible."

"No freakin' way! Who's talking to you?"

Jane didn't answer but started up her car.

Elle knew a code of silence existed among the caregivers. They knew things; they talked and also helped each other find work. "Why would I still be searching for the logbooks if I had already found them?"

Jane looked straight ahead. "Geena Louise is filling in at Hospice. Compassionate Care and Prayer was fired over missing fentanyl patches, and Geena Louise is not filling in there anymore. That's all I can say. I can't lose my job."

Elle lowered her head and closed her eyes for a second. "Thanks, Jane." She put the paper bag in her purse and limped as fast as she could back to her car. Her brain was tired. She had struggled to rule out suspects, without success. Could Mary Beth's diary shed some light on who tried to murder Charlie and who might be behind her own death?

When Elle knocked on Charlie's door, he was slouched in an armchair next to his hospital bed, clean-shaven, wearing a light cardigan sweater and sturdy walking shoes.

"Hi, Charlie. I'm early."

"Come in, doll."

"Sumpter's coming at five." She walked in and closed the door. "I raced over so I could talk to you first." She found the soap and washed her hands at his sink.

Charlie rose from his chair with a wobble. At six feet, his bent frame still towered over hers.

"You look crazy strong," she said and laughed.

He beamed and gave her a handshake. "I'm not dizzy … and stronger every day." He patted his belly. "Not your typical hospital food."

He offered her a chair next to his and stood patiently until she sat down.

"Such a Southern gentleman." She moved her chair so they faced each other.

He gave her a questioning look. "I'm always glad to see you, but …"

"I have Mary Beth's diary," she said, taking the book out of her purse.

"Mary Beth … the young nursing student who died?"

"That's right."

"That's private, isn't it?"

"It is, but it was given to me confidentially by a friend of yours. I think Mary Beth would have wanted you to hear this." She opened the diary. It was fairly new with mostly blank pages. Mary Beth had printed in short, abbreviated strokes using a black pen. The first few pages were mainly about friends at the university in her program. "There's one entry I want to talk to you about. The day of your wedding."

"I seem to remember. Mary Beth was at the wedding."

"I was hoping it would help you remember more," Elle said and flipped to the page. "I'd like to read some of what she wrote and hear your side of the story."

"Fire away," he said, staring at her.

"Her entry was October 6, 1996—this was about a month ago."

"Can you read it with a Southern voice?" He smiled and shifted in his chair.

Elle nodded and continued.

> Strange day. I helped a client to his wedding, and he didn't even know what day of the week it was. Drugs and marriage—not a good mix, but I followed the orders and gave them. Sweet Jesus, it just wasn't right. He struggled to stay awake the whole time.

Charlie looked at her attentively. "I remembered the dimly lit courtroom. I was slumped over in a wheelchair."

Elle nodded. "Go on, Charlie."

"I remember facing the magistrate," he said. "When the man opened his mouth, his upper denture fell. My vision was cloudy, but I saw him use his thumb to push his teeth back up."

"Who was this guy?" Elle asked.

"Beats me. If I wasn't feeling so lousy, it would have been funny."

She hesitated. "Do you want me to go on?"

He nodded. "You get a C minus for the accent. I can tell you're one of those Nordic Midwesterners."

"Guess I can't help myself," Elle said with a smile. He was funnier and sharper, more engaged with every visit.

Charlie waved her off. "Keep going."

She started the rest of the entry.

> The room was impersonal. Creepy ... too close for comfort. I was scared. This was my first day on the job, and I was witnessing the wedding of my new client! The bride wasn't there when we arrived, so I left the courtroom to leave her a message that we were waiting, that we couldn't start without her.

Charlie leaned back and closed his eyes. "I was dizzy … confused. In my head, I couldn't figure out what was going on."

Elle noticed him start to hyperventilate. "Here, look at me, Charlie. Breathe … in … out. Another breath … you know."

"Here, let me see that!" His hands were shaking when he grabbed the diary, and he squinted at the words.

She picked up his thick glasses from the bedside table.

Charlie shook his head and handed the diary back to her. "I was looking forward to getting remarried to Amy and heading home where a nice lunch was waiting. Later, I would take an afternoon nap while she read one of her Elizabeth George novels. She liked this English detective."

"Inspector Thomas Lynley?" Elle asked, placing his glasses back.

"That's right." He glanced at her and gave her arm a pat. "Lynley. I don't read much. Not since my vision's gone bad. I remember waiting. Waiting and feeling dizzy."

He cleared his throat. "I was having dreams about the war … a day hasn't gone by that I don't think of that damn war." He pulled the back of his neck. "I couldn't see over my shoulder. Then she moved next to me, and I could see her silhouette. Floor-length dress, long sleeves, a veil that covered her face. Nice and simple. I recognized Amy's Chanel perfume." His eyes closed. "I remember the magistrate pronouncing us man and wife. And then he said, 'You may kiss the bride.'" Charlie paused and shifted in his chair again. "She slowly lifted the veil with her hands." He blinked. "I braced myself. An attractive face, but a face I wasn't expecting. She pressed her lips against mine, and I remember feeling a squeezing pain in my chest, like I had fallen on a grenade."

Elle shivered, like she was a ghost in the room. Not until now did she understand the confusion about the wedding. Charlie never guessed it was Susan. Unbelievable. He thought he had married Amy. She leaned in, her legs shaking. "You remembered after all." She wanted to hug him and tell him he'd be okay. That they would be okay. What now? She couldn't wait to tell Sumpter.

Sumpter stood in the doorway of the stark-white hospital room and heard Elle's voice. She was telling a story to Charlie, as if talking to a long-lost friend over a cup of coffee. The noise from the intercom and conversation from the hallway could be heard in the background, even after he closed the door.

"I'm so glad to meet you, Charlie," he said as Elle introduced them. "I've heard so much about you over the years." He shook Charlie's hand. "I wanted to see you earlier, but this nice lady was standing guard until you were ready."

Charlie smiled and motioned Sumpter to take the empty chair. "Do you want some tea or coffee?"

Sumpter declined and pushed a chair next to Charlie's and sat down. He was nauseated from the super-clean smell that covered all of the foul smells of sickness and death that happened here. He hated hospitals. He remembered his own stay after his heart attack. Unless he was staying at a sandy beach somewhere, he was happy sleeping at home.

"How are you doing, Charlie?" Sumpter asked.

"My blood pressure's up; doctor's increased my medication. They shot me full of B12; come to find out, I'm not crazy, just anemic."

Sumpter wasted no time with chitchat. "We need to discuss a couple of legal issues." He pulled a document from his folder.

"I'll let the two of you talk privately," Elle said as she stood up.

"No, I want you to stay," Charlie said.

"He's right, Elle," Sumpter said. "We have a hearing on Monday. It's clear Charlie trusts you. Plus, you have a big role to play."

Elle sat back down.

"Recognize this?" Sumpter showed Charlie the signed marriage license.

Elle reached for Charlie's thick glasses and his magnifying glass on the bedside table, then turned on the illuminated magnifier while Charlie adjusted his glasses. Charlie put the magnifier close to his right eye to bring the document into focus.

"Is that your signature?" Sumpter asked, pointing to it.

"It's my name, but I don't remember signing a marriage license," Charlie said, then handed the document to Elle. "I can't see the fine print."

"That's okay," Sumpter said, holding up his hand and taking the document. "Think hard, Charlie. The question is whether you signed this document or someone else faked your signature."

Charlie looked hard at the signature, turning his head from side to side and turned off the magnifier. "I wouldn't have signed something I couldn't read."

"You're sure?" Sumpter pressed.

"For God's sake, I'm a businessman."

"Tell him what you remember about the wedding," Elle said.

Charlie looked at Elle and shook his head. "I was such a fool. You might wonder how I could make a mistake like that. But my aide told me I was meeting Amy. I thought Amy realized the divorce was a mistake."

"Which aide was that?" Sumpter asked.

"The young one. She was as surprised as I was."

"Did you ever talk to Amy about this?" Elle wondered.

Charlie shook his head.

"Talked to your kids about it?" Sumpter asked.

Again, Charlie shook his head. "I was too embarrassed." He hesitated. "I've been in a bad place since Amy left, and then the divorce ..."

"I met Geena Louise yesterday," Elle said in a bid to move the conversation along.

Sumpter watched Charlie scratch his head.

"You went to see Amy?"

"She did so at my request," Sumpter said.

"How is Geena Louise?" Charlie asked. "You know, she doesn't work with me anymore."

"She was on her way out to buy groceries, so I didn't get to talk to her much," Elle said. "Did Geena Louise tell you that Amy wanted to remarry you?"

"I don't remember, but she did tell me that Amy never wanted the divorce," he said with a sad glance.

Sumpter was encouraged by their meeting. Charlie looked every bit his eighty years with his thick glasses and magnifier, his difficulty with hearing and memory, but he followed their questions with answers that made sense. Even though Charlie needed his magnifier to read, Sumpter was convinced that Charlie understood the issues at hand. The marriage license troubled Sumpter; Charlie not acting of his own free will troubled him, but he knew Charlie had the stamina to sit through the hearing.

Sumpter pulled Elle into the hallway. He wanted to tell her that he never wanted to spend his last days in a hospital. He could explain that later. Now he had to get the hell out of here, before the walls started closing in. "Keep a close eye on him, Elle. Other than Las Vegas, how many people do you know who wake up the next day married to someone they never planned to marry?"

# Chapter 16
*Friday*

An urgent knock on his door startled Charlie. He was sitting in a chair, having a nice talk with Melinda in his hospital room when Robbie's voice called out from the hallway. "Can you get that?" he asked his daughter.

Melinda opened the door.

"Well, I'm glad my new hearing aids are working," Charlie said as Peggy stood in the doorway and waved at him. When he looked straight ahead, her face was swimming. Yet as he scanned the room, her yellow coat looked just fine.

An angry Robbie drove his electric wheelchair into the room. "Melinda."

Melinda stepped back from the door as Peggy went back into the hallway, leaving her alone with Robbie and their father.

"Where were you?" Robbie glared at Melinda. "We had an eight a.m. appointment with Daddy's attorney."

Melinda's silence filled the room. Finally, she spoke in a bitter tone. "Daddy has Alzheimer's. Have you read Dr. Woodham's medical letter supporting his guardianship?"

Charlie looked at his wall clock: 9:45 a.m. The room still smelled like his eggs and bacon. Things could sure turn on a dime. He tried to speak, but Robbie broke in.

"So you're gonna fight us?" Robbie asked.

"He needs Susan." Melinda eyed her brother suspiciously.

"You just don't give a shit, do you?" Robbie said.

"Robbie, don't be a pain in the ass."

Charlie stood slowly from his chair. His hips told him it was gonna rain.

"If I support you, we'll lose Susan," Melinda said.

"Go home, Melinda. Daddy and I don't need you."

"Hey, you two," Charlie said, putting his hand up. "Stop."

Melinda gave Robbie a sarcastic smile.

"Fuck you, Melinda. If you oppose us at this hearing, I'll make sure you live to regret it," Robbie said.

Charlie loosened his stiff legs and turned toward Robbie.

"And you, I'm sick of you feeling guilty about her childhood," Robbie said, turning to Charlie. "That was my childhood too."

"Listen to me," Charlie said, but it was too late.

"Peggy!" Robbie's wheelchair beeped on and off as he pitched it in reverse and headed toward the door in a rage. Charlie shook his head. Hopefully, Sumpter could get him out of this mess.

By the time Elle showed up at the hospital, the sky was gray. She had stopped by Hospice on her way, looking for Peggy Blackwell, and was told she no longer worked there. The new Hospice director had refused to tell her about any missing fentanyl or anything else.

Amanda, with her matte red lipstick and fake lashes, was sitting at her desk buried in charts when Elle walked into the nurse's station.

"Morning. How's Charlie?" Elle asked her.

"He's great, you know, for a Reagan Republican. Thank God he never supported Bush."

"Why is that?" Elle asked with a smile.

"Cause Bush raised our taxes and took us back to war."

"Does that mean he voted for Clinton?"

Amanda chuckled and raised her hands in question. "His family's here. Son and daughter. Together." She made an ugly face.

"Thanks for the warning."

Amanda turned serious. "A detective stopped by to talk to us. He asked if we knew anyone who might have had a grudge against Dr. Norris."

Elle hesitated. She didn't want to scare Amanda, not after she had worked with Dr. Norris for all those years. She shrugged, reached across Amanda's desk, gave her a quick hug, then left for Charlie's room.

What leads were the police following? She didn't know. What she did know was that she and Sumpter had their own investigation going on. And that included tracking down the missing box of fentanyl.

Elle spotted Peggy standing outside of Charlie's hospital room, ear to the door. She couldn't believe her good luck as she walked down the long hallway toward her. "Hey, Peggy, gettin' ready for the storm?" Elle gave her a friendly smile.

Peggy looked up. Her curly hair was pulled back in a ponytail, a yellow rain jacket draped over her right arm. Her wide brown eyes were watering.

"Melinda's her know-it-all self," she said, shaking her head. "I'm glad she came to see her daddy, but she drives Robbie crazy. They're blowin' up a storm in Charlie's room. I wouldn't go in there if I were you."

Elle wondered if Peggy had been crying. "I just wanted to talk to you and Robbie before the hearing on Monday." She cleared her throat. "Maybe I can help," she said, surprised at the pleading in her own voice.

Peggy shook her head again. "I've been a member of this family for almost thirty years. You get used to it."

Elle respected Peggy's position. Daughters-in-law were often more objective. Especially when sons and daughters were overwhelmed and thought they couldn't help anymore. She leaned forward and started to speak, but Peggy interjected.

"Robbie's only willing to talk to his daddy's attorney."

"And I'm working with Sumpter—"

"You don't understand," Peggy said, rolling her wide eyes. "He's scared. We all are."

"Why would Robbie—?"

"He recommended Mary Beth to Susan when they were doing the caregiver interviews, and now she's dead. He's afraid of being a suspect."

"Peggy, do you know if Hospice has reported a box of fentanyl patches missing?"

Peggy stared at Elle for a long time. "They had a dying patient with bone cancer. The patient was in a lot of pain. What I know is that Geena Louise was doing staffing relief through Compassionate Care and Prayer. She had only been assigned to the patient for two days. The patient died the last evening she worked, and that's when a box of fentanyl went missing."

Elle stopped herself from grabbing Peggy's arm. "So what do you think happened?"

Peggy stiffened. "You'll need to ask Geena Louise."

She gave Peggy a puzzled look. "I just wondered—"

"What does this have to do with you?" Peggy's voice turned cold.

"I mean, it could ... maybe it was the source of Charlie's patches." Elle regretted her response, even though it was true. She heard Robbie's voice calling out behind the door.

"Peggy!"

Peggy's hand opened the door. An electric wheelchair accelerated out of Charlie's room, the wheels squeaking on the floor as Robbie turned sharply into the hallway, the motor whining at full speed.

"Hey, Robbie. Wait!" Elle said. He narrowly missed her foot as she dodged him and bumped into the wall.

"I can't talk to you," Robbie said.

"It's our last chance." Elle gave him a panicked glance before he went whizzing by.

"I've gotta get out of here, Peggy."

*Holy cow.* How did Robbie expect her to support him in court?

Peggy slipped into her raincoat without looking back and chased the wheelchair down the hall. Elle thought about other family members who had appreciated her help. They mostly told her more than she needed to know. *Look for the evidence,* Sumpter told her. Geena Louise had access to fentanyl patches. Geena Louise, the one caregiver she hadn't yet interviewed. Could she have stopped by Charlie's the morning of his attempted murder? Well, Elle definitely needed to move her up on the suspect list.

Charlie shuffled in short steps, closing the door quietly. His eyes turned to his daughter.

"And how does this leave me?" Melinda asked.

"My head's clearer than it's been in months," Charlie said, sitting back slowly into his chair.

"You don't understand about your disease, Daddy, and I won't do anything to push Susan away."

He thought of the upcoming hearing. "I don't need no damn guardian, Melinda. Could y'all just let me go home?"

"Okay, Daddy," Melinda said. "You just do that. It's nuts for me to stick around."

She picked up her shoulder bag and started for the door.

"Melinda. Twenty years ago, you walked away—"

"Because y'all made me crazy."

"Please stay ... stay through the hearing."

"I'll think about it. Right now, I need a drink. To deal with this family, I need several," Melinda said and stormed out.

Charlie fumbled his way back to his hospital bed that was no bigger than a single. He climbed in and leaned against the pillows, like the army pillows issued during the war. Damn uncomfortable. People were messin' with him, and he didn't know who to trust. He stretched for the phone with one hand and watched as his stubborn fingers punched in a number. God, he wanted to go home. His best memories were in that house, and he wanted to hold on to them. He tried the number again and heard a ring, then a familiar voice.

"You know you're old when you dial a number from the hospital and it makes you tired," he said and closed his eyes.

"Mr. Charlie, how good to hear your voice."

"Geena Louise, I'd like you to come and work with me." He listened to a muffled response and shook his head. "What? Speak up! After the hearing? Yes, I want you to meet me at the courthouse after the hearing." He sighed. Just listening to her voice put him in better spirits. "I think I need protection. I'll pay you extra."

There was a knock on his door.

"Charlie?"

He turned his head to see better and recognized Susan, wearing more new clothes: a lavender dress, matching heels, and a long black trench coat. Her image was a little wavy, but he could still see the colors.

"Hi, Charlie! There's a cold front comin' and severe thunderstorms. This is a good time to go home."

Charlie walked over to the window and smiled at the idea of being home in a storm. His battalion had crossed the Rhine in a storm under severe enemy fire. It had been a winter of intolerable cold. Snow blanketed the roads, and the wind ripped through the valley. His feet were wet, and he was bone-tired from not sleeping. He remembered how cold he was, how hungry. But mostly he remembered how his buddies died in front of him, fighting so close that their bodies and the bodies of German soldiers were in the same foxholes. His heart pounded in his throat and stayed there.

Jolted back, he looked around and saw Susan. He looked at the wall clock. It was 3 p.m. He had himself a get-out-of-jail card. "Okay, what do we do now?"

Susan explained that she and Melinda had quietly arranged for his discharge while Melinda was still at the hospital this morning. It wasn't that he wanted to stay; he was just surprised that they convinced his doctor to let him go home so soon.

"I can't believe I'm on my feet. That's right. I'm happy to be walkin' out of here." He stood as tall as he could when Susan introduced him to his discharge planner, Ginny, and he shook her hand. Ginny went over a handout that listed instructions for Charlie at home: his blood pressure pills and an iron supplement for his anemia; a follow-up appointment with Dr. Woodham next Tuesday. It took less than an hour.

He watched Susan as Ginny explained things to him. Susan loved being in the center of things. He could tell that the social worker made Susan feel important, in control. Of course, he would let his attorney know he was home when he got there. He had to look out for himself. He had to stay focused on his plan.

Charlie sat at his kitchen table and watched as Susan scrambled eggs and fried bacon at the stove. She was still petite with hair that shone like a copper penny. He looked around his kitchen, relieved to be out of the hospital. "It's hard to believe I'm here, like *The Twilight Zone*."

"I dreamed about the night I stopped by your farmhouse and invited myself into your kitchen, Charlie—almost forty years ago. I was still a wild twenty-four-year-old. When I woke up this morning, I wiggled my toes and pinched myself to make sure this wasn't a dream," Susan said and looked down at her diamond ring.

"You were beautiful, Susan, but—"

"And you were tan and fit from a life of farming … a handsome man," she said.

He closed his eyes and could still see her in that old house. Sexual—the way she smiled, the way she moved. And her advances? First her hand, then his hand. Her mouth, then his mouth, as if they were in a chess game. And later in Charlie's bed, lying naked, trying to catch their breath. She had taken him by surprise, as if he were suddenly waking up from a long winter's sleep. "I was an unhappy man … and we drank too much."

"But I wanted you. Not just for that night, but every night after. You were like the finest thoroughbred. I knew if I placed my bet on you, I'd find myself in the winner's circle."

"We need to talk about this."

She gave him a soft smile. "Breakfast is the only meal I cook anymore." She sizzled the bacon till crispy, but not burned, just the way he liked it.

"I made a coffee cake especially for you," she said as she brought out their breakfast plates. "I'm sure you'll sleep better in your own bed."

"Thanks, Susan." Mostly, he felt sorry for her—caring for him. Her wanting to help Robbie and Melinda. Holding on to one night so many years ago. Occasionally, though, he wondered if she could be a gold digger. After, he felt guilty. He had to admit, he worried about his money. He didn't want anyone stealing it, and that included his family.

Susan ran a sharp knife around the edges of the coffee cake and loosened it from the bottom of the pan.

He breathed in the sweet sugar and cinnamon. He knew Susan wanted them to work as a team. She and Melinda were friends, even confidantes. They talked on the phone, mainly about him.

"I never felt close to my own family," Susan said, stacking the pieces of cake on a floral plate.

Charlie took a deep breath and craved a cigarette, even though he didn't smoke anymore. He knew Susan wanted to get this damaged family reconnected. His whole life had been a crisis, starting with the war and his first wife's suicide. Last he knew, Melinda was going through the Betty Ford Center out in California. He hadn't seen her in twenty years until now. But why in God's name did she and Susan petition for guardianship?

The bedroom was warm, the way Charlie liked it. The shutters were closed. Susan helped him into his bed, fluffed up his pillow, and pulled his blankets around him. She brought him a glass of ice water and placed it on his bedside table.

"You know, I toyed with the idea of becoming a nurse years ago, even had some training," she said once he was settled. "It's too bad I never did."

He offered her a tired smile. "I didn't sleep again last night."

"Charlie, once I've moved in—"

"You can't live here, Susan." He shifted uneasily in his bed.

"I've tried to be here for you in every way ..."

"I—I'm grateful, but I never wanted this."

189

She pulled out her prescription bottle and took out two pills. "Here, take these. Two Valium—"

Charlie raised his hand in protest. "Jesus, no more pills."

She stood there, staring down at him. "Charlie, I have stayed true to my marriage vows: in sickness and in health, till death do us part. For the past month, I've tried to reason with you. Lord give me strength. And now Robbie's causing problems. He wants to take control over you. Control for himself so he can make all the decisions. Is that what you want?"

"Susan, somehow in my mind, I didn't realize we were getting married. I fucked up. If you need money, I'll be happy to—"

"Charlie, you could have died. I'm afraid of what's going to happen to you."

"I'll be fine—"

"You're not fine. You're sick. We can talk about this later." She dropped the pills back in the bottle.

"I just need some sleep," he said. He wanted to say more, but it was too late for that.

After Susan left his bedroom, Charlie felt such longing. He stared out the window at his planned backyard, now overgrown with weeds. The grass had grown several inches from what he could see, and the sky had shifted to a dark gray, filled with thunderclouds. The truth was, he missed Amy. He missed his old life.

Sliding his legs out of bed and planting both feet firmly on the floor, he pulled open the top drawer of his bedside table. He looked at a faded picture of a young woman with chestnut brown hair and took out a small bottle of scotch and set it on the table. After drinking the glass of water, he replaced it with two fingers of scotch, placed it on the table, and, at a snail's pace, dragged his body back into bed.

How many times had he and Amy shared cocktails before dinner, listening to their favorite music? How many nights had they crawled into bed together, tired and grateful at the end of the day? What kind of husband was he if he couldn't keep her close in his heart? Despite the heartbreak, his best memories were here in this house; here, where he remembered her best.

He finished his scotch and looked out the window again. He would make plans, after the rain, to find a new gardener, but for now he just needed sleep. He placed his pillow under his neck and relaxed his back as he drifted off. He knew his time was running out. Some of his memories were disappearing too, but he never forgot her. He smiled, remembering how they met that spring of 1945.

It was dawn. Standing alone at his post, he closed his eyes, fighting off sleep. Then he heard footsteps. Startled, he raised his gun as she walked up and held out a cup of steaming hot coffee. He studied her young face, the fear in her dark eyes, and instinctively lowered his gun. God, she was lovely.

He fixed his eyes on her chestnut brown hair, in curls falling to her shoulders. She wore a short pleated skirt and shoes with thick wooden soles. Then out of nowhere, like a wave of nausea, he was homesick—homesick and tired—suddenly remembering he was just a farm kid from North Carolina. He swallowed the strong coffee.

"A little whiskey would be good in this."

She smiled.

"I'm sorry, but the warmth of French gratitude will have to do for now."

"Do you live around here?"

She described how she was raised in France. How she came to the small village of Zhuri to visit her aunt and uncle who owned a small bakery by the river. It was 1938, and then the war started.

For four days, they met over coffee during that cold spring. It was so damp and miserable—she shivered—on their last day together.

"Are you cold?" he asked her.

She nodded. "Yes."

Standing behind her, shielding her from the wind, he placed his hands gently in her coat pockets and kissed her hair.

And then his orders came, a change in direction. He had to move on. She promised to find him. *We're just so young.*

How many times in his life had she appeared to him like that?

The sixteenth floor was quiet when Elle arrived at the office at 3 p.m. Grady greeted her in a Pearl Jam T-shirt, holding fifteen messages. She thanked him and reviewed the messages one by one. Mostly clients and family members. Nothing was urgent except for one. Mr. Johnson's brother was canceling her services since she hadn't returned his call from this morning and because she hadn't been available all day.

"Available 24/7, on the spot, that's what he wants," Grady said.

She nodded like she agreed. "Can you hold any new calls until after four?" It wasn't that she didn't want to talk to anyone, and she needed every single client for her business to survive; she just had a deadline of 4 p.m. to get the Blackwell report faxed over to Sumpter, and she couldn't solve multiple problems at once.

"Fatigue is real," Grady said and walked out, giving her a sideways glance as he closed the door behind him.

He was right. Her brain was exhausted. She sat down at her computer and began the final editing of her report. She followed with her own evaluation, which was already written, and then her observations. Finally, she attached the functional assessment instruments.

Her mind wandered. The problem was that Charlie had some tricky cognitive issues, a wife who believed he was incompetent, and a daughter and daughter-in-law who believed his wife. She shook her head. She had to stick to Charlie's functioning, what she observed, the objective data. That's what she was being asked to explain.

She flashed back to some studies she read in graduate school, studies that found nurses' rating of physical function the gold standard. Nurses were more accurate than older adults, their family members, and physicians—who were the least accurate.

She typed as fast as she could until 4 p.m., reviewed the report once more, and printed a copy for Sumpter. She faxed over his copy and called Julie to make sure the fax had gone through.

"I'm looking at a seven-page report with seventeen pages of your assessment. Now Elle, just relax this weekend," Julie said.

"Thanks, Julie," she said, sinking back in her chair. "I'll be spending the weekend preparing my testimony." That meant returning the fifteen phone calls now. Yet all she wanted was to sleep.

Sumpter walked into Doug Kilpatrick's sprawling law office in the tall Uptown tower around 5:30 p.m. He had let Kilpatrick know he'd be dropping off Elle's written report. What he really wanted was to punch the young son of a bitch in the face for getting a physician's order to discharge Charlie without talking to him first. How many times had Doug said, in that deep voice of his, that he would work harder to communicate?

The waiting room was empty except for an attractive woman wearing a bright pink satin suit and gold jewelry—elegant but overdressed for a visit with her lawyer. She sat, looking out the upper floor window at the busy city below. When she turned to look at him, he recognized her. He couldn't help but notice the strain on Susan's attractive face.

"Susan Blackwell. We've met before."

He walked over and shook her hand. "It's a great view, isn't it? To look down on everybody from way up here. Too bad about the fog and rain."

"Mr. Sumpter, do you have an appointment too?" Susan asked, straightening a pile of papers she was balancing on her lap.

"No, I'm here to drop off a document, that's all." He sat down next to her. While they waited, he noticed the Blackwell marriage license on top of her stack of papers. He waited, hoping she'd say something.

"Mr. Kilpatrick asked that I bring in our license and Charlie's previous divorce papers. I also have the bank statements that show how Amy was exploiting Charlie when they were married."

Sumpter merely nodded. She was not the one he needed to push.

"Doug Kilpatrick took our case as a challenge," she said. "He has much bigger cases to try."

"Did he tell you that?" Sumpter asked. He knew better. While bad marriages were making Doug rich, it was the high-profile clients like the wife of Charlie Blackwell who he was really after. And winning, of course. It was all about winning.

"I like being around powerful men," Susan said coyly.

Sumpter didn't respond. Doug had given her the utmost attention and respect, no doubt. He also suspected that the power Susan had over men was like a passion potion.

"Sumpter, come on in!" Doug shouted in his deep voice. He wore his trademark three-piece suit and winked at Susan. "I'll be with you in a minute."

Sumpter followed Doug into his office and closed the door. He stood in front of his desk and set his briefcase on the desktop. "You couldn't wait till Monday?"

"Charlie wanted to go home. Susan wanted him home," Doug said and sat down at his desk.

"You know you're risking his life." Sumpter handed him a copy of Elle's written report. "I'm sending Elle Larson out there right now to set up his meds and make sure he's safe."

"Don't be surprised if Judge Townsend throws Miss Larson's report out of the hearing. I've asked that she not be allowed to testify as an expert," he said, glancing at the report, his deep voice getting higher.

"Save it for Monday, Doug," Sumpter said, although he was worried. He knew that Townsend let favoritism influence his rulings, and leaning on judges like Townsend had been critical to Doug's success. Like his wife had told him, Sumpter had to play his cards right.

Doug propped his feet on top of his desk. "Townsend told me how proud he is of my rising career." He tipped his chair back. "So, game on."

"By the way, Susan's out there studying a signed marriage contract." Sumpter stared across the desk. He hated arrogance. He hated lawyers who relished hurting people for no good reason. "To let you know, there's an expert graphologist looking at Charlie's signature right now." He grabbed his briefcase. "Susan's not going to make you famous, Doug."

# Chapter 17

Charlie had been napping soundly when he woke to a grip around both arms. His body automatically resisted as a masked blur stared down at him. Two hooded figures hovered over his bedside, one pulling his arms together, the other binding his wrists with wide surgical tape.

"What the hell's goin' on here?" he yelled, twisting frantically in the dim light. Before he could utter another word, his mouth was taped shut. He struggled against the intruders who yanked him out of bed and twisted him into his wheelchair. His shoulders burned in pain.

Oversized sweatshirts, baggy sweatpants, and old sneakers. He couldn't place them, yet the shorter one moved more gracefully, swinging her hips and taking shorter steps. The taller one picked up the seatbelt and buckled him into his wheelchair. Then came the push and pull of the chair, out of the bedroom door, and a handoff to the backyard patio. Wearing boxer shorts and a sleeveless T-shirt, Charlie was cold as he hit the damp night air. Cold air on his chest and bare feet chilled him to the bone.

"You'd better go, or you'll be recognized," an unfamiliar male voice shouted close to Charlie. "Just drive the car around, and I'll meet you on the street."

The woman left through his backyard gate.

"Everything's gonna work out fine," the man whispered. "We're gonna get you out of here."

Charlie smelled cigarettes and stale alcohol. Thunder rumbled as the man grabbed his wheelchair from behind and shoved hard, pushing him toward the gate. He glanced around and tried to scream, to strike back, but all he heard was the moan of his voice muffled by tape. He raised his bound hands and struck back against soft flesh.

"Shit," the man yelled and yanked the chair around, then pulled it to a stop almost turning over the chair. "I musta been goddamn crazy ..."

He changed course and ran in the direction of the pool. "Hey, ol' man, you'll thank me for this," he said, breathing hard. "I'm savin' you from endin' up in a nursin' home."

Charlie heard the slap of running shoes against his deck, as the intruder pushed him to the deep side of the pool. He was reliving his worst nightmare. The tears started when he saw the water. Water had always been part of his life, and his pool—he'd swum laps in it for so many years. He closed his eyes and took a deep breath as he hit the water. He had no fear of water, until now.

Elle pulled on a pair of colorful wool socks, boots, and her waterproof rain jacket. There was only one way to know how Charlie Blackwell was doing ... and that was for her to see for herself. "Big ol' three-story mansion, look for the swing," she told Mac as he jumped into the passenger seat. Driving slowly with her window open, she looked at her watch. It was shortly after 6 p.m. Fog hung low, moist, and heavy. Without warning, the sky cracked.

The wind picked up as she turned onto Queens Road West and tunneled through the canopy of trees. Oak leaves gusted across the road. The Blackwell swing flapped about, agitated by the gale. She rolled the window down, enjoying the breeze.

Lights sparkled in the neighbors' windows, but Charlie's house looked gloomy through the fog. Mac whined as they slowed to turn into Charlie's driveway.

"Hey, champ. Just a cold front coming our way."

A midnight-blue sedan screeched out of the front drive and turned left onto the street in front of her. She saw the blur of a gray hooded sweatshirt.

She took a deep breath and tightened her grip on the steering wheel, then sped her wagon quickly into the drive.

"Stay, Mac." His brown eyes pleaded with her.

She reached for her purse and briefcase, then closed the car door behind her. Mac jumped into the driver's seat.

"Stay, Mac," she said, louder.

He growled and she placed her hand in front of his face. "Stay."

She pulled a flashlight from her briefcase and lit the path to the side terrace. At least she'd been here before. Approaching the side door, she knocked and waited. A desk light brightened the entryway, reflecting off the hardwood floor.

She entered the house through the unlocked side door. Soft lights illuminated the backyard pool.

"Charlie?"

She tried the kitchen light switch, and nothing happened. An outside door slammed.

"Charlie, it's me, Elle Larson."

A shadow moved outside. "Who's there?" She opened the French doors and scanned the backyard. Her cell phone rang, and she answered it.

"Let's go to a movie tonight," David said.

Before she could respond, Elle looked up to see a masked man in a hooded sweatshirt roll Charlie and his wheelchair into the pool with a splash. She screamed and let go of her briefcase.

"David! Call 911! Get the police to my client's house, corner of Queens Road West and Wellesley."

Elle ran out the kitchen door and dropped her cell phone as Charlie hit the water. His mouth was taped, and then his head disappeared under the surface of dark water and fallen leaves. Her heart pounded like the hooves of a runaway horse. It would take her at least six or seven seconds to reach him at a dead run. She tore off her jacket, kicked off her boots. "Mac!" She knew he heard her voice.

*Please don't hurt my dog.* She ran like hell toward Charlie, and the masked man turned and began running across the yard. She braced for the plunge, then jumped in feet first, right above where she could barely see Charlie. The water stung, then turned chilly but was not icy cold. Slimy leaves covered in dirt enveloped her body like seaweed. She caught her breath and closed her eyes just before she went under. *Hang on, Charlie.*

Elle slowly exhaled and sank lower, balancing with her arms, her navy pants and shirt billowed out like an inflating parachute. Still, her heart pounded harder. Her foot scraped Charlie's wheelchair. Bending low she found both armrests with her hands and positioned her feet over their flat coverings, balancing in a squat position by holding on to his shirt. Her legs were strong from skating. She groped for the seatbelt, her cold fingers fumbling the buckle. Seconds passed slowly. She fought against inhaling. If only she could get her head above water.

Grabbing the heavy-duty nylon with her left hand, she exhaled more and snapped the buckle open with her right. Instantly the belt gave way. Gotcha. She reached under Charlie's arms, then pushed off with her legs and yanked him up, leaving the wheelchair in their wake. As they surfaced, she gasped for air; her lungs ready to explode. She heard Charlie inhaling quickly through his nose, grabbed him in a spray of murky water, and pulled him to the side of the pool. She let go of the ledge, treading water for a second, just long enough to pull the tape from his mouth, then grabbed the side of the pool again. Charlie's mouth opened wide as he took several deep breaths.

"Are you okay?" She struggled to catch her breath and heard sirens coming up the drive.

"Don't let go. My arms are taped." He held on to the edge of the pool with his hands.

"Help!" she screamed, still gasping as her lungs expanded.

Minutes later, two uniformed officers were running toward them.

"Good rescue, miss. The paramedics are here."

"Did you know I was on the high school swim team?" Charlie asked between deep breaths and groans, as they cut away the surgical tape from his wrists and transferred him by stretcher to the waiting ambulance.

Elle followed with her hand on his stretcher, her body vibrating with adrenaline. "So you're a good swimmer," she said quickly between coughs and wheezes.

"Not like the old days," he said. "I can still hold my breath a good while, but I'm stiff as a poker." Charlie reached for her hand. "I saw you coming. For the second time, I saw you come to my—" He choked.

Elle grabbed his hand and wheezed.

"I have so much to live for," he said as they loaded him into the back of the ambulance, his voice overcome with emotion.

Hearing a low growl, Elle turned her head and stared at her dog, who was standing over the distressed man sitting on the grass. Mac's mouth covered his right wrist, holding him with just enough pressure to keep him from getting up.

"I fell and broke my ankle. Now he's trying to kill me." The guy screamed for help, his mask and hood lying in the grass. His sleeve was torn, exposing a tattoo on his left forearm with the initials B.S. He tried to move, and another low growl kept him in place.

An older police officer handcuffed the man's left wrist, but still Mac did not let go. He guarded the guy with a fierceness she hadn't seen before.

The police officer picked up the man's wallet. "Billie Sutton?"

"Shit, man. My ankle is killing me." He shook his head and groaned in pain.

"Miss, can you tell your dog we'll take it from here," the police officer said, trying to contain a small smile.

"I'm telling you; I broke my ankle!" The man stared at Elle with contempt.

Elle shot daggers at him—so pissed, she couldn't see straight. Maybe he was afraid of dogs. He looked flat-out terrified of Mac. "My dog knows you aren't tough. You're just mean and cruel."

"Miss, your dog needs to let go."

Elle looked up at the officer. "This man just tried to drown Charlie Blackwell. Did you know Charlie was an officer under General Patton in World War II? He's a real hero."

She walked over, bent down, and stroked Mac's square head. Looking down, she immediately recognized the guy's Reebok shoes, only now they were muddy. "This guy was at Dr. Norris's memorial service."

The prisoner tried to move away, and Mac growled again. "Look, he's trying to kill me."

Elle stood up. This was not going to be easy. She had forgotten Mac's liver treats at home. "Either stay here and work with these nice officers or come home with me." Mac's eyes looked up at her, but his head didn't move as he held on to his prisoner.

Elle turned to the officer. "I'll make a run for my car and see if he follows. I'll wait in my car to talk to you." She started for the car, carrying her phone, socks, boots, briefcase, and purse, her wet clothes sticking to her. "C'mon, Mac—let's go home!"

She wasn't sure when he decided to let go, but by the time the station wagon was running, he was at her door. Once inside the car, she buried her face in the curly hair of his neck and started to sob, gut-wrenching sobs, while Mac sat stoically in the passenger seat, as if guarding his post.

Sergeant Kate Harrigan opened the driver's door of Elle's Volvo and Elle stepped out. Kate stepped back when Mac leaned through the window to check her out. Elle put her arms around him to stop him from getting closer. "He's really friendly."

"You continue to surprise me. Any idea how the suspect got in?"

"The side door was unlocked when I got here. Charlie's been in the hospital all week. The plan was for him to stay until his hearing on Monday. And now if you'll excuse me—"

"Miss Larson, you can't leave until I've asked you a few more questions," Kate said.

"You don't understand, I have to be with my client. The ED physician will kill me if I don't show up!" Elle said, regretting her choice of words.

"You're a witness to this crime, and your memory of what's happened is more accurate now than it will be later."

Elle groaned. "Charlie can't come back here until his court hearing is over. We've got two people dead, and now there's been two attempts on Charlie's life."

"The suspect will be locked up—"

"Do you really think this guy's at the top of the food chain?"

"What do you think this is, *Law and Order*?"

Elle shivered in her wet clothes and the cold evening air. She raised the driver's side window to make sure Mac stayed and walked with Kate to the backyard as the officer handed out crime scene tape to her uniformed officers. Kate kept her eyes on Elle as if worried she might escape.

"Absolutely no one goes over to the pool without my permission," Kate said and directed the first-to-arrive officers to secure the area around the pool.

More than a dozen people were now gathering in Charlie's backyard.

"I thought you said this was a quiet neighborhood," Elle said.

Kate Harrigan barked out orders. "Touch nothing. Has anyone seen a weapon?" She gave Elle a blanket from one of the police vehicles parked in the driveway. "Here, put this on. I know you're strong willed and mad as a hornet, but you need to stay here."

Elle wrapped the blanket around herself and sat down on the wet grass after retrieving her phone. Her right knee throbbed. She needed to get out of her wet clothes. In all of the confusion, she had not talked to Sumpter. She opened her phone and called.

"Elle?"

She struggled to hold back the tears. This case was proving to be a disaster, like watching the cars pile up in a train wreck. She pulled the blanket tighter around her shoulders. "Sumpter, I … I just don't think I can do this anymore."

# Chapter 18
*Saturday*

At 8 a.m. Josh Geller made his way to the hospital cafeteria. Coffee, then home to shower and sleep. That was his plan. He could smell eggs and bacon from the griddle. The tables were filling with hospital staff. As he stood in the doorway and scanned the crowd, Susan Blackwell walked in on red stilettos, her black purse draped over a red silk dress.

"Hey, Dr. Josh," she said in her softest voice. "Nice to see you again."

"Hello," he said wearily. "I just finished my shift; coming in for some caffeine."

Susan pouted. "You doctors work so hard," she said, giving him a gentle pat on the arm.

They walked to a table and he pulled out a chair facing away from the crowd. He motioned for her to sit. "Coffee?"

"A glass of sweet tea, please."

He returned a few minutes later and took a seat next to her.

"You are such an attractive young doctor," she said and locked eyes with him.

He swallowed his coffee and studied her. "Thanks," he said. *She wants me on her side.* And for the sake of his patient, he wanted to know what was going on. In the back of his mind, he still wondered if Charlie's drug overdose made sense.

"What church do you go to?" Susan asked.

He hesitated. Religion was the last thing he wanted to talk about after working all night. "I'd rather not discuss that. I treat people of all religions," he said. "Mine is personal, and I don't let it affect the care I give."

"Well, I believe in putting things in the Lord's hands." She moved her chair closer and took a sip of tea. "And when the Lord is willin', he also helps those who help themselves. I'm so glad it was you workin' with Charlie last night." She reached for his hand.

"I'm glad I was able to help." He clasped her hand and patted it with his other hand, not sure where she was going with this but willing to play along. "So, tell me what it's like at home with Charlie?" he asked.

"Charlie's Alzheimer's makes it hard." She leaned in and whispered in his ear. "Especially when he gets aggressive toward me."

He could feel her squeeze his hand. She was coming on to him and was old enough to be his mother. He couldn't help but think about Elle.

"I'm afraid I can't care for him without medication," she said and gazed into his eyes. "He needs medication, and I do too."

For a second, Josh felt sympathy for her. There were tears in her eyes.

"If you could just give him some Depakote; give me some Valium or Xanax." She gave him her most suggestive smile.

"Who was giving Charlie his medication before he was hospitalized?" he asked.

"His caregivers made sure he took his medicine every day," she said.

"And before you were married?"

She explained how, as the scheduler for Compassionate Care and Prayer, she had set up Charlie's med box at the office for the past two years and dropped it by the house once a week. "The caregivers still give him his pills because I haven't moved in yet," she said.

He nodded. Now he was getting somewhere. "Susan, if you were in control of all of his meds, where do you keep his prescription bottles?"

"In my office. I hope you think I'm doing the right thing by Charlie." She held his hand while waiting for a response.

"You know, Charlie can't stay at home without your help." He tried to gently extricate his hand. "But last night he was nearly murdered."

"I can't talk about it … I'm so upset." She reluctantly let go of his hand.

Josh looked at his watch, gulped the last of his coffee, and stood up. He wanted to take a shower, but knew he needed to talk to Elle right away. "I'm meeting a friend, but I'll have a talk with Charlie's doctor about your request for medication." He needed Susan to believe that he valued her input. "We'll take good care of him over the weekend. Try to get some rest, Susan."

"Y'all take care … and thank you, Dr. Josh." Susan smiled. "I promise to pray for you."

He felt her eyes follow him as he walked away and returned the tray. *She's using me—served up with sweet tea and a prayer.* As much as he hated to admit, his first impression of Charlie had been wrong. Josh didn't look back as he headed straight for his car.

Elle woke from a sound sleep to Mac barking at the front door. She had taken him out for a walk at six in the morning, made coffee, and crawled back into bed before the coffee was ready. Her head ached, and dark images of being hauled out of Charlie's pool were swimming in and out of consciousness. Wrecked, she had cried herself back to sleep.

The doorbell rang and Mac growled fiercely as he jumped against the door. Throwing back the covers, Elle grabbed her terry robe and stumbled down the stairs.

"Coming." When she reached the hallway, she stared out her front door window. On the other side of the etched glass, a pair of puffy eyes surrounded by dark circles stared back at her.

"What time is it?" She unlocked the door and blinked in the bright sunlight. "It's okay, Mac." Her gaze fixed on a tired-looking Josh Geller in blue scrubs, holding a small deli bag that smelled like the pickling spices of St. Patrick's Day.

"How did you know where I live?" She rubbed her eyes and patted Mac's head until he calmed down.

"I called David." Josh crouched down. "Hi, boy." He patted Mac and looked at his watch. "It's nine o'clock."

"I was up late."

"Me too," he said dryly.

She smiled, knowing he had worked all night, and waved him in. She noticed the faint smell of his cologne and caught a glimpse of herself in the hall mirror. Semiconscious, a patch of thick hair sticking up, red-rimmed eyes, and decaffeinated—not bad, considering she and Charlie had almost drowned last night. She tucked the unruly hair behind her ears.

Josh strolled into her living room and stopped at the fireplace mantle to smile at the picture. "Who's this?"

"That's me. My graduation from graduate school. I was celebrating with my younger brother, Peter."

Josh placed the paper bag on her coffee table and settled into one end of her cozy couch. Mac followed and sniffed the bag.

"No, Mac," she said and turned to Josh. "He likes to finish food off the coffee table." She grabbed Mac's collar, "and only shares the couch with people he likes."

Josh ran his hands over Mac's coat of hair. "Rough night, huh?"

She nodded. "Is Charlie okay?"

"He swallowed a little water. I needed to make sure he didn't develop aspiration pneumonia. We kept him till a hospital bed opened up around four this morning."

"So he didn't get much sleep either?"

Mac thumped his tail.

"I ran into Susan this morning. I think she was trying to seduce me."

Elle looked at him with surprise. "Wait, let me get some coffee. I need to hear this. Milk, cream?"

"Just black."

She went to the kitchen and found two clean Gourmet Lutheran Coffee mugs. She poured cold coffee into the mugs and heated them in the microwave. *Why in the world is Josh Geller on my couch?* He had never been to her house before. She walked the mugs back to the coffee table.

"Sorry about the coffee. It's from early this morning. I took Mac out and never drank it." Slowly, she curled up on the other end of the couch and took a sip. "Still tastes good."

"Wait till Susan and the family find out that Charlie has twenty-four-hour security with no family or friends visiting until after Monday."

"That's brilliant," she said, folding her hands around her cup.

Between sips, Josh described his conversation with Susan. His brown eyes looked so gentle when he wasn't mad. And now he was sitting beside her on her sofa, trying to help her. Unbelievable!

"She has Charlie's prescription bottles in her office. She's been setting up his med boxes since long before the wedding," he said.

"She told you that?"

"Yep. She's behind the meds, and she's seeking more. She's gonna fight to keep that control."

"But wait," Elle said, holding up her hand for a moment. "Did she say she was actually replacing blood pressure pills in the med box with other drugs?"

He scratched his closely trimmed beard. "No, not actually."

Her mind raced. "Someone else could be replacing the drugs."

"I suppose so."

She had spent hours trying to figure this out. "Okay, let's say it is Susan. Why? You think it's the money?"

"Maybe as a means to an end."

"What then, being the wife of a wealthy man?" Elle asked.

"That and the attention she gets from doctors and nurses, her attorney."

Elle thought of Stevie Nicks's new release "Twisted." Crazy men and women, desperate for love. "Nice theory." She chuckled, throwing his words back at him.

He looked at her with a smirk. "Getting even?"

"Well, you're the one who doesn't reach conclusions without the facts." She smiled a little more and told him that Susan was at her attorney's office when Charlie was shoved into the pool. She closed her eyes for a moment, then opened them , trying not to relive last night all over again.

"I treated Billie Sutton in the emergency department last night."

"He was screaming that he broke his ankle."

Josh shook his head. "Just a mild ankle sprain. He left with two police escorts and his ankle wrapped up."

"Did you know that Mac caught him in Charlie's backyard?"

"Oh yeah. Did you know he's scared to death of dogs?"

She looked at Mac, who wagged his tail and kept his eyes glued on the bag resting on the coffee table. "And every time the guy moved, Mac growled."

"Mac, you're a good judge of character," Josh said, patting him on the head. "I'm happy to report there were no puncture wounds on his wrist."

"He knows not to bite people." Elle watched Mac's response to Josh, his tail curling up in a question mark and wagging back and forth like a metronome. His face said it all. He liked Josh.

Josh eyed her as he sipped his coffee. "Coffee's heavenly," he said, reading the mug's fine print. "So, how does this Billie Sutton guy fit into the picture?"

"I think I recognized him from the memorial service for Dr. Norris."

"That's great, a real suspect."

"Well, we know he pushed Charlie into the pool, but the police have no suspects or witnesses to Dr. Norris's murder." She tapped her fingers on her mug. She had put the rest of her life on hold for this case, and still couldn't get ahead of it. "I nearly quit this case last night."

"But why?" His dark eyes were expressive. "Charlie needs us."

"I was overwhelmed." She realized how much she wanted them to be friends, to be colleagues. Was he finally seeing them as working together? "I'm still trying to figure out who Susan trusts: Charlie's daughter, Melinda, for sure; I think Peggy too."

"But they're hardly insiders."

"The paid caregivers are insiders. His ex-wife was an insider, but she hasn't been in the house for the past year." Elle knew Josh focused on facts, and he didn't know about the caregivers. She went to the kitchen, pulled her caregiver summaries from her briefcase, and gave the list to him.

"The caregivers are all certified nursing assistants. Two worked with Charlie before he married Susan, two after." She moved closer to him as she sat back down. "And the weekday caregiver, Mary Beth, who Susan and Robbie hired, started the day of the wedding. I think she was murdered."

"How does this all add up?" he asked, scrutinizing her list.

"Once again, we're back to the meds. According to Florence Benson— who worked for Charlie every weekend for two years before the wedding— the med box was always filled. She never saw who filled it, but assumed it was Amy, Charlie's ex-wife. She also assumed that Charlie's pills were for his blood pressure."

"I thought you said Amy was out of the house for the past year."

"I did." Elle stood and paced around the coffee table, one hand wrapped around her coffee cup. "Florence also denied knowing about fentanyl. I haven't interviewed Geena Louise yet. She worked for Charlie during the week for the past two years. She's been too busy working to come to the office. I'm not scheduled to meet with her until after the hearing."

"Okay, then who is this Jane Hale?" He folded and put her list in his pocket.

"She's the current weekend caregiver, only worked with Charlie for the past month. She thought Mary Beth was filling the med box. So we have several stories here."

"You need to talk to this Geena Louise now, before the hearing," he said, his dark eyebrows arching into his forehead. "You need to find out who's telling the truth. And if Susan's been replacing his antihypertensives."

Elle wasn't convinced that the dots were connecting. "Even if Susan was in control of Charlie's meds, she wouldn't have access to fentanyl without a doctor's prescription." She kept pacing. "And why would Susan want to murder him? She's already his wife. What would she have to gain?"

"You must be working up an appetite." He smiled. "Why don't you sit down before you wear a hole in your carpet."

She stopped pacing but went on. "Geena Louise works with Amy during the week. I'm sure she knows who was filling the med box before the wedding."

Josh opened the bag. "Charlie could die. You can't quit this case now."

Elle took a step closer. He pulled a half of a corned beef sandwich out of the bag and handed it to her. "Eat a little something. You'll feel better."

Mac stared at him, then at her, sniffing the air between them.

Elle laughed.

"Not exactly Katz's delicatessen, but it's the best in Charlotte," Josh said.

"I've never heard of Katz's." Elle sat back down. He was right. *I can't just quit now.* Suddenly, she was starving.

"They have the quintessential corned beef sandwich." He told her about Katz's on Houston Street, the boundary to the old Jewish neighborhood in New York City. "You should go with me sometime. Deli food for dinner." He told her how as a young boy he went there with his family. "You ask, 'So how's the corned beef today?' and the butcher behind the counter carves off a piece and hands it to you."

Elle took a bite of the layered slabs. They were warm and spicy, overflowing the warm rye bread. She closed her eyes, tasting the salt and brine, the mustard seeds, peppercorns, and cloves. He'd given her something that felt like a piece of his soul. She had always loved New York City. Like Chicago—different ethnic neighborhoods and old-world atmosphere, reminding her of her own family roots and traditions. She opened her eyes and watched him yawn, then she blinked and took another bite.

There was a word in Norway, *kos,* that her mother had taught her that described the feeling of warmth and friendliness that happens when two people who like each other share simple pleasures. It might be sitting in front of a roaring fire with a good crime novel or sharing corned beef on her sofa with a sleep-deprived guy she was just getting to know: exciting, yet comfortable.

"I've gotta go and get some shut-eye. I'm working all weekend. Monday too," he said and leaned over to kiss her gently on the cheek. "You have a really nice dog."

Elle blushed and turned toward Mac. She wondered if there was something more.

"In my next life, I'm coming back as a chef," he said and yawned again.

"Goodnight, and thanks for taking such good care of Charlie," she said as she walked him out the door. It was funny how his gentle face, up close, made it hard to remember the negative thoughts she'd held over the past year.

Elle parked her car in the driveway off Laurel Avenue in Elizabeth, where Geena Louise lived. Elle had called several times before Amy's current caregiver agreed to sit down for a ten-minute interview.

The modest brick home, freshly painted beige, sat right behind Fenwick's, Elle's favorite go-to place for comfort food with David. She recognized Geena Louise when she opened the door. The same furrowed brows and small eyes. Only today she looked like a middle-aged, stressed-out soccer mom in her brown velour tracksuit.

"I need to use your bathroom," Elle said on a crazy whim.

"I was planning to speak with you on the porch ..."

"I'll be out in a flash." It was true. She did have a full bladder. It was also true that she was tired of bending over backward for people who beat around the bush and hid things from her.

"My son is staying with me, and he's asleep. I really don't want you in my house right now."

Elle limped past her. She had been nursing her knee with rest, ice, and elevation that afternoon but still found it painful to walk. "Please, I can't hold it ... which way?"

Geena Louise sighed. "First door to the right."

Elle entered a living room of unframed paintings clustered on all four walls, taking up every square inch of space. She took a deep breath. The dark blinds were closed, giving the place the look of an art museum, poorly arranged. The paintings reminded her of old-world art collected by people with means.

She found the bathroom, closed the door, and sat down on the toilet. What was she looking for? Geena Louise had hung incredibly old paintings, like original artwork, above the empty towel hooks and in the bathroom corner, while a woman's portrait was set on the side of the tub. Elle peed and washed her hands at a dirty white sink.

She opened the unlocked medicine cabinet and shook her head. "Jeez." Her eyes counted ten unlabeled clear jars, like baby food jars, filled with little pills of different shapes and sizes. Prescription Valium, Xanax, Ativan—as if it were the most normal thing in the world to have all of these drugs at home. Elle felt a flash of pride that she still remembered the names and shapes she had to memorize in her pharmacology class, but she didn't see any of the same drugs found in Charlie's system. *Hmmm*. She reached for one of the jars, then stopped. *I don't need my fingerprints anywhere.* Was Geena Louise a petty thief? Grady had checked her references. Her criminal record was clean. Or was her son a drug dealer?

Elle stepped out of the bathroom; her right leg buckled and she caught herself.

"What are you doing?" Geena Louise was standing in front of her, hands on her hips, breathing hard.

Elle stiffened. The possibility of Geena Louise giving Charlie sedating drugs that weren't prescribed made her cringe.

"My husband left me money. I paint on the side, and I know art—I collect. The collection is my retirement, and my son has a drug problem. That's why I don't invite people into my home."

They headed outside where Elle leaned against her car, facing Geena Louise. "Your son has a drug problem, and you have all of these prescription drugs in your bathroom medicine cabinet?"

Geena Louise lowered her eyes. "The drugs are my son's doing, not mine. I—"

"I'll get right to the point, Geena Louise. Did you fill Charlie's med boxes when you worked with him?"

"No, Susan's been filling them."

"For how long?"

"The past two years."

"Okay, so have you been giving Susan sedating drugs to replace Charlie's blood pressure pills, the pills he hasn't been getting for at least the past six months?" Elle met her eyes and thought she saw guilt or fear settling over Geena Louise's face.

"No! I ain't been giving Susan any medication. She gets all of Charlie's drugs from Dr. Woodham."

*Ahhh, finally.* "Did you know the drugs in Charlie's med box were not his blood pressure pills?"

"God, no." Geena Louise shook her head. "Y'all know I'm a nursing assistant. I can't dispense medication, and I believed Susan when she told me those pills were for Charlie's blood pressure."

Elle nodded, but she was not finished. "I also know that you had a Hospice patient who died during your shift. And after she died, her box of fentanyl went missing."

Geena Louise flinched. "I … I was accused of stealing the fentanyl, but the box was still there when I left at the end of my shift." She looked pale, as if she had seen a ghost. "I didn't do it," she whispered. "But they wouldn't give me a chance to explain." Her shoulders sagged as she looked down at her driveway. "You know how the wrong job, the wrong childhood, can work against you like a bad record playing over and over?"

Elle was still trying to piece things together when Geena Louise slowly walked back to her front door. There were more prescription drugs in that house than any one person could take. Elle didn't know what to believe, but certain things just didn't add up. She glanced at her watch: 6 p.m. and getting dark. She started her engine, wondering what she had learned that might help her in the courtroom on Monday morning.

Hours later, Elle sat on her bed, briefcase in hand, and flipped through her folders. It was such a relief to be home. She could set her clock by Mac. At 9 p.m. he had climbed the stairs and pushed open the bedroom door. By nine thirty he had rumpled the duvet cover and burrowed into it at the foot of her bed. He lifted his head slightly, followed her with his eyes, and laid his head back down as if he were in some zone that was neither asleep nor awake.

She thought about the best way to prepare for her testimony. She had organized separate folders for her written report—the seventeen-page assessment and the progress notes. There were folders for Charlie's medical records and for the neurologist and neuropsychologist evaluations. A final folder held interviews of family members and paid caregivers.

She was rubbing her tired eyes when her cell phone rang. She recognized Melinda's voice.

"I've spent the week visiting Daddy in the hospital, and now I can't see him ... what idiot is trying to keep me away?"

"Melinda, the twenty-four-hour security was a physician order. To keep your daddy safe until the hearing."

"I think you're behind this."

Elle was quiet for a minute. Swept with dread and panic, a repeat of her underwater rescue triggered once again. "The police arrested a man named Billie Sutton. He tried to kill your daddy."

"I don't believe it," Melinda said, slurring her words.

"Do you know him?"

"No, but I don't believe you."

Melinda sounded half drunk. "He pushed Charlie into the pool strapped in his wheelchair."

"Were there any witnesses? Daddy has dementia and—"

Elle raised her voice. "Melinda, I saw the whole thing happen myself."

"All the more reason Susan needs to be Daddy's guardian.

*Don't start explaining. She won't hear it. Breathe, breathe.* Elle steadied her voice. "When you're ready, I'll tell you how I arrived just in time to rescue your daddy. But right now, I'm putting my notes together for the hearing on Monday, so unless there's something I can help you with—"

"I wanted to stop by our old farmhouse. I … I couldn't bring myself to do it." Melinda's voice was suddenly calm. "Can you give me a ride out there tomorrow?"

Elle sighed and leaned back against her headboard. She wanted the rest of the weekend to prepare, but tonight she was too tired to argue. *Oh well*. "I can pick you up at noon."

"Thanks; I'm staying at The Morehead Inn."

Elle said goodnight and pulled out an article from her briefcase. "Destroy the Witness, Discredit the Message" was written by a trial attorney, Mark Johnson, and examined the use of expert witnesses in the courtroom. Sumpter had asked her to review it before the hearing.

Mr. Johnson wrote, "Expert witnesses could not win trials, but they could lose trials and often did by destroying their own credibility." He described how expert witnesses were taught to believe they must defend their opinions and conclusions under any circumstance. Experts were usually too confident or stubborn to admit when they were wrong and were unable to change their position, creating a toxic combination. Most attorneys relied on the content of expert witnesses to provide evidence for their own cases while trying to discredit the opposing experts.

Elle called David on his home phone. "Hey, it's me. What would you make of an article titled 'Destroy the Witness, Discredit the Message'?"

"Is this a trick question, or are you running for office?"

She laughed. "I just want your opinion."

"'Destroy the Witness, Discredit the Message,'" he repeated. "Well, I would say that somebody was out to shoot the messenger."

"So if I'm the messenger …"

"And I don't believe in you, I won't believe in what you have to say."

"Okay, what if you were told you had to testify in a courtroom, and it was going to get nasty? The lawyer's goal was to discredit anything you say. And what if you were told that what you had to say didn't make a difference in terms of winning the case?"

"What's this about, Elle? Sounds like you need a legal opinion here, not mine."

"But I want yours."

"Well, I would ask myself, 'Why am I doing this?' "

She laughed again and looked at Mac. His paws and tail twitched in his sleep.

David was glad she called him. He invited her to his place Monday night, after the hearing.

"I'll invite Josh and make dinner for the three of us, say about seven p.m.?"

"What if he can't make it?"

"Then it'll be you and me, missy. We need to celebrate the end of this case. I'll be glad when it's over."

"Any word on Billie Sutton?"

"Billie who?"

"Billie Sutton, the guy who pushed Charlie Blackwell into the pool."

"Oh, him. He's not talkin'—but the contents of his wallet connect him with military service. He's a washed-up army private who's terrified of dogs. That's all we know so far."

She thanked him. Feeling more confused than ever, she said goodnight and went on reading. "Juries made up their minds within the first thirty minutes of the case. From then on, they listened only to the evidence that supported their position." She looked for tips to prime her for the hearing but didn't find any. What was Sumpter trying to tell her? She flipped to the front and back pages of the article. No mention of any journal or book as a reference.

She felt squeezed, as if a blood pressure cuff had inflated around her head, causing her pressure to rise. It was crazy enough that Charlie's family was battling for control. Opening Sumpter's copy of the North Carolina guardianship law from her briefcase, she read the definition out loud to

Mac, who was waking up: "If a person lacks sufficient capacity to manage his own affairs or to make or communicate important decisions regarding his person, family, or property, he can be found to be incompetent."

Mac's tail thumped on the bed. He liked the sound of her voice. She reached over and rubbed his belly, then went on to read about the three components experts on both sides would give testimony on. The first was Charlie's medical condition and whether it met the definition of incompetency. The second component focused on cognitive impairment and whether Charlie was able to make and communicate decisions. The third component focused on functional impairment and whether he was able or not to manage his affairs. Elle saw these components as different sides of the same coin. Charlie's medical conditions impacted his cognition as well as his abilities to communicate decisions, manage his finances, and balance his checkbook.

She commented to Mac, "It's like putting a picture frame around a moving picture." She ran her fingers through his hair.

At 9:45 p.m. her cell phone went off again. She reached to the bedside table and fumbled for the ringing phone; her nerves were getting the best of her. "Hi, don't tell me you're still at the office?"

"No, on my way home," Sumpter said. "I need a copy of your résumé and copies of the articles you've published, Elle. You're my only expert witness."

Elle sat up straight. "Wait, what? What about Lynne Singleton?"

"Refusing to testify."

"You're kidding?"

"No, someone's been calling her late at night, threatening her if she testifies."

Elle thought about the guy who came to her door and the fall she'd taken at the ice rink.

"Lynne also had a terrible experience with Kilpatrick once before and doesn't want to sit in judgment of physicians—says she relies on their referrals, doesn't want to make waves."

Elle leaned back onto her pillow, her heart beating faster. She also relied on referrals. And now she was the only freakin' expert witness? Sumpter offered to drive her to the courthouse after he picked up Charlie from the hospital, but she declined. "I'll meet you there," she said.

"Sure. Have you found something else?"

"No." She told him about reading the article as she tucked it into her briefcase.

"Attorneys bring in expert witnesses to hurt the other side," he said without pausing. "It works both ways. Just don't underestimate your role, kiddo. I'll see you Monday at ten."

His phone clicked. Short and to the point, that was Sumpter.

"This case is not as simple as just proceeding with evidence," she said to Mac, who had jumped off the bed, gone downstairs to grab his leash, and was back in the bedroom doorway with eager eyes and the leather strap dangling from his mouth. His tail wagged widely from side to side.

"Okay, okay." She laughed, distracted and reassured by his behavior. "I wish I could take you to the courtroom."

She took Mac for a quick walk in the park, ironed her new white blouse, and laid out her mother's pearl necklace and earrings. She crawled into bed and thought about Sumpter's words. She knew how to use the medical records to support her evaluation. Could she use them to hurt the petitioner's case? Who would Doug Kilpatrick bring in as an expert witness? Dr. Woodham for sure. Was Sumpter asking her to undermine Dr. Woodham's credibility? She thought for a minute, looking down at Mac, already sleeping in his bed. Woodham had given Charlie a diagnosis of Alzheimer's disease. It was Susan's story that led him to the diagnosis.

There was something else tugging at her. Something about Dr. Woodham's notes. She called Sumpter back on his cell phone. "Hey, there's something else missing from the medical records. I may have some additional information. I have to check it out first."

"Fine, just no surprises."

"I'll be at the courthouse by nine thirty a.m." What she needed to look into had been staring at her this whole time, but it now stuck out like a sore thumb. "We'll have time to talk, right?"

"I'll pick up Charlie, and we'll meet you in the courtroom. Just come and get me right away."

"Perfect," she said.

After saying goodnight, she read through Dr. Woodham's notes one more time.

# Chapter 19
*Sunday*

Elle drove down Morehead Avenue with Mac harnessed in the back seat of her Volvo. She cracked his window, so he could sniff the outdoor air, and pulled into the parking lot of Morehead Inn. Melinda stood up slowly, appearing glassy-eyed and disheveled—*hungover*. Elle watched her slump into the passenger seat, wearing the same orange paisley top and tight flared jeans she'd worn at the airport. She reeked of stale alcohol, sweet and sour, a bit like the ketosis smell from Mary Beth's car.

Mac sniffed the air around Melinda as she settled into the seat directly in front of him.

"There are definitely ghosts in this place," Melinda said, not even turning around to greet Mac.

"Ghosts!?" Elle said.

"A white apparition wandered into the garden last night."

"Were you outside?"

"No, just sitting at the window." Melinda pointed to a second-story room above the garden.

She didn't want to hear about the ghost, especially when Melinda had accused her of keeping her away from Charlie. "Are we heading right to the farmhouse?"

"No, the abandoned mine. It's close to the farmhouse. You know, Daddy never went back to the farm once he moved out."

"And you?"

"No, but I've always wanted to go back." Melinda rubbed her red eyes.

*What are your secrets?* Melinda hadn't been to the farm in twenty years, yet she needed to go the day before the hearing, and she wanted Elle to drive her. *Why?*

Melinda stared at her with a weird smile and impatiently shifted her hips from side to side. Elle put the car in reverse. Mac wagged his tail and barked as they started out for the old farm. To him, riding in the car was another exciting adventure.

A voice called out as Melinda directed Elle to the unseen mine shaft on the outer edge of the Blackwell farm. Elle was surprised to see Gordon Thomas wearing steel-toe boots, a safety vest, and a bandana under his hard hat. He gave them a quick smile and waved them into the mine.

"Did you plan to meet Mr. Thomas here?" she asked Melinda.

"Of course."

"My dog's friendly," Elle said, walking Mac on a tight leash, her backpack slung over her shoulder. The arched entrance was dark and low into the earth. Elle bent her head to enter, stepped into darkness, and waited for her eyes to adjust.

"You never want to do this alone," Mr. Thomas said with the bright beam of light from his headlamp leading the way.

It was a horizontal mine shaft dug into the rock, a relic from the gold-mining past. Mac pulled against her to sniff all of the new smells, as Elle gave him more leash so he could walk in front of her. They followed Mr. Thomas single file through the entrance.

"There's always a risk of cave-ins."

"It's so cold down here," Elle said, her voice quivering as she listened to their footsteps on the gravel.

"Between fifty-five and sixty-five degrees year-round," Mr. Thomas said.

The mine was much bigger below than it looked from the entrance and reminded her of being in a cave—a long, deep cave. Opening her backpack, Elle pulled on her wool sweater and grabbed her penlight, shining a soft beam on the gravel path as they walked through the dark.

"I found some shiny rocks and hid them," Melinda said as they followed Mr. Thomas through one of the tunnels with Elle bringing up the rear.

"When did you say you hid these rocks?" he asked.

"It was sometime in the 1940s."

"So you think these rocks had gold in them?"

Melinda shrugged her shoulders. "It was a long time ago. I was five or six and didn't know anything about gold … Mother and Daddy were farmers. They didn't know about gold either."

"Well, your daddy sold the farm to me in 1960, so if we can find those rocks, they're yours," he said with a jovial grin.

Elle wondered if he meant what he said.

"Lots of mines around here were gone by the fifties, except for the ones bought up by old prospectors and geologists who were out on their own, like me."

"Did the gold dry up?" Elle asked, hoping they had reached the end of their walk and could retrace their steps. They were deeper underground than she imagined.

"No, the gold never dried up. A new international monetary system was introduced, back in 1944, to create stability in exchange rates."

"Wasn't that the Bretton Woods agreement?" Melinda asked.

"That's right, Melinda. Fixed the price of gold at thirty-five dollars an ounce, and gold mining down here was no longer profitable."

"It's spooky down here," Elle said, touching the solid rock wall with a hand, feeling the cold all around her. Her heart pounded as they walked along, and Melinda's labored breathing and heavy steps were amplified in front of her.

"It's probably haunted—" Melinda began, but Mr. Thomas cut in.

"This mine was shut down and boarded up in the fifties. Did your daddy know you were out here foolin' around back then?" He shot Melinda a curious glance.

"It was Daddy who brought me here. It was our little secret."

"That was risky," he said, pointing to a sign: Danger, Open Shaft. "This shaft is partially collapsed, but once it was thirty feet deep." He shook his head. "There are still some vertical shafts hidden here, so you need to follow me carefully."

Elle looked in the direction of the shaft and stopped. She imagined falling thirty feet. Bad idea ... especially following Melinda, who believed in ghosts. She shivered. "So where are these rocks we're looking for?"

"I found the rocks in an old gold vein in the back of the mine and hid them in a leather pouch," Melinda said.

"Well, let's go and inspect a couple of veins. There's some gold-embedded quartz back there," he said, his headlamp pointing a steady brightness toward the back of the mine.

"I've never done this before," Elle said, forcing a smile, her feet still planted. She wanted to head back, but it was too easy to get turned around in the tunnels. *Mac can find his way out.*

"Just stay close," Mr. Thomas said, stopping at one of the veins. "You can see this gold vein laced into the rock." He traced a thin gold line, the width of a skinny straw. "There's been a cave-in here; I reckon from water seeping through the mine and rock erosion."

Elle imagined a cave-in where water rushed in, trapping them all. She cautiously stepped forward and looked into the darkness. *We can't die down here.* The hearing was less than twenty-four hours away.

"This is it!" Melinda shouted. She picked up a couple of rocks and moved them to the side.

Mr. Thomas hunched over, shining his light on the rock floor. The dust rose where the rocks were disturbed.

"Can you help me?" Melinda asked Elle.

Elle nodded. "Sit, Mac."

He sat on his hind legs, and she gave him a dried liver treat.

She dropped his leash, tucked her penlight into her sweater pocket, and lifted a giant rock with both hands, piling it on top of Melinda's rocks.

"Look at this." Melinda pulled out what looked like a hammer with a square head that curved down to a single point. The metal was rusty with age.

"An old rock hammer." Mr. Thomas took the hammer in his free hand and examined it. "What in tarnation! I've been all over this mine … never came across this before." A look of delight crossed his face. "Look, your dog is starting an excavation project."

Elle stared at the place where the hammer had been removed. Mac was digging with his front paws, shoveling dirt under his belly and behind him, in one powerful motion after another. The muscles strained in his shoulders and legs as he kept digging. He jammed his black nose deep into the hole. "Mac, no!" she ordered and squatted on her legs, gripping his leash as tight as she could. He didn't stop. She grabbed his harness, stood, and pulled back. "Stop." After a couple of seconds, he pulled his nose up and panted in excitement, dirt covering his bearded mouth and tongue as well as his legs and underbelly. She looked over his shoulder into the hole and noticed a saucer-shaped bone at the base of what looked like a skull, still embedded in rocks. The sides of the skull were packed with dirt and rocks. Mr. Thomas noticed it, too, and bent over.

She grabbed her penlight and beamed it over a break in the cranial bone—the kind of fracture that occurred from a sudden trauma to the base of the skull. Was this a human skull that had been hit from behind by a single point of a hammer, a hammer like the one Mr. Thomas was now holding? That kind of blow was usually fatal.

Mr. Thomas reached out his hand.

"Don't touch it!" Elle said. It was one thing to come looking for gold; it was another thing to find a skeleton buried in this old mine. "This is a crime scene! Put that hammer down. Now!" She reached for her cell phone. "I'm calling 911."

Standing in front of the mine, Elle finally had enough service bars to call 911. She breathed the outside air again, fresh oxygen. Only two days ago, she had been holding her breath underwater, in the pool with Charlie. She never wanted to take breathing for granted again. Never, ever.

She pulled Mac tight against her and gave him a cool bowl of water from the car and another treat from her pants pocket while they waited for the police. She felt like she was dreaming—a horrible dream where she was a suspect in one of those cold cases from *Forensic Files*.

Two officers from the Davidson Police Department showed up, and one was taping off the mine as a crime scene. The other was interviewing Melinda and Mr. Thomas across from the mine entrance in front of his police car. More officers arrived. Elle stood, waiting beside Mac, who had flopped down on the grass. She could hear Melinda arguing with an officer about going back into the mine to find her leather pouch. The officer stood there taking notes and politely refused.

Elle took out her cell phone and called David. "Hey, it's me. I'm in Davidson … we found an old rock hammer at the back end of an abandoned mine. Then Mac started digging and found a fractured skull … human."

"Elle, stop! Davidson is out of our jurisdiction. You need to call Davidson PD right now."

"The police are here. Long story—I'll explain later—but there's this guy who went missing thirty-six years ago. No one ever heard from him again."

"Who went missing?"

"Jackson Walker. He was the realtor who hired Susan and sold the Blackwell farm to Gordon Thomas. Fast-forward to now."

"Okay."

"The Davidson police found no wallet or money, no driver's license or credit cards, but they did find a plastic laminated ID—Jackson Walker's ID—in the remnants of his backpack. The plastic survived. Weird, right?"

"Plastic always survives. You think it's his body?"

"Well, the skeleton needs to be examined."

"And I suppose the hammer was used to fracture his skull."

"It's going to be examined as well. I know it's full lunacy, but I seriously think this is related to our case."

"Elle, you're inside the Davidson County line—"

"I know. I know it's not your jurisdiction. I'm just asking you to introduce yourself to the detective that wants to question me. Explain that I'm for real." She heard him chuckling on the other end.

"Just don't give him sass, missy, or you'll be posting bond. And I wouldn't go sharing your conspiracy theory ... not just yet."

"Why is it, when I'm trying to connect the dots, you act like I'm a loon?"

They ended their call, and Elle opened the back door to her car. Mac leaped into the seat, excited at the idea of another car ride. She was too exhausted, emotionally, to say anything. She fumbled her key into the ignition, started up the engine, and turned on the radio's old-school R&B station with a trembling hand. *More PTSD.* Her brain was unable to focus.

A short time later, Melinda took her place in the passenger seat, and they hit the road. At first, Melinda was quiet, looking out the window. Ten minutes into the ride back to Charlotte, she opened up. "I've spent the week visiting Daddy in the hospital and looking back on when we were a family. I've made so many choices without much thought at all ... reacting in the moment."

"We all make different choices than we thought we'd make," Elle said, trying to be supportive and thinking about her own life.

Melinda reached for a prescription bottle in her purse, and Elle met her glance as she tossed a few pills into her mouth and swallowed. Tears welled up in Melinda's eyes.

"Most of my life, I've blamed Daddy. Yet now, sitting here, I think it was my mother who was too deep in her own depression to see what I needed."

"When your parents die, your life changes forever."

Melinda didn't answer.

"Sorry we didn't find your rocks," Elle said, knowing Melinda thought she'd be the one to find gold. The old farm wasn't Charlie's dream; it was Melinda's. After the first domino had fallen, they all started falling. Charlie sold her beloved dream a week after Carol's suicide. Melinda packed up and moved away; her mother's death had severed the bonds between them all. Then Robbie became paralyzed. He married, and Charlie remarried too.

"You know Daddy sent letters to me … I never answered them," Melinda said after another long silence.

Elle thought about the Blackwells' separate lives. She thought about her own parents. They didn't choose to leave her and Peter behind. Different issues, different families.

"Only now can I see some of my mistakes. It's like looking in a rearview mirror." Melinda began crying. "What a waste."

Elle handed her a box of tissues and clenched the steering wheel with both hands. All this guilt and conflict over being so angry, for misplaced feelings.

Tina Turner started belting out "What's Love Got to Do with It." Melinda whispered the words about not needing hearts only to have them broken.

"As a young girl, I learned to take care of Mother. But when Daddy got sick and separated from Amy, I couldn't come home. I couldn't be the one."

"Did you ever call Amy, I mean to find out what happened?" Elle asked.

"I didn't have a relationship with her. I'd call the caregivers, usually Florence."

"Florence Benson?"

"Yes, ma'am. She worked with Daddy on weekends."

"And what did she say?"

"He was usually asleep, but she was always willing to talk to me. 'Your daddy's not doing so well,' she would say, or 'He's getting more confused.' The day that Daddy married Susan … I was so relieved."

Was it relief that Susan would take care of him or relief thinking Melinda's stress would be over?

"And here I am. The drugs and booze are how I've escaped the pain, but … I'm still havin' a hard time figuring out what happened."

Elle glanced over and smiled. "It's not too late to start over, Melinda. Your daddy needs you in his corner."

# Chapter 20
*Monday*

At the courthouse, Sumpter opened the door to the clerk's office and found Doug Kilpatrick sitting alone in the waiting room, dressed in his best Hugo Boss suit, head down. His hair was shorter by an inch since Friday, and he was clean-shaven.

Sumpter didn't want to talk to Doug and leave Charlie waiting for him at the hospital, but Doug looked up and spotted him.

"Bad news, Sumpter. Judge Townsend's in the emergency department with a horrible case of the flu."

"Hey. Yeah, I just heard." He eyed Doug's pained expression as he walked over to him. He imagined Doug cruising down Providence Road in his black Mercedes earlier this morning, listening to Frank Sinatra and feeling the good life. Sumpter smiled with deep satisfaction.

"I hate last-minute changes," Doug said.

"Elaine Kincaid's replacing Townsend?" Sumpter checked his watch.

"So I hear ... She can't be the only one available."

Sumpter shrugged. "Would you prefer Townsend throwing up in our courtroom?"

"I'd take him sick over Kincaid any day."

"How well do you know her?"

"I'm certainly not friends with her, if that's what you're asking." Doug's face turned red, in anger. He looked around shaking his head, then pounded his fist on the arm of his chair.

Sumpter knew Judge Kincaid well enough to know she'd be great. While she had less experience than the other judges, she'd practiced as an elder law attorney and had three years of guardianship experience.

"That's not why you hate this," Sumpter said knowingly. Elaine would have sole authority over the case. Of course, her choices of action were limited by statutes and case law ... He sighed in relief. "She won't like your tactics."

Doug kept shaking his head back and forth. "As far as I'm concerned, women have no business being in the role of judge, attorney, or expert witness—not in our courtroom."

"Well, she's enjoying her new role, and she's improving with every case." Doug waved him off. "I don't want to hear it."

"I gotta go and pick up Charlie." Sumpter gave him a two-finger wave and walked away. *Holy shit.* Doug Kilpatrick no longer held all the aces!

Elle left home and drove to an old two-story brick building off Providence Road. She had reviewed all of her notes for the hearing. Normally, she would have driven straight to the courthouse while everything was fresh in her mind. But unanswered questions lingered, and she sensed more danger, like someone was going to creep up on her at any moment. She looked at her watch—8:40 a.m.—just enough time to visit Dr. Woodham's office.

She pulled to the curb and parked in front of the entrance. A week ago, the weather had been warm, the fall color at its peak, and now it was cold and pouring rain. She opened her red umbrella and carried her briefcase into the building, then walked past four offices down a dark hallway. The clicking sounds of her heels echoed off the tile floor.

The building smelled musty, like it hadn't been cleaned in a while. Three empty offices were real estate agencies. They weren't open till 9 a.m. The fourth was unmarked. Dr. Woodham's office was the very last, at the back of the building, his name engraved on a plaque adjacent to the double glass doors. She peeked through the door and knocked.

Elle hid her surprise as Florence Benson approached on the other side of the glass and unlocked the doors.

"Why, Miss Elle, can I help you?" Her voice dripped sugar.

"Hey, Florence. Charlie Blackwell's hearing starts this morning." She tried to make her request sound important. "I need to talk to Dr. Woodham's nurse."

"We don't open till nine a.m. Let me see—" Florence left and came back. She had pulled on a lab coat over her navy-blue scrubs. "Sonya, his office nurse, says to give her ten minutes." Florence looked down the hallway and back at Elle. "I guess you can wait in Dr. Woodham's office."

Elle followed Florence past two exam rooms along the way. She could feel her blood pressure rising. Florence opened the door to his private office with her set of keys and flipped on the light.

"Does Compassionate Care and Prayer have the office next door?" Elle asked, trying to make small talk.

"No, that's Dr. Woodham's pharmacy. We share a small room." Florence pointed to a closed door off of Dr. Woodham's office suite. "It's about the size of your office."

Elle smiled, remembering Florence squeezing in at her table. "So are you working for Dr. Woodham, now?"

"No, he has his own staff. We help him when he needs it."

"And what do you do?"

"His receptionist is on vacation. I'm filling in for her—the Pain Clinic on Mondays and Fridays." Florence looked at the wall clock. "I better get back to my desk."

Elle thanked her, then closed the office door. She took a deep breath and looked around. Charts were stacked everywhere: his desk, the sofa ... even the floor. Dr. Woodham's practice looked legit: a waiting room, exam rooms, potted plants, and his own private office. But his own pharmacy next door? *Red flag.*

A Harris Teeter grocery bag sat on his desk. It looked out of place among the scattered charts and two computers. She walked over and then, facing the door, peered inside. The bag was filled with stacks of prescription pads. She stopped. The room was quiet. It wasn't right for her to snoop, but she had a good reason for looking through those scripts. Standing there, even though she felt guilty, she rationalized it was the right thing to do, since red flags were popping up all over the place. And Sumpter had told her—no surprises!

Still facing the door, she lifted the first pad out of the bag and thumbed through carbon copies of scripts written for last week. After leafing through a couple more, she decided to peek at them all. Her breath quickened as she found what she was looking for, near the bottom of the bag. Prescriptions for oxycodone and clonazepam. But not prescriptions for Charlie ... they were for Susan, Charlie's wife. *Good enough.*

She carefully placed the pads back in the bag. A stack of billing sheets was hidden under the bag. Her senses sharpened. She moved the bag and scanned through last Friday's billing sheets, one by one. Other than the names of the patients, they looked pretty much the same: oxycodone 100 pills, oxycodone 240 pills. Without an explanation, she wasn't sure how to interpret them, but the charges looked excessive.

Elle heard two women talking outside the door. She quickly dropped the billing sheets and sank into the chair next to Woodham's desk. The door opened. A Latino woman with short brown hair, wearing a white lab coat, introduced herself.

"Sonya Brown," she said in a husky voice.

"Elle Larson. I work with Charlie Blackwell." She shook her hand and noticed a black ink tattoo that ran up Sonya's wrist, half covered by the sleeve of her lab coat. She handed Sonya her copy of Dr. Woodham's October 20 notes.

"Where'd you get this?" Sonya's dark brows furrowed as she looked over his notes and turned on the desktop computer.

"From the court lawyer. I'm an expert witness for the hearing that starts this morning."

"With Dr. Woodham?"

Elle nodded, feeling another pinch of guilt. Sonya didn't need to know they weren't on the same side. "I need to understand the Blackwell records … I'll be asked about them today." That was true. She gave the quick explanation she'd played over and over in her head. "I don't want to make any mistakes in court. I'll be under oath …"

"What's your question?"

"I didn't see where you recorded vital signs on the October 20 visit." Elle's heart was pounding. "In case I'm asked, was Charlie Blackwell seen on that day?"

"Let me see, I worked that day." There was a questioning look on Sonya's face as she pulled up the date on the computer. "Ah, that's right," she said as the schedule popped up on the screen. "Dr. Woodham didn't see Mr. Blackwell on October 20—only his wife, Susan—which explains why I didn't record any vital signs." She smiled with satisfaction.

Elle nodded, acting like it was no big deal. She wanted to hug this Sonya Brown.

"You know Susan's been a longtime patient of ours. She needed our help to petition for guardianship."

Elle nodded again, feeling like she had just bought up all the orange and red properties while playing Monopoly.

Sonya's cell phone rang. "Excuse me a moment." She stepped into the hall.

"Birds of a feather," Elle said under her breath and quickly put the grocery bag back on top of the billing sheets, hoping Sonya hadn't noticed.

When Sonya returned, she remained in the doorway and sent Elle a searing glare. "Dr. Woodham says you are not to be in his office."

Elle looked at her in surprise. Her face flushed. It was go time. "Guess he's not worried about me telling the truth."

"I'm asking you to leave now," Sonya said with a chill in her voice.

Elle held her breath and grabbed her copy of the medical records without saying anything else. No more poking the bear. Once outside the office, she ran down the hallway and didn't look back. Adrenaline surged as she hit the pouring rain and hopped inside her car for a quick getaway. The courthouse was a brief ten minutes away. Her heart was now racing, and she was short of breath. *Oh no. I left my umbrella.* Suddenly, she didn't care. She had more evidence for the hearing.

Elle pushed through the bronze double doors of the nine-story glass-and-concrete courthouse. Large blocks carried the message: *To Secure the Blessings of Liberty.* Once inside the recessed entrance, she turned left at the information desk and followed the shorter of two lines through security, taking out her flip phone and placing it, along with her purse and briefcase, on the conveyor belt. Security was necessary; it just felt like judgment day. Her knees were already trembling as she watched the metal detector scan her belongings.

"Having a good day, miss?" the security officer asked.

"I sure hope so," she said, smiling weakly.

As she walked through the atrium, hundreds of footsteps echoed. She took a deep breath and looked up through the eight floors of courtrooms to the ninth floor. Tourists loved this place. So why did she find it so intimidating? On top of the vibe of the building itself and the anxiety about Charlie, there was the dread of being an expert witness. She just didn't belong here. *Slow down, focus … breathe.*

Jostled by the crowd, she escaped in a small group and took an elevator to the third floor. When the elevator door opened, she walked across the hall to the clerk of court's office.

"You're in Hearing Room A," Keyanna said from behind the clerk's desk.

She had not met the young deputy clerk before, but then she only came to the clerk's office once or twice a year. Keyanna pointed out where the hearing room was and then where the ladies' restroom was, after Elle asked.

Inside the bathroom, Elle sighed at her mop of wet hair that was sticking up all over. She was never going to be a barometer of fashion. Pushing strands behind her ears, she felt her heart quicken and took a deep breath. It was 9:30 a.m. Thank God she had some extra time to pull herself together before entering the courtroom.

Elle hadn't been to court in the past year, but the first time she had, she thought it would be like *Perry Mason*, the series her dad had watched every week. But guardianship hearings had smaller rooms, modest and simple, not like *Perry Mason* or the grand lobby downstairs. The glow of ceiling lights illuminated the room into a small stage, drawing attention to the small front table where the clerk of court presided.

And there was Charlie, sitting next to Sumpter at a cherry-finished table along the left side wall. Susan and Doug Kilpatrick would sit across from them at a cherry table along the right wall. Bibles were stacked on each table, in groups of three, as if the Gideons had paid them a visit.

Elle silenced her phone as she walked over and sat next to Charlie. Elle, Charlie, and Sumpter, all in a row.

"Hey, doll. I'm guessing only the important people get to sit here," Charlie whispered. He placed his arm around her shoulder.

She was overcome by the sight of him, noticing how nice he looked in his camel jacket. It sure was good to feel his hug and hear his voice—a reminder of why she was here. "I like your red tie," she whispered back.

"Thanks, kid. My battle tie."

"Battle tie?"

"Yes, ma'am. Always wore a tie; part of the uniform. We'd be chest high in cold water, wearin' a tie."

Elle shivered.

"You'll do fine. Just think of all those young soldiers in the Middle East. They're not sure they'll survive another day, let alone come home. Believe me. I know."

She tried to relax, but thinking about her brother, Peter, didn't help.

Sumpter leaned over and rapped his knuckles on the table. "Okay, here's how this works. There's no jury in a guardianship hearing. There's a judge and there're attorneys representing both parties. The petitioner is the person filing the action. The petitioner has the burden of proof. Elle, what does that mean?"

"That means that Susan's attorney has to prove to the judge that Charlie needs a guardian." She was glad she had reviewed the North Carolina guardianship definitions over the weekend.

"Well, if I need a guardian, I'll be damned if it's going to be her," Charlie said.

"Susan's attorney needs to show clear and convincing evidence," Sumpter went on, "but he doesn't need to show beyond a reasonable doubt."

"So, how does he do that?" Charlie asked.

"By trying to prove you're incompetent. But we are the opposing party. Charlie, you are called the respondent, the person who may need guardianship."

"I don't need a guardian!"

"Well, it's Elle's responsibility here to testify about your functioning; what you can do and, more importantly, what you can't do for yourself. That will help Judge Kincaid decide."

Elle looked at Charlie's angry, puzzled face and smiled reassuringly at him. This would be hard, talking about his weaknesses while sitting beside him in a courtroom full of people. How would he feel about her after the hearing was over?

Her thoughts were interrupted by a warm-faced, broad-shouldered man in a tailored three-piece suit entering the courtroom. He walked over and shook hands with Sumpter.

"Charlie Blackwell, this is Doug Kilpatrick. He represents Susan."

"Nice to meet you," Kilpatrick said in a soft baritone, extending his hand. Charlie shook his hand but remained silent.

Doug Kilpatrick. This was the first time Elle had ever seen him. He was big—a foot taller than her—looking more like a Chicago Bear linebacker. He was attractive in a clean-shaven, muscular sort of way. Kilpatrick smiled at her, his large capped teeth as white as his shirt. She smiled back and lowered her eyes. Her legs began to tremble again.

"Your witness is kinda young, isn't she, Tom?"

"She's good, Doug."

"Hell, if she was that good, she'd be on my team," Kilpatrick said and turned, walking back to his table on the right.

Elle was getting used to the talk that went on between attorneys in the courtroom, like preparing their teams for the big game. She noticed Doug's Italian leather shoes. What was it her father had told her? "You could tell a lot about a man by his shoes." Or was it Sherlock Holmes who said that? She swallowed hard. Sumpter leaned past Charlie and whispered to Elle, as though he could read her mind.

"Don't let his looks, or his voice, deceive you."

She shot Sumpter a serious look. He looked sharp in his dark gray suit and full Windsor knot pulled all the way to the top of his shirt line, his salt and pepper hair combed back, not a hair out of place.

"Can we talk privately for a few minutes?" she asked.

Leaving Charlie at the table, they moved from the courtroom and found a couple of chairs outside the clerk's office and sat down. She pulled out the medical records and flipped to Dr. Woodham's notes. Sumpter put on his reading glasses.

"There's a diagnosis of Alzheimer's disease and memory loss, right?" Elle pointed to the end of the October 20 note.

"Right," Sumpter said. "We know that."

"Well, Dr. Woodham was the first and only physician to make that diagnosis, and he did that without seeing his patient."

"What?"

"Usually, the physician takes a medical history, does his exam, then orders lab tests and a CT scan or MRI. We knew he didn't order the lab work or X-ray."

"But what makes you think he didn't see the patient?"

"My first clue was rereading his notes." She fingered over to the top of the note. "See? No vital signs. Here's where his height, weight, blood pressure, pulse, and temperature would have been recorded. The office nurse would have recorded his vital signs at the beginning of the visit."

Sumpter looked at her proudly as if she were uncovering the big reveal.

"Then there was no mention of what Charlie told him during the visit."

"Only the story from Susan," Sumpter added.

"Right," she said. She loved this part of her job. Interpreting medical records as if they were hiding secrets. "Usually, the physician wants to hear the patient's history in his own words."

"Even if he has dementia?"

"Even if he has dementia," Elle repeated. "So this morning, I stopped by Dr. Woodham's office and talked to his office nurse." She took a deep breath. "She confirmed that Charlie didn't come to the office on October 20."

"The date he gave Charlie a diagnosis of Alzheimer's disease?" he asked as a smile spread across his face. "The same date he wrote the letter in support of the petition." Sumpter's eyes brightened with intensity. "Sounds like the beginning of a malpractice case."

*Awkward*. It wasn't her place to decide. "If he didn't feel comfortable doing the dementia workup, he should have referred Charlie to a neurologist."

Sumpter studied her face. "Was Dr. Woodham there?"

"No, but the receptionist put me in his office, where I waited until his nurse had time to talk to me." Elle hesitated before going on. "While I was waiting, I snooped. I shouldn't have done it, but I couldn't help it. There were about thirty prescription pads sitting on his desk." She neglected to tell him that they were in a grocery bag, and she had to take them out of the bag. "I thumbed through the carbon copies of scripts he'd written—prescriptions for oxycodone, 100 pills, 240 pills. Based on what I saw, there were too many pills ... too many people being seen on the same date."

Sumpter raised his eyebrows. "Go on."

"I was looking for a script for Charlie, but I didn't find one. What I did find were two scripts for Susan, oxycodone and clonazepam, the same drugs that showed up on Charlie's drug screen. So Dr. Woodham writes a script for Susan—"

"And she gives her pills to Charlie. They've been fucking up his brain … Was Woodham marking up the price of drugs?"

"I only saw charges on the billing sheets for oxycodone. I called Charlie's pharmacist on my way over here. The charges on those billing sheets were like three times higher." She shook her head. "Dr. Woodham has his own office pharmacy. Funny, right?" She shrugged her shoulders. "There's no way he could have seen that many patients in one day."

"He's a drug pusher, charging visits that never happened and keeping Susan happy? He needs to be reported to the licensure board," Sumpter said, looking at her as if they were finally getting to the truth. "But first I'm going to get a subpoena and send the police out to his office. That lousy piece of shit."

Elle breathed deeply and exhaled. Sumpter swearing in the courthouse gave her a sense of confidence for the moment, like skating down the ice rink.

"I'm glad I'm not going to be here this afternoon when you cross-examine him," she said, knowing that she would be leaving after her testimony.

Sumpter's brow furrowed, and he rubbed his chin. "I want you back here at one thirty sharp to hear his testimony. I promise, it will be a learning experience."

"I really need to get back to work. I'm scheduled to see Naomi at McCrory's Five and Dine—"

"I know, I know, but this is important too. Important for you, Elle. You've done some badass work here."

"Woodham's nurse also told me that he's been Susan's physician for years."

"So Woodham compromised his professional standards to do what Susan asked him," Sumpter said.

"How does all this fit into our case?"

"I'll figure it out. We've got to get back, Elle." He stood to escort her back to the courtroom.

"Wait, I just need a minute." Alone in the ladies' room, Elle put both hands on a sink and looked in the mirror at her new navy suit and white blouse that she had saved for the courtroom. *Your face looks scared.* She pretty much knew how this would work. Kilpatrick would ask questions. She would be eager to answer them and provide a better understanding of what had happened to Charlie. Wasn't that why she had been called to court anyway? Meanwhile, the judge and everyone on hand would be watching. But Kilpatrick wasn't interested in her evaluation. He wanted her to make mistakes; he would set her up. He would discredit her in front of her client, in front of Sumpter ... in front of the judge. And the worst part? She would have to go along. She couldn't be defensive or hostile.

She reapplied some lip gloss to her dry mouth. So what could she do? *Strong back, soft knees, good for pushing,* was what her skating coach had always told her. Maybe if she relied on muscle memory and adrenaline. *Push through.* That's all she could come up with. She tapped her mom's pearl necklace for luck, pushed open the door, and walked to the courtroom.

# Chapter 21

By the time Elle opened the courtroom door, the chairs lined up theatre style at the back of the room were already crowded with Charlie's family and friends. Elle recognized Charlie's neighbor, Georgia Harris, dressed in her sage-green coat. Her frizzy hair stuck out from her matching hat as she held hands with Amy Blackwell, who was looking pale and tired but pleased.

Elle bent down and thanked them for coming.

"It's so good to see my dear friend," Georgia said.

"I'm only going to stay a little while," Amy said. "I thought it would be good for me to hear what you have to say, Elle." She gave her an encouraging smile.

Elle smiled weakly and walked back to Charlie and Sumpter. She wondered about backing out. No, that was lunacy. How would Charlie spend his holiday? How could she ever enjoy Thanksgiving?

Elle watched Susan walk into the courtroom. A vivid blue suit, a brown sable fur coat draped over her shoulders, her face poised as if she were waiting for a camera flash. Elle could smell her French perfume as Susan walked past. Kilpatrick motioned Susan to sit next to him, extending his hand to take her fur coat, which slid off her petite frame like she was stepping out on the red carpet in strappy heels. She looked like an aging actress still vying for center stage. It was clear that Susan liked the limelight. It gave her power, and that power was an aphrodisiac that drew people to her. Holding Kilpatrick's hand, she sat down with the same grace Elle remembered from their first encounter.

Susan was the same size as Amy. Given Charlie's poor vision and hearing, Elle could see how he had mistaken her for Amy during the wedding switch: Susan wearing a veil that covered her face and hair, even wearing Amy's perfume and camouflaging the truth, bright lipstick and lip liner—lots of lip liner.

Robbie Blackwell, wearing a wool winter cap, rolled in; Peggy walked beside him. A pale Melinda walked in behind them, pulled on dark glasses, and announced that she wanted to sit in the back.

"I'm neutral, like Switzerland," she said to no one in particular. She sank heavily into an empty chair in the back row and took out her trusty bottle of Xanax.

The courtroom was pretty much full when Judge Kincaid entered. She shuffled her tall and lanky frame over to Charlie, who stood and gave her a hearty handshake. She looked to be in her late thirties with baby-fine hair standing up in one- and two-inch razor-cut wisps all over her head. Her oversized earrings and black-framed glasses gave her a bold and bright look.

"Smart and serious," Elle whispered to Charlie as the judge walked to the head table and sat down.

"She's so young," Charlie whispered back.

Promptly at ten, the bailiff announced that court was in session.

"Good morning. My name is Elaine Kincaid," the judge said once the room was quiet. She poured herself a glass of water and introduced the bailiff, Clay Guthrie. "We are here on the matter of Charlie Blackwell."

Judge Kincaid gave Charlie a kind and thoughtful look. There was a formality to her voice. She weighed each word before she spoke. "Doug Kilpatrick works for the petitioner, Susan Blackwell." She looked from Kilpatrick to Susan and then turned to Sumpter. "Tommy Sumpter represents Charlie Blackwell, the respondent."

She explained how the rules of evidence were more relaxed in guardianship cases, but how it was helpful for the judge to hear all issues of concern. "It helps me determine who is to be the guardian, if one needs to be appointed today."

Elle felt the seriousness of the judge's decision down in her bones, and she leaned forward to take it all in.

Judge Kincaid softly drummed her pen on the table. "But this is not family court, and what needs to be proven is whether or not there is incompetency." She paused and again glanced at them individually. "If there is incompetency, then there needs to be a guardian of the person and a guardian of the estate. And we will need to decide who are the most suitable guardians. These are the questions we want to answer today."

Elle grabbed her pen and notepad and began taking notes. She was glad Judge Kincaid was explaining the rules before she had to testify.

When it was time for her to be sworn in, Elle placed her left hand on the Bible and raised her right hand. Judge Kincaid told her she would be testifying at the table. She was happy to stay seated next to Charlie and Sumpter.

Kincaid then asked Doug Kilpatrick to summarize the petition. He picked up his copy and began reading.

"The petition filed by Susan Porter Blackwell asks that she be named guardian for her eighty-year-old husband, Charlie Blackwell. The petition alleges that Charlie is suffering from dementia caused by Alzheimer's disease and, as a result, has been susceptible to being exploited by his ex-wife."

There was an awkward silence. Kilpatrick went on to tell them how Amy Blackwell stole more than $200,000 in the past year and with the divorce, just one month ago, received a substantial settlement. Elle looked at Amy in the back row, shaking her head.

"Charlie still has access to his checkbook, credit cards, and savings," Kilpatrick then explained with a scowl on his face. "And that's gotten him in big trouble."

Charlie leaned over and whispered something in Sumpter's ear.

Judge Kincaid looked up and adjusted her thick glasses, then took a sip of water. "Since the petitioner has the burden, they normally would go first. However, I understand that the petitioner's expert witness is unable to testify until this afternoon. Mr. Sumpter, I'd like to start by having you question your expert witness. I understand we have reports from the neurologist and neuropsychologist to review. We'll break for lunch around noon and then ask for Dr. Woodham to testify around one thirty p.m."

"Thank you, Your Honor. I'd like to call Elle Larson to testify," Sumpter said, turning to offer Elle a small, encouraging smile.

Elle stated her name for the record and began answering Sumpter's questions, starting with her educational background.

"Can you tell us about the type of work you do?" he asked.

"I own a small care-management company in Charlotte. We coordinate care for aging and disabled adults, mostly for people who need help but want to stay at home."

Elle knew that Sumpter needed to lay the foundation for her testimony by asking background and employment questions—all routine. *All good.* She just wanted to get this over with.

"Do you yourself review medical records and perform assessments?"

"Yes, I do."

"Can you please describe your typical assessment?"

Elle explained how she reviewed her client's medical records, then she assessed their capacity and functional abilities to determine what level and type of care they needed.

"Were you asked by me to conduct an assessment of Charlie Blackwell?"

"Yes, I was," Elle said. *Relax and breathe.*

"Can you describe your assessment of Charlie Blackwell?" Sumpter asked.

She picked up her written report with a trembling hand and slid it directly in front of her on the table. She looked at Elaine Kincaid, who sat with her pen poised, listening to every word.

"On November 6, I was asked to assess Mr. Blackwell and review his medical records. I saw Mr. Blackwell at nine thirty a.m. that day. When I saw him, he had five fentanyl patches on his body. He was too deeply sedated to assess. The fentanyl was life threatening and—"

"Objection, Your Honor," Kilpatrick said, his baritone voice breaking over her explanation. He leaned forward. "Miss Larson is not being asked by her attorney to render an opinion about Mr. Blackwell's medication." His voice was ice cold.

"Your Honor, her opinion is based on what she directly observed," Sumpter said.

Elle glanced over at Sumpter, who looked calm and neutral.

"Overruled. Please go on, Miss Larson."

Elle could feel the shift in tension around the courtroom. Kilpatrick had cut her off before she could mention oxycodone and clonazepam were discovered on Charlie's drug screen later that morning. She wasn't sure how to go on. She waited for someone to speak.

"Miss Larson, how did you find Mr. Blackwell on your next visit?" Sumpter asked.

She cleared her throat and explained how Charlie's long-term memory was good, even as he still had some difficulty with short-term memory. "His short-term memory has improved significantly since the non-prescribed fentanyl, oxycodone, and clonazepam have cleared his system. Those were the drugs that sedated him during my first visit to the point that he lost consciousness."

"Miss Larson, please go to your written report and let us know when you finally were able to do your assessment." Sumpter opened his copy of her report.

Elle turned to the judge. "On November 11, during my third visit to see him, and then on November 14, during his rehospitalization."

"Please summarize your evaluation and review of available records," Sumpter said.

She started with Charlie's major functional limitations: decreased vision, decreased hearing, and mild cognitive impairment. She went on to describe his medical diagnoses, including anemia, hypertension, macular degeneration, and mild dementia due to multi-infarct dementia, also called vascular dementia.

"How did you specifically evaluate Mr. Blackwell's cognitive functioning?"

Elle talked about the different cognitive screening instruments she used, and then she compared them to the tests conducted by the neurologist and neuropsychologist. In her mind it was her cognitive screening and subsequent testing by Dr. Norris and Dr. Singleton that told the real story.

"Can you tell us what the tests revealed?"

She talked about the various scores, what the testing meant, and how that translated into Charlie's functioning. "He still experiences some difficulty with short-term memory recall and visuospatial ability, yet he's able to register current information, which means he knows what's happening to him as it happens. He has good attention and calculation skills as well as good language skills."

"Are there any limitations to the screening instruments you used?" Sumpter asked.

"Yes," she said and nodded. "The Folstein, one of the screening tools I used, helps to stage the level of dementia, but it doesn't test abstract thinking skills, such as the executive function skills of insight and judgment. That's why the neuropsychologist further evaluated Charlie."

Sumpter picked up Dr. Singleton's report and looked at it, his eyes widening. "There's a lot of medical terminology here. Can you explain to the court what you mean by 'executive functioning'?"

She knew what Dr. Norris would have said if he were still alive. *Start there.* "Executive function involves planning functions. It's Mr. Blackwell's ability to take past and current information and plan for the future." She thought hard. Executive function was difficult to understand, so she decided to explain it in a way that made sense to her. "Executive function is like the air traffic controller of the brain. A pilot needs air traffic control to guide his plane down the runway. Our brains rely on executive function the way a pilot relies on air traffic control. For example, Charlie Blackwell knows he needs services, like help with his medications, but he also needs help coordinating those services."

"And how crucial are these skills in his overall cognitive functioning?"

"They keep Mr. Blackwell from making poor decisions with regard to personal care and health care, as well as financial and legal matters."

Sumpter continued his questions. "Can impairment of these skills increase his risk of making serious mistakes or even being exploited by others?"

She took a moment to think. "Yes. It's my professional opinion, based on the neuropsychologist's testing, that Mr. Blackwell is at risk for undue influence and financial exploitation."

"And what was Dr. Singleton's conclusion?"

"It was her professional opinion—"

"Objection, Your Honor," Kilpatrick interjected. "Miss Larson is not qualified to give us the doctor's opinion."

"Overruled, Mr. Kilpatrick. Miss Larson can give her opinion as an expert," Judge Kincaid said.

Kilpatrick rolled his eyes.

"You have the neuropsychologist's report in front of you. I have no further questions," Sumpter said to Judge Kincaid and for everyone to hear.

"Mr. Kilpatrick, would you like to cross-examine this witness?"

"Yes, Your Honor." Kilpatrick's prominent jawline was framed by tobacco-colored hair, pushed back behind his ears. He tightened the knot of his tie as if he were going in for the kill.

Elle's hands shook and her legs trembled again. This guy probably came out of the birth canal with his fangs bared and claws poised. She had heard about his nasty divorce cases and knew he had a reputation for being contentious. She also knew he had little experience with guardianship, but that didn't make her feel any more comfortable. He knew how the law worked, and he seemed quite at home.

Sitting at the courtroom table, Elle imagined the room as an ice rink and Kilpatrick as her partner rather than her adversary. Skating was about going for it … reaching. Like a team of dancers leading each other around the ice: push, pull, transition, turn. She held her breath for his first question.

"Miss Larson, do you understand that you are under oath?" Kilpatrick asked, again leaning forward, his eyes like lasers burning a hole into her brain.

She looked at his nose, avoiding his stare, and thought of an old blues song her dad used to sing, "Sweet Home Chicago." It calmed her a little.

"Miss Larson, do you understand what I've said to you?"

"I do," she said and straightened her posture.

He asked about her age, how long she had been in Charlotte, and when she had started her company. She told him she was twenty-nine, thinking she was getting older by the minute. She had been in Charlotte for five years and set up her company that same year, in 1991. Yes, she had testified in guardianship hearings before, but this was her first contested case.

"You testified regarding the mental capacity of the client?"

"Yes, sir," she said and gave him a brief list of target areas she evaluated. "Cognitive, emotional, social, and physical functioning."

"Okay."

"Home environment and family dynamics," she added. Where was he leading her? Sumpter had already asked her these questions.

"Isn't it true, Miss Larson, that you're not a doctor?" he asked with a look of amusement.

"I'm a nurse practitioner with a master's degree." She clasped her hands under the table.

"Just answer the question, yes or no. Are you a doctor?"

"No," she said. *Remember, answer only the freakin' question.*

"Isn't this just your lay opinion, Miss Larson?"

Before Elle could answer, Sumpter interrupted.

"Objection, Your Honor. She has been asked to give her professional opinion. She has testified as an expert witness in guardianship hearings in the past. She does these kinds of assessments every day in her job."

Judge Kincaid looked from Sumpter to Kilpatrick, her keen expression changing from thoughtful to stern.

"Mr. Kilpatrick, ask your questions. If Miss Larson can answer them, she will."

"Miss Larson, I believe you stated that you have a degree from the University of Illinois. Isn't it true you're not licensed in the state of North Carolina?"

"Yes, I am," Elle blurted out as Sumpter objected.

"Her license is a matter of public record," Sumpter said. "The court can take judicial notice—this has already been provided by her résumé."

"There's no basis for your questions," Judge Kincaid said, looking displeased at Kilpatrick. "Counsellor, get to your point. We don't have all day."

Elle was impressed by the judge's confidence. She knew Elaine Kincaid had ethical rules she had to go by. She also had the power of the court behind her.

"According to this report, Alzheimer's disease alone accounts for about seventy percent of all dementias," Kilpatrick said, reading from a piece of paper.

"Objection, Your Honor," Sumpter said, still maintaining his calm composure. "Kilpatrick is not the witness. He's testifying here. Is there a question?"

Kilpatrick then held up another page. "Mr. Blackwell's personal physician is Dr. Woodham." He presented Elle with Dr. Woodham's note from his most recent visit. "Dr. Woodham diagnosed Mr. Blackwell with Alzheimer's disease, didn't he?"

"Yes" Elle said. She thought about Dr. Woodham and reminded herself not to say anything that would get her in trouble.

"Yet, your report fails to include this diagnosis. How can you believe with absolute certainty that he does not have Alzheimer's disease?"

"The tests that were done—the evaluations by Dr. Norris and Dr. Singleton, who are experts in this field—indicated that Dr. Woodham misdiagnosed Mr. Blackwell."

Kilpatrick held up the petition and glared at Elle. His eyes darkened. The strong natural arch of his thick eyebrows gave him a sinister look. She imagined stepping onto the ice and pushing through her leg tremors, trying to figure out how they would move together. *I have my space; he has his.* Sharing, but maintaining the tension of the circle.

Kilpatrick smiled a Cheshire cat smile.

"This petition is a legal document. Do you understand what that means?" he asked, holding up the paperwork.

Elle pieced together the documents in her mind: the petition, the medical letter from Dr. Woodham, and his medical notes from his October visit with Susan. They were the foundation for what? A house of cards? She looked at her copy of the petition again and sighed loudly. "I understand it's a legal document. But if a clinical evaluation was not done and the information provided to the physician was false—"

"What are you saying, Miss Larson?"

*Oh my God.* Sumpter hadn't told him? Finally, she responded, "I'm saying Dr. Woodham's notes reflect only what Susan reported. And that makes the petition inaccurate. The narrative is word for word what Susan reported in his medical note."

"Susan is his wife. She lives with him," Kilpatrick said. "You don't—you conducted an isolated evaluation. I'll ask you one more time, Miss Larson. What are you saying?"

Elle looked at Charlie and wanted to hug him. He deserved better than this. She turned and glared at Kilpatrick. "I'm saying this petition is fiction. It's not true."

There was a pause as Kilpatrick looked at his notes. The silence seemed forever. She shot a pleading look at Sumpter. He smiled and nodded his head, as if to say she needed to keep answering his questions. Her whole body was trembling now, like a vibrating cell phone. Kilpatrick was setting her up with leading questions, and the arrogant tone of his voice was wearing her down.

"Miss Larson, there was an incident where you found fentanyl patches on Charlie Blackwell. Is that correct?"

"Yes, that's correct."

"And those patches were turned over to the police for fingerprint analysis. Is that correct?"

"Yes, sir." Her first crime scene was still vivid in her mind.

A flash of anger crossed Kilpatrick's face. "We were notified of the analysis this morning: The only fingerprints found on the fentanyl patches were your own. Did you place those patches on Charlie Blackwell, then take them off, making it seem like you came to his rescue so you could be the hero in the courtroom today?"

"Objection, Your Honor," Sumpter said and cleared his throat. "He is badgering the witness. She is not on trial here."

"Enough! Enough, Mr. Kilpatrick!" Judge Kincaid took off her glasses, rubbed her eyes, and shot him an irritated look.

Kilpatrick's face was red.

Elle glanced at Sumpter gratefully.

"Thank you for your testimony, Miss Larson. I have only one more question. If it's determined at the end of this hearing that Mr. Blackwell needs a guardian, would you support Susan Blackwell in that role as guardian of the person? She is, after all, his current wife."

Elle looked at Kilpatrick, who again gave her a Cheshire smile. Her legs bounced up and down. Careful, there was still time for him to trip her up. He would love nothing better than to disqualify her as an expert—if her testimony crossed over the line. *Think. Think.* Sumpter had reminded her that this was a guardianship hearing and other issues would need to be saved for another day. She took a deep breath.

"Can you repeat the question?"

"Miss Larson, do you need to have your hearing checked?" Kilpatrick asked.

"No, sir, I'm just surprised that you're asking me—"

Sumpter intervened. "Miss Larson, please answer the question as best as you can."

Elle nodded at Sumpter and cleared her throat. "I think it would be crazy to appoint Susan." She pointed to the woman in question. "She's exploiting him."

"Objection, Your Honor," Kilpatrick said in his deep baritone, pounding both fists on the table. "I move to strike. This information is prejudicial."

"Your Honor, Miss Larson's opinion is based on objective facts," Sumpter said, looking first at Kincaid and then at Elle with a matter-of-fact look on his face.

"Overruled," Judge Kincaid said. "Mr. Kilpatrick, you asked for her opinion ... the witness's opinion is relevant. Please proceed, Miss Larson."

Elle thought for a minute, trying to sort out the courtroom theatrics. Kilpatrick needed to object because her testimony could hurt his client. That's what prejudicial meant, right? Fair enough, but the judge wanted her to continue; she also wanted no-nonsense control of her courtroom.

Elle had the strongest urge to blurt out that Dr. Woodham hadn't seen Charlie. No, it was time to finish this—save the October 20 visit for Dr. Woodham to explain during his own testimony. "It is my opinion, Your Honor, that Susan Blackwell has been setting up Mr. Blackwell's weekly med box with sedating drugs that have been given to him on a daily basis without a physician's order—until we intervened."

"I see no mention of this information in your report, Miss Larson," Kilpatrick said.

"I was not asked to address that in my written report. I have shared the information with Mr. Blackwell's attorney," Elle said.

She looked over at Charlie. He had a puzzled look on his face. She wished she had told him more about what she had discovered since the weekend.

"And why should we believe you, Miss Larson?" Kilpatrick blurted. "You never met—"

"No, I never had your permission to meet with her." Elle shivered all over. "I met her once—"

"Just answer the questions, Miss Larson!"

She looked up at Kilpatrick. He glared at her, only to be interrupted by the judge.

"Let me remind everyone, once again, this is not family court."

"Answer the question, Miss Larson," Kilpatrick repeated through clenched teeth.

Suddenly, Elle lost it. Without hesitation she blurted out, "Susan substituted Charlie Blackwell's blood pressure medicine with sedating drugs and drugged him for the better part of a year. She took her scheme further by finding a way to marry Charlie without his consent. The wedding was premeditated. Now she's rich. Cha-ching! She's, like, stealing his life! Takes his money, buys herself new clothes, a new car ... and buys the best attorney. Why? So she can take his rights away. She's not only exploiting Charlie Blackwell, she's abusing the court system on his nickel." She gasped for air. She didn't care if Susan was looking at her. She glared at Kilpatrick. He didn't interrupt her ... then she realized why. She turned to Sumpter and thought she saw a look of disappointment. He made no comment.

"Thank you, Miss Larson," Judge Kincaid said, looking thoughtful. "Before you leave, I have one more question. If it's determined that Mr. Blackwell needs a guardian, who would you recommend?"

*Oh my God.* She felt the gravity of her answer. Someone making decisions for Charlie in the final years of his life. Elle thought about the times when family members were hiding things or were unwilling to talk to her. Robbie and Melinda had been difficult to work with despite her best efforts, despite Charlie's best efforts. Of the two, only Melinda seemed to recognize that Elle even played a role here. It was all very sad, but then the fracture between them started long ago.

"Your Honor, Robbie's been unwilling to talk to me, and Melinda has a problem with alcohol and has been estranged from her father in the past." She paused, trying to reclaim her composure. "I recommend Amy Blackwell as guardian of the person and a reputable attorney as guardian of his estate, to protect Charlie from any future financial exploitation."

"Thank you, Miss Larson," the judge said, her expression changing from thoughtful to surprised. "We will take your recommendations under consideration. I think we need to take a break now. I would ask those of you who are staying to be back here in fifteen minutes."

Elle stacked her folders and slipped them into her briefcase. She said goodbye to Charlie and Sumpter, then stood up and fought back tears as she made her way out. She'd blown it. This was not going to end well, and Sumpter would never want to work with her again. Five years of running her small business—up in smoke. Not to mention the money she had spent to start it. Money that she didn't have.

She walked out of the courtroom, her head down, exhausted. At least it was over. The armed bailiff, Clay Guthrie, waited for her outside the doorway. His eyes looked at her sadly.

"Miss Larson, please allow me to escort you out," he said in a soft and kind voice. He walked with Elle through the lobby and out of the courthouse.

Once outside, she stopped trembling and glanced at his thinning hair, his kind face, and double chin hiding the tight neck of his uniform. His short legs and full torso made him look top heavy when he walked.

"Can I walk you to your car?" he asked.

"That's kind of you to offer, but I'm okay," she said, knowing that he only had minutes before getting back to the courtroom. "I guess I blew that one."

"I wanted to thank you for your testimony today but also tell you something else," he said while continuing to walk with her across the street, to the parking deck.

She stopped and faced him. She opened her mouth but couldn't speak.

His eyes stared into hers as if to say he, too, had seen much over the years. He shook his head, an urgent expression on his face, and smiled sadly. "I wanted you to know that Charlie's first wife, Carol, was my sister." He looked around to make sure no one was listening. "And she did *not* commit suicide."

# Chapter 22

David sipped his cup of Earl Grey and sat back, using the end of his pen to open up the mail piled high on his desk. It had been a busy Monday morning, and he was waiting for Elle and her new assistant; he promised to give them a quick tour of his unit over the lunch hour.

He had worked all weekend: a shooting on North Tryon, a couple of robberies and aggravated assaults, but the kicker was the dead body found at home—suspected overdose. He was taking pictures at one crime scene when he got the call and had to leave his team to collect evidence on the other. He estimated the man's body had been decomposing for days. The image and smell—rotting meat and eggs—had tormented him all through the night. Yet here he was, feeling sleep deprived with his list of cases growing, the ones he'd been working on and the new ones coming in the door. He spent the morning processing evidence from the weekend with no time to process seeing that dead body.

He opened an envelope from the lab and unfolded the report. Results for Mary Beth Abbott, Age: 23, Gender: Female. He read through to the bottom of the page. Normal saline. *Damn it*. Someone had tampered with the insulin bottles, confirming Elle's suspicions.

He heard Elle's voice and her footsteps, then she was in his doorway, looking subdued. He swallowed, refolded the report, and tucked it into his desk drawer.

"For once, I'm early," she said, without her usual cheerfulness. Her normally broad shoulders slumped forward. She introduced Grady, who shook his hand.

*Hmmm ... cute guy. Young, but surprisingly good-looking—a twink and skinny as a rail.* "Come in," he said and motioned them to have a seat.

Grady placed a dozen Krispy Kreme glazed donuts on top of his desk, and they pulled up two metal chairs and sat down.

"Cops like doughnuts, right?" Grady asked.

"Thanks. They do, but I'm not a cop," he said, taking a doughnut for later. "But I'll make sure they get these."

"David's a crime scene investigator," Elle said.

"C'mon, I've got a bit of stuff to show y'all." David walked them out to the vehicle bay just outside his office where several smaller—and two huge—white vans were parked. "This here is where we process all murder or robbery vehicles."

"Da bomb," Grady said, his face lit up like a Christmas tree.

"Da bomb," David repeated and walked up to the largest white van.

"And this ... this is our mobile crime scene lab." He had washed the van this morning—his pride and joy.

"Not exactly *Law and Order*," Grady said.

"Well, we've upgraded to Chevy vans," David said and winked at Elle. "This ain't like what you see on TV." He opened the side door and extended his hand.

"How's it different?" Grady asked after they stepped inside.

"Like, we don't solve crimes in ten minutes, and crime scene investigators don't carry guns or arrest people."

"How fast can you drive this—"

David interrupted before Grady finished his question. "We don't run emergency traffic, either. We never, ever, run blue lights unless there's a visibility problem."

"Oh," Grady said, disappointment evident on his face.

"What we do is collect evidence."

"That's all?" Grady asked.

David opened up the cabinets and, standing in front of the shelves, pulled out evidence placards to mark scenes, stickers with letters to mark blood on the wall and holes in the door, evidence envelopes, and fingerprint tape. He showed them how to use the metal detector and camera tripod for nighttime photography. He reached for the dental stone used for casting footprints, mixed it to a consistency of pancake batter, and poured it into a plastic bag. Then he gently poured it into a footprint that Grady had made in the dirt outside the van and turned it into a shoeprint.

David looked up. Elle's eyes were watching him work, but she seemed distracted, and she hadn't said a word.

Grady whistled as he examined the cast. "It's perfect!"

Then David showed them his goodies for buried bodies.

"Shovels and trowels—looks like garden tools," Grady said.

David entertained them with stories from his training at the body farm in Tennessee where he had learned to study decomposition rates and recognize different bodies by their bones. By twelve thirty, the tour was over.

"Hey, David, can I borrow a pen?" Elle asked, after they returned to his office.

He handed her a pen that was lying on his desk. "I think this was found at a crime scene, but I cleaned it," he said with a wink.

Grady looked at the pen in Elle's hand. "Can I have it when you're done?"

"Sorry, we've got to go," Elle said, tossing the pen to Grady after writing herself a note. "Even though I cleared my schedule to see you, I've got to be back in court by one thirty. Sumpter let me know this morning. He's insisting that I hear Dr. Woodham's testimony."

"Thanks, David," Grady said, examining the pen. "This has been wicked."

"Grady, I need to ask you to do one more thing," Elle said. "You know those driver's license photos that you blew up and copied? Could you run them to Rock Hill this afternoon and show them to the manager, Naomi, at McCrory's Five and Dine?"

Grady looked surprised that he had been asked to help. "Good to go. I'll take the afternoon off!"

"It's a big deal. I was supposed to meet Naomi this afternoon. See if she recognizes one of the caregivers."

"Far out." His eyes twinkled with excitement.

"Naomi saw someone with Susan Blackwell, and we need to know who."

As they stood up to leave, David wished Grady good luck and gently nudged Elle. "Can we talk privately for a second?"

"Sure," she said, searching his face. She handed Grady her keys. "I'll meet you at the car."

"Yes, ma'am." Grady shook David's hand. "I think I'd like to do what you do."

David raised an eyebrow and smiled. All of the violence and death—it took a special person to do this job and to separate work from home, to walk out the door at night and leave it all behind. And those who couldn't did not last long, like his new evidence tech, Rachel Harper: gone in a week.

After Grady left, he handed Elle the report from his desk and watched her eyes grow larger as she read down the page. "Detective Slater will be following up on this," he said.

"Jeez, David. Normal saline instead of insulin, no wonder Mary Beth died."

"Your theory is plausible, but ..." He closed the door and looked at her exhausted face. "Are you okay?"

"I lost it during the cross-examination. I was expected to give unemotional responses ... just the facts." She shook her head. "God, I'm scared for Charlie. What if they appoint a guardian?"

"What's the damn deal with this guardianship? We have two unsolved murders," he said slowly, his frustration with her mounting. She didn't even recognize the danger she was in.

"And two attempts on Charlie's life—"

"Screw the guardianship." He shot her a sharp look. "We need to find out who murdered Mary Beth and Dr. Norris before anyone else is killed!"

"Isn't that the police department's job?" she asked, her voice cracking. "You seem behind on that investigation. It could take you weeks ... months, right?"

He nodded. "I'm just saying, let's keep a sense of perspective here."

"Well, if Charlie's found incompetent, the very person who's trying to kill him could be appointed his guardian ..."

He saw her eyes well up. "When is that decided?"

"This afternoon. I mean, c'mon, man. None of this is going to bring Mary Beth or Dr. Norris back. But there's still justice for Charlie. Why do you think I feel so responsible?" She blew out a breath and raised her hand as if to say she was one step beyond what she could handle. "Thanks again for showing Grady around."

"I'll talk to you later," he said as she walked away. She was overwhelmed. David understood. He was surprised by his anger, though. They both saw death more than most people their age. Tonight he'd call her, before she came to dinner, and find out what happened. He picked up the box of Krispy Kremes and headed to the next floor to look for Kate. A new murder investigation to open ... they hadn't put additional manpower into it, but they would now.

# Chapter 23

Elle entered the courtroom at half past one as Dr. Woodham was being sworn in. Judge Kincaid was sitting at the front table, eyes glued on the doctor. Elle looked around the room. Amy Blackwell and Georgia Harris were gone. Robbie and Melinda were now sitting side by side, brother and sister, with Charlie and Sumpter. *That's a first.*

Charlie turned and waved. He looked happy to see her, and she quickly waved back. Across from them, Susan sat close to Doug Kilpatrick and whispered something in his ear. Dr. Woodham sat on the other side of Susan, forming a threesome in the standoff across the table. Elle walked over and slid into an empty chair at the back of the room next to Peggy, where she had a clear view of Dr. Woodham on the right.

The doctor was middle-aged and short with excess visceral fat around his stomach, which put him a good six inches away from the table. His thin and stringy hair hung down to his shoulders—an unhealthy and unprofessional look, even in a lab coat. She felt better already.

Dr. Woodham held his head proudly as Doug Kilpatrick began questioning him. He cleared his throat and refilled his glass of water. Yes, he was a Charlotte family practice physician. He'd practiced for over twenty years and had worked alongside his father until his father died, two years ago. Now, as a solo practitioner, he'd been Charlie Blackwell's physician for the past six weeks, taking over after Dr. Parker retired.

"Can you please tell the court about Mr. Blackwell's Alzheimer's disease?" Kilpatrick asked Dr. Woodham.

After another sip from his glass, Dr. Woodham described the gradual decline with Alzheimer's and how Charlie filled in the blanks of what he couldn't remember, making Susan's observations more important in getting at the truth.

Elle started watching Susan, who smiled at Dr. Woodham as though his attention filled her up. She smiled at Kilpatrick and gave him flirty looks whenever he looked her way. She was holding court, radiating in the energy from both of the men who sat beside her.

"And how would you describe your observations of Charlie Blackwell during your visits?" Kilpatrick asked.

Dr. Woodham explained how Susan had brought Charlie in for the first time on October 2. No, he had not seen him act inappropriately. He had not noticed any aggression toward him that later was reported by Susan during the October 20 visit. It was because of this decline from October 2 to 20 that he was concerned about Charlie taking his medication, concerned about his safety and the safety of his wife.

"In your opinion then, does Mr. Blackwell lack the capacity to manage his own affairs?"

"Yes, he lacks that capacity," Dr. Woodham said, coughing.

Elle looked over at Peggy and shook her head. Kilpatrick clearly wanted to paint Dr. Woodham in the best light. *Good luck with that.* She had never seen a doctor who looked so sick and out of shape, as though his eating, drinking, and smoking habits had caught up with him.

There was a moment of confusion when the courtroom door opened. Sumpter's wife, Julie, entered and, spotting Sumpter, made a beeline for his table. Handing him a sheet of paper, she whispered something in his ear that Elle couldn't hear, then turned and walked out. Elle glanced at Sumpter, who was smiling patiently and waiting.

The questioning took on a different tone when Sumpter began his cross-examination. He told the court he wanted to ask about the medical letter.

With a copy of his letter and notes in front of him, Dr. Woodham answered, "Yes, I dictated the letter and signed it. Can't you see that's my letterhead? I'm the only physician listed."

"And how long did it take for you to dictate that letter?"

Dr. Woodham coughed again and hesitated before responding, then admitted that the letter had taken him only a few minutes to dictate. He had been in a hurry because of other patients waiting to be seen.

Sumpter picked up his copy of the letter and appeared to read it. He looked up at Dr. Woodham. "So this is your conclusion?" he asked.

"Yes," Dr. Woodham said, chest puffed out and arms crossed.

"On what did you base this conclusion?"

Dr. Woodham looked at his notes, then scowled at Sumpter. "His wife said he was combative. I can't move into their house to see what's going on. I accepted what Susan said."

"Did you see the patient on October 20?"

"I did not," Dr. Woodham said and looked at Judge Kincaid, rolling his eyes. She locked into his gaze but said nothing.

Elle squirmed in her seat and leaned over to Peggy. She saw fear in Peggy's eyes.

"So you gave Charlie Blackwell a diagnosis of Alzheimer's disease without seeing him?" Sumpter asked, his voice encouraging and without judgment.

"Yes, that's right."

Elle closed her eyes and took a deep breath. It was too painful to watch even though Sumpter in action was always a learning experience for her. He continued in his neutral voice.

"Is it standard practice to base your diagnosis totally on what you are told rather than to independently evaluate the patient?"

At this point, Dr. Woodham became defensive, his voice brittle with anger. "Susan was hysterical when she met with me. She was not happy until I gave her a prescription for oxycodone and clonazepam."

"So, the first time you saw Mr. Blackwell, he was fine. Yet less than twenty days later, without seeing him, you reached the conclusion that he had Alzheimer's disease and needed guardianship. Is that correct, Dr. Woodham?" Sumpter asked.

For the first time, Elle heard a hint of judgment in Sumpter's voice.

Dr. Woodham looked down and continued talking, his voice struggling for control. "Susan was having difficulty moving into the house because Charlie didn't recognize her anymore, didn't want her living there. She didn't feel safe. She asked me to place Charlie in a dementia unit, but I refused."

Elle opened her eyes and looked at Charlie, who was glowering at the doctor.

Sumpter smiled politely. "Dr. Woodham, have you ever assisted in a guardianship or a guardianship hearing before?"

"No."

"Any involuntary commitments?" Sumpter asked.

"Yes, I've done three or four involuntary commitments, when the patient was confused and combative," he said, defending himself.

"Without examining them?" Sumpter wrinkled his forehead.

"Objection, Your Honor," Kilpatrick said.

"Overruled," Kincaid said. "Go on, Dr. Woodham."

"I'm a busy physician. I can't be expected to remember every patient."

"Dr. Woodham, please try to remember and answer the question," Judge Kincaid said.

"Like I said, I've had to accept what is true based on what the family tells me."

"I have one more question, Dr. Woodham. Do you routinely prescribe opioids to your patients without seeing them?"

Kilpatrick slammed his fist on the table. "Objection, Your Honor. This question is not relevant to this case!" He glared at Sumpter.

"Your Honor, the witness has a self-serving interest in prescribing narcotics with a high risk of addiction. This question goes to his integrity, his character, and his willingness to be truthful," Sumpter said.

"Overruled," Judge Kincaid said. "No more drama, Mr. Kilpatrick!"

Elle glanced at Kilpatrick, who said nothing more. He looked deflated for the first time since the hearing began.

"Is that a yes or a no?" Sumpter asked Dr. Woodham.

"Yes, I suppose so," Dr. Woodham said, sagging in his chair.

"Well, the police are searching your office right now. I just got word that they're turning evidence over to the FBI."

Elle was glad she came back.

Dr. Woodham gasped for air, like an out-of-shape wrestler.

"No further questions," Sumpter said, smiling at the judge.

Elle glanced from Sumpter to Judge Kincaid, who was holding her head in both hands. Her pale skin looked white, as though she'd seen a ghost. Or were her worst thoughts being confirmed? Elle stood quietly, whispered goodbye to Peggy, and stepped out of the courtroom without glancing at anyone. Woodham had been handing out pain medication like it was candy and locking up patients in psych wards without seeing them, not to mention giving them diagnoses that would follow them wherever they went. *And he's okay with that?* She had heard enough.

It was midafternoon when the judge announced a thirty-minute break in the courtroom. Susan stood up and watched as everyone else left, leaving her alone with Doug Kilpatrick as he finished writing his notes. She felt blessed that he was helping her get Charlie declared incompetent. He cared about her. "You best know, I adore watching you in the courtroom."

He gave her a puzzled look. "I'm sorry. I just need to finish things up here."

"I understand. I'm gonna go now."

"Just be back before the end of our break," he said and went back to writing.

She pulled on her fur coat, caressing it lovingly, and walked behind the crowd, heading for the front doors. She had known she could fool Doug Kilpatrick. After all, she had been working her magic since her father had abused her mother as far back as she could remember. She was twelve when she figured out how to make him forget his anger.

Having control made her feel important, like she was part of the team—the medical team, the legal team, the Charlie-and-Susan team. After all, she had helped Charlie one night thirty-six years ago. He may have walked away from her then, but now they were together, and he was making her the kind of lady she always dreamed of playing. *Yes, I will be Lady Blackwell for the rest of my days, even if I need to live a parallel life.*

Susan walked out of the courthouse on Fourth and McDowell and moved into the crowd. She looked at her new watch. It felt good to fight for Charlie. In less than two hours from now she would be his official guardian.

Across from the courthouse, Susan sat in her new BMW on the second floor of the concrete parking deck. It took her two minutes to cross the street from the courthouse doors, walk up the stairs, then walk to her car. She timed it. While she waited, she picked up her shoulder bag from the floor of her car. She opened the leather flap. The gun was heavy, making the bag heavy too.

The floor rumbled as cars drove by. She refocused her thoughts. *Maybe two hundred steps from here to the courthouse.* All she needed was for her paid accomplice to show up and carry her bag to the double doors.

Susan closed the flap over her bag and took a deep breath. She'd been looking forward to this day. Dreaming about being a legal guardian. She placed the bag back on the floor of the passenger seat and picked up her phone. "Hey, Susan here. I'm leaving my car unlocked. You need to go to my car and pick up my bag. Keep the top flap closed and drape the leather strap across your chest." She didn't say that the top flap concealed the gun, or that it was loaded and ready. "Before Charlie and his attorney exit security, you will push through the double doors, stand inside against the wall, and wait for me."

Susan sighed. "Don't worry, you'll get your money when this is over. All you need to do is hand me my bag and leave immediately. No one will ever see you in the crowd." She swung her legs out of the car. "It's time for me to go." Slowly, she stood up and closed the door. "This is our backup plan, so don't leave your car unless you get my call."

With another sigh, she pulled her fur coat tightly around her and walked back to the courthouse.

# Chapter 24

A block away from the courthouse, Elle's cell phone rang. She pulled over and placed her car in park. It took her a few seconds to get to her phone. "So, what's the verdict?"

"The judge ruled in favor of guardianship," Sumpter said, sounding dead tired.

The blood drained from Elle's face. Guardianship was supposed to be a last resort. Sumpter always sought a less restrictive alternative to guardianship. *This is so unfair.*

"Elle, are you there?" Sumpter asked.

"We lost. Charlie didn't deserve this." She thought of all that Charlie had lost already, all that he'd been through.

"Hold on," Sumpter said calmly.

"He's stuck with Susan." How could she face Charlie?

"Elle, this means that Charlie was mentally incapacitated at the time of his divorce."

She paused. "Does that mean he was never legally married to Susan?"

"We'll need future court hearings to make those decisions."

"But my report—"

"Your report was a roadmap for the judge's decision," he said strongly. "In light of the exploitation and his problems with executive function."

"Oh my God," Elle said, still convinced that the court had been unable to protect Charlie. All he needed was a power of attorney if the family had been willing to support each other.

"Robbie Blackwell will be guardian of the person," Sumpter said. "And having a lawyer as guardian of the estate will prevent Charlie from being exploited again."

Elle just nodded in her car, realizing Charlie was probably sitting there, right next to Sumpter.

"The other good news is that the judge has requested that you continue to work with Charlie in the role of care manager, setting up his medications, taking him to doctor appointments, and reporting back to Robbie."

"What does Doug Kilpatrick think about all this?" she asked, taking her car out of park.

"He filed the petition and hates losing, but he's finally realized that Susan was lying to him from the beginning."

Elle's adrenaline was pumping. "I've been told that Charlie's first wife was murdered," she said in a low voice. "I want to talk to you about this, but not while you're there with Charlie."

"I'll call you later," Sumpter said. "But first Charlie and I are gonna get out of here. Can you pick him up at the front entrance, say, in ten minutes? Robbie and Peggy will be staying with Charlie tonight. Robbie's still up in the courtroom talking to Melinda."

"I'll be there in five," Elle said. She would need to reschedule a client appointment she had made for later that day.

It had been a long day, and when the hearing was over, Susan kept thinking about the judge's decision. Judge Kincaid left her with no choice. As she put on her sable fur, she thought back on the past two years. A physician had told her she had borderline personality disorder. She saw him in the emergency department and requested an antidepressant. He referred her to her own primary care physician, Dr. Woodham, who told her she had anxiety. He gave her antianxiety medication and told her that different doctors give people with mental illnesses different diagnoses all the time. To get it right, he relied on the patient's history, and that's when she first thought of her plan.

She studied Alzheimer's disease for weeks and made another appointment to see Dr. Woodham. When she did see him, he gave her whatever prescriptions she wanted. He believed her, but he had failed her today. All three men whom she relied on—her physician, her lawyer, and her husband—had been in the courtroom with her and failed her. The promise of guardianship had been broken.

Susan fingered the inside of her jacket pocket for her pill bottle, flipped off the cap with her thumb, and took the last three Valium, working them under her tongue. She grimaced. The taste was bitter, but she needed a quick fix. In a few minutes she would feel a little bit drunk, more relaxed.

Dark thoughts about Elle popped up in her head. Elle cheated her out of Charlie's guardianship—power that was rightfully hers. Without it, she couldn't protect Charlie. And she damn well wasn't going to give up her control. If her dream were to end, *she* would say when it was over, not some judge ... or attorney ... or expert witness. No way.

Susan looked over her shoulder and saw that Peggy was still standing in the doorway, watching her. Robbie and Melinda were talking to each other in the hallway. Charlie and his attorney were also standing with them, getting ready to leave. She looked at her watch: 4:40 p.m.

Susan took quick steps in her heels, down two flights of stairs and through the atrium with its massive chandelier glittering like shiny coins in the light. If only she could dance with Charlie under this light and hold him close to her one more time. She imagined dancing in a shimmering peach gown, her hair swept up in curls with an audience applauding in admiration. Applauding because of how important and beautiful she was ... how much more she loved Charlie than anyone else. They would see that Charlie could not live without her. And she was not going to let anyone undo their marriage. But now she couldn't tell Charlie what she had to do. It was strange. Her heart was pounding, but she wasn't afraid. Like Scarlett O'Hara, she wouldn't worry ... time would run out soon enough.

Elle pushed her way inside the courthouse entrance as jurors, lawyers, and county employees squeezed their way out of the bronze double doors for the day. She had parked in the Fourth Street parking deck. There was no need to go back through security, as she was meeting Sumpter and Charlie right here. She spotted Geena Louise, who managed to find a place against the entrance wall, avoiding the crush of the crowd. Geena Louise looked away as she was jostled by a woman trying to leave the building.

"What are you doing here?" Elle asked, pressing against the crowd and trying to avoid a lady lighting up a cigarette.

Geena Louise looked up. Her eyes widened. "Susan left her bag and all the client schedules."

"Elle!"

Elle turned her head when she heard her name, and she waved at Sumpter. He and Charlie headed toward her, just steps from exiting security. The top of Charlie's balding head bobbed above the crowd. From her peripheral vision, she saw Robbie ride out of the open elevator, followed by Peggy and Melinda. A vibration grabbed Elle's attention, and she answered her phone.

"Oh man, Elle, the meeting went like this: I spread out all five pictures on the counter, and the waitress, Naomi, watched me."

"Hey, Grady, can I call you back? I'm at the courthouse—"

"Wait, wait! Naomi identified the picture—the person who's been meeting with Susan."

"What?"

"Jesus, Elle, it was Geena Louise."

"Geena Louise?" she said, pressing a hand over her ear to block out the background voices.

"Yeah, Geena Louise. This is freakin' awesome—"

"Grady, oh my God!" So that's how Susan pulled off the wedding, with Geena Louise doing her bidding from inside Charlie's home.

Elle turned as Susan grabbed the black bag from Geena Louise's shoulder. The bailiff, Clay Guthrie, shouted something she couldn't understand and pointed to the bag Susan dropped on the floor. Elle started shaking. *Susan is making one last stand.*

In slow motion, Susan's gaze turned blank as she stared at Charlie. She stepped forward and raised the gun. "We're in this forever, Charlie. You and me." She steadied her hand. "There's no other way."

"Susan, don't do it!" Elle bent her legs and sprang, pushing Susan violently into the wall.

Susan's arm smacked back, and she pulled away. "If I'm going to die, I'll die as Lady Blackwell!" Susan yelled, still holding the gun.

"Drop the gun!" Clay Guthrie crouched down, his own gun raised as he advanced a couple of steps.

"Don't fuck with me," Susan said and aimed her gun at him.

Elle charged again and grabbed a large chunk of Susan's hair with both hands, pulling her head down as hard as she could. Two cracks, like fireworks, rang out—the sound heightened by the small space of the courthouse entrance. Elle cried out after the second shot, a bullet ripping into her left shoulder as she tackled Susan to the floor. Elle went down with a crash, a searing pain in her shoulder, blood soaking the sleeve of her white blouse. Her head hit the marble floor.

People screamed as they fought their way out of the double doors. Charlie reached for Elle's arm and stumbled. She blinked her eyes.

A voice on a radio shouted, "Shots fired, two down."

A security officer reached Susan, but not before another crack sounded. He forced the gun from Susan's hand and cuffed her behind her back.

An acrid smell filled the air as screaming people poured out the doors. Hundreds of footsteps, running, falling—trying to get out. Clay Guthrie was lying on the ground, blood oozing from his abdomen. Elle blinked again and tried to get up, but her arms and legs failed her.

Charlie was now standing, leaning hard against Sumpter's shoulder, who was holding the older man up by his jacket. Charlie looked shell-shocked. "Susan, how could you—?"

"I only wanted to make you happy, just ask your first wife!" Susan growled.

Elle's throat tightened as she struggled against the scorching pain. She stared at Susan's glassy eyes, half-drunk with power. "Go on, Charlie. The paramedics will take care of me," she said.

"I'm not leavin'," Charlie said, reaching for Elle's hand. He stumbled once more to his knees and struggled with his balance.

Elle couldn't raise her arm. "Sumpter, tell the police that Geena Louise is in on this. She brought the gun to Susan."

Sumpter looped his arm through Charlie's and attempted to pull him up.

"No, I'm staying. Peggy, come and help her," Charlie said, still kneeling like an old veteran, refusing to leave the war zone.

Visibly shaken by the scene, tears streaking her mascara, Peggy moved in as Robbie followed close behind in his electric chair, and Melinda brought up the rear. Peggy grabbed on to Charlie's arm. "This is over, Charlie. Let's go home. The paramedics can take it from here."

Elle winced in pain as she tried to sit up. She gazed up at Charlie.

Wide-eyed, Charlie turned to Peggy. "The last time you stooped over and touched me was early that morning ... in my bedroom." He shook his head. "It was you! You put those patches on me."

Robbie stared at Peggy. "What's he talking about?"

Elle winced with pain. *Of course ... the mitered corners on Charlie's bed, the fentanyl patches, the heating pad.* It all made sense as more pieces of the puzzle clicked into place: Peggy had been the invisible force that almost killed Charlie.

Robbie gave Peggy a horrified look. "But why?"

"I did it for you," Peggy blurted out. "He would have died comfortably in his sleep."

"You tried to murder Daddy?" Robbie asked, in disbelief.

"Susan was after your money. The money you were about to inherit."

"That's not true," Robbie said, looking away.

"You couldn't see what she was doing." Peggy sobbed. "We needed that money, Robbie."

Elle lifted her head. The emotional chaos of the moment had cracked the dam of Peggy's defenses. *An excited utterance.* They had survived the god-awful hearing and now this.

The courthouse started to spin. Elle closed her eyes and lowered her head back to the floor as Stevie Nicks's voice sang "Twisted" in the background of her brain. She prayed Susan's bullet was not going to kill her and leave her brother all alone. She fought for her breath. The last voice she heard came from the man with a radio: "Shots fired. Three down: an officer down, the shooter is down!"

# Chapter 25

Geena Louise pushed her way through the crowd, trying to escape. "Stop that woman," Sumpter yelled. "She's involved in this."

An armed officer grabbed her, and her legs buckled as she crashed under his weight. After cuffing her, the officer read Geena Louise her rights and began escorting her to the door. She tried desperately to yank her arm out of his vice grip.

"Wait! I need to speak to you," she yelled out to Sumpter.

"Two minutes," the officer grumbled once Sumpter made his way in front of them.

Geena Louise started to cry, but Sumpter didn't feel sorry for her. "Why in the hell did you bring a gun to the courthouse?"

"It was Susan's gun. I didn't know it was in her bag. You need to understand ... Susan deceived everyone, including me." She wiped her eyes with her hand. "Ain't no one crazier than Susan and Billie. It was a big mistake for Susan to bring him in on this."

"Who's Billie?" Sumpter asked.

She looked up at him, the sleeve of her T-shirt torn from the fall. "Billie Sutton ... Susan's son. Susan didn't want Charlie's neurologist testifying in court, so Billie shot and killed him."

The officer moved closer to her.

"Before you say anymore, Geena Louise, you may want to contact an attorney," Sumpter said.

"I don't need an attorney," she said, gasping for breath. "I have lots to tell ... and I need to get out from under this."

This was great news. Sumpter loosened his tie and tucked it into his pocket. He was exhausted. He was finally giving the police a missing link they could sink their teeth into. He turned to the uniformed officer who hadn't said a word since Geena Louise started talking. Sumpter shook his head. "You can take her away."

Elle sat up in the emergency department of Presbyterian Hospital, her left shoulder bandaged and propped up by pillows and a scalp wound on the back of her head that Josh Geller had just sutured—six stitches, but superficial. He insisted she stay in the bed, but it was the terrible headache and shoulder pain that made her comply. She tried not to think about the afternoon in the courthouse.

Josh washed his hands at the sink, walked over, and pulled the curtain around the hospital gurney to give them some privacy. "You okay?"

"I know I'm lucky." She was still groggy, but ready to go home.

"Sorry I can't give you anything for the pain … not until we rule out a concussion."

"I've had a serious concussion before," she said, feeling the back of her scalp and touching the sutures.

"When was that?"

"During the car crash with my parents." She took a deep breath. The memories were as fixed in her brain as the stitches in her scalp. If only her mom and dad were here. Peter too.

"What were your symptoms?"

"Initially, panic attacks, memory loss, even some dyslexia. They said I had depression too, but I think it was grief."

"Any residual symptoms?"

Elle thought for a moment. "For a long time, even after I felt better, I tired easily. Sometimes the symptoms came back if I was really tired."

"And now?"

"This is different: just the headaches and shoulder pain, no dizziness. I don't feel lightheaded ..." She closed her eyes a moment. "Have you heard anything about the bailiff who was shot?" she asked, changing the subject.

"Clay Guthrie was the first one here from the courthouse." Josh held his finger a comfortable distance away from her eyes.

"So I guess I'm the second."

He nodded. "He's in surgery. We're waiting to hear."

She pictured the bailiff lying on a surgery table, the blood still oozing from his abdomen. "You know, he's a retired detective, and his sister was Charlie's first wife—"

"Elle, I need you to stop talking while I do this. You know the drill. Follow my finger with your eyes only."

She followed his left index finger with her eyes. He would continue these neuro checks as long as she stayed here.

"Now follow my finger in as I move it toward the bridge of your nose."

She followed his finger, trying to keep her eyes open.

"Any problems with your vision?"

"No."

With the back of his left hand, he displaced her left breast upward and moved the diaphragm of his stethoscope into position with the palm of his hand.

"You're left-handed." She looked at his face as he focused on his stethoscope and moved it again and again over her chest. His expression was totally professional.

He nodded. "Shhh ... just relax. I don't want your heart rate to go up."

She continued to watch his face as he listened and counted. She could feel her heart pounding against her chest wall.

"Heart rate's up, not surprising with the pain you're having."

"If this is our first date, I think it's going pretty well." She grimaced and sat forward.

He chuckled and met her glance. "If I screw up here, you'll never give me another chance." He tucked his stethoscope into his lab coat pocket.

"When do I get to go home?"

"Just need to wait on the results of the head CT. Then we need to observe you overnight to rule out a possible concussion."

"I can't stay. Mac hasn't been out all day."

"Why don't I let Mac out on my way home? I'm going home after my shift, and I'm off tomorrow."

She missed Mac and her own bed. She needed a break from all of this scrutiny. "I need to go home."

He shook his head. "Can I get your keys, please?"

She wanted to slide off the gurney, put on her clothes, and leave. Instead, she held out her purse with her right arm. He leaned over and pulled the keys from an inside pocket.

She felt a rush of gratitude and, pressing her face into his cheek, whispered in his ear. "Thank you … for everything." He was doing the right thing. She knew it. If she needed to stay here till tomorrow morning, at least she could accept his offer to rescue Mac.

It was not until 10 p.m. that a droopy-eyed Sumpter stopped by the ED. He was still dressed in his suit, although his tie was missing.

"Sorry about this," Elle said, "but I'm still waiting for a room." She knew he hated hospitals and the lack of privacy.

"Last time I was here, I had to leave before the walls started closing in. I'm letting you know if I hear a patient moaning or smell vomit …."

"So tell me what you know?" She waved him to a chair, but he remained at the foot of her bed, as though he might need to leave at any moment.

"The police searched Peggy and Robbie's apartment and found the fentanyl box and wrappers in Peggy's desk."

"Charlie was right. It was Peggy!"

"The patches were Peggy's idea … Geena Louise was assigned to Peggy's Hospice patient the day she took the patches because Compassionate Care and Prayer was filling in for the girl who was out sick. Peggy blamed Geena Louise and she was forced to resign."

Elle imagined Peggy trying to take an inventory of drugs after her Hospice patient died and blaming the missing fentanyl on Geena Louise. "But why?"

"As Robbie's wife, Peggy thought she would inherit Charlie's money through her husband."

"But Sumpter, I thought the will stated that Robbie and Melinda would inherit Charlie's estate."

"Until Peggy explains it, we can only assume she was worried about the will being updated and the amount of money Susan was spending. But there's more." He told her of the other evidence of insulin tampering they found in Peggy's desk. "Two more insulin bottles with Mary Beth's name on the labels and a bottle of normal saline."

"Assuming it was Peggy, we know how she could have done it." Elle could see from Sumpter's expression that she needed to explain. "Peggy needed to get Mary Beth out of the house so she could pull off her fentanyl stunt. Oh my God. What is Robbie going to do?"

"The detectives offered Geena Louise a deal. Come clean, and she might get some leniency. They also checked Susan's apartment and found prescription bottles of oxycodone and clonazepam. And the caregiver logbook and schedule."

Elle nodded thoughtfully, thinking about the pieces that were still missing. "But why the shoot-out in the courthouse?"

"Susan was so angry with the judge's decision—"

"She wanted to be Charlie's guardian." Elle paused for a moment.

"Susan wanted the spotlight," Sumpter said. "And nobody was going to stand in the way of her fifteen minutes to shine."

"And have it all." Elle tried to get more comfortable in bed and moaned when she leaned on her left shoulder. "I'm okay. Don't leave yet … really, I'm okay."

"Stop moaning then. Why do you think Charlie's first wife was murdered?"

Elle sat forward, lessening the pain, and told him what Clay Guthrie said about Susan. "Charlie's first wife was Guthrie's sister."

"You're kidding."

"Nope. Clay Guthrie is also the retired detective who worked on a cold case in 1960. He was investigating a missing person case years ago. It was Charlie's realtor. He thinks Susan murdered Charlie's wife and realtor." Suddenly she was exhausted, and the tears started to flow.

"I'll call the police and tell them Susan needs to be a suspect in the death of Charlie's first wife."

"All I know, Sumpter, is that Clay Guthrie put himself in harm's way and took a bullet for the rest of us."

"Well, I want you to write this story and think of some up-and-coming actress to play your role when it gets made into a movie," he said.

"More like a horror show."

"The legal battles may go on for years, Elle. But right now, Susan's been arrested for what she did today—arrested with the gun still in her hand."

"Jeez," Elle said, draping her left shoulder against the pillow.

"By the way, you know that article on expert witnesses?" Sumpter asked.

"Were you trying to scare me?" She laughed.

"No, I wasn't, but I knew Kilpatrick would." He smiled kindly at her. "I was worried you'd be too eager to help the other side. I thought the article would bolster your confidence and caution you on giving out too much information, that's all."

He had been so supportive in the courtroom today. Sure, she'd made mistakes, but she also learned so much. "Thanks, Sumpter. I know I can do better next time."

When Josh Geller pulled up Elle's driveway, Mac's square face was peering out the front door window, his bearded mouth holding his leash. "You are too funny." Josh chuckled as he got out of his car.

The leash dangled from Mac's mouth as he dragged it up and down the hallway while Josh continued to look in the window and struggled with the door key. He opened the door and reached for the leash. "Remember me?"

Mac bolted out the door and lifted his back leg with calm dignity on the flower bed at the bottom of the steps, still holding the leash in his mouth.

"Good boy," he said, looking at Mac's tan and jet-black hair as the dog came back in the house, wagging his tail, the leash still in his mouth. Mac had a deep chest and strong bladder. Still, he had been waiting since this morning. If the plants died, c'est la vie.

Josh found kibble in a small storage container on the floor of the kitchen pantry. He took a scoop, filled Mac's bowl, poured his water, then found a mini bottle of Chivas Regal in the cabinet next to the refrigerator. He filled a tumbler half full of ice and poured himself a scotch.

His day had been long and exhausting—yogurt for breakfast and caffeine in between patients. Hungry and tired, he opened Elle's refrigerator: milk, eggs, a plate of smoked salmon, another of boiled potatoes with meatballs, and a jar of lingonberry sauce. He helped himself to the potatoes and meatballs and left the lingonberries. He didn't know what they were, definitely not Southern fare.

He plopped the cold meatballs in his mouth one at a time. Yum, comfort food. Onion and nutmeg. After a sprinkle of salt and pepper, he finished the potatoes. He liked her simple taste. She seemed fun and funny, smart, and attractive ... and he loved her sweet-natured dog and his undeniable charm.

"I'm sorry, Mac. You must have been starving," he said, sitting at the end of the kitchen bar with his scotch, watching Mac grab his food and swallow it whole, spilling kibble on the floor. He thought about Elle lying in her hospital bed, her soft, down-turned eyes looking right through him, and how she had been grazed by a bullet and sent to his emergency department. Sipping his scotch thoughtfully, he was relieved that her injuries were minor.

"Make sure the bedroom door is open, or he'll scratch all night to get in," she told him when he left her at the hospital.

Josh looked around for the TV. The kitchen was tiny with built-ins, blond wood cabinets, and a hanging rack for pots and pans. Wooden mixing spoons were stacked up in the corner by the sink next to her Gourmet Lutheran Coffee mugs. He liked her minimalist look, as if she hadn't fully moved in, and the understated décor reflecting her Scandinavian heritage. He felt emotionally safe here, appreciating more of who she was, down-to-earth and straightforward—the real deal.

Mac finished his kibble, then came over with a wet mouth and worn-out tennis ball. Mac tossed the ball in the air and caught it himself. Josh found the TV, in the back of a shallow niche at the end of the bar against the wall. He turned on the eleven o'clock news. The courthouse drama was the leading story.

"The suspect started shooting before walking through the security checkpoint," a clean-shaven male reporter said, standing in front of the courthouse. "What was highly unusual about this shooter ... she was a woman."

There was a pause as the TV screen cut to the area surrounding the courthouse. Josh could see a terrified crowd of people running and screaming, blocked by police cars and yellow tape.

"A nine-millimeter Glock handgun was brought to the shooter by an accomplice," the reporter added.

Josh started on the last meatball and glanced over at Mac, who was now lying down at his feet, watching him as if he expected him to share his food.

"Police have not released the names of the shooter or any of the victims, as they are still notifying family members and continuing the investigation," the reporter added.

The screen cut to the inside of the courthouse.

"David!" Josh yelled and sent a confused Mac running for the front door to see who was there. Josh finished the last meatball and watched as David, wearing his large moon suit, unloaded toolboxes and other equipment from his mobile lab. "Mac, he's on live TV dressed like a giant banana."

Mac came back to the kitchen and thumped his tail against the bar stool as Josh stroked his head. He hoped Elle was watching from her hospital bed.

"The shooter was taken into custody," the reporter said.

The camera showed David counting bullets, looking for discharged cartridges.

The reporter added, "The shooter, a White woman in her sixties, was the wife of the man involved in a hearing at the courthouse."

Josh rinsed his glass and placed the dirty plate in the dishwasher, then turned off the TV and the kitchen light. He wondered how Elle would manage tonight. She looked so vulnerable lying there in a hospital gown. It struck him—all the hours they spent together this past week—he had started thinking with more certainty that she was the one, or else he was dumbstruck.

Before he left, he went to the windows and closed the shutters. "She's gonna be okay, boy." He started for the second floor to make sure the bedroom door was open.

Mac ran up the stairs, spun around, and stood in the open bedroom doorway, curling his upper lip, as if protecting something valuable. He growled, a possessive warning in his throat.

"You don't know me well enough for a sleepover?" He smiled. "This is where you draw the line."

Josh wasn't about to push his luck. The next day was his day off. He'd be back to walk Mac in the morning and later meet David at the hospital. He locked the front door quietly and started his car.

Mac's face popped into view, standing at the door, as he watched Josh even after he backed out of the drive and pulled away.

"G'night, Mac," he said. If Elle and the bailiff could survive the courthouse shooting, surely he could win over this dog. He needed to believe that. But right now, he needed to get some shut-eye and pray that tomorrow would bring the best possible news from the hospital.

# Chapter 26
*Tuesday*

At dawn, Elle woke up sobbing in a panic. She was sprawled out over the hospital bed, her head smashed against a too-stiff pillow. Another bad dream ... and trouble waking up to reality. But unlike other dreams where it was a relief to wake up, this had been a dream about the case. It was real, and the loss in the courtroom was real.

Turning, she pushed up from her blood-stained pillow with a giant headache and her left arm in pain. It was still dark as she dragged herself to the bathroom, looked in the mirror at her pupils, her bandaged shoulder, and realized how seriously she needed a haircut. Someone had woken her every two hours and flashed a light in her eyes to check her pupil reaction.

She called her brother on her cell phone and got through on the second ring. "I'm in the hospital with a possible concussion."

"What?" Peter yelled.

She closed her eyes and told him about the hearing, the shooting, her fear of leaving him alone in the world, and everything she remembered before she lost consciousness. After losing their parents, she was a lot more fragile.

"Oh my God, Elle—"

"Look, I need to know some things from you ... about the accident ... did the brakes fail? Was it Dad's fault?"

"Elle," he groaned. "How is this going to help—"

"I can't remember, Peter." She leaned into the phone, hoping he'd give her an answer. "It's stuck in my brain like a loop, but I can't get over it."

"Okay," he said, "but I'd rather us be face-to-face ..."

"God, I've missed you," she said, her voice wavering. "When—"

"Look, I wanted to surprise you, but now is as good a time to tell you: My leave came in."

"I'm feeling better already." Why did she worry about letting him down when he seemed so sure of himself? *Mom always wanted me to protect you.*

"I'll be in Charlotte by Thanksgiving."

"Awesome." *Unbelievable. Together again ... after all this time.* "I should be fully recovered by Thanksgiving ... love you. Be safe."

At seven, she was sitting up in bed, her thoughts on Mac and Peter, when David and Josh walked through the door, single file.

David walked up to the side of her bed, where she could see his friendly face. "You left this at the crime scene," he said and placed her leather briefcase on the bed next to her. "Next time you get shot, don't leave your shit everywhere."

She laughed and winced at the pain in her left arm, then turned to Josh. "Verdict?"

Josh sat close at the side of her bed, gently touching her rumpled bed hair but avoiding her scalp wound. "No concussion. Your discharge is planned for ten a.m."

"That's great news," she said, trying to put on a brave face.

"And who looks as good as you do in the hospital!?" David said. "Nobody."

Was he teasing her, or did he mean it? She didn't know, but she couldn't imagine life without her friend.

Josh bent down and grabbed something he had hidden by his feet. He placed a white bakery box and a small blue hydrangea plant on her bedside table. "I drove to Reid's on Providence Road and picked up a Carnegie Deli cheesecake," he told her.

"What about my breakfast tray?" Elle asked, smiling at all the attention.

"Staff will grab it. I said they could have the leftover cheesecake too."

She fingered the hydrangea.

"Jewish guilt. I felt guilty after eating all your meatballs last night."

"How nice," Elle said. "The guilt, I mean."

"You ate her Swedish meatballs?" David chuckled and opened a bottle of French champagne, chilling on ice, hidden in a plain paper bag. "It's Lady Rose, in your honor." He handed her and Josh their bubbling glasses and added a splash of fresh-squeezed OJ.

"I told him you couldn't take pain medication while they were monitoring you for a concussion." Josh turned on her TV to the morning news.

David clinked his glass with them. "Cheers."

"*Skål,*" Elle said with a slight bow of her head.

"*L'Chaim,*" Josh said, a twinkle in his eye. "And to no brain damage."

She breathed a sigh of relief. "To life is right and to suddenly feeling lucky."

"Hey, Elle, you've got to see this," Josh said.

A reporter for NBC Channel 6 stood in front of the courthouse and announced the shootings of Clay Guthrie and Elle Larson. This time they identified the shooter by name. Susan Porter Blackwell, sixty-three, had been involved in a contested guardianship hearing with her husband. The screen showed Susan firing on Elle at the courthouse entrance while a throng of people ran for safety and others huddled behind the information desk. Elle could see the back of her head.

They watched the entire news report as David added commentary. "Gunshot residue is volatile—we only have a four-hour timeframe to test it. Otherwise, it's gone." He pointed at the screen. "See how the sheriff's deputies controlled the doors and provided security?"

"If the sheriff's department provides security for the courthouse, how did you get notified?" Josh asked David.

"Our officer responded to 911. Homicide gets involved because the bailiff was shot. Homicide notified the Crime Scene Unit."

After the report, they toasted again, this time to Clay Guthrie.

"He's in ICU but doing well," Josh said.

"I know him," David said. "He's a retired detective. He would stop by our department and tell us how much he enjoyed being in the courtroom. He loved working there—since he wasn't working with us anymore."

"Any kids?" Elle asked.

"No. He was widowed. I think that's why he kept on working," David said.

"Here's to Charlie and to some good things happening out of bad," Josh said. He raised his glass once again.

"The gun was a nine-millimeter Glock," David said. "There were five casings. We found all five projectiles. We also did fingerprints."

"And it takes more than a week to get them back," Elle said and grinned at him. The champagne was making her warm and relaxed.

David went from describing the crime scene to describing his one-pot paella. "You cook the sausage before adding the chicken, and then the chopped vegetables, herbs, and spices before the rice. The mussels and shrimp are added at the end."

"Don't forget the saffron!" Elle said.

"Sounds like an all-nighter," Josh said. "When do we get an invite?"

"This is all still rattling my brain," Elle said. "I was there ... now we're here ..."

"It's gonna take time," Josh said, giving her an encouraging smile.

Elle nodded, imagining them having dinner together, hanging out like this. "I'll be happy to chop vegetables for the paella."

"And I can chop the onions," Josh added.

"Well, I think we can make it in an hour, if we work together," David said.

Josh pulled up a chair beside her, and they went back to talking about the case.

"How would you not recognize the woman standing next to you in her wedding dress?" David took another sip of his mimosa.

Elle looked at him and shook her head. "Charlie's in his eighties. He's got macular degeneration and trouble with hearing. Plus, he was getting sedating medication without his knowledge. It could happen to any of us." She was glad to see her own brain was still working.

Josh shook his head. "Susan was so evil." He held the cake knife under hot tap water and cut a slice of cheesecake, wiping the blade dry before cutting the next slice.

"I think it's complicated for Charlie ... he needed help." She smeared a small bite of cheesecake on the inside of her mouth, tasting as it melted slowly. "Once Charlie realized what happened, he didn't want to be married to her. But in his mind, she had also helped him sell the farm and become a wealthy man."

She thought about Charlie and some of her other male clients, not recognizing how vulnerable they were.

David, his deep blue eyes dancing, topped off their glasses with more bubbly.

"Here's to being a guy," she said. "Often wrong, but never in doubt." She chuckled with satisfaction.

David smirked; Josh laughed.

"If you think about it, it made no sense, Elle, for Amy to be the guardian when she was in such poor health," David said. "Appointing someone else was a good idea."

"I agree," Josh said. "That way Amy and Charlie can just love each other."

"I got ahead of myself, thinking that he wasn't really married to Susan. You know, he didn't initiate the divorce from Amy. And he sure didn't initiate that freakin' wedding to Susan. Sumpter says Susan forged the documents."

"You botched it," David said.

Elle gazed up at David, then looked at Josh, his brown eyes smiling. She felt proud. They had helped her get through the case. "Well, at least I was right about Charlie."

They both grinned but didn't respond.

She knew they wouldn't give her that satisfaction. "Okay, guys, I should at least get credit for taking a shot for the team."

"Cheap shot," David said with a poker face.

"I agree ... cheap shot," Josh said, trying not to smile. "You stayed overnight because you hit your head on the courthouse floor and passed out, not because you were shot."

"What would it be like ... to be pushed into a pool while strapped into a wheelchair?" Elle asked, changing tack.

"Maybe that's what you're worried dating will be like," Josh said.

Elle laughed. Her biggest fear had been not being able to breathe under-water. Her next biggest fear was being an expert witness in a courtroom. She had survived both. Maybe dating wouldn't be so bad after all.

Today the sun broke through with only one week to go before Thanks-giving. It was two days since her hospital discharge, and Elle was feeling much better, fueled by caffeine and a good night's sleep. David had called this morning and read the report from the Davidson police. The bones that Mac had dug up in the abandoned mine had been identified. They did in fact belong to Jackson Walker, the realtor who went missing thirty-six years ago, and would be evidence in a new murder investigation.

She called Sumpter right away and gave him the news.

"Geena Louise told the homicide detectives that Susan killed the realtor," he said, "after he refused to give her the commission from selling the Blackwell farm as promised."

"Jeez, so that's when it all started." She wondered if they would ever prove that Charlie's first wife was murdered. Did Susan really think Charlie would end up with her, after his first wife was out of the way? In Susan's mind, she did it all for love.

Later that day, Elle picked up Charlie to make a special trip to see Amy so she could take him to dinner at the retirement home. He had dressed up and was wearing Amy's favorite disco shirt under his jacket. She drove while Charlie asked about Mac and made small talk for a few minutes, then they were quiet. She knew he was grateful. She was grateful too. They had been locked together in moments of sudden violence and crisis that neither of them would forget. Charlie was tough in ways she hadn't been. She was strong in ways he couldn't be. She glanced over at him and smiled. It's like the Blackwells had been stuck as a family—frozen in time. And the worst trauma, in her mind, was what had happened between him and Amy, but he never let go.

"It's room 426," Charlie said when they entered The Pines. Elle walked by his side through a long hallway, his ambulation careful and deliberate. He put his arm on her good shoulder, leaning for support.

They took the elevator to the fourth floor. In the hall, they met a man in a dinner jacket and a woman in dress pants, presumably heading out for dinner. Charlie greeted the couple as they walked by.

"Here it is," Elle said, feeling as if the heart-aching conclusion to his story was about to be told. Or was it a new beginning? She took a step back and stood behind him as he walked up to the door.

"How do I look?" he asked her.

"You look awesome, Charlie."

Charlie knocked. "My last chance." He glanced at Elle while they waited.

Finally, Amy opened the door, and they stood facing each other without speaking. Elle glanced around. Amy's new apartment looked like her, the French painting above the sofa holding a prominent spot in the living room. Sentimental French music, accompanied by the soft sound of an accordion, played gently in the background.

"Your hair is shorter," Charlie finally said. "But still a chestnut brown."

She nodded, her cheeks glowing. She handed him her belted camel coat. "This feels like the first time we met."

"The French coffee," he added.

"That cold and snowy spring."

As he held up her coat, she turned around to put her arm in the sleeve.

"Are you cold?" he whispered in her ear.

She nodded yes and turned to put her other arm through the second sleeve. He adjusted the jacket and wrapped himself around her, holding her close, bringing tears to Amy's eyes.

There was a gentleness between Charlie and Amy that only two frail people, who were wise and weathered, could express. On the drive home, Elle thought about the guardianship hearing. Back then, she had no idea that Susan, Billie Sutton, Peggy, and Geena Louise would all be arrested, or that Dr. Woodham would be investigated for fraud. In the end, the courthouse shooting had been far worse than the hearing. Miraculously, she and Charlie had survived. So had Clay Guthrie.

It had turned into a Carolina-blue-sky kind of day. She would continue working with Charlie and try seeing things more like him—happy just to be alive. Letting go of being so afraid. And speaking out when the situation demanded it. Sumpter had referred another case her way, and she accepted. She thought her parents would have been happy about that.

Mac was waiting for her when she got home. She opened the front door and looked into his eager brown eyes as his pink tongue licked her fingers. "We need some fresh air, don't we, boy?" She put on his leash and followed him to the porch, where they looked over the park and the towering city in the background, the city where the streets were paved in gold. She put her arm around him. "Hey, champ. Let's go chase some squirrels."

# Acknowledgments

I would like to thank Editor-in-Chief Amy Ashby, who was thrilled to publish this story, and the dedicated team at Warren Publishing, including President Mindy Kuhn and Marketing Director Lacey Cope. Thanks also to Erika Nein for her copy/line editing and Chris Kinsley for her final proofreading. They made this book possible.

Many thanks to my early readers. I thank Ellen Montgomery, Kari DeRohan, Korin Waltersdorf, Kara Knutson, Ryan Knutson, Eric Knutson, Jacqui Barbaras, Patricia Padgett, Kathy Comess, and Matthew Holt. Special thanks to attorneys Kim Bonuomo and Mandy Rosenblum for their legal reads of the later drafts. I would like to thank my talented writers group, Chris Quarembo, Pamelia Stratton, Kimberley Leahy, Cynthia McGroarty, Gus Cileone, and John Newlin who have read every chapter. I can never thank all of them enough for their literary suggestions as well as their friendship.

Deepest thanks to my mentor, Kaaren Boothroyd, editor of the Journal of Aging Life Care, and to Mark Spencer, Elizabeth Kracht, Lisa Regan, and Carole Lawrence for their editorial eye during the many rounds of editing when I thought the manuscript was finished.

Thank you so much to Roy Patterson for meeting with me and answering all of my questions about crime scene investigation, and to Kris Touchstone for allowing me to interview her about her role as a female police officer in a mostly male field.

Heartfelt thanks to the many clients and their families I had the privilege to work with over the twenty years I lived in Charlotte. They taught me so much about aging, loss and abuse, and World War II. They also inspired my story.

Writing this book took me down various research paths. I am very grateful to Historic Site Manager Larry Neal for his tour of the Reed Gold Mine, our conversations on the discovery and history of gold in the Charlotte region, and his great suggestions for the fictional mine in my own story.

To Milan Jisa, curator at the Patton Memorial Pilsen in the Czech Republic—thank you for showing me and my husband the museum and for driving us two hours to and back from the battlefield in Zhuri, the place of one of the last, but little-known, battles in World War II.

Special thanks to my family for their love and support and their many hours of listening to me talk about the writing of this book!

And finally, with deepest heartfelt gratitude and love to my first reader, my perpetual editor, and the one in my corner from the first word, my husband, Steve ... the biggest storyteller I know.

www.ingramcontent.com/pod-product-compliance
Lightning Source LLC
Chambersburg PA
CBHW020542020726
47494CB00006B/1884